HARD KNOCKS

ZOË SHARP

ISIS

LARGE PRINT

Oxford

First published in Great Britain 2003
by
Judy Piatkus (Publishers) Ltd.

Published in Large Print 2012 by ISIS Publishing Ltd.,
7 Centremead, Osney Mead, Oxford OX2 0ES
by arrangement with
Gregory & Company Authors' Agents

British Library Cataloguing in Publication Data
Sharp, Zoë, 1966–
    Hard knocks.
    1. Fox, Charlie (Fictitious character) - - Fiction.
    2. Detective and mystery stories.
    3. Large type books.
    I. Title
    823.9'2–dc23

ISBN 978–0–7531–8954–2 (hb)
ISBN 978–0–7531–8955–9 (pb)

Printed and bound in Great Britain by
T. J. International Ltd., Padstow, Cornwall

For Andy, who's stopped me giving up altogether
on occasions too numerous to mention . . .

Acknowledgements

Many people have let me trawl through their collective experiences in order to put together this book. Former VIP protection officer Brad Blake was one of them, as was Glynn Jones. The people at the Revere Gun Range in Pompano Beach, Florida, also helped, but never knew it. I'm still drawing on the lessons learned during self-defence classes with Ian Cottam and Lee Watkin.

Key pieces of German information were provided by Derek Harrison and Armin Mohren. Technical info vital to the plot came from Tim Enderby and Ike Flack at SAS; and Ian Hill and John Whitehead at Hiteq. Thank you also to Chris Brown at Alpine Electronics (UK) for explaining the finer points of their navigation system. Any factual errors are all my own work.

Once again, many people were kind enough to offer their opinions during the early stages, including Iris, Jean, Sheila, and everyone at the Lune Valley Writers' Group. The usual pre-publication vivisection was carried out by Peter Doleman, Claire Duplock, Sarah Harrison, Clive Hopwood, and Tim Winfield. Keep on digging, people, and don't mind me sqealing . . .

As always, the biggest thank yous go to my husband, Andy, who has a lot more to put up with than he lets on about; to my editor Gillian Green; my publisher Judy Piatkus; and my copy editor Sarah Abel, who spotted all the bits that everyone else had missed.

Once again, grateful appreciation goes to Steve Calcutt and Maggie Heavey at the Anubis Literary Agency, for putting up with even more *cries de foi* from me than normal.

CHAPTER
ONE

It rained on the day of Kirk Salter's funeral. Hard cold rain, close to sleet. Driven down off the moors by a frenzied wind, it rampaged through the gravestones of the bleak little Yorkshire churchyard and buffeted the sparse group of mourners clustered round the open grave.

I stood a respectful distance back from the family, listening to the droning voice of the vicar, nasal with flu. The rain stung my face, plastering my hair flat to my scalp. As I tried desperately to stop my teeth from chattering I wondered, not for the first time, what the hell I was doing there.

It was two days after Christmas. Yesterday morning I didn't even know that Kirk was dead. We hadn't kept in touch since our army days, and I'd had absolutely no wish to do so.

The last time I'd seen him all I remember was being scalded by a white-hot rage, an impotent fury at his actions — or lack of them. He was a fucking coward, I'd yelled at him. A traitor. I hoped he died screaming.

Be careful what you wish for.

It was Madeleine who'd broken the news that Kirk had been shot dead in Germany. She turned up quite out of the blue at my parents' house where I was reluctantly spending the holidays. That was what surprised me most about her unexpected appearance. I hadn't told anyone I was going to be there.

In fact, until recently, I would have done just about anything rather than be found within a fifty-mile radius of the family fold in Cheshire. It certainly wasn't the obvious place to start looking.

For various reasons, my relationship with my parents had fractured about the time I got kicked out of the army. It had taken the best part of five years before it had begun to knit back together again. If the warehouse building next to my Lancaster flat hadn't caught fire in early December, it probably would have taken longer.

Still, it's amazing what the prospect of being homeless at Christmas does to your pride. I'd swallowed mine dry and accepted my father's coolly delivered invitation.

It hadn't been easy. My mother, aware of how fragile was this truce, had greeted my return with a twitchy delight that was almost hysteria. By Boxing Day, if I listened carefully enough, I could almost hear her rack-tight nerves snapping quietly behind her apron strings. My own were not far behind.

And then, into this scene of agonising tension, had come Madeleine.

"There's a funeral tomorrow that I think you might want to go to," she'd said carefully, her face solemn.

She knew — I'm damned sure she did — whose death I'd instantly assume she was talking about. I'd had no contact with Kirk for nearly five years. Why on earth would I think of him? Besides, she was too good at digging out such information not to have known I'd be only mildly interested at best in his untimely demise.

No, I'd thought she meant Sean, and the shock of the blow I'd felt at that moment had quite literally taken my breath away. I've never fainted in my life, but I came pretty close to it then. It was only afterwards, when I caught her studying my reaction, that I realised she'd broken the news that way deliberately.

Sean Meyer. Madeleine's boss. Now there was a name I'd spent so long conjuring with I was practically eligible for entry to the Magic Circle.

Madeleine worked for Sean handling electronic security and surveillance. When I'd first met her I'd believed there was a lot more to their relationship than strictly business. Bearing in mind my own shattered affair with Sean, a certain antagonism from that assumption still lingered. I couldn't seem to put it aside.

I told myself it was a relief to have an excuse to get away from my family. That Sean's relayed request for my presence at the service was no deciding factor, but maybe I was still feeling too shaky to put up much of a fight.

It would have been difficult to refuse in the face of Madeleine's stubborn determination, in any case. Sean hadn't dragged her away from her Christmas dinner to spend the best part of a day tracking me down, she told me grimly, to have me back out now.

She'd practically stood over me while I'd thrown some suitably sober clothing into a bag and borrowed a

3

black coat from my mother that contrived to make me look bulky without actually keeping me warm. Then we'd headed north.

As we'd crawled across the Pennines in freezing fog, Madeleine had filled me in on how she'd come to be involved in Kirk Salter's life and the aftermath of his death.

"He came into the office to see Sean in early November," she explained. "He was back in civvy street and looking for a job."

Somehow I wasn't surprised at the news. Since he'd left the army himself, Sean had moved into close protection work. If you're ex-Special Forces and you're an expert in your field, there aren't many alternative career choices open to you. Sean had, it seemed, found immediate success, and Kirk had certainly been big enough to have been useful as a bodyguard.

"So what was he doing in Germany?" I asked. When she'd initially told me the location and manner of his death, I'd automatically assumed it was military. "Was he on a job for Sean?"

"Sort of," Madeleine said. "He'd gone to do a VIP protection course over there. Since they banned handguns in the UK most of the bigger training schools moved to either Holland or Germany, as you probably know."

I hadn't known it, but I wasn't inclined to correct her. "So what happened?"

Madeleine flicked her eyes to the rear-view mirror before she pulled out round a slower moving truck in the centre lane. "We're not entirely certain," she said, offhand. "I'm sure Sean will fill you in."

I watched the gloomy humps of other cars appearing out of the fog alongside us and reflected idly that Kirk should have been too experienced a soldier to get himself shot so carelessly. *Well, hell, it couldn't have happened to a nicer bloke.*

I hadn't always felt that way about him, of course. When we'd been undergoing Special Forces training together everyone wanted big Kirk on their squad for any exercise. Particularly if there was any heavy lifting involved. I'd have sworn he was solid, dependable, one of my comrades. Someone to trust your life to. Mind you, I'd have sworn that about the others, too.

Donalson, Hackett, Morton, and Clay.

I almost winced as the list unrolled inside my head. I'd managed to go without thinking about my quartet of attackers for a couple of months and now it was like they'd never been away.

The four of them were part of the same intake of trainees. We were supposed to form the kind of bond that would see us all attending reunions together in fifty years. Then one night they'd drunk enough to tip them over into macho bravado and I'd taken on the shape of prey.

After they'd raped me, they'd sobered up enough to realise I could finish them, if they didn't finish me first. I remember lying there, half-senseless from the beating and the pain, and listening with remote interest while they'd discussed the best method of disposing of my body.

And that's when Kirk had stumbled upon us.

He may not have been the sharpest tool in the shed, but he was certainly one of the heaviest. Even four to one, the others hadn't had the courage to go against him.

Kirk had stayed with me like a big dog, holding my hand until the medics arrived, until they'd scraped me up and poured me into the ambulance. I never dreamed for a moment that when it came to the court martial he would deny everything he'd seen and heard.

But he did.

My shoulder blades gave an involuntary shudder and I shook myself out of it. A junction sign flowed past my window like a wraith, but I couldn't recall the last few miles.

I twisted back in my seat. "Madeleine," I said, my voice level, "you must know I didn't give a damn about Kirk Salter, alive or dead. Why don't you cut to the chase and tell me exactly why Sean wants me at his funeral?"

She gave a rueful half smile. "I wondered when you'd ask," she said, "but the truth is, I don't know. Sean rang me from Germany yesterday morning and said he needed to talk to you urgently. Something to do with Kirk. He didn't say what."

She was concentrating on the road too hard to notice the twitch her words provoked. It occurred to me for the first time that Kirk might have told Sean more than I realised about my shambolic eviction from the army. What other reason could there be?

6

I fixed my attention on the slap of the wipers across the glass in front of me. I'd had the opportunity once before to explain to Sean the full tawdry details of my attack. I'd bottled out. He already had the bare bones, but when it came to the true extent of my injuries I'd been rather more economical with the truth.

He knew I'd been beaten up, but he didn't know it had gone so much further than that.

What if Kirk had told him the rest?

Madeleine had booked rooms at a small hotel on the outskirts of Harrogate and that's where we spent the night. The following morning we drove the rest of the way through pretty but desolate countryside. The rain had started almost immediately, slashing in sideways across the landscape, turning it icy grey. Even the sheep looked cold.

Sean was already at the church when we arrived. I hadn't seen him since we'd climbed out of a riot together two months before. He was looking good, on the whole, with no sign of the shoulder injury that had so restricted him then.

He'd favoured me with a brief nod as we'd walked into the tiny church, but his eyes, dark enough to be almost black, were cool and flat. There was something formidable about the set of those wide shoulders that made me instantly wary. I knew that look. It meant nothing but trouble.

Question was, who for?

He'd spent his own Christmas in Germany, Madeleine had told me, untangling the inevitable

7

shroud of red tape that had delayed the retrieval of Kirk's body. That would have been enough to piss anyone off, but I had the nasty feeling there was more to it than that.

A burst of alarm flashed through my system, translated as a sudden warmth despite the bone-numbing chill. It was only a degree or so above freezing inside the church but at least it wasn't raining much in there. The whole place smelt of mildew and mothballs like my grandmother's wardrobe.

Madeleine and I trailed after the coffin as it was carried out. I hung back purposely, but there were no faces I remembered among the pallbearers.

There were none I'd tried hard to forget, either.

By the time we got to the graveside the ground was slick with mud. The tracks of the Bobcat mini digger they'd used to scratch out the requisite pit had left gouges in the surrounding earth that were deep enough to make you stumble. They'd lined the edges of the void with strips of artificial turf, its harsh bright green the only splash of colour against the greys and blacks.

Someone was fighting to hold an umbrella steady over the vicar's head, but the wind lashed the rain in under the side of the canopy, the spray coating his glasses. "Man that is born of a woman hath but a short time to live and is full of misery," he croaked, with an uncommon depth of feeling. "He cometh up and is cut down like a flower, he fleeth as it were a shadow, and never continueth in one stay."

As they put Kirk into the ground Sean stood in the second row back with his head bent, staring at nothing.

He didn't seem to notice the rain sliding in rivulets along the angles of his cheekbones.

Afterwards, when clods of sodden earth had been shovelled in on top of the coffin, he spoke only briefly to Kirk's parents. They thanked him without any sign of resentment for bringing their boy back to them so quickly.

Their intensely grateful manner disturbed me. If Kirk had been working for Sean at the time of his death, as Madeleine had implied, I would have expected a reception that held more bitterness, more blame.

Sean solemnly shook their hands and, with every sign of urbane sophistication, bent to kiss the pale cheek Kirk's mother offered. Then he turned and walked across the patchy grass towards us, and that air of quiet civility just seemed to drop away from him.

He moved like he always did, covering ground with a long, almost lazy stride, but something had hardened in his face, like he didn't have to pretend not to be angry any more. My system kicked up a gear as I fought down the impulse to back away from him.

I'd spent most of the previous night lying awake trying to get my head round finally getting things out in the open with Sean. I'd thought I'd come to terms with it.

Looks like I'd been wrong.

Half an hour later, I found myself sitting huddled into the open fireplace of an otherwise deserted country pub. My mother's coat was spread across the chair next to me. It was dripping puddles onto the stone flagged floor and steaming gently in the heat. I hoped it wasn't dry-clean only.

Madeleine had disappeared at her earliest opportunity, no doubt eager to get back to what was left of her Christmas break. Sean would take me where I needed to go she'd said, almost cryptically. I'd transferred my bag into his car, another of the Grand Cherokee jeeps he seemed to favour, and allowed myself to be ushered into the passenger seat without argument.

We hadn't talked of much on the drive to this middle-of-nowhere pub. Nothing of any note, anyway. We scratched the surface of his recovery, which was well under way, and his troubled family situation, which was going to take rather longer to resolve.

Now Sean came back from the bar, stooping to avoid the lower beams that spanned the ceiling, and put two cups of coffee down onto the oak bench in front of us. He shrugged out of his overcoat and loosened the top button of the starched white shirt that suited him just as well as fatigues had ever done. I knew he was gearing up to get right to the point, and I almost braced myself.

"I suppose Madeleine has told you what this is all about?" he said, sitting facing me and stirring his coffee slowly.

"Some," I hedged. I was shivering, not entirely from the cold, and I clamped my hands together in my lap so he wouldn't see them trembling. "She said Kirk came to see you."

"Yeah." He lifted his cup, eyed me over the rim. The silence stretched and snapped. "Salter talked about you, Charlie," he said at last, softly. "He told me what happened."

Inside my head I heard a sound almost like a sigh. *So, it was out at last.*

I sat back in my chair, feeling my face setting. I forced a shrug even though my shoulders were so tense the movement nearly cracked them. "So?"

"So, I can understand that you're not going to like what I'm going to ask you," he said, hesitant. I'd never seen him so uncertain. He'd always been supremely self-confident. The change made me nervous, stepped up my heart rate. The beat of my blood was so loud in my ears that I missed his next question and had to make him repeat it.

"I said, I want you to go to Germany for me and find out what's going on at that school."

He'd veered so far off track that the shock of it turned me slow. "What school?" I said blankly.

"At Einsbaden. It's a little place just outside Stuttgart." He paused, frowning as though I should have known all this. "It's where Salter was doing his training. The place where they claim he wasn't killed."

Come on, Sean, for God's sake don't keep me hanging on like this! If Kirk told you I was gang-raped by the same group of people you were training, that they used the unarmed combat techniques you'd been teaching them to overpower and restrain me, then just get it over with . . .

"Wait a minute. What do you mean 'claim he wasn't killed'?" I demanded, catching up belatedly. "Who else could have been in that coffin?"

"Oh it was definitely Salter. I saw the body myself," he said, voice grim. "But he was found dumped in the forest a few miles away from the school. They're saying he left at the end of the previous week and they thought he'd flown home, when I know for a fact that they'd asked him to stay on and do some kind of work for them. That's only the first of the anomalies."

It dawned slowly that he wasn't being deliberately cruel.

He didn't know.

Whatever else Kirk had told him, it wasn't that.

The relief and the disappointment was like sweet and sour on my tongue. I struggled for composure, to stay with the programme. I reached for my coffee, took a sip. The top was covered in a layer of froth, fooling me into thinking that the liquid underneath had cooled to a drinkable temperature.

"What anomalies?" I managed.

Sean must have thought the question implied more interest in the circumstances surrounding Kirk's death than I actually meant. He gave me one of those quiet smiles, the ones that started out slow yet put out heat. The ones that made me wish I could wipe out our disastrous history together and begin again from new. But I couldn't, that was the problem.

"He rang me a week before he died, just as the course was finishing up. Said he'd got a job to do out there, a short-term contract, and could he start for me after he got back. He sounded different. Distracted somehow, evasive." He ducked his head like a boxer

12

avoiding a punch. "Maybe I should have pressed him harder."

"Pressed him harder about what?" I shut my eyes for a moment, took a breath. "Sorry, Sean, I'm missing a few steps here. I thought Madeleine said Kirk went to Germany to train so you'd give him a job with your outfit. What else was going on?"

He leaned forwards, resting his forearms on his knees and staring into the flames. The action revealed a large-faced Breitling with a polished steel strap. It was a far cry from the battered old watch he'd always worn when I'd known him before, seeming to suddenly emphasise the distance travelled.

"I need somewhere to train my people," he said. "I've been using a place in Holland, but it's small and the facilities there are limited. Then I heard about Einsbaden Manor. They've got everything I need and they used to have a good reputation, but in the last year or so things have gone off the boil. They had a pupil killed in a driving accident early last year, and there were rumours that it wasn't quite as accidental as it could have been. I needed someone to check the place out." He shrugged. "Salter offered."

For a moment the silence hung between us. The logs shifted and spat in the cast-iron grate.

"So what happened?"

"Nothing — to begin with. He rang me twice with progress reports. He said they like to play mind games with you. Like seeing how you react. And they were putting too much emphasis on firearms drills, by the sounds of it, but Salter was a proficient man round weaponry, as I'm sure you can recall. He reckoned he could out-shoot the instructors with just about everything they were using, and I could well believe that."

Sean paused, took a sip of his coffee. The side of my calf nearest to the fire had started to burn. I hutched round in my seat to a cooler spot, and waited.

"During his last phone call, when he'd told me he was going to be late coming back, he mentioned your name. Said he wished he'd stood up for you. That it had been on his conscience and he wasn't going to make the same mistake twice. I've no idea what he meant. Then he said, all joky, that if anything happened to him, would I see him right."

"Premonition or preparation?" I wondered aloud. I didn't probe into Kirk's reference to me. I didn't have the courage to. Instead, I said, "What was the job?"

Sean shook his head. "He wouldn't say. Next thing I know I get a call from Salter's parents telling me he's dead and can I help get his body home."

"And what does the school say they think happened to him?"

"They're claiming they've no idea why he should still have been in the area, but perhaps it was an accident. Illegal hunters."

"But you don't believe that." It was a statement, not a question.

Sean glanced at me. "He was shot three times in the back," he said, voice neutral. "Right hip, spine, left kidney." He formed the first two fingers of his right hand into a gun and plotted the diagonal course.

I sat up straight as old memories surfaced. "They used a machine pistol," I murmured. I'd fired fully automatic guns often enough when I'd been in the army to recognise the way the rounds tracked, stitching across a target from low right to high left. It was almost impossible to hold one steady.

Sean nodded. "Not the kind of thing you'd use for hunting, however illegal it was. But, the school supposedly don't use machine pistols either. The pathologist recovered the rounds, by the way. They were hollowpoints."

He was watching my reaction as he said it. Hollowpoint rounds were designed to mushroom and distort on impact with soft tissue, maximising damage. Nasty, whichever way you squared it.

"If he was shot in the back, that implies he was running away from something," I said slowly. "What? What had he found there that made him stay on and what was so important that they killed him for it?"

"I don't know," Sean said. "I got the impression when he first told me he was going to be delayed that it was the school that had offered him a job, but now I don't think so."

"What do the German police think?"

He gave me a wry look. "They're playing things very close to their chest," he said. "They're still investigating and therefore can't give me any information, but I get the feeling they're not too interested. It's just —" He broke off, opening his hands in a gesture of frustration.

"I send people into dangerous situations all the time," he began again. "But they know the score. It's their job, their choice, and they're well paid for it. All Salter was doing was scouting the place for me. I never considered for a moment it would get him killed. That's why I need you to go and find out what happened to him."

He looked up. "The only way in is as a pupil, and I'm too well known in the industry to do it myself. They'd suss me out straight away. I don't have anyone else I could send who's sharp enough for the job, Charlie. Not at this notice."

I gazed into the fire again, long enough for my eyes to dry out and my cheeks to begin to cook. Not quite long enough to successfully tamp down the anger that was rising at the back of my mind.

"Why would you think that I would give a damn about Kirk Salter, after what he did?" I asked at last, without meeting his eyes.

"He was under pressure, Charlie," Sean said gently, and the hairs came up on the back of my neck. I felt them riffle against my collar as I turned my head. "He was having his strings pulled all the way along the line. It wasn't his fault."

I half rose, shoving my chair backwards. "I don't care whose *fault* it was that Kirk shit on me," I snapped. I put my fists on the table and leaned in close, adding in a savage whisper, "All I know is that he did, and I only came to his funeral to make sure the bastard really was dead! If you think I'm going out there looking for justice for him, you've got another think coming!"

Sean didn't react to my outburst, just caught and held my gaze, level, steady. "I'm not asking you to go for Salter's sake," he said quietly. "I'm asking you to go for mine."

Not quite what I was expecting. I almost fell back into my chair, deflated. "I —"

That was as far as I got before the shrill interruption of Sean's mobile phone. Without taking his eyes off me he reached into his jacket pocket for a unit about the size of a cigarette lighter, flicked it open. "Meyer."

He paused for a moment, wincing at a burst of static that even I could hear. "Hang on, the signal's awful," he said. "Let me go nearer a window."

He stood, moved away across the stone floor. I watched him lean against one of the wooden shutters, speaking too quietly into the phone for me to hear. He was back in control again, cool, hard. There was no hint of the fact that a few moments earlier he'd been almost pleading. Sean Meyer was not a man who begged often. Not for anyone.

But he'd come close to begging me.

I glanced back into the fire, as though I'd find my answers there. Somebody once told me that you always regret most the things you *didn't* do.

If I said no, what would happen?

Sean would incline his head politely, make some throwaway comment. Of course, it was too much to ask. Then he would deliver me back to Cheshire and he would drive away. And I knew, instinctively, that I would never see him again.

If, on the other hand, I agreed, what then?

I could go to Germany for him and do my best, whatever that might turn out to be. If nothing else it

17

might tell me if I'd been a fool when I'd turned down Sean's last offer of a job. As it was I couldn't be sure, and I'd rued my decision more or less ever since. This might be my only second chance.

I thought of my burned-out flat and the stiff, uncomfortable prospect of another week in my parents' company.

Sean needed my help. Needed me. I hugged the thought to me, felt the warmth of it, and the excitement. I probably would never have got in touch with him if he hadn't made the first move, but now he had, how could I let it go?

And he didn't know.

He didn't know about the utter humiliation I'd suffered. Whatever else I saw in his eyes when he looked at me, it wasn't going to be pity.

I twisted in my seat and took advantage of his distraction to watch him as he spoke to some unseen colleague. When the call was over he flipped the phone closed and moved back towards me. As he sat down again there was just a tinge of resignation about him, and of disappointment.

My chin came up.

"OK Sean," I said calmly. "OK, I'll do it."

CHAPTER
TWO

A week later, just after New Year, I flew to Germany.

I took a BA flight out of Heathrow to Frankfurt, then caught a Lufthansa connection for the internal on to Stuttgart. It wasn't the most direct route, but at that kind of notice, it was the best Madeleine could organise.

Things had moved fast since the day of Kirk's funeral. Sean had driven me back to Cheshire, but only to collect the rest of my stuff and pack up. My parents had greeted his appearance with surprising equanimity, considering they'd once warned him off ever contacting me again.

They took my announcement that I was taking off with Sean for an indefinite period with less composure, though. My mother just bit her lip and looked away, but I had to weather my father's aloof disapproval. I imagine it was the same kind of reaction enjoyed by his motorcycle accident patients when they told him that although he'd expended hours of his undoubted surgical skill piecing them together, they were getting back on their bikes again.

Nevertheless, they didn't actively try to stop me. Which was just as well, really, because I don't think they would have succeeded.

Regretfully perhaps, I left my Suzuki RGV 250 motorbike in their garage, tucked away behind my father's Jaguar XK-8. I didn't like the idea of abandoning my independent transport, but at least the bike would be safe there until I got back.

Sean rang Madeleine on his mobile once we were on the road again. By the time we got down to his base of operations in King's Langley on the outskirts of London, she had sorted me a room in a small privately owned guest house nearby. The owner turned out to be a slim, upright chap in his eighties, a retired Royal Marine Commando with a line in war stories that kept me riveted late into the evenings.

My days were lost in whatever groundwork Sean could devise. He ran through roughly the kind of syllabus he expected them to teach until my head swam to overflowing with information I couldn't hope to digest.

On the practical side, I reckoned my biggest problem was going to be the defensive driving section. My passion for motorcycling meant I hadn't seriously driven anything with four wheels since I'd left the army. I was badly rusty, and it showed.

Sean didn't seem to share the same concerns. "As you stand now you're as good, if not better, than most of the people who come to me having completed one of these courses," he told me, but I had a feeling he was just trying to bolster my confidence.

He and Madeleine both came to Heathrow to see me off and Sean had one last piece of advice to offer. "Don't forget, if this is as dodgy as we think, they're most likely going to be expecting you," he said. "Not you personally, but someone. And they're going to be expecting them to be good. You're going to have to tone it down, Charlie. Play it quiet and you'll be OK."

I wasn't so convinced.

Outside Stuttgart airport, I snagged one of the line of Mercedes diesel taxis, and gave the driver the address of the school. As he pulled out into traffic he radioed to his controller, in German, complaining about the distance he was having to travel outside town.

"If it's too much trouble, *mein herr*," I said, a little tartly, "then please tell me."

I saw his eyes flick sharply to meet mine in the rear-view mirror. It was only then that I realised the old cupboard in my brain had fallen open. The one where I stored those years of school German lessons. I'd forgotten it was there, let alone what might be still inside.

It took just short of an hour to reach the little village of Einsbaden where the school was located. At normal speeds it probably would have taken two, but once we were out onto one of the main twin-lane roads my driver put his foot down. He cruised with the speedo needle quivering at a hundred and sixty-five kph. I did some mental juggling from klicks back into miles per hour and found we were doing a sliver over a hundred. Even at that speed he was constantly being flashed out of the way by other drivers.

Once we'd got away from the uniform industrial drabness of the city itself, the countryside was surprisingly pretty, even if I was holding on too hard most of the time to really appreciate the scenery.

He flashed through Einsbaden village itself hardly lowering his speed. The little I saw of the place was picture postcard stuff. A square with a fountain, a small café, a couple of shops, a bar. Then the houses thinned and we were back into thickly wooded countryside again.

A couple of klicks the other side of Einsbaden the driver finally slowed and swung the Merc between a pair of tall stone gateposts with poised griffins on the top of them. There was no signage, but the driver seemed confident over direction.

The driveway was narrow, pocked with water-filled ruts. It twisted out of sight into the forest that surrounded us. The driver proceeded with caution, and I let go of the centre armrest for probably the first time in the journey, edging forwards in my seat to peer out of the windscreen.

The afternoon was slipping away and the light level had started to drop fast. Under the thick, evergreen canopy it was downright gloomy. The driver switched on his headlights.

Just round the next bend there was a small security checkpoint, like some throwback to the Cold War. The lowered barrier across the road gave us no choice but to stop.

We braked to a halt alongside a hut that looked as though it had started out in life as a large garden shed. A figure in camouflage gear emerged, carrying a clipboard. He and the driver spoke together too quickly for me to catch the words, and the driver grunted.

"He says this is far as I go," he said to me. I paid the seemingly exorbitant fare without complaint, even though it bore no relation to the amount displayed on the meter. It was Sean's money I was spending, after all.

I grabbed my kit bag and climbed out into a temperature that was cold to the point of hostile. The driver didn't bother to wave goodbye as he performed a rough five-point turn, his headlights bright enough now to carve swathes and shadows through the trees.

The wood went back much further than the reach of the lights, shrouding the sound of the Merc's engine and tyres so there were no echoes. It hinted at a scale that was monumental, like something alive and breathing. Something implacable in its patient pursuit, and without mercy.

"What's your name?" the man asked. He was short and dark, with an aggressive Northern Ireland accent that made his words sound like an invitation to a fight. He had a long scar that ran from the lobe of his left ear across his cheek to his nostril, then curved down to his upper lip, so maybe someone else had felt the same. I gave him my details trying not to hold my breath.

Madeleine was something of a master hacker and there wasn't much she couldn't get out of — or add into — anyone's computer records. She had managed to slip my name to the top of a standby list of people waiting to go on courses at Einsbaden Manor. Sean had called in favours to make sure there was a suitable dropout. Some unsuspecting would-be bodyguard from another agency would be waiting for the next intake before they could undergo their training.

The man ticked my name off without any apparent alarm bells ringing and I let my breath out slowly, like I was on false papers. He jerked his head towards the shed. "Wait in there."

Inside, it was bright, clean, and surprisingly businesslike. A fan heater was going full blast, provoking heat and condensation in roughly equal measures. It was sitting precariously propped up on the narrow bench which was fixed along one wall.

There were two other people already in the shed, a man and a woman. My arrival made it cramped. The woman had taken the single folding canvas chair and she didn't look set to relinquish her prize without a struggle.

I didn't have to hear her speak to know she was German. Even sitting down she was tall and solid, with dark hair cut in a ruthless bob, and wearing glasses with thin rectangular frames. The man was lounging against the bench, youngish, much more casual, with wavy mid-brown hair brushing his collar. By the looks of her stiff discomfort, and the obvious amusement dancing behind his eyes, the man had been trying to hit on her.

"Ah," he said as I came in, "another willing victim to the slaughter." He was Irish too, but in contrast to the gatekeeper his voice had the soft flows and rhythms of Dublin running through it. "Will you not come in, darlin', and make yourself at home?"

I shut the door, and set my canvas bag down next to the other cases. If this was all their luggage, everyone was travelling light.

"I'm Declan, by the way, Declan Lloyd," the Irishman said, holding out his hand for me to shake.

"Elsa Schmitt." The woman's grip was firmer than his. Behind lenses which had a faint pink tint to them, her eyes had that watchful quality. It set up a warning jangle somewhere in my subconscious.

"I'm Charlie Fox," I said, perching on the edge of the bench and hoping it was up to the weight of two of us. "How long have you been waiting?"

Declan shrugged. "Not so long. They don't seem to know quite what to do with us."

I was about to ask more, but the door opened and the scarred man with the clipboard stuck his head inside.

"OK," he said. "They want the three of you to head on up to the house now."

We picked up our bags and stepped back out into the rapidly encroaching darkness. After the stuffily overheated shed, the cold was dazzling.

Declan shivered, looking round. "So where's the transport?"

"There isn't any," the man said, with a certain amount of relish. He waved a hand along the barely discernible track towards some hidden point in the distance. "It's only a kilometre or so. You walk."

The three of us looked in the direction he'd pointed. The sky had darkened through indigo towards an inky darkness, but above the jagged black outline of the tree tops, a waxing moon had risen.

"Oh you have to be feckin' kidding me," Declan muttered.

Elsa squared her jaw. "If you want to stay, stay," she told him, dismissive, "but *I* am going. Charlie?"

I hoisted my bag higher onto my shoulder. "I'm with you," I said with a smile.

Declan groaned. "Ah well, I suppose I can't let you two ladies venture out alone on a night like this."

Elsa threw him a withering glance and set off at a determined pace. I fell into step alongside her. Within a couple of strides, Declan had caught us up.

He immediately started up the conversation, as though he was using the sound of voices to keep at bay whatever might be lurking in the trees. He asked where we were from, and I learned that Elsa was born in Bochum, and had lived most of her life there. Declan's family owned land outside Wicklow.

"Before you arrived we were swapping our life stories," he said to me then, grinning suddenly in the silvery light. "So, Charlie, what do you do in the outside world that bores you so much you want to be a bullet catcher?"

I returned his grin. It was difficult not to. "I work in a gym," I said. Supervising weight-training programmes was something I'd only begun in the last year. It kept me occupied and fit, although lately I'd found the monotony suffocating. Sean had warned me against telling anyone about my army background, or the women's self-defence teaching I'd done after that.

"*Keep it simple, but keep it light,*" Sean had said. "*Invent as little as possible, just leave a lot out. They'll be watching the best and the worst more closely than the middle ground. You're just going to have to hold back a little, and keep to the centre of the pack.*"

"*What if they check up on me?*" I'd fretted.

"*Don't worry,*" he'd said. "*Madeleine will make sure they only find out what we want them to.*"

"So what's your story, Declan?" I asked now.

"Oh, my old man is in this business — works out in the States wet-nursing rock stars. He wanted me to join up first. You know, see the world, meet lots of interesting people, and kill them." He laughed. "I thought I'd miss out the rough-arsed bit where you have to spend four years cleaning out lavatories with your toothbrush, and go straight to baby-sitting the Hollywood babes."

"What about you, Elsa?"

She inclined her head slightly. "I was a policeman here in Germany," she said, and although I caught the dim flash of Declan's smile, we neither of us corrected her. "I left to get married, hoping to have many babies but, my marriage did not work out." She shrugged. "And so, here am I."

The simple words belied a good deal of pain, I considered. Even the Irishman didn't come back with a smart remark to that one, and for a few minutes we trudged on in silence. Until Declan put his foot into a particularly deep pothole, and picked up a bootful of cold dirty water for his pains.

"Oh Jesus, will you look at that?" he complained. "What the feck do they think they're doing leaving us to wade through this shit? And to think I've paid out good money for this."

"Don't whine, Declan," Elsa said calmly, "it will probably be the same for everyone."

"So, Charlie," he went on, ignoring her, "what's your story? I'm escaping from dead boredom, Elsa here is escaping from a dead marriage — what's your little dark secret?"

I didn't get the chance to think up a believable lie.

"Ssh!" Beside me, I almost felt Elsa tense and come to an abrupt halt. "Did you hear that?"

"Hear what?" Declan said, although I, too, could have sworn I caught the quiet crackling of dried branches, somewhere off to our left in the trees. "Oh don't start getting paranoid on us now, Elsa," he said, but there was a nervous tickle to his voice, "you'll be giving the lot of us the jitters."

He went on a few strides, moving close to the edge of the track. "Hello, hello," he called, out into the forest. The trees took his voice and sucked the power out of it, handing it back to him somehow small and lonely. "Are there any ogres, wolves or bogeymen out there?" He turned back towards us. "You see, fair ladies, noth —"

Out of the blackness a dark shape flowed up. In less than a second it seemed to utterly engulf the Irishman, taking him down like an animal kill. He fell as a dead weight. The only sound made was the breath exploding from his body as he hit the ground.

Memories and images I'd thought were buried deep reared up, vivid as a nightmare. Shock and fear clutched at me, and it was the fear that held on hardest. It gripped my heart, my throat, my gut, with steel-tipped talons. Just for a second it stopped my breath, and froze my limbs.

Then, almost in unison, Elsa and I dropped our bags and started to turn. Instinct made me keep low as I spun round and I felt the slither of something sweep across my back. An arm. It gave me a bearing and I lashed out, chopping the side of my fist into a leg at the knee. I was rewarded by a grunt of pain.

I dived sideways, hearing the German woman's wrenched-off cry as she was overwhelmed by the shadows. They seemed to swallow her up whole.

And then there was just me.

I rolled to my feet, tensed into a crouch, eyes raking the darkness. My blood was thundering through my veins, scrambling oxygen to my muscles. Every nerve and instinct told me to flee while I still had the chance.

Then, in the back of my head a tiny thought flared. "*They like to play mind games with you,*" Sean had told me. "*Like seeing how you react . . .*"

Another heartbeat. The shapes surrounding me converged another step. The edge of the tree-line was less than two metres to my right. I could still make it . . .

I straightened up, stood still, and let them come and get me.

★   ★   ★

They were rough, I reflected a short while later, but they were efficient, I had to give them that. Declan, Elsa and I were rolled onto our stomachs in the mud. I could feel the dampness of the ground leaching insidiously through each layer of my clothing. Our hands were fastened tight behind our backs with thin cord. Thick cloying hoods were dragged over our heads so that hearing became my only available sense.

Beside me, Declan was swearing under his breath, running through a list of saints and curses. Over the top of our heads someone else was muttering through clenched teeth. Probably the man I'd hit.

Well, good.

Up ahead, an engine vibrated resentfully into life, a big commercial diesel. Somebody grated the gears badly as they engaged the clutch. It was difficult to judge distance because of the muffling effect of the trees and the hood, but it seemed close by, and getting closer, rumbling the ground under us. *So, they were waiting for us. This was always going to be an ambush.* Somehow, the thought made me feel better.

Hands grabbed and hoisted us quickly into the back of the truck. It seemed a long way off the ground, with an iced bare floor that shivered as the lumbering engine was revved. I heard a flapping noise like a slack sail, and realised the truck had a canvas tilt. An army truck. I'd been in plenty of those.

"Where the feck are we going?" Declan demanded.

"No questions!" A boot scraped across the steel, connecting with the vulnerable softness of a body.

Declan groaned and went back to cursing under his breath again.

I lay on my side with my head resting on somebody's shin and concentrated on finding a position that lessened the pain in my chest. Two months previously I'd cracked my sternum. The injury had been without undue complications and had largely healed, but having my arms forced back like this made my ribcage feel as though it was being slowly torn apart up the middle. I closed my mind to the possibilities of what might happen if they were planning on manhandling us at the other end.

After only a few minutes the truck swung round in a half circle, the engine cut before we'd stopped. Doors opened, people jumped down, doors slammed. The latches of the tailgate were shot back and we were hauled out.

I managed to roll so that I landed mostly on my feet, going down onto one knee. I was dragged upright and hurried over gravel, concrete, and up a short rake of steps at such a rate that I tripped blindly over my own feet. Then I was being forced to my knees. Someone jostled into me and I heard a hiss of indrawn breath that sounded like Elsa.

The change in temperature was enough to tell me we were indoors, never mind the squashy layer of carpet under me. Even through the hood I could tell the light level had gone up dramatically. I tried to prepare my eyes for the change I knew was coming, but it couldn't be done.

When the hood came off, the brightness stung like when slicing strong onions. I screwed my eyes shut for a moment or so, then opened them cautiously. In front of me were probably twenty-five people, including another two women. They were all watching the three of us as we knelt there coated in filth and anxiety. There were some smiles, but it was mostly sympathy I saw spread among them.

A man was standing in front of us, wearing immaculately pressed khaki trousers and a green army jumper with a regimental belt over the top of it. He had smartly brushed back fair hair, a long aristocratic neck, and the kind of crinkled up eyes that he would like you to believe are more suited to staring out over a battlefield, or an ocean.

"Good evening, ladies and gentleman," he said, smiling a wolf's smile, revealing teeth too white and too even to still be his own. "I'm Major Gilby. Welcome to Einsbaden Manor."

"Oh for feck's sake," I heard Declan breathe, "can the man not just shake hands?"

The Major nodded to the men who'd brought us in. Two of them moved forward to release us. The rest fell in neatly to one side, as though this was a show they put on often enough for everybody to know their places by heart.

Now I had a chance to look at them in full light, I saw they were all big men, dressed in black assault gear, with cammed-up faces and woollen hats.

One of them had pulled a combat knife from a sheath on his thigh and sliced through our bonds. I swear I heard my breastbone creak as the pressure on it eased. At least they helped us up with rather more care than they'd shown putting us down.

"You may think this is a little drastic introduction to the course," the Major said, nodding, as the three of us eased our shoulders and surveyed our sodden clothing, "but I assure you that everyone here has been through just such an experience."

He glanced round. The other people who were obviously not staff were grinning at us in rueful embarrassment that they, too, had been caught out. Gilby turned back to us and switched off the smile, fixing us with a serious gaze.

"Let there be no mistake," he said, "by the time you've completed your training here you can be absolutely certain that nobody will be able to take you by surprise like that again!"

CHAPTER
THREE

It seemed that Declan, Elsa, and I were the last ones to arrive at Einsbaden Manor. Major Gilby launched into his full induction talk right away.

The Major might have been a charismatic speaker, had not someone obviously once told him what a charismatic speaker he was. As a result he tried too hard and found his own jokes just a little too funny. Most of us dutifully folded our lips back and showed our teeth to order, but for the instructors it was apparently harder to feign amusement. Maybe they'd just heard it all too many times before.

When he was done he told us we had an hour to get settled in and changed into dry clothes before supper. Elsa and I would be sharing a room with the two other women on the course. We were shown the way by one of the men who'd ambushed us. His name, he told us, was Rebanks, and he would be teaching weapons' handling.

"You're in the east wing and the blokes are in the west wing," he said as we followed him up the main staircase.

He turned. He had dark reddy-coloured hair over a slightly pointed face which made me think of an urban fox. Intelligent, but sly. "The instructors' quarters are in the middle, so you'll have to get past us first if you fancy any extra-curricular activity."

Elsa and I studiously ignored the knowing smile he flashed in our direction, but the predatory gleam was all too familiar.

Getting past anyone wasn't going to be easy, though. Einsbaden Manor had that slightly neglected air about it, like a seaside hotel in a resort long past its heyday. The carpeting was worn so thin in places you could no longer determine the colour. Under it, the creaking floorboards were loose and the way they rubbed against each other as a result gave them the shifting quality of sand beneath your feet. Making progress silently was not going to be easy.

We seemed to tramp for half a mile along corridors that all looked the same, the woodwork painted an institutional cream. The tied-back curtains at the long windows were so frail I doubt you could have successfully drawn them.

I noticed that the usual mandatory notices for fire exits were all in English first, German second, almost as an afterthought. Madeleine had told me that the school had transferred from Wiltshire after the gun ban. I hadn't realised that relocation had been almost wholesale.

Eventually Rebanks pushed open the door to a large room with a high ceiling. There were four single beds in opposite corners, lost among the floor space. Each bed had a lockable cabinet alongside it and a trunk at the foot.

"There you go, ladies, home sweet home for the next fortnight," Rebanks said with another grin. "Make yourselves comfortable." I almost expected him to linger, but with that he departed, pulling the door closed behind him.

Two of the beds were obviously already taken. I threw my bag on the nearest of those that weren't and sat down gingerly. The metal frame squeaked and the mattress sagged deeply in the middle.

Elsa had pushed open a small doorway in the far wall. "It's a bathroom, I think," she said, with some doubt in her voice. "Do you want first risk of the shower, or do I?"

In the end, I took the first turn, finding to my surprise that although the plumbing appeared as ancient as everything else, the water pressure was good and the temperature was consistently high.

"Please don't wait for me," Elsa said as I dressed again in clean jeans and a shirt. "I will follow you down in a short time."

I listened until she set the shower running again, then quickly unpacked my stuff. In the bottom of my bag was the mobile phone Sean had given me before I left. It would work all over Europe, he'd explained, and if I kept it switched off when I didn't actually want to make a call the battery would last for quite a while without needing to be recharged.

He'd programmed the number of his own mobile into the memory and told me to call him any time, night or day, if I needed to. He wouldn't contact me unless it was absolutely necessary. There was an answering service for when the phone was off that would automatically activate and replay the message as soon as I next switched it on again. He would keep in touch that way.

I flipped the phone open, hit the power button, and then hesitated. Finally, I switched it off again, hid it away in the cabinet. I hadn't enough to report to make the call worth while. With a final glance round to make sure my stuff was all out of sight, I left the room and headed back for the stairs.

On the way I looked for the quietest bits of the floor. I had a feeling that I might need to do some sneaking about and it was good practice. The edges of the carpet were much less worn than the middle and if you took it slow and careful the boards under them could be walked on without making enough noise to drown out a thunderstorm.

As I crept onto the open landing I saw a man about halfway down the staircase and I recognised the reddy-coloured hair of our friendly weapons' handler. He'd just reached the lower treads when he was halted by a harsh whisper from one of the doorways on the ground floor.

"Rebanks! Where the hell have you been?" It was Major Gilby who stepped out into the light, hands tight by his sides.

The man shrugged, on the sidelines of insolent. "I've been helping the ladies settle in," he said lazily. "I think I might be in with a chance there."

I peeled back my sleeve and checked my watch. It was thirty-five minutes since he'd delivered us to our door and disappeared.

"Oh for God's sake, Rebanks, take this seriously!" Gilby snapped. He looked up then and I shrank back behind the nearest wall, just peering round the corner through the balustrade. He lowered his voice again, but the tiled floor of the hallway ensured that it carried up to me. "You know how things stand at the moment. No one goes anywhere on their own. Not for any reason! Understood?"

"Yes *sir*!" Rebanks said, but there was laughter in his voice.

Gilby went white. His fingers clenched briefly and he took a step nearer, pushing his face in close to Rebanks.

"Until this thing is over, you follow orders," he said tightly. "I don't have to remind you of the consequences of —"

He broke off, and I heard it, too. Creaky footsteps from the corridor opposite my hiding place, which led into the other wing. I hopped back a few strides, then began walking normally. The floorboards under my feet crunched noisily like packed-down snow. I'd just got to the head of the stairs when Declan appeared from the direction of the men's quarters.

"Charlie, me darlin'! Have you been waiting for me?" he greeted me. He seemed to have recovered his bounce. "Are you ready to eat? After all that pillocking about in the woods, I'm starving."

We walked down together, passing the two school men with only a short nod of acknowledgement. I tried to act casual, but I found Gilby watching us with a narrowed stare. Perhaps it was my guilty conscience, or maybe he just didn't like Declan's cheek.

The dining hall had the same high ceiling of the rest of the house. It was huge, with a massive ornate fireplace at one end that cried out for a pair of sleeping wolfhounds in front of the blazing logs.

There were two long tables laid up, one on the main floor and the other up on the dais which ran across the opposite end of the room from the fireplace. The instructors, naturally, were taking their places at the high table. It was interesting that they felt the need to emphasise their elevated position with such heavy-handed lack of finesse.

There was a hot buffet to one side where people were already helping themselves. Declan and I joined the end of the queue.

Seeing that Einsbaden Manor was being run on military lines, I'd expected the worst of the food, but I was pleasantly surprised. It was more like the fare in a decent pub carvery. Three large cuts of meat and plenty of vegetables that actually *hadn't* been cooked long enough to lose all structural integrity. I piled my plate high.

More by accident than design, Declan and I drifted together towards a couple of empty chairs at the nearest end of the long table that was set for the pupils. There didn't seem to be a seating plan. You just found a space and got on with it.

Declan took the chair to my right. To my left was a big man with fair hair cropped close at the sides and gelled into a flat-top. He ate single-mindedly, resting his elbows on the table and shovelling it in. He had arms that were nearly as thick as my thighs, straining the sleeves of his T-shirt. He glanced at me as I sat down and I gave him a brief nod and a smile.

He didn't smile back. His pale blue eyes flickered over me once, then he turned his attention back to his plate, as though I wasn't worth the effort. With a shrug, I dug in to my own food and ignored him. Another of life's charmers.

Declan, however, wasn't so easily deflected. He looked around at the faces nearest to us, and instantly struck up an easy conversation.

I stayed quiet, letting them talk around me, but kept my eyes open. The instructors were drifting in now, filling up their plates and taking their seats on the dais. Now that they'd washed off their cam cream and hung up their woolly hats for the day, they looked human for the most part.

Rebanks arrived with Gilby still glowering after him, although the Major's expression settled into cool command as soon as he was among the students, like the professional smile of a politician.

I picked out another face I recognised. The scarred Irishman who'd greeted us at the gate. As I watched him climb the steps onto the dais I caught him pause fractionally and grimace in pain. It was only a small gesture, quickly covered. If I hadn't been watching him, I probably would have missed it. But the Major had seen it, too, and there was something darker and deeper in his eyes than the incident should have provoked.

It seemed that the scarred man wasn't the only one of the Einsbaden team who was below par. Another of the instructors entered the dining hall. A tall, wide-shouldered man with a slight but distinct limp. Half of the pupils at the table watched his progress across the room.

Or we did until he turned and glared at us, at any rate. He had sunken eyes under full black eyebrows that met as a single feature across the bridge of his nose, emphasising the slightly Neanderthal bulge of his forehead.

But something about the way he moved reminded me of Sean. They shared the same kind of cohesive control. I marked him out as dangerous without quite knowing why.

"Now there is a man whose lessons we will not enjoy, I think," said the beefy man next to me, suddenly breaking his silence. He had a deep voice with a trace of a German accent.

"Who is he?" I asked.

The German didn't look inclined to answer until he saw a couple of the others also waiting for his reply. "His name is Blakemore. Apparently he will be teaching us unarmed combat," he said then, shrugging. "It was probably not a wise move to antagonise him so early in the course."

For a moment my heart jumped. He'd seemed to direct that last comment in my direction.

"Who's been antagonising the man?" Declan asked. He raised his eyebrows at me. "Did he not like the way we fell in the mud at his feet?"

But the German nodded across the dining hall towards Elsa, who had just entered, freshly showered with her immaculate bob dried into place. She looked fit and self-confident.

"When they picked the three of you up I understand that she put up quite a fight," the man said. He went back to his food, spearing three or four carrots onto his fork. "Mr Blakemore has an old knee injury that has been aggravated and he is not a happy man."

I remembered the shape that had swung at me and the blow I'd managed to land. When I glanced up, I saw Blakemore studying Elsa with bleak interest that I didn't like the look of. I could only hope that the unwitting German woman wasn't going to get too much stick for my actions. But if I wanted my cover to stay intact there was no way I was going to hold my hand up.

The next morning we started our training in earnest. At five o'clock the next morning, to be precise, when Gilby's merry band of instructors came rampaging through the dormitories. They made a point of producing twice the quantity of noise that was required to get us out of our beds. And at three times the volume.

I was shocked into wakefulness as the overhead lights were slapped on and by the nastily cheerful voice of Todd, who had been introduced after supper the night before as the head physical training instructor.

He was short, almost stocky, with hair clipped razor-thin to his scalp. Not because he still hankered after his undoubted previous army career, but because he spent half his life in the shower after exercise. He had the air of someone who's fitter on a daily basis than you'll ever be in your life. And knows it.

"Good morning ladies," he barked, swivelling his bull neck to survey the room's occupants with just a little too much attention. "Outside in your running kit in fifteen minutes, if you please!"

The door slammed shut behind him and for a moment I continued to lie still, concentrating on slowing down my heart and preventing its imminent explosion. I've never liked loud alarm clocks and this was worse. It can't be good for you to surface from sleep with such suddenness and ferocity. The wake-up equivalent of the bends.

"Come on then girls," Shirley said briskly, sitting up in her bed opposite mine and reaching for her sweatshirt. "We can't let the boys think we're not up to the job."

Shirley Worthington was from Solihull, the archetypal bored housewife. She was a bouncy woman who wouldn't see forty again except in the rear-view mirror. Within five minutes of our meeting last night, she'd been handing round photographs of her grandchildren. Not exactly the kind of person I'd expected to find studying to be a bodyguard.

To my left I heard a quiet groan, and then Elsa pushed back her bedclothes and sat up wearily. The German woman looked like death, but I had a feeling I was probably seeing a fairly accurate picture of myself. Only Shirley seemed irritatingly alert.

I glanced over towards the room's fourth occupant, who was little more than a vague outline under the blankets. Even Todd's violent incursion hadn't made an impact.

Elsa heaved herself out of bed and padded across the squeaky floor. "Jan," she said loudly, shaking the lump by what appeared to be a shoulder. "It is time for you to be waking up now, please."

Jan King made a muffled comment that probably contained at least four expletives. I'd never come across a woman with such a wide vocabulary of swear words. Or a man, for that matter. And I was used to hanging out around bikers.

Judging from her dulcet tones, Jan was from the East End of London. She was small, sallow-skinned, and intense, with the stringy skinniness of a long-distance runner and very bad teeth. She didn't look much like a bodyguard, either.

By the time the four of us had scrambled into our clothes and got down the main staircase, the men were already outside on the gravel. They stood in a huddled group, their collective breath rising like steam from winter cattle under the floodlights.

The stars were still glittering above us. By my reckoning we were still a good two and a half hours away from sunrise. Why, I wondered bitterly, couldn't Kirk have got himself killed on a summer course?

"Ah, so good of you to join us at last, ladies," Todd's voice was sneering as he jogged up in a dark blue track-suit. "Too busy putting your make-up on, were you?"

Jan's response was short and to the point, but I don't think the reaction she got was the one she was hoping for. If she'd thought it through that far.

"Physically impossible, I would have thought," Todd said mildly, then his face tightened. "Get down and give me ten press-ups."

Jan's face mirrored her surprise. She put her hands on her hips. "Or what?" she demanded.

"Or you can pack your bag right now and bugger off back home, love," Todd said. He gave her a nasty smile. "Better make that fifteen press-ups."

"You can't order me about like that," Jan said, but there was a note of uncertainty in her voice now, underlying the belligerence.

"You didn't read the small print when you signed up for this, did you?" Todd asked. He raised his voice, speaking to the group of us. "We need hundred per cent effort from you lot. Anyone who isn't prepared to put the graft in and you're straight out." He waved an arm towards the edge of the gravel, where it faded out into the gloom in the direction of the forest track we'd come in on.

He turned back to Jan. "It's a long walk out of here, but you can use the time to reflect on what a failure you are. On how you haven't got the guts and the dedication to make it." He shrugged. "Makes no difference to me. So, what's it to be — twenty press-ups, or the next flight back home?"

They continued to stare each other out for a moment longer, then Jan dropped slowly and reluctantly to the frozen gravel.

Todd watched her complete the first three, then turned away. How many press-ups she actually managed to achieve was immaterial, I realised, it was the capitulation he'd been after.

Oh God, one of those . . .

I'd come across enough of Todd's type — the control freaks and the macho bullshitters. First in the army, and then in the brief period I'd spent working the doors in a local nightclub. I'd found out early that I didn't like playing the game their way. Sean had warned me to keep a low profile, but if this was their attitude, it wasn't going to be easy. Perhaps it was a good job there was someone as bolshy as Jan to do the answering back.

"OK people, listen up," Todd shouted. "We're going to start out nice and easy with a straightforward little jog . . ."

His idea of a little jog, we quickly discovered, involved several klicks of rough forest tracks, at a pace he must have known hardly any of us could hope to sustain. The ground was frosted hard enough to concuss your joints with every stride. If it had been wet, the mud would have been impassable.

As it was, within the first kilometre we became widely strung out. I was thankful that I'd spent most of the previous year working at the gym, and so was fit enough to keep up with the middle of the field, at least. I didn't have to put the brakes on in order to stick to the inconspicuous position Sean had recommended.

Two of the other instructors played sheepdog. Todd showed off his superior stamina by roaming up and down the line, goading us on. Sometimes he fell back almost to the rear and sometimes he'd sprint past to harangue those at the front.

I was surprised to see Blakemore lead off at the head of the group, despite the comments of the big German the night before. Blakemore was quick enough but he moved with a slight awkwardness, compensating for his damaged knee.

Bringing up the rear was the Belfast man, whose name I'd learned was O'Neill. I remembered his unguarded gesture last night at supper and wondered how he'd come by the hurt he was so obviously trying to mask. It surprised me that these two were the ones out running with us. If the Major didn't even allow for injury time among his instructors, how was he going to treat the rest of us?

Without breakfast, my body had just about used up its available reserves after around five klicks. My thigh muscles were blocky and buzzing and I could feel my pace weakening with every stride. The cold air was murderous as I sucked it down into my lungs, burning my chest from the inside out.

When the man in front of me started to slow, I couldn't have been more grateful at that point. More and more of us fell back to a walk, then tottered to a stop. I bent over, hands braced on my knees, and tried to drag air into my system through tubes that suddenly seemed totally inadequate for the job.

"What the fuck's going on?" Todd demanded as he came pounding up from giving them hell at the back. He didn't seem to be out of breath and was barely sweating. "Have you pathetic lot given up already?"

For a moment there was a silence that was almost fearful, then someone dragged up the courage to speak. "We're not sure of the path, sir," he said.

"What?" Todd roared. "Who's that? Where's Blakemore?"

"Er, I'm McKenna, sir," the same man supplied. "Mr Blakemore, he, er, just sort of dropped back." He spoke hesitantly, in case he was blamed for the bad news. "I think his knee might have been giving him some trouble."

Todd swore under his breath. "Come on then," he said sharply, and led off at a furious pace. I dragged in a final lungful of stationary air and forced my quivering limbs back into a jog. It was worse starting up again than if I'd kept running.

When we got back to the Manor, Todd and O'Neill had us doing ten minutes of star jumps and sit-ups just off the gravel, on the icy grass. We were doing full army sit-ups, which I never recommended to anyone when I was working at the gym. I didn't think it was a point worth mentioning to these two.

It was only then that Blakemore reappeared. As he came past me I noticed he was moving the same as he had been when he set out, with no apparent increase in his limp.

O'Neill must have seen that, too, because he broke off shouting vicious encouragement and grabbed Blakemore's arm, spinning him to a standstill. "Where the fuck have you been?" he said, keeping his voice low. "Todd's been doing his fruit."

48

"Don't panic," Blakemore said calmly. His mouth twisted into a derisive smile. "He's just mad 'cos he didn't think of it himself."

O'Neill skimmed his eyes over the nearest of us to see if anyone was obviously listening in. I forced a bit more effort into my latest sit-up. "You know what the old man said about us sticking together," he went on, speaking quietly through clenched teeth. "He's going to go ballistic if he finds out you've been off on your own."

"So don't tell him," Blakemore said, careless now.

"Yeah, and if anyone else finds out, that makes us both look bad, doesn't it?" O'Neill muttered.

Blakemore shrugged his arm away. "Well," he said coldly, "I'm not the one with secrets. How about you?"

CHAPTER
FOUR

After we'd showered and grabbed breakfast, they hustled us straight into the classroom. Gilby conducted the first lesson himself. He announced it, in the manner of someone expecting a round of applause, as an introduction to the art and science that was modern close protection work, and a debunking of the myths. Basically, it was an extended version of his welcome speech from the night before.

He was only mildly condescending towards the women in the industry, even admitting that they might have their areas of particular suitability. I smiled sweetly when he caught my eye, and tried not to show how much I was grinding my teeth. But, almost to my surprise, the more he spoke the more interested in the subject I became.

Annoyance and curiosity were useful emotions. They kept me awake. After the cold and the exertion of the morning, the stuffy heat of the classroom began to have its effect. Some of the students were visibly struggling not to fall asleep.

At one point McKenna nodded so hard that he nearly fell off his chair. He only got away with it by turning the movement into a violent coughing fit. He was a skinny youngster with a pale complexion that seemed to go pink at the slightest provocation. By the time he'd finished he was flushed from his prominent Adam's apple right up into the roots of his hair.

Gilby paused and momentarily closed his eyes during McKenna's performance. The show of mild irritation was natural enough, but that wasn't what bothered me. It was the sudden utter immobility that came over him.

The way he did it made my skin tighten.

I'd come across men before who had that same innate stillness and it always put the fear of God into me. Gilby may have carried off a civilised gloss, but underneath was something dark, that coiled and slithered. And just for a moment his flash of temper had let it show. I'd thought him another out-of-touch officer, a borderline upper-class twit, but I'd been wrong.

I glanced sideways at the others, but the majority of them hadn't noticed the change that had come over him. The ex-policewoman, Elsa was one of the few that had, I saw. Declan was just looking bored.

"The days of muscle-bound heavies in dark glasses are over," Gilby continued, as though nothing had happened. "There will always be occasions when you're called upon to provide a visible deterrent, but most of the time you'll need to blend in with the rich, the famous, and the powerful." He cast a critical eye over the disparate bunch of us as we wilted in our chairs. "I imagine for some of you that's going to take quite some learning."

He checked his watch, nodded sharply, then swept up his papers and walked out with his back ramrod straight.

"I wonder how well your man there blends into a crowd," Declan muttered as we gathered our notebooks. "You'd spot him for army brass even if he was wearing a dress."

We went straight from there into a class for unarmed combat with Blakemore. The instructor must have been using an ice pack on his knee since the morning's run, because when he sauntered into the room designated as the gym there was no sign of the limp.

After spending more than four years teaching self-defence classes for women, it was interesting to be on the receiving end. Blakemore was showy, I considered, but with the underlying grace that denotes an expert. The coarse construction of his face, the heavy layout of his features, could have fooled you into thinking he was little more than a thug. I hadn't been expecting such finesse or delicacy of technique, but it would seem my first impression of him had been the right one.

Now, he demonstrated half a dozen moves for restraint and removal of someone who might be approaching your principal in a threatening manner.

I was surprised to see that he was using O'Neill as his guinea pig. The Irishman was clearly unhappy to be put into repeated arm and headlocks, and then dropped onto the crashmats under foot. A couple of times I caught him passing a hand over his ribs as he got to his feet. The looks he levelled towards the impassive Blakemore should have been enough to make him shiver.

Blakemore, however, absorbed each barbed glance without reaction. When he was done he picked up a pair of big sparring pads and tossed one across to the other man hard enough to almost make him stagger. *What the hell's going on here?*

"OK," he said, turning to the rest of us, "that's the kind of thing we're going to be showing you over the period of the course. To begin with, though, I want to find out what kind of a punch you can pack. Form two lines and let's see what you can do."

I watched the big blond German I'd sat next to the night before line up in front of Blakemore. He had a bodybuilder's stance, with his arms pushed out away from his sides slightly by the sheer over-development of his upper arms and lats.

I'd learned that the German's name was Michael Hofmann and he was ex-army, from an elite regiment that was the German equivalent of the Paras. No great surprises there, then.

Now, he squared up to Blakemore, who was holding the pad up across his chest and stomach with his arms tensed through the straps on the back. He was leaning hard into it, feet braced wide apart. Everybody stopped and watched as the big man moved forwards to take his first swing.

Hofmann smiled very slightly, and hit Blakemore with an explosive uppercut that compressed the thick foam pad almost to its fullest extent. It was a testament to the instructor's upper body strength that he didn't so much as shift his feet under the onslaught. Even though he rocked back from the force of the blow and let out a grunt of effort.

Hofmann looked vaguely disappointed, a frown creasing his brow as if he couldn't compute why the other man was still standing. When someone the size of Hofmann hits you, you generally fall over and stay down.

By comparison, Shirley — who was next — barely made a dent in the pad. Blakemore grinned at her.

I turned my attention to the row I was in. Ahead of me, McKenna flailed wildly at the pad O'Neill was holding, to greater noise than effect. When he'd exhausted himself it was Jan's turn.

She stepped forwards and I noticed O'Neill's attention was elsewhere, that he was more interested in what was happening to Blakemore. I don't know if Jan saw this, but she hit the pad low and right, at a point that corresponded almost exactly to the area I'd seen O'Neill favouring when Blakemore had been playing with him. She was only slightly built, but somewhere along the line she'd learned how to punch, keeping her wrist locked straight, putting most of her body weight behind it.

O'Neill wasn't prepared for the force of the hit. It rocked him. He had to take a step back to counteract it, to regain his balance. I saw the surprise and anger in his face.

As she walked to the back of the line Blakemore called across, "Hey — Jan, isn't it?"

54

She paused, turned.

A smile spread across his face as his eyes flicked to his fellow instructor. "Nice punch," he said.

Jan nodded briefly and as she turned away she was smiling, too. She knew, I realised, that O'Neill was injured and yet she'd deliberately set out to hurt him. *What does that say about you?* I wondered. *What makes you tick that way?*

I was still mulling that one over when it was my shot. O'Neill eyed me warily, but I made sure I produced a suitably lacklustre blow.

He treated Jan's second turn with caution, too. This time she throttled back so that he nearly over-compensated for her unexpectedly feeble fist. That didn't serve to endear her any more than the harder blow he'd clearly been expecting.

It was only as we finished up the class, when O'Neill handed his pad back to Blakemore, that he touched a hand to his side. He pulled a face as he moved his fingers gently, like he was testing a tender area of skin.

"You all right?" Blakemore asked him, although there was no concern in his voice.

O'Neill let his hand drop away. "I'm fine," he said shortly. "Just fine. Leave it."

With a brooding stare, Blakemore watched him walk out of the gym and vanish in the direction of the instructors' quarters.

As the rest of us milled out into the main hallway Major Gilby put in an appearance. He informed us, to varying shades of dismay, that we'd each have to present a short talk to the rest of the class that afternoon.

"And what would that be about?" Declan asked.

"I would suggest that it has some relevance to the course you're on," Gilby clipped, with a fraction of a smile. "Some modern or historical event that illustrates close protection in one form or another. I want to see your take on the job. There have been plenty of assassinations or attempted assassinations to choose from. Look at all the political hits that have taken place over the past fifty years — Sadat, the Kennedys, Earl Mountbatten."

He dropped the last name in with a flickered glance at Declan, as though the Irishman had been personally responsible for the terrorist bomb attack that had killed the Queen's cousin. *Did he needle O'Neill like that, too?* "I'm sure I can rely on you all to come up with something different."

Declan was too laid back to rise to the Major's little dig. "And just where are we supposed to find out all the gory details at this kind of notice?" he said instead.

Gilby smiled at him, more fully this time. "There's plenty of information in the library," he said. "You'll have an hour after lunch to do your research."

Then, with his usual curt nod, he turned and disappeared again.

We had ten minutes to kill before lunch. Some of the students headed straight for the library, but I needed some fresh air. I grabbed my jacket and slipped out through the main doorway, trying not to shiver at the cloak of cold that instantly wrapped itself around me.

It was just before noon and in theory the sun was at its height. In reality it was practising low-level flying techniques, barely skimming over the tops of the trees to the south of me.

I stuck my hands deep into the pockets of my jacket and hunched down into the collar, trying to make a windproof seal. It didn't work particularly well.

There was a selection of cars on the forecourt, most of which apparently belonged to the instructors. There was one motorbike among them, a black Honda CBR900RR, a FireBlade, and I felt myself irresistibly drawn over to have a closer look.

The bike was a nearly new model, with less than four thousand kilometres on the clock. I didn't know who owned it, but whoever it was they certainly rode it with more guts than I would have done.

The back tyre was worn right to the edges on both sides and the hero pegs on the ends of the footrests were roughed up. You don't get them like that unless you've been scratching them on the road surface round every available corner.

With a regretful thought to my RGV sitting abandoned in my father's garage, I straightened up and strolled across the gravel towards the corner of the house. I had no particular aim or destination in mind, and I took the opportunity to get a feel for my surroundings in daylight for the first time.

Now I could see it properly Einsbaden Manor was a magnificent old place, imposing and severe, in grey stone that hadn't weathered enough to lose the detail of the original carvings. Two large flat-roofed wings extended outwards from a semicircular central tower, with three rows of evenly spaced windows laid out with almost military precision.

I realised as I looked round that I had no more idea now about who had shot Kirk dead and why, than I did when Sean had first told me about it. Where on earth was I going to start looking? I had to admit that I didn't have a clue.

Round the corner the gravel scattered onto a concrete path that followed the contours of the house. The air smelt clean, faintly of wood and pine needles.

Another ribbon of concrete stretched away across the grass towards a group of buildings about two hundred metres away, on the edge of the trees. As I watched, a man emerged from a doorway in one of the buildings, carefully locking it behind him. I was too far away to recognise who it was.

As casually as I could, I carried on further round the house. Towards the rear it lost its architectural neatness, became more random. The ground behind it dropped away sharply into what I should imagine were once formal gardens, but they'd been covered over with an all-weather surface. This was scored with tyre tracks. A group of slightly battered-looking, dirty vehicles were parked, haphazardly, to one side. Ah, the dreaded defensive driving arena. I still wasn't sure how I was going to cope with that one.

Reaching out from the ground floor at the back of the house was a walled terrace, raised a couple of metres off the ground so that it overlooked this glorified car park. Several of the students were already occupying this eyrie, despite the cold. As I drew nearer, I realised why.

All of them were furtively smoking. Gilby had made it clear from the outset that the whole of the Manor was strictly a smoke-free zone. It was a sign of their dedication to their habit, I thought, that they were prepared to brave such cold to enjoy it.

The bitter wind whipped over the exposed terrace, dragging the smoke with it. The last vestiges blew over me, tainted my nostrils. I decided not to advance any further.

All the ground-floor windows had deep external window ledges, and I settled myself onto one. At least it was partly shielded from the weather.

As I watched, Jan came out onto the terrace. She had the collar of her coat pulled up with one hand as a windbreak, trying unsuccessfully with the other to light the cigarette in her mouth. After she'd made a few failed attempts I saw Hofmann lever himself away from the balustrade and offer her his lighter.

There was what seemed to be a long pause while they just looked at each other, before Jan reached out and took it. From the little I'd got to know of her, I'd worked out that Jan was the kind of girl who didn't like accepting help from anyone, but least of all from a man.

Whatever make of lighter Hofmann owned, though, it was designed for outdoor use. It sparked and flared first time. She gave it back to him quickly, with a reluctant nod of thanks, before hurrying away.

Elsa was the next person out onto the terrace. She arrived with the only Norwegian student on the course, a surprisingly small guy called Tor Romundstad. I'd always thought the Norwegians were all strapping individuals, descended from Vikings, but he was a good six inches shorter than Elsa. He'd attempted to compensate for his lack of stature by cultivating the most enormous bushy moustache, like a seventies porn star. Elsa must have come out for the conversation rather than the nicotine, because although Romundstad was smoking, she was not.

Elsa's attention wasn't completely on her companion, though. I noticed her head kept turning towards Hofmann, who was still standing by the edge of the terrace, staring out over the grounds. After a minute or two longer she excused herself and went over to him.

I was too far away to hear their voices. The wind brought occasional snatches, but too faint and few to piece any words together. I had to work on body language instead.

From that I got the impression that Elsa asked Hofmann a question. One that he either didn't know the answer to, or didn't want to give it. Whichever, he met her enquiry with a dismissive shake of his head. She persisted, and it was then that Hofmann's manner changed. He bent his head, leaning in to her and speaking fast.

I saw Elsa's body jerk with the shock of his reaction, her face blanking. No one else on the terrace seemed to

60

have noticed what was happening. I started levering myself forwards, but as quickly as it had started, it was over.

Hofmann threw down his cigarette end, stamped it out, and headed back inside, leaving Elsa standing forlornly behind him on the mossy flags.

I hopped down from my window ledge and walked the rest of the distance onto the terrace, crossing to the German woman. She didn't seem to notice my arrival until I was almost on top of her. I touched her arm.

"Are you OK?" I asked.

She nodded vaguely, then glanced at me and seemed to pull herself together. "Yes, Charlie, thank you. I am OK."

"I saw you talking to Michael Hofmann, and he didn't look happy about it," I said. "What happened?"

"I thought I knew him," Elsa murmured. Her glasses had darkened in the light so it was difficult to read her eyes, but her voice was off-kilter, almost a babble, and her face was too pale. "You know how it is, you think you recognise someone and then you feel foolish when you are mistaken."

She looked up at me again, as if to see how I was swallowing the lie. Not well, she realised. "Please excuse me," she said. "It is time for lunch and we must prepare our little talk for afterwards, no?"

Before I could stop her, she'd hurried inside, letting the partly glazed door slam behind her. Romundstad also watched her go and he turned and raised an eyebrow at me, as though I was the one who'd upset her.

"Well now," I muttered to myself, "what the hell was *that* all about?"

The Major was right about the Manor's library. There was indeed all the information we could wish for on the subject of assassinations — failed and successful. I decided to go for the attempt on US President Ronald Reagan by John Hinkley Jr in March 1981.

Not only was it well documented in the library's files, but I felt it gave me plenty to talk about on the subject of his close protection team — both good and bad. After all, Reagan's secret service bodyguards had missed the fact that his would-be assassin had been hanging around all day outside the Washington Hilton Hotel looking highly suspicious.

On the plus side, when the attack did happen they'd reacted textbook fast. Three of them, including Reagan's Press Secretary, had even managed to get themselves shot in the process.

The members of the team who were still left standing had bounced on Hinkley, while another had thrown their injured principal into his limo and hustled him away from the scene.

What I didn't add, because it wasn't included in the Manor's information, was that if Hinkley had chosen a revolver with a longer barrel and a higher muzzle velocity than the Rohm R6-14 he'd been using, the explosive-head Devastator rounds he'd loaded might just have had the effect their name implied. Scratch another US president.

"So, Miss Fox, what conclusions do you draw from this?" Gilby asked when I'd finally ground to a halt.

"That Reagan's close protection team were good in a crisis, but not so hot at planning and prevention," I said. "They should never have let it happen in the first place. But, it does make Reagan unique — he's the only serving US president to date who's survived actually being shot by an assassin."

He smiled. "Excellent," he said, the praise pleasing me more than it should have done. "Who's next?"

I regained my seat next to one of the tall windows that looked out over the rear of the house. Elsa stood up, gathering her file of papers, and walked to the front of the classroom. The students were all sitting at tables, but the instructors, including Gilby, had lined themselves up along the back wall.

They had listened to all the presentations so far, mine included, with poorly disguised boredom. I got the impression that this was one of Gilby's pet ideas as far as the curriculum went and nobody else could see the value of it.

Elsa was the last to go. She reached the desk at the front and put her papers down neatly. "Good afternoon," she said, sombre. "We have heard already about many famous events, but I would like to speak about one that is not in your library records. It is more recent, and not so well known. My subject is the abduction of a young girl called Heidi Krauss."

The name meant nothing to me, but it was instantly apparent that it did to Gilby and his men. It was as though someone had passed an electrical current through the wall behind them. Every one of them jerked upright and Gilby even took a step forwards, as though he was going to try and prevent Elsa from speaking.

The German woman looked up. "Is there a problem, Major?" she asked, without inflection.

The rest of us followed the exchange like the crowd at a top-class tennis match, heads following each volley from one end of the room to the other. Gilby must have realised almost immediately that to stop her now was going to look more suspicious than letting her continue. "Of course not, Frau Schmitt, if you feel it's relevant," he said stiffly, allowing a trace of doubt to enter his voice.

Elsa brushed it aside. "She was taken from her own bed, in the middle of the night, from under the noses of her bodyguards," she said, coolly now. "Yes, I think it is very relevant, don't you?"

Gilby recognised defeat when it was staring him in the face. Without further demur he stepped back to his place and waved her to continue. I twisted round slightly in my chair so I could watch the instructors as much as Elsa.

The German woman had come well prepared for her lecture and she didn't get it from the Manor library, that's for sure. There was an elderly photocopier in there, which we'd all used to produce grainy pictures of our main protagonists, taken from the newspaper cuttings and books.

Elsa already had photographs, which meant she could only have brought them with her. She tacked a line of them up onto the dusty blackboard for us to see.

"This is Heidi Krauss," she said, indicating an awkwardly posed studio picture of a girl who looked barely sixteen. "This is her father, Dieter, a successful and wealthy industrialist, and this is their home on the outskirts of Düsseldorf."

She delivered the details in a flat, almost clinical style, the way I imagine she used to report to her superior officers when she'd been in the police. She hardly referred to her notes and barely glanced at Gilby or his men as she spoke.

Dieter Krauss, she told us, was away in the Middle East on the night his daughter had been kidnapped, just two weeks before Christmas. I realised with a jolt that she was talking about *this* Christmas. Heidi was at home with three household staff and four personal bodyguards. Of a Mrs Krauss, there was no mention.

There had been trouble with the movement sensors round the perimeter of the property. They had been badly adjusted so that small animals had been causing a number of false alarms. When the system was triggered again shortly before eleven on that evening, the man on duty did not immediately alert his colleagues to a possible security breach.

Instead, he had taken a torch and gone out alone through a side entrance to check the grounds for himself. There, a small force — more than four, it was reckoned, but less than eight — had overpowered him and gained entry through the open door.

Leaving a man guiding them towards Heidi's location using the internal security cameras, the intruders had closed in on her. They had used a taser stunner to instantly incapacitate her, then wrapped her in a blanket and started to carry her out, with the rest of her security team oblivious in the next room.

Had the housekeeper not stepped out into a corridor at the wrong moment, that's where the story would have ended. As it was; the woman started screaming. The intruders shot her in the neck, killing her instantly.

The close protection team had responded immediately to the alert, drawing their own weapons, but they had been understandably reluctant to become involved in a gunfight when the risk of accidentally hitting their principal was so high.

Hamstrung in this way, they'd stood little chance. One of them was also shot and killed, while another received a leg wound which had resulted in amputation. They had exchanged fire but, Elsa reported, they were doubtful that they hit anyone. Certainly none of the intruders had been injured sufficiently to prevent their escape — with Heidi.

Elsa paused and looked around at us. She didn't seem to be aware that she held the absolute attention not only of the class, but of the instructors as well. They had frozen up like a Madame Tussaud's exhibit, only not so lifelike. If Gilby clamped his jaw shut any tighter he was going to shatter those perfect teeth.

"So, Frau Schmitt, what conclusions do you draw from this?" he managed to grit out from between them.

Elsa closed her folder and shrugged. "That the bodyguards were careless and that they totally underestimated the level of threat to their client," she said at last.

Gilby took a breath as though he was fighting to control a temper that was rising like fire. He won, but I was sitting close enough to see the cost of that victory manifest itself in the tremor of a tiny muscle at the side of his jaw.

He nodded, jerkily. "Very good, Frau Schmitt," he bit out. His narrowed gaze swept across the rest of us, just in case we were thinking of making any smart remarks. "Class dismissed!"

He stalked out of the room with the instructors following him in a wave. I looked round and saw that most of the students were staring blankly at each other. Like me, they knew something was going on, but they had no idea what.

"Well, Elsa my darlin', I don't know what it is that you've said that should upset the Major so much," Declan remarked as he got to his feet, "but I don't think he'll be round to bring you a cup of tea and a biscuit first thing tomorrow morning, *that's* for sure."

CHAPTER
FIVE

On Day Two the four of us thought we'd spike our instructors' guns by setting our alarm clocks half an hour earlier than the six o'clock they'd told us would be our wake-up call. We should have known that wasn't the way things were going to work.

Todd came barging in at 5a.m. anyway, just like yesterday.

When Elsa sleepily protested we had been told we had another hour in bed, he launched into a screaming fit that any drill sergeant I've ever come across would have stood back and admired. As he ranted, flecks of spit sprayed from his lips like a nobbled racehorse. We scrambled out of our beds and fled into our running gear before he had a full-blown embolism.

As we hustled down the stairs I wondered briefly if Declan was right and Todd's reaction did have anything to do with Elsa's lecture of the day before.

Physical training this morning involved our usual merry little five-kilometre jog, followed by twenty minutes of sprints and press-ups. Todd only finally called a halt when one of the most unfit actually threw up. I think he'd been waiting for that as some kind of signal.

"If that's what makes him let up on us, remind me to puke after about ten minutes tomorrow morning," Jan said wearily as we hauled ourselves, groaning, up the staircase and headed for the showers. It might just have been the floor creaking as we traipsed along the corridors to our dormitory, but I wouldn't have sworn to it.

A few minutes later I was standing under water as hot as I could bear it. As I let the stinging spray pummel the back of my neck I recalled my brief phone conversation with Sean the night before. He'd asked if I was getting on OK, coping with the regime. I was beginning to think that even my cautious yes might have been over optimistic.

I'd hesitated over ringing him so soon, as though I didn't have enough to say to justify the call. His tone when he picked up seemed a little distant, and I'm not just talking about him being half a continent away.

I greeted him coolly and realised I could hear the same restraint in my own voice.

Still, when I'd filled him in on Gilby's reaction to Elsa's report on the Heidi Krauss kidnap, he'd seemed interested enough in that.

"I'll get Madeleine onto it straight away," he'd said. "I should have something for you the next time you call."

"I didn't know if it was relevant, but the way they clammed up, you never know." I'd shrugged, feeling oddly pleased.

"No," he'd said, "if there's anything you think I should know, then call me. I need to talk to you regularly, Charlie. I need to know you're OK, that nothing's happened to you."

My heart jumped, then I remembered Kirk. Of course, Sean was just protecting his interests. Keeping his conscience clear. "No problem," I'd said, casual. "I'll talk to you tomorrow evening, then?"

"Charlie, are you OK in there?" Elsa's voice, just outside the shower curtain, made me jump back into the present with a start.

"Er, yeah, fine," I said, hastily rinsing shampoo out of my hair. "You head on down for breakfast. I'll be with you in a minute."

I almost reached for the towel that I'd hung over the rail above me, just in case she pulled the curtain aside, but it wasn't modesty that drove me.

I'd been very careful so far to make sure that I dressed away from the view of the other women, keeping my neck and upper body covered. I knew that if I didn't do so, I would have to answer awkward questions about the number of scars I possessed, and their origin.

But how did I begin to explain about the one that curved a full five inches round the side of my neck from a point below my right ear to my Adam's apple? How did I drop it lightly into the conversation that I'd got it fighting for my life against a madman who'd already committed murder and who'd been more than willing to do so again?

I'd thought of lying, telling people it was from an operation of some sort, but the line of it was too ragged for that to be believable. And then they start to wonder what you're really trying to hide.

On the other side of the curtain I heard Elsa move away and close the bathroom door behind her. I sagged back against the tiles in relief, and wondered on the chances of getting through the entire two weeks at Einsbaden without having to explain what had happened to me.

I could only hope so.

When I arrived in the dining hall less than ten minutes later, I was alarmed to find the place almost empty.

"Where is everyone, Ronnie?" I asked one of the cooks who was expertly flipping fried eggs on the hot plate.

He grinned and jerked his head towards the front of the house. When I crossed to the window I saw a group of students and instructors clustered round a car that was just being unloaded from a transporter.

Our first class after breakfast was down as vehicle security, then we were into the driving. I checked my watch, but according to that I still had half an hour to go. Dammit. Another of their switched timetables.

I almost ran through the hallway, out through the front door and down the steps onto the gravel. I jogged across and nudged my way between the press of bodies.

When I got through I found they were just standing around like a group of eighteen-year-olds when the oldest buys his first second-hand Vauxhall Nova SR. Nobody was doing anything interesting to the car. It was the car itself they were looking at.

I didn't recognise the shape, but if it's got more than two wheels any other details tend to pass me by anyway. Even your most amazing supercar can be out-dragged and outmanoeuvred by your most average superbike, at a fraction of the cost. I know where I'd rather spend my money.

I had to admit that this one had a certain brutish charm about it. The car was big and squat, in a metallic shade that looked expensive enough to qualify as platinum, rather than silver. Not wanting to show my ignorance, I craned my neck until I could see the badging on the rear end.

"But it's a Nissan," I said, and my voice must have well given away how nonplussed I was by this fact. I'd been expecting something a lot more exotic. Maserati at the very least.

"Do you know nothing, girl?" demanded Declan, who was nearest. The reverential tone in his voice was slightly scary. "This is a Skyline GT-R R34 V-spec."

It was little more than an unlikely collection of letters and numbers to me. I shrugged. "What's so special about it?"

A couple of the others sniggered. Declan rolled his eyes. "Two-point-six litres, twin turbos, computer-controlled four-wheel drive," he listed, speaking slowly. He saw I wasn't cottoning on and broke off, shaking his head. "Your man's a lucky bastard, I'll say that."

"Whose is it?" I asked.

"Oh this is the Major's new toy. Apparently he's just had the engine tuned to over five hundred horsepower. The acceleration on this thing will be feckin' stunning."

I did a quick bit of mental arithmetic. My elderly quarter-litre Suzuki produced sixty-two brake horse.

Multiply that up to two-point-six litres, and it came to the equivalent of a smidgen over six hundred. It wouldn't work out like that in real life, of course, but the theoretical superiority made me feel better.

"You're really not impressed at all, are you?" Romundstad commented with a smile. I recalled him mentioning that he'd done some ice rallying in Norway. "I'd have thought you'd be into all things mechanical, Charlie."

I nodded my head across the gravel to where the black motorbike I'd seen the day before was parked at a rakish angle. "That," I said, "is what impresses me. A Honda CBR900RR FireBlade. A hundred and thirty horsepower from less than one litre, bog standard. A hundred and eighty miles an hour top end. Something that takes real balls to ride to the limit." I waved an arm to the Nissan. "Not something that has a computer doing it all for you."

"Thank you for your comments, Miss Fox," said the Major's acidic voice from behind me. My heart sank. He weakened enough to allow sarcasm to creep in. "I'm sure we're all utterly fascinated to hear your opinion."

I turned to find Gilby approaching. And there was I thinking you couldn't sneak up on anyone over gravel. He was eyeing me with all the favour of something he'd just scraped off his shoe. Behind him, Blakemore was glowering.

Gilby stalked past us and dealt with the transporter driver in rapid-fire German, signing paperwork and taking hold of a set of keys.

"Right, people," he said then, his voice businesslike. "I would suggest you get yourselves fuelled up because in precisely twenty-three minutes you'll need to be out here again and Mr Figgis will be taking you over vehicle security checks before we get you into the cars."

We drifted away from the Nissan. Gilby climbed into it and slammed the door. Even I had to admit that the engine note had that throaty growl when he turned the ignition key.

Despite the four-wheel-drive system Declan had mentioned, as he set off the Major managed to kick up a shit-load of stones halfway across drive. Hm, temper temper.

I realised that Blakemore had moved alongside me. He looked from the departing Nissan to the FireBlade, and back again. "So you'd really rather have one of these," he said nodding to the bike, "than one of those?"

"Yes."

I saw his face begin to crease, and I realised he'd been fighting down a big grin in the presence of his boss. The Blade, I surmised, must be his.

As I turned away he nudged Rebanks, who was standing next to him, and I heard him say, "Now *that* is my kind of woman."

"I don't think in all the time I've been teaching here that I've ever come across a more useless hopeless case behind the wheel of a car than you, Charlie," Figgis said two hours later, his long face mournful. "Have you actually *got* a driving licence?"

74

It was the fourth time I'd stalled one of the school Audis. This to the obvious amusement of the three other pupils squashed into the back seat and the increasing exasperation of our instructor.

The combination of unfamiliarity with cars of any description, plus left-hand drive, was doing its worst. Still, I wasn't the only one having problems. Shirley had gone out with Blakemore in one of the earlier sessions and had apparently been reduced to tears by his scathing criticism. I was determined not to let it get to me, however much of a hash of things I was making.

"What?" I said now, as I restarted the engine, feigning astonishment. "*Driving* licence? Oh, I thought it said you needed a *diving* licence. I can do scuba."

Romundstad called from the back, "The way you are going I would not be at all surprised if we are all ending up in a lake, for sure." And there was more laughter.

He wasn't so far away from the truth. We were out on the roads around Einsbaden, which seemed to be made up of a mixture of twisting humps and dips, and deceptive fast open stretches like a rally stage. Working out one from the other was the tricky part.

If you got it wrong there was an interesting selection of landing sites on offer, from solid-looking sheaves of timber to rocky drop-offs deep enough to qualify for the title of ravine. Some of them did indeed have water in the bottom of them. Great. Survive the fall and you drown. All in all, it was a combination designed to make the most proficient driver nervous.

I was terrified.

The idea was that we were there to practise our general driving skills and observation. In theory, I was supposed to be giving a running commentary on the sparse other traffic and spotting possible obstacles or likely spots for an ambush. In reality, I was just hanging on for grim death to the mechanics of actually controlling the car.

Fortunately, Figgis proved less hair-trigger than the other instructors. Maybe because he realised that if he yelled to the point where one of his pupils froze, they were likely to put their foot down and head for the trees.

Out of a vehicle he was a tall, almost ungainly figure, with rounded shoulders and arms that seemed to swing loose and disconnected around his body. Put him behind the wheel, though, and there didn't seem to be anything the man couldn't make a motor car do.

He'd given us a demonstration drive before we started and his skill was uncanny. He'd make some casual, unhurried movement with his hands and feet, and all of a sudden the car had swapped ends and you were hurtling backwards, but still going in the same direction that you had been. The easier he made it look the more difficult I knew it was going to be for any of us to replicate the manoeuvre.

"That's much better," he said ten minutes later, when I'd successfully navigated my way along a contorted stretch of open road. "You've got a great eye for a line through a corner, Charlie. It's just your clutch control that stinks."

"It's not logical," I complained. "Why on earth do you operate something as straightforward as a gear shift with your hand, but something as delicate as a clutch with your boot? Now on the bike it's —"

Another car overtook us suddenly then, so quick and so close that the shock of it made me twitch towards the side of the road and Figgis had to grab the wheel to steady us. I caught the briefest snapshot of a big dark saloon with four men in it as the driver flashed past. They all seemed to be staring intently at us.

"Somebody's in a bloody hurry," Figgis muttered once we'd straightened out again and my nerves had settled, but his eyes had narrowed. He shifted round in his seat. "Right everyone, tell me everything you remember about that car. Every detail. You first of all, Charlie. How long's it been following us?"

I did some frantic mental searching. "He closed on us at such a rate that I'm not entirely sure," I admitted, "but we passed a crossroads on a long straight about two klicks back, and I'm pretty sure he wasn't behind us before that."

Figgis nodded, and Romundstad gave him the fact it was a black Peugeot 406. Someone else had caught the registration number. They'd noted the number of occupants, too.

"This all part of the exercise, yes?" Romundstad asked.

Figgis grinned at him. "We like to see how awake you all are."

But as he faced front again I caught the anxiety in his face, the deep frown. As though aware of being watched, he flicked his eyes sideways and I jerked mine back onto the road ahead.

Something about his expression niggled at me, but it wasn't until we got back to the Manor that I put my finger on it.

We pulled up to change teams on the rough car park behind the house to find another of the Audis already there, stopped at an angle with the doors open. Everybody was standing around the car watching two men face off as if for a fight.

I stopped quickly and we all jumped out. Ran across to see what was happening.

McKenna had his nose stuck under Major Gilby's and was yelling at him, arms waving. The lad's pale complexion was slashed with pink across his cheekbones as though he'd been slapped, and all the cords stood out in his neck. The Major was so stiff you could have ironed shirts on him. O'Neill was trying, not too successfully, to calm McKenna down and pull him away.

"What the hell's going on?" Figgis asked Blakemore, who was standing watching the tableau with his arms folded, not making any moves to intervene.

"Oh, they were buzzed by some heavies in a Peugeot," I heard Blakemore reply. "Nearly ran them off the road, apparently, and McKenna's gone off at the deep end about it being dangerous."

"Is that so?" Figgis murmured. "The same thing happened to us."

Blakemore glanced at him sharply, and it was then that the niggle unfolded fully. I realised why I'd had the feeling that Figgis was lying when he'd said our near miss was all part of the game plan.

I've always been good with faces. I knew I'd caught enough of a glimpse of the men in the Peugeot to recognise them if I saw them again. But, if they were all part of the Einsbaden staff, how come I hadn't known them already?

I don't know how truly unnerved Gilby was by McKenna's outburst, or by the fact that his pupils were being harassed. He was either being very calm about it, or he didn't fully realise the dangers that had been involved.

Either way, after that he sent the cars out in pairs. There were no more sightings of the black Peugeot or its occupants. Even though we were keeping more than a careful eye out for them.

Trouble was, that didn't necessarily mean they weren't there. Maybe they were just being a lot more stealthy.

CHAPTER
SIX

"They're pushing us hard," I said. "All those damn silly exercises that are designed to break you rather than get you fit. It's like being back in bloody basic training."

"And I know how much you enjoyed that," Sean said, his voice made vaguely unfamiliar by the limitations of the mobile phone. "Didn't stop you passing out top of your class though, did it?"

It was difficult to read the hidden shifts and meanings in his tone without being able to see his face as he spoke. I couldn't tell if I was reading too much into his words, or was taking them too lightly.

"Yeah," I murmured. "It was a laugh a minute."

I shivered more closely into my jacket, jamming the phone against my ear to keep out the wind. I'd wanted somewhere private to call Sean after supper and the only place I could be sure of getting it was outside, despite the dark and the cold.

I'd found a staircase leading to the roof and a door that was only secured by bolts, rather than lock and key. Almost the entire roof of the Manor was flat, with a low wall that made up the façade of the building.

I sat in the lee of a chimney stack with my back against the stonework, and kept one eye on my exit. If anyone found the door open and shut it again without me realising it, I was likely to freeze to death up there before morning.

"So how are you coping?" Sean asked.

"With what?" I said, a little sharply. Somehow I knew it wasn't just the training he was talking about. It put my back up that he could still so accurately pinpoint my weaknesses. It had always been his speciality.

Right from the first moment I'd seen him I'd known that Sean Meyer was a danger to me. I was one of only three women who'd fought their way through selection to make it onto the Special Forces course. Sean, like the rest of the instructors, seemed to instantly zero in on the three of us as the candidates mostly likely to be the first drop-outs. There was nothing natural about the means of their selection.

"Well, with being back in a military atmosphere, I suppose," he said now, careful. "I wasn't sure how you'd react."

"So why did you send me?"

"I didn't send you, Charlie," he said, and there was no mistaking the mild reproof. "I asked you to go."

Same difference, I thought. "So why didn't you ask Madeleine instead," I snapped. "I'm sure she would have coped just fine. If you're worried I can't hack it out here, Sean, tell me now."

He sighed. "I know you can cope, Charlie," he said, ignoring my latest dig about Madeleine, as he always seemed to do. I wondered if that was why I kept making them. "I'm just worried about what it's costing you. I can imagine how difficult it must be for you, that's all.

Pretending, holding back. I think that's the part I'd find hard. I don't like deceit."

I stiffened, as though he was talking on another level. As though he'd guessed that I hadn't told him the truth about Kirk and what had happened before I'd left the army.

I searched for the right words to begin to tell him, but they wouldn't come. It really wasn't the kind of thing you could do over the phone. Mind you, I didn't think I'd have the bottle to tell him face-to-face, either. Stalemate.

The silence hummed along the wires between us.

At last, he said, "Yesterday you asked about the Heidi Krauss kidnap."

"Yes," I said, realising almost with relief that I'd missed my chance.

"Madeleine's been doing some digging. Apparently Heidi isn't the first to have been taken. There have been six abductions in the last year that match the same pattern. Snatched by a small but heavily armed group who aren't afraid to shoot first and ask questions later. They've left a trail of bodies halfway across Europe."

"Elsa said the housekeeper and one of the bodyguards was killed in the raid," I agreed. I glanced up. The wind was sending clouds rushing past the face of the moon, making the light level rise and fall across the roof like a swinging lantern.

"It isn't just bystanders." I could feel rather than see Sean shaking his head. "According to my source, four of the victims turned up dead as well, regardless of whether the ransoms were paid or not." He paused.

82

"Not encouraging odds as far as the Krauss girl is concerned."

"So why did Gilby's bunch go off at the deep end when Elsa brought the subject up?" I wondered aloud.

"That's not a difficult one," Sean said. "The bodyguard who died was one of his former pupils. So was the lad who lost a leg."

"Nasty." Hardly surprising that the Major had reacted like someone had just jabbed him with a cattle prod. I wondered if Elsa knew the connection when she prepared her little speech and, if so, what she'd hoped to gain from it. I made a mental note to ask her the first chance I got.

"Yeah, that's what happens when you get shot with a hollowpoint," Sean said. "It tends to do a lot of damage."

Hollowpoint. "Just like Kirk. Is there a connection, or are hollowpoints just this year's dumdum fashion accessory?"

I heard the smile in Sean's voice. "I doubt it," he said. "There are a lot of them about. Some people prefer them because they dissipate their energy into the first body they hit, rather than passing on through to the next man. Less chance of hitting someone on your own team."

I pondered on that one for a moment. "Any ideas who's behind the kidnappings?" I asked.

"It looks like the handiwork of a guy called Gregor Venko."

"I've never heard of him," I said. "What kind of name is Venko?"

"I'd be worried if you *had* heard of him. Nobody seems to know exactly where he came from, but he walked out of the ruins of the former Yugoslavia with a dubiously acquired personal fortune and an organisation that the Mafia would — and have tried to — kill him for. He's involved in everything from gunrunning to political assassination, drugs, prostitution, illegal immigrants. If there's money to be made out of it, just about any place in eastern Europe, then good old Gregor's had a hand in the deal somewhere."

"Sounds like a real charmer," I said. Another vicious blast of wind sliced its way through my jacket and embedded itself firmly in my ribs. I shivered, pulling my collar up more tightly around my chin.

"He is, by all accounts. His ex-wife spends all her time sozzled out of her skull in a resort on the Black Sea, and his son —"

As he spoke there was a noise from somewhere below. A bang like that last gust of wind had caught an open door and slammed it shut.

"Wait one," I interrupted. I put the phone down next to the chimney and rose cautiously to my feet. I crept over to the low wall that looked down over the back of the house and peered over the top of it.

Below me, walking quickly along the path that led away from the house towards the armoury and the ranges, was the figure of a man. The moon had darted out into view and was bright enough to lay a sharp-edged silhouette along the ground behind him.

The man was wearing a greatcoat that came almost down to his ankles, but even so I recognised Gilby's distinctive upright gait. He was carrying something, but I couldn't quite make out what it was.

I watched for a few moments longer and was just about to move away when another figure detached itself from the shadows of the house and made off after the Major. This second man kept to cover like a pro, moving swiftly and quietly.

As though warned by some sixth sense, Gilby stopped, circled slowly as though expecting to find someone behind him. I saw his head rise, scanning the windows of the house and even the roof line. My imagination made him pause over my location, made my heart bounce with fright. Then he turned and carried on.

I let my breath out shakily and edged back over to my chimney.

"What is it?" Sean demanded, tense, when I was back on the line.

"I heard a door. Looks like Gilby's off to the ranges, though it's a bit late for weapons' practice. Somebody's following him."

"Did you see who it was?"

I shook my head then realised, as Sean must have done, that it was a pointless gesture. "No. It's too dark and whoever it was he wasn't trying to be seen, if you get me. If he goes again tomorrow night, I might try to get a closer look."

I could have been mistaken, but I thought I heard Sean suck in a breath. "You be careful," he said.

I frowned. "It's what I'm here for, Sean."

"I know it is," he said, and there was no doubt about his serious tone. "But just remember it was what Salter was there for, too."

"I hardly think," I said dryly, "that I'm likely to forget."

"Has anyone mentioned Salter?"

I paused. So much seemed to have happened since my arrival in Germany that the death of Kirk Salter had almost been pushed to the back of my mind.

"No," I said at last, "but we don't get out onto the gun range until tomorrow. I thought that might be a good time to bring the subject up."

"How are you going to play it — with the shooting?"

"Like one of the hopeless and pathetic females they already assume me to be," I said, and couldn't entirely help the sneer in my voice.

"More fool them for underestimating you," Sean said softly. "You watch your back though, Charlie."

There was a warmth there that threatened to turn my brain a little mushy.

I shook it off.

"Don't worry," I said. "I always do. And speaking of watching my back, I picked up an interesting tail during my driving lesson today." And I told him all about the four men in the Peugeot.

"It certainly rattled everyone, although Figgis tried to make out it was all part of the set-up," I said. "The Major's trying to play it cool, but he goes off at the deep end if any of the instructors disappear on their own for too long."

"It begins to sound like the place is under threat," Sean murmured. I could almost hear his brain beginning to turn over.

"I did wonder," I agreed. "What if we consider the possibility that Kirk wasn't killed *by* the school, but because he was here? Some kind of warning, perhaps?"

"If that's the case why dump his body and cover up the connection? If Gilby's being threatened by an outside source, surely having one of his men shot dead would put the authorities on his side?"

"It could also shut him down," I pointed out. "Maybe that was the intention. Does Gilby have any opposition round here who might want him out of business? Or failing that, who's he upset in a big way recently?"

Sean promised to try and find me some answers before we spoke again. We didn't linger over our goodbyes. I switched off the phone when I'd finished the call, preserving the battery even though the indicator was still showing it fully charged.

I crossed the roof grateful to be getting back inside. I pulled the outer door closed behind me, and slid the bolts back into position, then I turned.

A man was looming behind me in the gloomy stairwell.

I gave a gasp of shock, took a step back, and felt my feet shifting into a stance almost of their own volition. I had to stop myself from bringing my hands up. Had to abort the blow I'd been about to launch.

There had been a time when I would have gone for a defensive block before I'd have ever thrown a punch. It was what I'd taught my self-defence students. And I'd believed it was the right way.

Painful — not to say nearly deadly — experience had taught me that a pre-emptive strike was by far the best defence. To hell with fair play. To hell with waiting for the other man to make the first move. This wasn't sport. He wasn't your opponent. He was your enemy.

And if there were consequences, well so be it. Consequences could only be faced if you were around afterwards to face them.

"Now just what would you be up to, Fox?" demanded the thick Belfast tones that could only be O'Neill. He spoke softly, let the accent threaten by association.

I put my hand on my chest and noticed that his eyes followed it. I made a play of trying to steady my breathing. "Christ, you frightened the life out of me!" I said. "Don't *do* that."

O'Neill moved forwards into the light and grinned. The scar pulled his face into a lopsided tilt, but he wasn't to be deflected. "Well? What were you doing out on the roof?"

I shrugged. "Doing a recce," I said. "Major Gilby told us that we should learn the layout of the Manor for this exercise he's planning for us next week."

I was suddenly thankful for such a decent excuse. It was so much more convenient to use the truth rather than have to invent a lie. "The roof's a great vantage point, and you could get to the rooms on the second floor via the balcony, no trouble. I thought it was worth checking out."

He eyed me shrewdly, head on one side. "You're not just a pretty face, are you now?" he said slowly. "Up here alone are you?"

I remembered Rebanks's sly comments about having to get past the instructors if we wanted to investigate the men's quarters. I felt my face begin to colour. "Yes," I said, more than a little defensive.

"Hm, so you didn't bother to share your thoughts about the roof with anyone else then?" He regarded me for a moment longer and it was hard to know if he was impressed or disappointed. "Not much of a team player are you, Fox?"

The following morning, right after the usual punishment that was phys, we had our first introduction to firearms. Sean had told me to expect a motley collection of old Bulgarian Makarov pistols, but when we trooped down to the indoor range I discovered that Gilby had updated his armoury since then. A line of very new-looking Sig Sauer nine-millimetres were waiting for us on a bench to one side.

"Now then," Rebanks said, "hands up anyone who has ever handled or fired a gun of any description before?"

About half the group raised their hands. This included Hofmann and Elsa, which I would have expected given their backgrounds. More of a surprise was Jan, who also put her hand up. After a moment's hesitation, I raised mine, too. I reckoned it was easier to fake a reaction as a bumbling amateur, rather than as a complete beginner.

"OK, in that case most of you will already know that these are lethal weapons. They only have one purpose in life, and that's death. You fuck about with these, you don't take them seriously, and you will end up killing someone," Rebanks said with an evil grin. "Do I make myself clear? OK, let's get on with it."

He ran quickly through the different parts of the weapons, how to load and unload the magazine, how to tell if they were safe and clear, what to do if you had a stoppage.

"One last thing," Rebanks said as we were each handed our own gun and a box of shells. "Quite a few people who come on these courses decide they'd like to take a couple of live rounds home with them as a souvenir." He eyed the group. We all tried to look innocent, as though that was the last thing to cross any of our minds.

"If that thought had occurred to you, forget it!" he went on. "For those of you who'll be going back to the UK, they take a pretty dim view of it over there now anyway and we don't appreciate you nicking it from us, either. So, at the end of every session here you'll be required to give what we call a range declaration, right? If you're then found with anything on you that you shouldn't have, you take the long walk out of here. Clear?"

We all murmured our understanding. It was the same procedure as I'd followed on every army range I'd ever been on. Except the penalty then was somewhat more severe.

Blakemore, O'Neill, and Todd were acting as Rebanks's assistants for the class. They fitted us out with ear defenders and eye shields, which were loaded into a universal plastic carry tray with a handle in the middle. It was a good way of keeping everything together and also, I acknowledged, it stopped us putting things into our pockets.

I was put into the first group to shoot. We moved through a pair of soundproof doors into the range itself, a low-roofed slot of a room with scarred walls and a huge sand berm heaped up at the far end to catch the fired rounds.

There were eight lanes marked out, with a solid counter about four feet high that ran right the way across the firing position. I picked the far left-hand lane and plonked my carry tray down on the counter top in front of it.

McKenna was in the lane next to me. After his outburst of the previous morning, he seemed quiet and withdrawn.

"OK, I won't ask you to try and produce groupings at this stage," Rebanks said, condescending. "Just aim for the target and that'll be enough for me. Fire when you're ready."

I took my time over getting sorted, fussed over making sure my ear defenders were in the right place, aware all the time of Todd standing behind me. I didn't know if it was my imagination, but the big physical training instructor seemed to be watching me more than the others.

Once my ears were covered, the sound of my breathing became loud and rasping inside my head. I concentrated on slowing the rate for a moment or so before I picked up the Sig and slid the magazine into the grip, pinching back the slide to chamber the first round. I hadn't fired the P226 model before, but as soon as it settled in my fist it felt right. It fitted.

I held the gun in both hands, bringing it up until I knew by instinct that the front and rear sights had come into alignment. We were using standard military paper targets that showed the head and shoulders of a snarling soldier. They were pasted to a flat board and set at the seven-metre distance on the range.

To my right, McKenna fired his first shot, jerking the trigger and only just managing to clip the extreme top edge of the board, which splintered wildly. Out of the corner of my eye, I saw Todd shift to stand behind him instead.

I let out my breath and squeezed the trigger, aiming for the eye of my target. The gun fired with a muffled bang, but very little recoil. The trigger action was smooth and progressive.

When I checked my target, the eye was gone.

I glanced sideways and saw that the rest of the targets were gradually filling with random holes. I carefully emptied the rest of my magazine in what I hoped was a haphazard pattern around the board, deliberately bypassing it altogether with the last two, which I put straight into the berm at the back of my lane.

"OK everyone," Rebanks called. "Safeties on. Let's have a look how you've done."

We all pulled off our ear defenders and eye shields and the outside world suddenly got brighter and louder again. There was a wisp of smoke drifting inside the range, even with the extractor fans switched on. I breathed in the faintly familiar cocktail of cordite, gun oil, and nervous sweat.

Rebanks sauntered along the line, dishing out comments and criticism. Mostly the latter.

The standard varied enormously. Shirley must have been holding her gun with the barrel drooping, because she'd only managed to get two onto the target at all, right at the bottom edge. After her poor performance in the driving session that morning, she was looking thoroughly dispirited.

Hofmann came out on top, placing all his shots within a four-inch square area right in the centre of his target, and he was looking pretty smug about it. Rebanks made much of him, but to be honest I would have expected better from an ex-military shooter, particularly at such close quarters.

"OK, that was only mildly horrible," Rebanks said cheerfully when he'd finished. "Now let's try and get some groupings going, shall we?"

We reloaded and fired again. Two lanes down Declan had a stoppage which he struggled to clear. He didn't have the brute strength to force the slide back to eject the jammed round. In his desperation he started getting careless about where he was pointing the business end of the barrel as he wrestled with the gun.

Rebanks stopped us all shooting immediately while he tore the Irishman off a strip. "You have a problem, you keep the pistol pointing down the range at all times, is that clear, Mr Lloyd?" he yelled. "This is not a toy, it's a deadly fucking weapon. We've never had an accident yet where anybody's been injured on this range, but you do that again and I'll shoot you myself. D'you understand me?"

Declan mumbled his reply. Rebanks took the gun away from him, cleared it in one movement, and thrust it back into his hands with a darkly contemptuous look.

We've never had an accident yet where anybody's been injured . . .

I turned the words over as I resumed my slapdash firing. Their choice was an interesting one, and they'd been delivered with just a hint of self-consciousness. Almost as if Rebanks was trying to convince himself, rather than the rest of us. I wondered how, in the face of that statement, I was going to be able to throw in my casual question about Kirk's death.

I found to my alarm that I hadn't been concentrating on the last three rounds and I'd planted them so close together in the centre that the holes overlapped each other. Damn. I was going to have to be more careful.

"OK, that's enough for today, I think," Rebanks said when we'd all ground to a halt. "Under the counter in front of you, you'll each find a pot of glue, a brush and a bag of paper squares. Go and paste the squares over the holes in your targets so the next lot can use them, then you can go with Mr O'Neill. He'll show you how to strip your weapons down and clean them."

We all dutifully went through the door at the far right-hand side of the counter and out onto the range itself with our glue pots in hand. Shirley was done well before the rest of us, by dint of the fact that she'd managed to create very few holes.

When I'd finished my own target, I walked back down my lane and put the glue onto the counter where I'd been shooting, rather than carry it round.

As I did so, a bright object on the floor caught my eye. It was tucked hard up against the bottom edge of the counter, completely hidden from view from the normal firing position. I dropped the bag of paper squares close to it, quickly stooping to pick it up.

I palmed it quickly and forced myself not to look round to see if anyone had noticed what I'd done. I joined the others, casually wiping my hands. My fingers were black with ingrained powder and oil.

Back on the other side of the counter I loaded my gear into the plastic carry tray and headed for the doors out of the range with the others.

"Hold on a moment, Miss Fox," Rebanks said from behind me. "Aren't you forgetting something?"

I turned slowly, trying not to panic. "Am I?"

"Your declaration, if you please."

"Oh, sorry," I said. It was hard not to stand to attention as I rapped out, "I have no live rounds or empty cases in my possession, *sir*."

"All right, all right, on you go," he said, grinning as he waved me through.

It wasn't until later that afternoon, when I had chance to examine my discovery more closely, that it really came home to me how easily I'd been able to lie to Rebanks.

Still, he'd lied to us, too, so I suppose that made it evens.

The object I'd picked up and carried away with me, against all the rules, was a single live round. It must have rolled off the front edge of the counter when someone was loading up, or maybe clearing a stoppage, as Declan had failed to do.

But you often find the odd live round on a range. That in itself wasn't unusual. It was the round itself that gave me pause for thought because, according to Sean's information, the school didn't use them, or even list them as being held on the premises.

It was a hollowpoint.

CHAPTER
SEVEN

I was intending to call Sean at the earliest opportunity about my discovery, but when I walked into the dormitory to change before supper, I could tell at once that something was wrong.

Elsa was sitting on Shirley's bed with her arm around the older woman's shoulders. Jan was leaning against the wall near the head, looking serious and uncomfortable. All three of them tensed up when I opened the door.

I paused with my fingers still on the handle. "What's up?"

"Oh, it's nothing, dear," Shirley said, and I could tell by the thickness in her voice that she'd been crying. She sat up straighter, opening out a crumpled tissue and blowing her nose fiercely, as though she was annoyed by the need to do so. Elsa let her arm fall away.

"Shirley wishes to leave," the German woman said bluntly, her voice giving no clue as to whether she was happy about this occurrence or not.

I glanced at Jan, but it was difficult to know what she was thinking at the best of times. She caught my eye and shrugged.

I sat down on the bed opposite Shirley. "Why did you want to come here in the first place?" I asked gently.

Elsa made an impatient gesture. "What is that to do with it?"

I ignored her and held Shirley's eye instead. I wanted to find out if her reason to stay was stronger than her reason to go. "Well?"

Shirley swallowed, stared up at the corner of the room over my head, biting her lip as though that would keep the tears trapped beneath her eyelids. "I wanted to do something different," she said at last. "I wanted to get out there into the real world and do something exciting, just for once. Something that would matter."

She skimmed her gaze over me briefly, then let it fall. "I've always been really good at organisation," she said, now talking to the worn carpet in front of her feet. "I can plan and organise a children's party, a conference, a fundraiser."

She glanced at the three of us briefly and gave what might have been a self-derisory laugh. "All three at once, if you like. It's easy. Multitasking, my daughter-in-law would call it. Somebody told me that was what ninety per cent of close protection work was all about. Organising security during transport, hotels, restaurants. That's what fascinated me about the job. Not all this running around in the mud and the dark, being screamed at by a bunch of thugs."

Her face collapsed again, and she brought her hands up to cover it. Elsa put her arm back around Shirley's shoulders and gave her a helpless squeeze. She flashed me a look of reproof from behind her glasses.

"Anybody on the job would give their right arm to have you co-ordinating all that kind of stuff behind the scenes for them," Jan said suddenly. "It's not all gung-ho bullshit. You hang in there, girl, and don't let the bastards grind you down."

In spite of herself, Shirley smiled wanly but looked no more convinced. We tried for another half an hour to talk her into finishing what she'd started. When the memories of the cold and the tiredness and the bullying had faded, she'd always berate herself for giving in. What was a few weeks of discomfort, compared to a lifetime of regret?

In some ways, I had done exactly the same thing. Given in when the going had become too difficult. Maybe the sense of disappointment I'd felt then went some way towards explaining some of my actions since. My occasional stubbornness to the point of stupidity. My disinclination to just let things go, however prudent a move that might turn out to be.

When we left her, Shirley seemed more positive, but there was an underlying sense of defeat about her. I knew we hadn't really got the message through.

Shirley wasn't the only one who was feeling low. There were a lot of subdued faces in the dining hall that evening. Lack of sleep and a punishing regime of exertion and mental fatigue was taking its toll. As I ate I had the chance to quietly observe the people around me. Even Declan was looking miserable.

I was beginning to pick out faces from the crowd. They were becoming more individual and distinct, and so were their abilities. McKenna had started out badly and gone downhill from there. It wasn't so much that he was sitting a little way apart from the others, as they were sitting apart from him. He was picking at his food, with his head down and his eyes fixed to the tablecloth in front of him.

A couple of places away was a big Welshman called Craddock. He was an ex-Royal Engineer with a robust sense of humour, who was sailing through the course with a calm that sometimes seemed almost drug-induced. The more Todd had ranted at him that morning, the more serenely Craddock had taken it. I wondered if it was a deliberate ploy.

The German contingent were all very competent, with Hofmann probably in the lead, but Elsa not far behind him.

Of the rest, Romundstad was the quiet one of the bunch, but I had a feeling he might turn out to be a very useful player in the long run. He'd certainly been the best of us during the afternoon session. We'd spent part of it on more driving drills, and the rest learning immediate first-aid from Figgis for dealing with our damaged principal.

I'd done first aid before, from simple stuff right up to full scale simulated casualty exercises with the army. I'd even had to cope with more genuine medical emergencies — involving myself as well as others — than I liked to think about.

At the Manor, though, things were slightly different. Figgis had headed up the usual priority checklist of Breathing, Bleeding, Breaks and Burns with another point of consideration. Being Safe.

"If you're still under fire, or in a position where there is still a threat, it's pointless trying to start CPR on the guy," he'd said. "You *must* make sure you're secure before you do anything else."

We'd all nodded, sober, then he'd added. "Oh, and the most important rule. What do you do if it isn't your principal who's hit, but another team member?"

There was a moment of silence. I think we all knew the answer he was looking for, but nobody had wanted to actually come right out and say it.

It was Romundstad who'd spoken, frowning as he tugged at he trailing end of his moustache. "Nothing?"

Figgis nodded, looking round at the various degrees of discomfort and distaste on the faces of the class.

"That's right. It doesn't matter if he's lying in the middle of the street screaming. You get your principal to safety first, then you help your mate, but *only* if you can do so without putting your principal in danger. If you can't, you leave him where he's fallen. It doesn't matter if he's your brother. It's the first rule of BG work. Your principal is the only one that matters. OK?"

"Penny for them?"

I shook myself loose from my recollection and found Rebanks hovering next to my chair. He'd finished his meal and was carrying a mug of coffee. "Sorry?"

"You look deep in your thoughts," he said, grinning. "I was just offering you a penny for them. Did old

Figgis come over too graphic on the blood and guts front today?"

I smiled back. "No, he was very restrained," I said. "Hardly anybody fainted."

He hitched his hip onto the table next to me, made himself at home. "You don't strike me as the fainting kind of girl," he said. He eyed me momentarily over the rim of his mug as he took a swig of his drink.

I waited a beat, then said sweetly, "I was talking about the blokes."

The instructor's grin grew wider.

Now, I thought, would be a good time to ask my awkward questions. "You said this morning that there'd never been an accident on the range."

"That's right," Rebanks said smartly. "And I aim to keep it that way, which is why I don't appreciate pillocks like Mr Lloyd."

"I did hear," I said, as offhand as I could manage, "that there was something that had happened recently. That somebody was killed out here?"

"Where did you hear that?" Rebanks tensed, then took a drink of his coffee, making a real effort to relax.

I shrugged. "It was just a rumour."

"Yeah," he said with a touch of bitterness about him, "and we know how easy those start."

"So," I said, "any truth in it?"

He shook his head, but his body language shouted that he was lying. "Nah. You don't want to believe all the gossip you hear."

Undeterred, I tried a different tack. "So, is it true we'll be firing hollowpoints on the range next time?"

102

"Hollowpoints?" Rebanks said, his voice almost a yelp. He swallowed before he went on, more calmly, "You lot? No chance. Where did you hear that?"

"Oh, someone mentioned it, that's all," I said, waving another vague hand in the direction of just about everyone else in the room.

"Well they're talking bollocks," Rebanks said firmly. "We don't have any in the armoury."

There was a pause, then he turned the tables on me. "So," he said, "you did pretty good this morning. Where did you learn to shoot?"

I laid my knife and fork on my empty plate and pushed it away from me slightly before replying. "I did a bit at a local gun club — before they closed it down, obviously," I said.

"No military stuff then?" he asked, voice a shade too casual.

Physically, I sat still but mentally, I jumped. What had I done to give myself away?

My mind threw a rocky excuse together with all the care and skill of a third-rate cowboy builder. "We've an army camp with an outdoor range near where I live," I said. "I went there once to see if I fancied joining the Territorials and we had a go with nine-mil pistols." I shrugged. "I enjoyed that, but I didn't fancy the weekend soldier bit much."

He nodded. "I thought you'd done some before," he said. "You've got some promise, Charlie. Bit inconsistent maybe, but I reckon we could do something with you. A few more weeks here and you could be quite a passable shot."

For a woman. I heard those extra words. Even though his lips didn't move and no sound came out.

Blakemore paused by the side of us then. "The boss wants you for a team briefing," he told Rebanks, jerking his head towards the door from the dining hall. He passed a dark gaze over me, as though I'd been the one who'd stopped Rebanks to chat.

The weapons' instructor gave me a last grin and tilted back the last of his coffee before getting lazily to his feet. "Be seeing ya," he said with a wink.

But the two of them exchanged words before they reached the doorway and Blakemore turned back to lance me with a brooding stare before he followed the other man out.

I watched the two of them leave with a sense of foreboding that tightened my chest. I'd tried to be low key. I'd tried not to stand out from the crowd. Hell, I'd gone out of my way to miss the target. How on earth was that showing promise?

I got to my feet and dumped my plate with the pile of dirty crockery in one of the plastic bowls to one side of the room. Then I went slowly upstairs wondering what I'd learned, and at what cost?

I decided not to risk the roof again as my location to call Sean that night. Instead I went out onto the terrace, down the steps to one side, and walked across the rough car park where we'd first practised our driving drills. I ended up enveloped by the shadow of the trees on the far side.

From there I could see the whole of the rear of the Manor laid out in front of me, the windows streaming light into multiple shadows across the ground. It was quiet out there, removed from civilisation and cold enough for my breath to cloud in front of me.

And if Gilby came this way again I would see him — and his stealthy follower — long before he saw me.

At least, that was the theory.

Sean's mobile was on divert to a land line, which he answered on the fourth ring. His voice when he picked up was lazy, relaxed. In the background a soaring choir of voices swelled and broke. Either Sean had his stereo system wound up or he was hosting a very unusual house party.

"Hang on Charlie," he said, "let me just turn this down."

I heard him lay the receiver down onto a hard surface with a click, just as the main soprano took flight in the background. The male and female chorale swept in behind her, creating a rush of emotion, an overwhelming wrench of sadness. Then the voices died and were lost, and all I could hear were Sean's returning footsteps.

"Sounds cheery," I said dryly.

"It's a John Rutter requiem piece, so I don't think it's supposed to be," he said. "I was looking after a guy in the States last year who was really into it. When you've heard it night and day for a month you either grow to love it or hate it."

He paused and I knew I should have brushed the comment aside and got on with my report, all business, no personal asides, but I found I couldn't do it.

The stark realisation surfaced that I needed this brief snatch of respite with Sean. I'd missed the reassurance of his voice, even at the other end of a phone line, hundreds of miles away, from another country.

It was not an admission that made me proud.

"Don't apologise," I said now, catching a hint of embarrassment that I'd caught him listening to classical music. "It sounds interesting. You'll have to let me have a listen to the whole thing when I get back." And just so he didn't think I'd let him off the hook entirely, I added, "I wouldn't have put you down as being into that kind of thing."

He laughed softly and batted that one straight back, a return blow that made me squirm. "Well, Charlie, as I recall when we were together we spent more time making music than listening to it."

Memories came bursting up along with his words, fragments of other times and places. A host of stolen moments, always in a hurry, always against the clock. We'd never had time just to be together. Never had the chance to find out if we fitted anywhere else except in bed.

Haste and secrecy had brought us together in a shower of sparks, with a kind of emotional violence that had left me shaken to the centre. I'd never experienced anything like it, before or since.

Especially not since.

I was glad of the darkness, and that I was alone in it. I blushed scarlet to the point where I could warm my chilled fingers on the heat coming off my face. I stuttered some incomprehensible reply and hurried the conversation on.

Across my babble Sean asked, "So how did it go on the range today?" I could still hear the amusement in his voice.

"Interesting," I said, thankful to be on safer ground, and I told him about my discovery.

As I spoke I took the round out of my pocket and turned it over in my fingers. There was just enough light bleeding into the trees from the house to be able to make out the bullet's cylindrical shape and the characteristic hole in the nose.

"There isn't a good reason I can think of for Gilby to be using hollowpoints," Sean said, all trace of that teasing humour wiped out of his voice. "OK so they tend to ricochet less, and they don't go through body armour as easily —"

"Which would be useful to us *if* we happened to be wearing any," I interrupted.

"Which you're not," Sean agreed. "Gilby just wouldn't be using them for training. Hollowpoints generally don't load as freely, so you tend to get more stoppages, and they're too expensive to waste on target practice. It doesn't make any sense."

"Unless he's using them to get rid of people who get in his way," I said, my voice grim. "Did you make any headway finding out what Gilby might have to hide?"

"We're still working on it," he said. "How did you get on today anyway? Did you shoot sloppy?"

"Sort of," I said, remembering again those three closely-grouped rounds when I hadn't been paying enough attention. Had that little lapse been enough for them to rumble me? "Not sloppy enough, it would seem. I'm not sure what I did, but Rebanks asked me this evening if I'd ever done any military shooting."

Sean sucked in his breath. "What did you tell him?"

I repeated my TA story then asked, anxiously, "Is there any way he can check up on that?"

"No, I don't think so," Sean said slowly. "Hang on." He must have put his hand over the receiver. There was the sound of muffled voices in the background, but I couldn't catch the other one clearly. "I've just got Madeleine onto it."

"She's working late," I said. I didn't think I brought anything sharp to the statement, but I must have been wrong about that.

Sean sighed. "It's just work, Charlie," he said, but his voice was gentle. "You should know that by now."

"OK," I said, aiming for a level tone, offhand. The logical half of my brain recognised the truth of it. The emotional half sulked and glowered and stuck its bottom lip out. I slapped it down. "Have you found out any more about these kidnappings?"

"Not much," Sean said. "The last kid to be taken before they snatched Heidi Krauss was a Russian businessman's son. He disappeared about three weeks before she did, on his way home from school. They forced the car off the road, shot the bodyguard who was driving, and burnt the wreckage with him still in it. They had to identify the guy from his dental records. The kid's fifteen. He's still missing."

"Gregor Venko again?"

"Hm, possibly," Sean said, but there was a hint of doubt in his tone. "I've been reading his profile and if it *is* Venko who's behind these kidnappings then it's just not his usual style. He's always been ruthless, but this is beyond that. It's nasty. Vicious."

I realised I was still turning the hollowpoint round over and over in my fingers like a worry bead. I slipped it back into my pocket.

"D'you think there's any connection with what happened to Kirk and these kidnappings?" I wondered aloud. "You mentioned that Heidi's bodyguards were shot with hollowpoints. Do you know what kind of weapons the kidnappers were using?"

"Machine pistols," Sean said, "But that doesn't prove much. The close protection team were using something very similar."

"The same weapon that was used to kill Kirk." A cold little ghost scuffed its feet all the way down my spine. "Are you sure he might not have been involved in some way?"

"Salter was many things Charlie, but I don't think he'd quite lowered himself to criminal status," Sean shot back. "Besides, just about every thug in eastern Europe can pick up a machine pistol and a box of hollowpoints these days. It's common. I wouldn't read too much into it if I were you."

"Nevertheless, we know that there *is* some connection between the Manor and Kirk's death, and whatever's going on here they might be prepared to kill to keep it covered. Bearing that in mind," I went on with a studied mildness, "you might want to get

Madeleine onto another little research topic before you finally send her home for the night."

"What's that?"

"Well, if this all goes pear-shaped," I said, my voice calm and even, "how do you propose to get me out of here?"

CHAPTER
EIGHT

Gilby didn't show.

After I'd finished talking to Sean I waited for another forty minutes before the cold finally got the better of me and I sloped back into the Manor.

I ran into Jan in the hallway. She had her cigarette packet and lighter in her hand, and had obviously just been out onto the terrace for a crafty smoke. We compared our reddened noses and whitened fingers.

"I keep threatening to give up the soddin' cancer sticks and if this doesn't make me, nothing's going to," she muttered. She checked her watch. "I've got my name down for the pool table in five minutes. D'you fancy a quick game?"

"OK," I said. "I'll just dump my jacket and I'll see you down in the mess hall."

The mess hall had once been another of the Manor's elegant drawing rooms, now stripped bare except for a tatty selection of easy chairs and a ripped and faded snooker table with a downward slope towards the bottom left-hand corner pocket.

On the far side of the room was a darts board of similar vintage. The wall around it was pockmarked like a woodworm-infested beam as a testament to people's general inability to throw a straight arrow. Looking at just how far away some of the holes were from the board itself, it was quite scary to realise that the same people were also given guns and expected to shoot straight.

Jan was setting up the pool balls in their plastic triangle by the time I arrived. She'd helped herself to coffee from the hulking vending machine that lurked in one corner and she offered me a cup.

I shook my head. I'd made the mistake of trying the coffee it dispensed early on. It turned out to be tasteless thin grey sludge with peculiar thermal properties which meant it was either so hot it burned your tongue or stone cold, without seeming to pass through any other temperature on the way.

Jan broke the pack with an aggressive thwack of the cue, scattering the balls in all directions, but not managing to pocket any. She reached for the crumbling cube of blue chalk as she stepped back.

I walked round the table with my eyes on the lie of the balls. There was an easy stripe near the middle pocket, but the others were in difficult positions. I chose a more difficult spot instead, lurking close to the bottom cushion. I was lucky, and I nudged it just far enough to topple into the pocket, wiping its feet on the way in.

"Nice shot," Jan said.

"Luck rather than judgement, I'm afraid," I said, bending to see if I could just squeeze the cue ball past the black without a foul.

"So, I hear you work in a gym," she said as I tried it. The white cleared the black by a fraction and a second spot dropped in.

"Yeah," I said as I straightened up. "Personal training, stuff like that."

"Not aerobics, then?" Jan said, and there was just a trace of a sneer in her voice.

It made me unwilling to admit to having taken such classes in the past. Besides, the gym where I'd been working during much of the previous year had not been the kind of place you'd imagine anyone skipping around in shocking pink lycra.

The lads who went there were all seriously into training hard with the biggest weights they could lift without rupturing themselves. Getting them to do proper warm-up stretches was as close as I ever came to introducing any form of aerobic exercise.

"No," I said, flicking her a quick smile. "I just sort out people's weight programmes and keep my eye on their technique." I failed to give my next shot enough pace and the slant of the table had it rolling way wide of the mark.

"So they listen to you OK, do they?" Jan asked, her tone dubious. "They don't give you any shit because you're a woman?" She was a canny enough player to leave the easy stripe over the pocket it was covering and pot another instead, putting plenty of backspin on the cue ball to bring it back up to the top of the table for her next shot.

"Not really, no," I said. Maybe it was because my boss was built like Schwarzenegger and always backed me up, right or wrong. Or maybe it was because all the regulars had seen the scar round my neck at one point or another, and between themselves had exaggerated the rumours about how it got there. Either way, I didn't get many clients who were prepared to argue with me.

"You're lucky." Jan put another two stripe balls away with gutsy determination. "I qualified as an engineer. Got a fucking good degree, too. Better than half the guys I was working with, but you try telling that to most of the macho numskulls and they just pat you on the backside and send you off to make the tea." As she spoke she let her eyes slide across to where the blokes were playing darts with much loud laughter and matey camaraderie.

I wondered how much of the attitude Jan had experienced was down to her combative stance. You have to show people you know what you're talking about, not just tell them. Besides, she was too touchy, too perfect a target for winding up. I could understand why they hadn't been able to resist the temptation.

She miscued her next shot completely and nearly snookered me. I was just about to try and play a tricky bounce off the far cushion when Major Gilby walked in.

The Einsbaden staff had their own mess hall in a different part of the building. Separate and segregated. For any of them to venture into the students' area was unusual enough to cast the conversation adrift and bring all play to a standstill.

Gilby looked round at the silenced faces. He was frowning, as though in disapproval of the fact that he'd

114

caught us relaxed and relaxing. His gaze seemed to linger in my direction. For a moment I wondered if he'd spotted me waiting for him out there in the tree-line and had changed his plans accordingly. If that was so, evidently it hadn't pleased him much.

In his hand was a piece of paper. He glanced down at it.

"We've had an alteration to tomorrow's schedule," he said, his voice deceptively mild. The kind of tone that doctors use when they say, "This won't hurt." It provoked an instant ripple of distrust and uneasiness.

"Directly after phys you'll all be taking part in a simulated casualty exercise," Gilby went on. "A test of your first-aid knowledge."

He turned to leave, skimming that steely gaze over us again. "You might find," he said, quiet yet somewhat ominous, "that your time this evening would be better spent on revision. Goodnight."

They started in on us after breakfast the next morning. Figgis was showing us how to check cars over for booby traps when the Major appeared with a clipboard and took Hofmann away.

Ten minutes later he was back for McKenna, then Craddock, and Declan, all at ten-minute intervals. None of them returned to the group. My nerves screeched under the tension. By the time my name was called, I was so nervous that I had no brain capacity spare to concentrate on Figgis's warnings of foreign objects shoved up exhaust pipes, or trip wires in the engine bay.

The Major led me into the hallway and motioned me to remain by the foot of the stairs. He disappeared through a side door and for a few moments all I could do was wait apprehensively for something to happen. I had the underlying fear that I was being manipulated, that events were moving beyond my control.

Still, at least I didn't have to wait long.

A door burst open and Rebanks came charging out, shouting like someone possessed. He practically scooped me up as he ran past and hustled me down a corridor so fast that he pushed me out of my stride.

We rounded a corner at the far end, with Rebanks still bellowing in my ear. Blakemore was standing by a doorway a few metres away, beckoning frantically. He was yelling, too. I skidded to a stop alongside him and looked in, heart thudding from adrenaline as much as exertion.

The clock stopped. I tuned out the shouting around me, had time to take in the whole scene. The room was a study, darkly decorated and dimly lit. The heavily curtained window was opposite the doorway, fronted by a sombre desk. The usual desk furniture was arranged across its surface — in and out trays, an old-fashioned black telephone, a leather-cornered blotter, and a hooded lamp. The lamp was the only thing that offered illumination, casting eerie shadows into the recesses of the room.

In the gloom I could make out the body of a man lying on his back in the middle of the carpet. He was wearing half a dinner suit, dark trousers with a satin inset along the seam, a bow tie and a formal white shirt. He would have looked smart if it hadn't been for the twisted mass of intestine spilled across his stomach. The front of the shirt was stained a livid scarlet. My heart kicked up another gear.

"Go on! Go on, that's your principal in there!" Blakemore's voice was almost a howl. I took a step forwards, innately following his command, then froze. Something was way wrong here, I could feel it.

He urged me on, his hysteria rippling the hairs on the back of my neck. I glanced sideways at him and found eyes wild with blood lust. I stepped back again, and thought he was going to burst a vein.

"It's not safe," I said, shaking my head.

"You coward, you fucking coward!" he screamed. "This isn't about your own safety. That's your principal in there. He's down and he's injured. You get in there and do your fucking job, you bitch!"

I staked him with a short, vicious glare, but stepped across the threshold, staying close to the wall. Everything smelt of a trap, I just knew it. I waited half a beat, straining to hear anything over the breathing of the men behind me. *Oh shit . . .*

I moved towards the man on the floor, squatted beside him. Through all the gore I recognised Ronnie, one of the cooks, and hoped that it wasn't part of our lunch he was wearing. I'd got as far as pulling back his shirt cuff to check for a pulse when I sensed movement in the shadows, closing fast.

I barely had time to glance up, to take in a big man dressed in black, saw him moving out from behind the open door. There was a balaclava concealing his face, leaving only his eyes exposed, but the jolt it sent through me was like an electric shock.

His hands were clasped together, stretched out in front of him. The silenced automatic let out a sharp, distinctive flup of sound that sent my reactions screaming.

The fear came down like a falling blade, slashing into me. My choices came down to fight or flight. I went for the latter.

By the time the second round was fired I'd hurled myself sideways. I rolled over the top of the desk, scattering half the contents, and dived under the lee of the big mahogany structure.

My breath was coming in gasps, horribly loud to my own ears. In the light from the doorway I could see his shadow moving silently round towards the side of the desk. He knew he had me pinned down, knew I didn't have a weapon. He knew he could take his time to finish me off.

I had nowhere to run and my hiding place was about to become useless. My options were running down like a tape machine with dying batteries.

"They like to play mind games with you. Like to see how you react . . ."

I shut my eyes for a moment, forced my breathing back into a regular rhythm.

This isn't real.

I almost had to whisper the words out loud in order to believe them. Whatever test of our reactions Gilby and his men hoped to achieve from this exercise, it

118

would not involve any real danger. I had to cling to that thought.

The barrel of the gun, extended by its silencer, edged into view at eye level round the corner of the desk, followed by the man who was holding it. Without speaking, he flicked his head to indicate that I should rise, and he stepped back while I did so.

But as I moved to pass him heading back for the doorway, he came in close, jamming the gun into my back to shove me down onto the surface of the desk. I landed face down, hard enough to bruise, hard enough to frighten, rammed into the smooth wooden surface.

Afterwards, I told myself I could have coped with that, with the rough pat-down search they decided to subject me to. I didn't like it, didn't see the need for it, but I could have stood for it, even so.

And then the man grabbed me at the back of my neck, and held me down.

Donalson, Hackett, Morton, and Clay.

I panicked totally. I couldn't help it.

Terror exploded into rage, expanding instantaneously out of nothing like a chemical chain reaction. Unstoppable and toxic. My emotions were banded by colours. White heat. Red mist. Black.

The heavy old-fashioned telephone was close to my right hand on the desktop. I closed my fingers around it, feeling the coldness and the weight. I heaved and bucked at the man pinning me, twisting under him as I brought my arm round at full stretch, like a pro golfer unwinding his best drive.

119

I'd selected target by instinct. At the last moment, the last fraction before I hit, I managed to connect with sanity long enough to shift my aim by a few millimetres. It was enough.

The phone smacked up under the side of the man's masked jawbone, snapping his head back with a nauseating crunch. The phone's internal bell reverberated as it hit and seemed to carry on vibrating for a long time afterwards.

The man shot backwards and sprawled across the leather Chesterfield sofa on the far side of the room, limbs flopping. I jacked my body upright away from the desk and went forwards automatically, ready to go again. He didn't move.

My "principal", Ronnie, had scuttled himself into a corner at the first sign of violence. He was now cursing with great fluidity and vigour for a man who only moments earlier had been pretending to be at death's door.

Rebanks and Blakemore had come charging through the doorway in sync by this time, flicking on the overhead lights. Blakemore went and pulled the balaclava off the inert figure on the sofa, bending over him to take the pulse at his throat. I recognised Todd. Strangely detached, I registered the blood around his nose and mouth.

"Get a medic in here," Blakemore told Ronnie. The cook clambered to his feet, dropping the offal that had been standing in for his guts into the waste bin as he went out.

120

Blakemore stared at me and his eyes were still very bright. I saw a feral excitement in them, and it sickened me. I looked away, ashamed. The smell of violence hung in the air dull and bitter, like burnt plastic.

Rebanks put his hand on my shoulder. "Are you OK?"

I swallowed, nodded, not trusting myself to speech. He carefully prised the telephone out of my clenched fingers and inspected it. Blood was smeared up one side.

He murmured, "Now what was that all about, hm?"

I let out a shaky breath, shrugged his hand away. I was beginning to come round, to snap out of it. "Well," I said, aiming for a relaxed tone, almost bringing it off, "you know what they say — it's good to talk."

He nearly made it to a smile, twisted into mocking. "In that case," he said, "remind me not to have a conversation with you."

His eyes had dropped from my face and I realised that Todd must have ripped my shirt collar, although I didn't remember him doing it. The material was gaping open across my shoulder, revealing the scar in all its lurid glory.

Rebanks's gaze lingered in that direction and when it shifted up to my face again, his expression was cool and calculating.

Ronnie returned with Figgis in tow, who went quickly to deal with Todd. Major Gilby wasn't far behind.

"What the hell happened here?" he demanded as he stalked in. His eyes flicked to my neck, then to my face, and back again.

Rebanks lifted the telephone. "Old Toddy went in a bit heavy and Charlie here made a collect call," he said, laconic.

The Major's nostrils grew pinched. "This is not a laughing matter," he snapped with a glance at Todd's unconscious figure. He jerked his head to Blakemore. "My study, the pair of you. Now." He favoured me with a last brooding stare. "You too, Miss Fox, if you don't mind."

"I think perhaps that you have some explaining to do, Miss Fox," Gilby said when the four of us were closeted in his inner sanctum.

I was in the centre of the room, trying to resist the urge to stand to attention. The other two men were slightly behind me, with Blakemore lounging against the door jamb and Rebanks slumped in an armchair with his legs stretched out straight before him.

The Major was sitting stiffly behind a desk not unlike the one in the simulation, although its surface was covered in a more realistic clutter of papers. He fidgeted a little, I noticed, straightening papers that were already neat, tidying a set of keys into a top drawer. He had an old-fashioned letter spike by his left hand and I noted its position almost unconsciously.

I could feel the location of all of the school men, without having to look. If things went bad I could estimate exactly how long it would take them to react and reach me. The fact that I was even beginning to think that way scared me to death.

"Todd should have kept his hands to himself," I said now, my tone on the defiant side.

"Very probably," Gilby said. He repositioned the leather blotter so that the corners were precisely aligned. "Although I would hazard a guess that you overreacted somewhat."

"That," I said coldly, "is a matter of opinion. Anyone who expects me to lie there and put up with him feeling me up has another think coming."

"Difficult to think when you've got concussion," Gilby rapped back. "Is that what happened when you had your throat cut?"

The sudden unexpectedness of the question took my breath away. I couldn't pull back the gasp his words provoked, nor could I speak.

"What do you mean, she had her throat cut?" Blakemore demanded. He moved away from the door, circled me with his eyes fixed on my jugular like a starving vampire. I did my best to ignore him.

Gilby nodded towards my neck. "That scar's not surgical," he said. He put his head on one side slightly, pursing his lips. "Knife, by the looks of it. A big one with a serrated blade. I would say you were damned lucky."

I felt my shoulders drop. "Yes," I said, "I was."

Gilby ducked his head, a small nod as though recognising my capitulation. "Thank you, Miss Fox," he said, gracious as a snake before it strikes. "Tell me, did this happen before or after you left the army?"

Now that had to be a stab in the dark. No way could he have known about that. Sean had promised me.

"What makes you think I've ever been in the army?" I stalled.

It was Rebanks who spoke, lazily throwing my own words back at me. "When we'd finished shooting yesterday you came straight out with, 'I have no live rounds or empty cases in my possession, sir,' without having to be told, didn't you?" he repeated with a grin. "It's a standard army range declaration, babe. No reason for you to have known it unless you were in."

He grinned at my consternation. "And before you try that excuse again, you must know as well as I do that the TA don't let you loose with weapons on any old open day. Not until you've been through basic training." He shrugged. "Sorry."

"So, Miss Fox, time to make a clean breast of it, don't you think?" Gilby said, brisk, but with a deceptive mildness.

"Yes, I was in," I said. "But the army didn't suit me, and I didn't suit the army. They chucked me out."

"Why?"

I hesitated. I was faced with three choices. An outright lie, which I hadn't prepared for and couldn't sustain for long enough to be convincing. I could tell them about Sean, which would be embarrassing, but probably believable. Or I could tell them the truth. I almost flinched at the thought of it.

"I had a fling with one of my instructors," I said at last, feeling my face colouring. "It didn't go down too well."

Rebanks looked me up and down slowly, insultingly. "Oh but I'm sure you did," he murmured.

The Major silenced him with a look of intense distaste and continued to stare at me for a while. I just hoped there was enough truth showing in what I'd said for him to accept it. Still, he was the type who was predisposed to believe that I'd done something so predictably female, so stupid.

In the end, he nodded. "All right, Miss Fox, we'll overlook this one, but if I find out that there's anything else you haven't been telling us, you'll be in more trouble than you can imagine. Is that understood?"

"Yes sir," I said, resisting the urge to salute.

So, what had Kirk found out that he wasn't supposed to know? Was that the kind of trouble the Major had in mind? The thought made my skin go suddenly cold and start to prickle.

"All right," Gilby said, glancing at his men in dismissal. "Now get her out of here."

Rebanks took me down the corridor to the students' mess hall where the others who'd been through the exercise were waiting. Shirley took one look at my face and my torn shirt, and came to put her arm round my shoulder.

"What on earth happened to you, lovey?" she demanded.

Elsa, though, was a little more observant. She waved a hand to my neck. "So, this is what you have been hiding under all those high collars," she said.

Her cool comment made everybody stare at me like I was a science exhibit. I glared at them, and all but those with the thickest of skins let their eyes drop away.

They were looking expectant, though. I knew I was going to have to tell them something or the rumour mill was going to be working overtime.

Question was, what?

And, more to the point, what the hell was I going to tell Sean?

CHAPTER
NINE

As soon as I could get away at lunch, I called Sean. He sounded surprised to hear from me during the daytime, his voice switching to wariness almost right away.

"Charlie, are you OK?"

"You'd better get Madeleine to plant some new information in this mythical past of mine she's been creating," I said.

"Why? What's happened?"

So I told him. I told him in detail how I'd slipped up on the range and given away my army training. I told him in somewhat less detail how I'd come to overreact during the first-aid simulation.

"You knocked him out with a telephone?" Sean demanded, and I could hear the faintest trace of laughter behind his words.

For some reason, the funny side totally eluded me. My temper was still edgy, close to the surface, and that was enough to spill it over again.

"I'm glad it amuses you, Sean," I snapped. "Meanwhile I'm the one out here taking the shit. I just want some reassurance that if they follow up on my story — and I think Gilby is the careful type — they'll find it checks out. At the moment I don't have a lot of confidence that it will."

Sean's voice dropped cold and serious instantly. "Why not?"

I shrugged, aware that maybe I'd said too much. "I just have the feeling that Gilby's men knew what they were looking for today," I said. "They seemed to know just which buttons to press to get me to let go."

"By the sound of it, Charlie, they're pressing everyone's buttons."

"True," I said. "But not like this."

I'd asked around and they'd given the others a rough ride also, but nothing quite as specific as the treatment they'd given me. Having said that, the sim had been the final straw for Shirley. She'd packed up her stuff and taken the long walk up the driveway and out of the Manor, struggling to carry her dignity along with her suitcase.

"Apart from that one slip-up on the range yesterday," I went on, "I don't think I've done anything that should have made them so suspicious — unless my cover story isn't holding water. Where else could they be getting their information from?"

"I'll check," Sean said, his voice clipped. Anger or concern? I couldn't tell. "Call me tonight. I'll try to have something for you then."

At lunch we found out that we'd all failed the first-aid simulation. Almost everyone had blundered straight in and been judged shot dead, too indoctrinated by their army training to question the order to go over the top.

128

Those who weren't hamstrung by a military background had simply been too intimidated by the frenzy of the instructors not to do as they were told.

Apart from me, only Tor Romundstad had perceived the dangers waiting in that darkened room. He'd point-blank refused all Blakemore's rabid inducements to enter the study. Some sixth sense warning the Norwegian to stay clear.

Despite this, we still failed. When Romundstad asked Major Gilby why, he was told it was because we'd obviously left our principal unguarded for long enough for him to be attacked in the first place. A real no-win situation.

I think I was finally beginning to learn.

Todd was back on his feet in time to eat, so it didn't seem like I'd done him any lasting damage. It was clear I hadn't made any friends in that direction though, and more than ever I regretted my instinctive violent reaction.

I found out just what a bad idea it was during the unarmed combat session that followed. Previously Blakemore had used O'Neill as his guinea pig, but when I saw the stocky phys instructor step into the gym in his place, I knew there was going to be trouble.

The thing that alarmed me most was the fact that there was nothing overt about the threat Todd exuded. There was no stare-out contest, no stamping of hooves in the dust, no throwing of salt into the air. He didn't even look at me. Not once.

But I could feel his enmity washing in like the cold draught from a broken window.

Blakemore had decided to teach us how to use extendible batons. In countries where we would not be allowed to carry firearms, he said, they were a viable alternative for disabling a would-be attacker.

In its collapsed form the baton was about eight inches long. It sat cold and heavy in my hand, the weight of the concealed end making it feel unbalanced.

Blakemore demonstrated the technique for opening it up, flicking his wrist so the two magnetically held inner sections telescoped out and locked into position with a solid click like a steel door closing. Fully extended, the baton was just short of two feet in length and weighed four hundred and fifty grams, nearly a pound.

The sight of it was enough to push sweat out all along my hairline.

A year or so previously I'd had my left arm broken in two places by someone using a metal rod that seemed very similar to the baton. He'd been aiming for my face at the time and if he'd connected I probably wouldn't be here to tell the tale. My forearm still gave me gyp when the weather was cold and I could forecast rain with it more reliably than the Met Office.

Listening to the fizzing sound of the baton parting the air as Blakemore made a few exploratory swipes with it brought that memory rushing back in all its sharp and bitter glory. It made my bones tingle, sent a ripple sizzling across my skin.

Blakemore and Todd moved onto the crashmats and sprang at each other, sparring with the batons and a liberal dousing of testosterone. They clashed with great energy but to little effect. Like a couple of stage actors indulging in a sword fight designed to make the audience gasp, but not to put either in any real position of danger. It looked impressive, though.

When they were done they stepped apart, breathing hard. Blakemore had put enough effort into the display for the sweat to track down his temple and he wiped it away with the back of his hand. He turned, caught my set face and grinned. "Don't worry," he said, "we don't expect you to practise on each other."

He and Todd dragged out a line of weighted mannequins and strolled among us while we went through the drills of deploying the baton and striking the dummies across the head, chest, and neck.

Once we'd got the feel of it, Blakemore moved on to set attacks and defences. As he'd done before he formed us into two groups. Instinctively, I graduated towards his side, trying not to make it look too obvious that I'd made a conscious choice.

Just as casually, it seemed, the instructors deliberately changed places at the last minute so I ended up in Todd's group anyway.

The first pass went fine. When I reached the front of the queue and stepped forwards onto the mat Todd walked me through the move without a hitch. I was to make a strike for him, which he would evade, and then I would counter, formal as a dance. He followed the same routine with everyone, and we lined up to go again.

It was only on the second pass that Todd deviated from the game. Instead of the move I was expecting he went for the hand holding the baton, grabbed and burrowed in with steel fingers, trying to force me to release my grip.

I'd taught my self-defence students more escapes from wrist-locks than just about anything else. I didn't have to think about my response, it was knee-jerk and immediate.

I twisted so the baton lay low across the back of his hand, then reached across to grasp it with my left, jerking the hard edge of the baton down and into his wrist, just where the bones protruded. It was a surprisingly delicate area, vulnerable to force in just the right spot.

Todd stiffened in surprise as the baton dug in, and I let the pressure off right away. I'd no wish to antagonise the man any more than I had done already.

I should have known better.

As soon as I'd partially released him Todd curled himself around my arm, tucked in to my body, and brought his elbow back, hard. I don't know if it was luck, I don't know if it was judgement, but the blow landed smack in the centre of my sternum.

The following few moments disappeared in a haze of pain. I don't remember letting go of the baton. I don't remember falling. My next recollection is staring up from the crashmats at a circle of faces above me.

Blakemore's was the closest, but I saw more curiosity written there than alarm.

I sat up, suppressing a groan that movement provoked, and the faces retreated a little way.

"Are you fit to continue, Miss Fox?" Blakemore asked. There was just a touch of challenge to his tone.

I looked past him to where Todd was lounging with his arm draped around one of the mannequins. In his hand he was swinging the baton he'd taken from me and his eyes met mine with a lazy arrogance. He'd made his point, I realised, shown me who was top dog. I would do well to remember it.

I nodded briefly to Blakemore, who condescended to give me a hand up. The other pupils were watching me with a bemused air, as though I was going out of my way to cause trouble for myself.

Somehow I got through the remainder of the lesson. The pain in my chest subsided to a dull throbbing ache that only hurt if I tried to fill my lungs to full capacity. I wondered how much more of this I was willing to put up with, just to act as a balm to Sean's guilty conscience.

Todd stopped me on the way out. "Feeling all right, are we?" he asked.

"I'm fine," I said, and was reminded of the way O'Neill had said the same thing to Blakemore after that first unarmed combat lesson. The standard lie.

He nodded, looked me up and down, then leaned in close to murmur a threat that was all the more dismaying for its totally unexpected nature. "Keep asking questions," he said softly, "and next time you won't get away so lightly."

Shock kept my face blank, but I was still turning over Todd's words as I made my way upstairs and back to the dormitory. Shirley's bed stood stripped to its mattress by the window, with the pillow and blankets stacked neatly at the head, and the locker empty beside it. I wondered how many more of us would jack it in before the course was up.

And for what reasons.

We had a reasonable gap in the timetable between unarmed combat and the next driving session, so I headed for the shower, standing for a long time under the stinging spray with my hands braced against the tiles.

The only question I'd asked that might have upset anyone was my casual enquiry about Kirk and my mention of hollowpoint rounds. Rebanks had sidestepped both casually enough, so why the big fuss about it now? It didn't make sense, unless Todd was just using that as an excuse to take me down a peg or two. But, did he really need an excuse for that?

I pushed my sodden hair out of my eyes and realised that I'd forgotten to bring my shampoo with me. Leaving the shower running I stepped out onto the mat and roughly towelled myself off, before hurrying through to the bedroom.

But as I opened the bathroom door I caught a glimpse of a figure rushing out through the main door into the hallway, letting it slam behind them.

134

I shot to the door and yanked it open, but surprise had slowed me down, and by the time I stuck my head out into the corridor, they were gone. With water dripping off me in puddles and only a towel for cover, I wasn't inclined to give chase.

I stepped back into the room and shut the door.

Whoever I'd interrupted had left my locker open, with half the contents scattered out onto the floor in front of it. The mobile phone Sean had given me was on the bed, switched on.

When I picked it up I found that they'd been scrolling through the dialled numbers. There weren't many to go at. In fact, the only one in there was Sean's own mobile. For a moment I stood there clutching the phone. Who was searching my stuff, and why?

And, more importantly, had they found what they were looking for?

I abandoned my shower, even though my hair was going to be uncontrollable for being wet and dried again without shampoo. I hurriedly put the contents of my locker back together again, checking as I did so that the hollowpoint was still where I'd hidden it.

I'd dropped it into the bottom of a sock which I'd then rolled back into a pair again. Not a ploy that would have held off a determined searcher for long. Now I picked the bullet out and looked quickly for a better hiding place.

Shirley's empty bed caught my eye. I lifted up the foot end and discovered that the narrow steel legs were hollow. If I turned the round sideways-on, it would just about wedge in place inside the leg. I made sure I repositioned the bed back exactly onto its original indentations in the carpet when I was done, and stood back. It wasn't perfect, but it would have to do.

I had to resist the urge to check that the hollowpoint was still in its new hiding place when we packed in for the afternoon and the three of us trooped wearily back to the dormitory.

I still had no idea who my mystery searcher might have been. During the afternoon's lesson I'd had plenty of opportunity to look round for guilty faces. Trouble was, just about everyone had begun to look shifty and suspicious all of a sudden, instructors as well as pupils.

Since Shirley's departure the cosy feel among the women seemed to have evaporated, too. I hadn't realised how much she'd held us together, cheered us along.

Now, Elsa headed for the shower without much by way of conversation and Jan picked up her cigarettes.

She paused by the doorway. "You fancy a game of pool in a bit?" she asked.

"Maybe," I said. I picked my phone out of my locker. "I want to call home first."

Jan eyed me with a rare smile. "I don't envy you your mobile bill this month," she said, fishing. "He must be something special, the amount of time you spend on the phone to him."

I grinned back. "He is," I said.

It was only when she'd gone out and closed the door behind her that I realised how little of that I'd had to feign. It made me cautious in my greeting of Sean when he picked up at the other end.

He matched his tone to mine and launched straight in. "We've been doing some checking," he said, businesslike. I heard the "we" and wondered if it was a deliberate attempt to put distance between us. "As far as we can tell your cover is solid. Someone's been looking, but they haven't broken past the stops Madeleine put in unless, of course, Gilby's working for the army."

My heart did a back flip. "What?"

"Don't panic," Sean said. "I don't think that's a likely one. It would seem that Major Valentine Gilby is not a popular boy in a variety of circles."

He filled me in on the Major's military career, which had been on a fast track until the Gulf War. "He was put in charge of a group of Iraqi prisoners who mysteriously ended up walking across a minefield. Which wouldn't have been so bad," Sean said, his voice dry, "except for the fact that a team from CNN happened to capture the whole thing on camera. Doing it was one thing, being caught doing it by the media was quite another. There was hell to pay."

"So he got the boot," I said.

"In very short order," he agreed. "But it's not quite that straightforward. Gilby only held the rank of captain then. It would seem he'd kept enough records to show that he was just following orders, and he threatened to go public unless they made him up to major and let him go with full honours."

"Sneaky," I said, with a certain amount of admiration. If only *I'd* had something so strong to hang over their heads things might have turned out very differently. But it confirmed that underlying ruthless edge I'd picked up from Gilby. I could well believe he'd not only force prisoners into mine clearance, but that he'd then resort to blackmail to escape the blame.

I glanced at the door to the bathroom. I could still hear the shower running. Looked like Elsa was taking her time in there. I moved over to the window anyway, just in case, and hitched my hip onto the window ledge.

From there, if I craned my neck, I could see across the forecourt to where Blakemore's FireBlade and Gilby's new car were parked on opposite sides of the gravel, facing each other. It was as though they were preparing for a duel.

As I watched I saw Gilby and Blakemore walk down the steps. Blakemore was in full leathers. The two men exchanged a few words, then went to their respective vehicles. The combined noise of their engines being started up was clearly audible, even at the other end of a telephone line.

"What the hell's that?" Sean wanted to know.

"Boys and their toys," I said. I watched Gilby perform another of his pebbledash starts with blatant disregard for a cold engine, heading for the driveway. Blakemore streaked the Honda across the gravel after him.

"Gilby's got a new motor that's supposed to be something special and he's trying to race a FireBlade with it," I said. "It's a Nissan Skyline R30-something or other, apparently."

"R30-what?" Sean demanded sharply. "Is it a thirty-two, a thirty-three, or a thirty-four? What does it look like?"

"Like a car. I don't know," I said, surprised. "I'm not sure of the number. R32, R34, what difference does it make?"

"At current prices, about forty-five grand," Sean said. "If it's an R34 he'll have paid a fortune for it."

Forty-five grand. "I think it is a new one," I managed weakly. "Forty-five grand? Are you sure? That's almost as much as a house."

"My God, Charlie, you do live in the impoverished north, don't you?" Sean said, and there was no mistaking the smile in his voice. It died fast. "Where the hell has Gilby got that kind of money from? The last financial info we dug out on him showed he was only holding himself out of the red by the skin of his teeth."

"There's no sign of the place being run on a shoestring," I said. "The food's too good. And someone's spent a fortune restocking the armoury here." I told him about the Sigs having replaced the old Makarovs he had told me to expect.

"I'll get Madeleine to look into it, see what she can dig out," he said. He paused, then, "There's something else come up that I think you ought to know about."

"What?"

"It would appear that we're not the only ones taking an interest in Salter's death. The Germans are in on it."

"What do you mean?" I demanded. "I thought you said the police here weren't bothered."

I was aware then that I could no longer hear running water from the next room. At that moment the door opened and Elsa came out, wrapped in a pair of towels. She smiled briefly at me and began collecting up clean clothes from her locker.

"It isn't the police I'm talking about," Sean said in my ear. "It's the security services. Apparently they've got someone into the school."

"That's interesting news, darling," I said, my voice a purr, "do tell me more."

For a moment there was utter silence, then Sean asked, "Do I take it that you're no longer alone?"

"Unfortunately not," I said. I gave a throaty chuckle. "But I can't wait until we are."

Elsa threw me a quick look of distaste. She gathered up her stuff and hurried back into the bathroom, closing the door firmly behind her. I heard her hairdryer start up almost right away.

"Don't make promises you're not prepared to make good on, Charlie," Sean said, and his voice was rich with promises all of its own.

"It's all right, she's gone," I said, ignoring that last remark. "Do you have any idea who this German agent is? Male or female, even?"

Sean sighed. "No, not yet. We're working on it. Do you have anyone in mind?"

I glanced at the closed bathroom door. "Possibly," I said. "It might explain why I nearly caught someone searching my stuff this afternoon."

140

"Did they take anything? Do you still have the round?"

"Yes, it's safe, but they had a good look at the phone, so they've got your number," I said. "You think that might be the Germans rather than Gilby's lot?"

"Probably, but the real question is not who, but why? I can't believe they'd be investigating Salter's death unless it was connected to something else."

"I'll see what I can find out at this end," I said, "although asking questions is not exactly making me popular."

I told Sean all about Todd's warning, and this time I didn't gloss over the events leading up to it.

"Are you OK?" Sean's voice was tight.

I shrugged. My chest was still sore. I could only hope that I hadn't done any lasting damage. "I'm fine," I said.

"Charlie, what did you mean earlier when you said they knew just which buttons to press? What did they do to you?" What could I hear in his voice? Weariness or anguish?

I had a brief, vivid flash of Todd holding me down on the desktop. An echo of the panic I'd felt then came clawing up my throat. It was a struggle to overpower it.

"It's nothing, Sean, forget it," I said quickly. "Don't worry about me. I can cope."

"How can I not worry about you, Charlie?" he asked gently, "I never realised when I asked you to go and do this that it would be so damned difficult." And there were turns and folds in his voice like melted chocolate.

"Part of me knows full well that you were one of the best soldiers I ever trained," he went on, "but at the same time part of me can't help but remember another side to you — soft, vulnerable." He broke off, took a breath. "If you want to give this up now and come home, I won't think any less of you," he said. "You've been hurt before because of me. I don't want it to happen again."

"That wasn't your fault Sean." I found to my horror that I was close to crying. "I'm OK," I said, stronger. Wanting to believe it. "And now I've started I want to see this thing through. One way or another."

If only I'd known.

CHAPTER
TEN

"OK, Charlie," Rebanks said. "Let's see what you're really made of." He moved back, folded his arms around his clipboard, and raised his voice. "Watch and shoot. Watch and shoot."

I held the Sig out in front of me, both hands clasped loosely round the pistol grip, and stepped out onto the Close Quarter Battle range. As I carefully advanced I was acutely aware of the eyes on me. Not just of Rebanks, O'Neill, and Gilby, who'd turned up to watch this lesson, but the other pupils' as well.

Those who'd already had their turn were lined up to watch the next victim. By now, they'd all found out about my army background. I'm not entirely sure how. Some, like Declan, took it all as a big joke. Others, like Hofmann, took it as a personal affront, as though I'd been trying to trick them. Even Jan and Elsa seemed more distant with me somehow.

So, this morning on the CQB range, I'd decided to drop the act. I was going to give it my best shot — literally as well as figuratively — and see where that got me. I didn't think I could be doing any worse.

Eight metres away to my left, the first of the targets swung into view, a hardboard cut-out of a half figure clutching a gun in both hands, his features hidden by a ski mask. I planted two rounds square in the centre of the forehead. By the time it folded away again I was already moving forwards, looking for my next target.

The Manor's CQB range had been built in a small gully in the woods with banks that rose to provide natural cover for wild shots on either side. All told, it was about two hundred metres long and affected by a stillness that was unnerving.

Regular gunfire obviously kept the animal and bird population at bay. The lack of life signs gave the ground a contaminated feel to it. Even the weak pale sunshine seemed reluctant to climb over the banks and wash down onto the floor of the gully. It was a place shunned by nature and to be avoided.

Trying to suppress a shudder, I walked on. I concentrated on keeping my shoulders easy, keeping my breathing light. Rebanks walked a careful distance behind me, keeping score.

The second target had been placed low and left. It burst upwards out of a pile of pine needles less than three metres away, with a suddenness that took me by the throat.

I just had time to put another two rounds into the head before it fell away as though responding directly to the hit.

Rebanks had explained to us at the pre-shoot briefing that there would be six targets, appearing at a variety of distances, and for random periods ranging from four to eight seconds.

He'd been lying.

Whatever they'd been doing for the others, I knew damned well that for me they were only holding their upright position for a two-second maximum. I wondered why that should surprise me. I should have expected special treatment.

All right then.

There was an old tree fifteen metres away to my right. The bark of its trunk was lacerated with pale scars. When the next target started to flip out from behind it I was already twisting into position. Even before it had locked flat I punched the first round through at an angle, raking out a two-inch splinter from the back board. Instinct told me the second was a clean hit, but the target wasn't around long enough for me to check.

Three and four came up so close together in time and range I nearly didn't get to them, but I was dialled in now. Utterly focused. And damned determined that they weren't going to beat me at this game. The Sig wasn't just in my hand, it was part of my hand, an extension of my arm, part of me.

By the time the targets dropped, Rebanks had another pair of kills to add to my total.

Kills. Somewhere out in these woods Kirk had been killed. Mown down either just as his back was turned, or when he'd already started running.

Running for his life.

Who shot you, Kirk? What did you see, or know, or do, that made you an unacceptable threat to them? My feet carried me forwards while my mind reached back, trying to understand the motivation of the men who'd gunned him down.

Target number five was a sneaky one, tucked away at the bottom of a log pile. I was almost at the far end of the range before six came up, a long walk designed to stretch and snap the nerves. This one didn't drop away after I'd slotted it, but remained upright and quivering, signalling the end of the run.

I lowered the gun, but kept the muzzle pointing straight down the range, aware for the first time of the buzz of tension in my neck and upper arms. I hunched them, hearing my vertebrae click and pop as they settled.

Rebanks came up on my right with a peculiar little smile on his face. He made a couple of marks on his clipboard and started to turn. As he did so, I saw the alarm bloom in his face.

"Look out, look out!"

He grabbed for my shoulders, started to pull me over to the side towards him. I ended up falling onto his legs in a tangle, taking him with me. I twisted as I went down, keeping the Sig level. Out of the corner of my eye I saw the outline looming in from the left, recognised the threat as another target. Number seven of a supposed six. Another of their mind games.

The sun was in my eyes, making the target little more than a dark silhouette. I aimed by instinct as I went down, but in that split second before I fired I realised there was something different about that target.

Something wrong.

I fought to twist my hand even as my finger tightened irrevocably on the trigger. The Sig twitched as it discharged with a force that jarred my whole arm. The moving parts locked back on an empty magazine.

Rebanks rolled out from under me and climbed to his feet without speaking. He batted the wet earth off his camouflage trousers before he glanced down at me.

"Congratulations, Charlie," he said then, his voice ironic. "Weren't you paying attention when we told you there'd only be six targets? That was your principal you've just hit, running to you for help and protection."

He waved towards the target. Still lying on the ground I turned my head and looked at the cut-out figure, less than four metres away.

I could now tell it was a fairly realistic picture of a frightened-looking young girl with long hair. She was not holding a weapon and did indeed seem to be running directly towards me, frozen in mid-stride.

The weak winter sunlight streamed through the hole I'd shot high in her right shoulder.

Nobody else managed to shoot the principal during the CQB exercise. Mind you, hardly anyone managed to hit all the other targets either, even though they stayed up for what seemed to me to be half an hour a go.

Declan was the last man down the range. His shooting was so wild that Rebanks stuck to his back like an overcoat in high summer, leaving no chance that the Irishman was going to swing round and clip him by mistake. Even Declan didn't manage to hit the girl at the end, although that was more by luck than judgement. He fired at her when Rebanks jumped him, but he missed.

Afterwards, O'Neill collected up the Sigs and he and Major Gilby climbed into one of the Audis and disappeared back towards the Manor without any comments about our performance. Or lack of it.

The rest of us got to walk back. I trudged along at the tail end of the group, a dark cloud of gloom settling over me. They'd set me up and I'd fallen for it. The thought sat badly on my stomach like a heavy meal.

"They weren't being fair on you," said a voice to my left. I turned my head to find Elsa walking alongside and watching me. I remembered my last conversation with Sean. Was Elsa the German security service plant?

I forced a shrug. "You try and stick your head above the parapet," I said, "you shouldn't be surprised when people try and blow it off."

"The targets stayed upright for much longer for everyone else," she said, as though I hadn't spoken, her voice thoughtful. "They weren't being fair on you," she repeated. "Yet still you managed to hit them all."

"Yeah," I said, casting her a tired glance, "even the one I wasn't supposed to."

"When that last one came up at the end for me, Rebanks just nudged my arm. He didn't grab me and pull me over." She was frowning now. "You never stood a chance of seeing that it wasn't the same as the others. They expected you to fail — but you know that, don't you?"

"Yes," I said, managing to find half a smile from somewhere. "They wanted me to, but I don't always do what people want."

148

"They're going to make it harder for you next time," she said, her face serious. "What have you done that they're trying to trip you up all the time?"

Now, *there* was a question. Did Gilby's men know about my dual role, or did they just not like it when they came across a woman who showed a spark. And why was Elsa so interested all of a sudden?

"I'm not the only one who's trying to make life difficult for themselves," I said, keeping my eyes on the needle-coated path in front of me.

I felt her stiffen. "What do you mean?"

"That lecture," I said, glancing at her. "You must have known Gilby was going to take it badly."

Either the German woman was a better actress than I'd given her credit for, or I'd genuinely thrown her off balance. She looked sincerely confused. "Why should he have done?" she demanded, and there was defiance in her lifted chin.

I stopped for a moment, staring at her, but could detect no hint of guile.

"You really don't know, do you?" I said slowly.

"Know what?" she said. Bewilderment gave way to frustration. "Charlie, please explain."

I turned and started walking again. We'd fallen a little way back from the rest of the group by now, and I felt safe to launch into the details Sean had given me about Heidi's kidnap, and the Major's involvement with the team who were guarding her. The trees had a convenient muffling effect, but I kept my voice low, all the same.

I suppose I should have been more wary about giving her the information, but I figured if she *was* secret service, she already knew it all anyway and if she *wasn't*, well I probably needed all the help I could get.

Elsa was silent while I spoke. It was only when I'd finished and checked out her face that I saw the closed-in anger there.

"Dumb fuck," she bit out quietly, and went on in German along what I gathered from the tone were similar lines. Her hands were balled into fists by her sides. "I knew I never should have trusted him."

Now it was my turn for confusion. "Trusted who, Elsa?"

She took a breath and made an effort to loosen up, even flicking me a short smile that didn't reach behind the lenses of her glasses. "One of my ex-colleagues," she said, with no small amount of bitterness. "One of my ex-husband's colleagues, also. Someone I thought was still a friend." She gave a derisory snort, shaking her head. "Obviously not."

We walked on another minute or so while I assumed she ran through a mental list of things she was probably going to do to her ex-colleague — not to mention her ex-husband — when she next got her hands on him.

"What did he tell you?" I asked then.

She sighed. "He told me he knew people who'd been on this course, that we would be asked to present such a lecture and he gave me the details of the Krauss case from the police file. He told me it was because he felt bad about how my husband had treated me and he wanted to help me. Now I realise he was just trying to

150

make trouble for me. To make sure I failed. So they could all laugh behind my back." She spat out another word in German that I didn't understand, but it sounded like a useful piece of abuse. I stored it for later. "Bastard."

"Elsa," I said carefully. "When I came back to the room yesterday, someone had been searching my stuff."

She frowned, distracted from her thoughts. "That's strange," she said at last. "I thought someone had been through my things, also. Nothing was missing, but some items were not quite as I remembered leaving them. Has anything been taken from you?"

I thought of the hollowpoint, tucked safely under Shirley's bed. "No," I said, "but you didn't see anyone hanging around our rooms did you?"

She shook her head. "No, only you, me, and Jan. No one else. Do you think we should speak to the Major about this?"

"I don't think there's much point," I said, giving her a tired smile. "If it wasn't any of us, who do you think that leaves?

I don't know if Major Gilby realised we were starting to go stir crazy by the end of the fifth day, but he announced over that evening's meal that transport had been arranged to take us into Einsbaden village to visit the local bar, if anyone was interested? He took our unanimous loud vote of approval with something akin to disappointment. As though he hadn't expected better of us, but had hoped for it, nevertheless.

They rolled out the same canvas-topped trucks that had picked up Declan, Elsa, and me on our arrival. Was it really only five days ago? We all began piling into the back.

Figgis and O'Neill were driving and the other instructors commandeered the comfy seats, leaving the rest of us with cattle class. Just as we were loading up Blakemore appeared in his leathers.

"You not riding with the rest of us then?" Declan called across to him.

"Nah, I'm riding in style, mate," Blakemore said, grinning at him through the open visor of his helmet. He threw his leg over the FireBlade like it was a cavalry charger, hit the electric start and short shifted his way across the gravel. I admit to a pang of envy before that rorty exhaust note was drowned out by the asthmatic rattle of the truck motor cranking into life.

It was only a relatively short trip into Einsbaden. It was too loud for conversation in the back of the truck. We sat and swayed and stared at each other in the dim light from the single flickering light bulb without attempting to speak.

The guys had that scrubbed up look about them. Freshly showered hair still gleaming wetly, designer shirts, and an air of hopeful anticipation. The mingling aromas of their liberal dousings of aftershave would have felled an anosmic ox at a hundred paces. It wasn't doing much for me, that's for sure.

The trucks rumbled into the village square like the advance party for an invasion force. If the locals saw them coming they certainly didn't hang out flags of welcome. When we'd rolled to a halt outside the one local drinking hole there was a stampede to be first to the bar which I didn't try to compete with.

As they burst noisily through the main doors, though, my fellow pupils discovered that, not surprisingly, Blakemore had beaten them to it. He was sitting at one end of the bar, looking very much at home, with a beer by his elbow and an open paperback on his knee. He grinned smugly at us when we came in, sliding a marker into the book and setting it pointedly aside as if to say, what kept you?

"What'll you have, Charlie?"

I turned to find Craddock had muscled his way through to the front and was standing at the bar holding a euro note in his hand. I hesitated briefly, but there was nothing devious about the Welshman.

"A beer would be great," I said. "Whatever they have is fine."

The landlord was on nodding acquaintance with the instructors, although he seemed neither pleased nor displeased to see his customer numbers so vastly swelled for the night. He greeted the few locals who ventured in with the same stolid lack of hospitality.

The original decorators of the place had gone for an alpine tavern look, all rough cut timbers, old-fashioned wooden skis, and cow bells. I snagged a table in a corner. It had ornately carved heavy wooden chairs at each end and rustic benches along both sides that had been polished smooth by the passage of years of hutching bottoms. I sat at one end of a bench, where I had my back to a wall and could watch the rest of the room.

Craddock returned from the bar with two bottles of lager and no glasses. Declan was with him, and we were soon joined by Jan, Elsa, and a couple of the others whom I didn't know well enough to confidently put names to. They all sat and we tilted the bottles.

"Ah, but that hits the spot," Declan said, his tone almost reverential.

The rest of the Manor crew, once they'd found there were no local women under the age of sixty to receive the benefit of their collective charms, lost their predatory boisterous edge and seemed to settle, mentally downgrading the evening from possible pulling session to night out with the lads.

I watched the change come over them and felt the tension ease out of my shoulders. I could almost hear the hiss as the steam escaped from my system. I hadn't realised how much I'd been holding it in.

The evening progressed better than it had any right to, given the circumstances. Declan bought a second round, then one of the other lads got a third in. A suitable while later, I got to my feet and waved a hand at the empty bottles cluttering the table top.

"Same again?" I asked. Nobody came over all chivalrous on me, so I headed for the bar.

When I returned, clutching two handfuls of lager bottles, I found O'Neill was in my place.

"She double-tapped the lot of them, just like that?" Declan was asking. "Now *that* I would have liked to have seen. Why the feck couldn't I have been one of the ones to go before her?"

I didn't have to ask what he was talking about. I put the beer down on the table top with more of a sharp click than I might otherwise have done. O'Neill looked up at me then and winked. He slid out of my seat and gestured for me to regain it with exaggerated courtesy.

"Please, be my guest," he said, grinning. "I make it a rule never to start a fight with a lady who could kill me just as easy with either a nine-mil or a telephone." But as he made to move past me I put my hand on his arm and stopped him.

"Why did Rebanks do it?" I asked him quietly.

O'Neill had the grace not to play dumb with me. He glanced across the room to where the weapons' man was sitting, and leaned in close. The move sent a waft of beer breath gusting over me that almost made me flinch.

"Because he didn't think you'd got a hope in hell of hitting them," he said, blunt with the truth of it. There was a certain amount of smug satisfaction in his voice, too. No love lost there. "I doubt he would have maxed out that one himself and he knows the position of those targets in his sleep."

He grinned at me again, and this time there was a hint of sly in his face. "It doesn't happen often that we get someone as good with a pistol as you, Charlie," he said.

I remembered Sean's comment, that day in the little pub in Yorkshire, about Kirk being able to out-shoot most of the instructors.

"So who was the last?" I asked.

O'Neill shrugged. "Big guy called Salter. He was here last month. Bit of a coincidence really," he went on, giving me a sideways look. "We get years of no-hopers, then two crack shots come along, one after another."

Before I could think up a response to that one, there was a crash of breaking glass from the direction of the bar and the kind of quick scatter of movement you only get in pubs when someone's just dropped a full pint, or just started a fight with one.

We all twisted round to look. In this case, it seemed that both option boxes had been ticked.

Blakemore was off his bar stool, tense with anger and surrounded by a sea of broken glass. Beer was splashed up the front of his leather jacket, and the front of the shirt he had on underneath was dark with it. Blakemore didn't seem to notice the mess. He had that head-down stance I knew well. The kind that counts down to violence like the timer on a bomb.

"What's going on?" Craddock asked, jiggling to see past me.

It took a moment for the people around the bar to shift enough for us to see who the other player was.

"Looks like McKenna's got himself a death wish," I said. "He's just squaring up to take Blakemore on."

"This I have to see," Declan said, hopping out of his seat.

After a second's pause, the rest of us scrambled after him.

"Looks like you've started a trend for attacking the staff, Charlie," O'Neill said, nudging my arm. I ignored him.

As we closed on them, McKenna was so unsteady on his feet that for a moment I thought Blakemore had already thumped him.

"You're not bloody fit to teach us anything," McKenna said, his voice slurred so that he ran the words at the end of the sentence together. He stabbed a finger towards the other man's chest. "You get careless and then people die, yer bastards. And you don't give a shit, do ya? You just don't give a shit. It won't be the first time that you've had to clear up the bodies, though, will it?"

My heart jumped. Was he talking about Kirk? And if not, who else had died here?

Blakemore stood there, vibrating with suppressed fury the way a big dog does, just before it launches itself straight for your throat. He didn't move, but under his heavy drawn-down brow his eyes had begun to smoulder like a dropped cigarette down the side of a cheap foam sofa.

Even Declan's eagerness to witness the bloodshed started to wilt in the face of this sense of burgeoning menace. Those nearest began to back way.

Alongside me O'Neill muttered, "Oh shit," under his breath. "He'll fucking kill him."

I turned. "Blakemore?"

"No," he said, and nodded.

I looked back and found that another of the instructors had stepped into the demarcation zone. Possibly the last one I would have expected.

Figgis.

"I think maybe you've had a little too much to drink, Mr McKenna," Figgis said politely. His voice was as calm as his words. His body language was calmer than that. "I think maybe you need a bit of fresh air."

McKenna lurched away like the floorboards had tilted wildly under his feet and mumbled, "F' cough will ya?" He waved an arm at Blakemore, the movement unbalancing him even more. "This is between me and 'im."

Figgis straightened up and seemed to come together in front of us. Normally he was a shambling figure, as if all his limbs were slightly loose in their attachment. Now, it was as though someone had threaded cord right the way through his body and suddenly taken up all the slack.

He ambled towards McKenna, took hold of him almost gently and went up his arm in a sequence of what looked like clips and squeezes that was never hurried, but at the same time was too fast to properly take in.

Figgis finished by lightly chopping McKenna under the sides of his jaw with the edges of both hands. If it had been an open-handed slap to the face, it would barely have been hard enough to bring tears to his eyes.

McKenna watched him make the moves with a mystified look on his face, then his eyes rolled back and he folded up almost gracefully, like he'd just fainted. Figgis caught him neatly on the way down.

"There now," Figgis said to the room at large. "Too much beer, like I said. Let's get the lad outside and get him some air." He glanced at Blakemore and added,

"No harm done, eh?" and there was a trace of something in his tone that might almost have been a warning.

Blakemore seemed to shake himself out of it, brushed off his jacket and made a careless gesture. "No," he said darkly. "No harm done."

A couple of the others helped McKenna out of the bar. He was conscious, but unaware, staggering blindly. Figgis turned to beam at everyone, and dropped back into the baggy skin that we'd all assumed was the real him.

We drifted back to our table.

"Now, I know we've all just seen that, but would somebody mind explaining to me exactly what the feck it is that we've just seen?" Declan demanded.

I could have answered his question, but I didn't choose to. I'd come across a few martial arts practitioners who used Kyusho-Jitsu pressure-point techniques, but I've never seen one take somebody out of a fight with them quite so easily. Figgis, I considered, was more than an expert. He was a master.

"Ah well," O'Neill said. "He's a bit of a dark horse is our Mr Figgis. Bit like Charlie here." He glanced sideways at me, but I didn't rise to that one, so he let it go. "Up until a few months ago Blakemore was teaching defensive driving and Figgis was your man for unarmed combat, but they did a bit of a job swap. It's a waste, so it is, because good old Figgis is absolutely fucking lethal. I wouldn't be wanting to go up against him."

I waited until everyone had settled back into their drinking. Waited until the boys who'd helped McKenna outside had returned without him. Waited until I could make my excuses to look for the ladies' room without it seeming obvious that I wasn't going there.

Then I slipped out of my seat and walked into the cold little back corridor where the toilets were located. I kept walking, moving past them and out through the back door at the end. From there I picked my way round the crates of empty bottles and aluminium beer kegs, and headed for the front of the building.

I spotted McKenna almost right away. He was standing leaning against the tailgate of one of the Manor trucks. If I was going to find out what he meant by his outburst, I reckoned, then doing it while he was half-cut and disorientated might be the best time.

I walked over to him. As I approached he dragged out a packet of cigarettes and lit one with a disposable lighter, cupping his hand around the flame. He still looked a little unsteady on his feet, but when he heard my footsteps he lifted his head and stared at me with perfect focus.

"What do you want?" he said. Not roughly, but with no sign of the slurring that had marked his earlier speech, either. It was embarrassment I could hear there, I realised, as though he'd fallen for some cheap stage hypnotist's trick in front of his mates.

"I just wanted to check you're OK," I said.

"I'm fine," he said shortly.

I waited a beat, but he wasn't going to follow that up with anything else. I stuck my hands in my jeans pockets and jerked my head towards the bar entrance. "So what was that all about?"

He shrugged, as if to loosen a stiff neck. "Just had a bit too much to drink, that's all," he said, sucking in on the cigarette and blowing the smoke out down his nostrils.

If that was the case, I thought, how come he was stone-cold sober now? I nearly left it there, but I couldn't let the opportunity slip. "What did you mean about people dying here?" I asked carefully, and so as not to lead him I added, "Who died?"

McKenna's face closed in. He took a final deep drag on his cigarette and dropped the half-finished butt to the floor, stamping it out with more vigour than the task demanded. Then he glanced up and stared at me, his eyes shrewd. "You really want to know?" he asked. "Why don't you ask them?"

He nodded to a point over my shoulder as he pushed himself away from the tailgate and headed back towards the bar.

I turned and followed the direction he'd indicated. Just in time to see a dark coloured Peugeot saloon on the other side of the square start up. It moved off fast, the driver not switching on his headlights until the car was nearly halfway down the far street.

Even so, there was enough illumination spilling out of the windows of the bar and the surrounding houses for me to recognise the outline of four men inside.

CHAPTER
ELEVEN

The next day, during rapid de-bus drills in the rain behind the Manor, Figgis was back to his usual relaxed self. So much so, in fact, that I began to wonder if I'd imagined last night. One look at McKenna's wary face told me I hadn't.

More than ever the youngster seemed to be avoiding contact with everyone else. Where another of the pupils might have brushed off his foolish challenge to Blakemore as drunken bravado, McKenna was finding it hard to let it go. Maybe the fact that he hadn't been nearly so drunk as he'd been pretending had something to do with it.

And with that in mind, what had he hoped to achieve by starting a fight with Blakemore, other than concussion and stitches? The more I turned it over in my mind, the more I came to the conclusion that there'd been something calculated about his words in the bar. They weren't just random ramblings. There was a point to them. A message. But was it about Kirk? And if so, who was it aimed at? I'd really no idea.

I'd switched the phone on and tried to reach Sean when we got back from the village, but his mobile rang out without reply until it finally clicked over onto his voice mail. Disconcerted, I'd left him a brief message, telling him I'd call him in the morning. I'd tried again before breakfast, but still he wasn't answering.

For the first time since I'd arrived in Germany, I felt cut off, and alone.

Phys seemed to be getting harder every day, which didn't help. This morning, one of the blokes had packed up and left shortly after our usual pre-dawn marathon, claiming he'd aggravated an old back injury. It was clear from Todd's dismissive reaction to his departure that the staff believed he simply couldn't hack it.

Now, I stood trying to keep the rain from sliding down my neck while a group of us watched Romundstad, Craddock, and two of the others pulling up fast in one of the school Audis and hustling Todd out of the back seat in a suitably protective scrum.

At a shout from Figgis that signified a gunshot, they had to get their principal back into his car, throwing themselves on top of him to provide body cover, and then get the vehicle away from the danger zone as rapidly as possible. They were piling in on top of the phys instructor with great gusto, eager to get their revenge for the punishing early morning regime any way they could.

"Do it again. That was crap," Figgis said mildly when they'd finished. "You're anticipating too much. This time there might be a threat, or there might not. I'll decide. And don't forget, you're supposed to be blending in with a big business atmosphere. If you do every de-bus like that, you'll give your principal a nervous breakdown inside the first day. Not to mention breaking most of his ribs."

He glanced round at the sheepish faces. "You're supposed to be giving him confidence, making him feel protected, not looking like you're expecting a full-scale assault every time. If you was looking after me like that, you'd be frightening me to death. Go on. Get back out there and do it again."

The rest of us stood and grinned as they set up for another run, but as I watched them swing the car round again I suddenly had the uncomfortable feeling that I, too, was being watched.

I turned my head to find O'Neill standing a few feet away. He was regarding me narrow-eyed through the smoke from his cigarette. When he saw that I'd clocked him, he took that as his invitation to come over.

"I was just thinking back to our little conversation in the pub last night," he said, a mite too pally in his approach.

I said, "Oh yes," in what I hoped were entirely neutral tones, while I frantically searched my memory for anything I might have said that he could possibly have taken encouragement from. After a few moments I gave it up as futile.

"Yeah," he said. He put his head on one side and looked at me with an expression of exaggerated puzzlement playing across his scarred features. "Y'know there's something familiar about you. I thought that first time I saw you. I keep getting this feeling that I know you from somewhere."

164

I cocked him a quick look to check that it wasn't a chat-up line. Believe it or not there are still some guys out there who think that kind of remark qualifies.

"I don't think so," I said, turning away. Jan, standing close enough to overhear the exchange, flicked me a sympathetic glance. Hofmann's group had started their approach now. I concentrated on watching them roll to a halt and begin their second de-bus.

"You sure about that are you now, Charlie?" O'Neill said softly. He'd moved to just behind my shoulder. There was something intimately knowing in his voice, the blur of it halfway between a threat and a caress.

"I guess I must just have that kind of face," I said through clenched teeth.

"Is that right?" O'Neill murmured. "Well I got to thinking about coincidences, and how I don't believe in them. Two crack shots, one after another," he repeated his words from last night, emphasising them with two taps on my shoulder. I suppressed the urge to scratch. "I *know* you from somewhere, no mistake, and sooner or later it's going to come back to me where that is."

I didn't reply to that and when I next glanced round, he'd gone. I found myself clutching a desperate wish for him to suffer sudden, total, and irrevocable amnesia.

After the driving we were in the classroom until lunch, learning about the organisation behind successful bodyguard work. Checking out hotels, restaurants, itineraries, schedules. It would have been right up Shirley's street, had she lasted that long.

Just before the lesson finished Gilby dropped it on us that we'd be back in Einsbaden over the course of the next few days, carrying out site surveys of the village.

"For the purposes of the exercise, your principal is going to be staying there. He wants to relax, see the sights, visit the local bar and café," he told us. "You need to know where the dangers could come from, and your best escape routes." He picked up his notes and gave us his usual parting cool stare. "You will be tested on this."

At lunch, ignoring the table manners that had been drummed into me since I was a child, I bolted my food as fast as I could shovel it in. It was efficient rather than stylish, but I managed to get my lunch finished before anyone else and almost ran up the stairs. This time, when I dialled Sean's number, it was picked up on the third ring.

"Sean!" I said, the relief like a weight lifted. "Thank Christ for that. Where have you been?"

"No, sorry," said Madeleine's ever-efficient voice. "He's not here at the moment. If you'd like to tell me what you need, though, I'll try and help."

"Where's Sean?" I demanded, feeling cheated.

"He's away. Rush job," Madeleine said carelessly. "Some Arab prince flew in for a quick shopping trip and he won't venture into the jungles of Knightsbridge without Sean by his side. Don't worry. He'll be back tomorrow."

Yes, but that's no good when I need Sean now.

I sat on Shirley's empty bed and stared at the rain slanting across the window. Below me I heard an engine and when I looked down I saw Major Gilby returning from some short run out in the platinum-coloured Skyline. He walked a couple of strides away from the car, then turned and looked back at it for a moment, disinclined to hurry despite the weather. I was too far away to see his expression, but I knew that look. Pride. New toy.

At the other end of the line there was silence for a second longer, then Madeleine said, "So, what's been happening over there?"

I vacillated over launching into the whole story, or waiting until Sean was back. In the end I decided any other viewpoint was better than none.

"We went out for a bit of R&R in Einsbaden last night," I said, "and one of the lads, McKenna, got a bit out of hand."

"With you?"

"No, he had a go at one of the instructors — guy called Blakemore." I could have added more detail, but some perversity made me want her to have to ask for more information.

"Blakemore. He's the unarmed combat man, isn't he?" she said. I should have known she'd be fully up to speed on all the major players in this drama. "McKenna's a brave boy. He must have been pretty drunk."

"That's just the thing," I said. "He was making out that he was completely sloshed, but when I caught up with him outside, he was sober as a judge."

"Hm, you wouldn't say that if you knew many judges," she said, and I could hear the smile in her voice.

Dammit, take this seriously. Out loud I said, "I need to know if the kid's got any connection with Kirk. He accused Blakemore of getting careless and then people dying. Something about it not being the first time. He can't have pretended to be drunk in order to take Blakemore on, because they never actually got to blows, so it must have been to deliver that little speech without repercussions. Can you check out his background for me? He's not exactly the chatty type."

"Of course," she said, all trace of amusement gone. "Anything else?"

"Yeah," I said. "That black Peugeot I told Sean about is back. They were hanging around outside the bar last night. Took off when they knew they'd been spotted. Any clues as to who they might be?"

"Mm, I've already been looking into that one," Madeleine said, and I heard her rustling papers in the background. "Ah, here we are. The car is registered to a German security company who, in turn, have their roots in Russia. I get the impression the German company's a front, but I'm still trying to get past the layers."

"Russia?" I echoed, almost to myself. "Why would the Russians be interested in Gilby?" Something stirred in my mind, but I couldn't pinpoint it. I shook it off.

"That's a good one. We're working on it."

"I don't suppose you've found out any more about the identity of this German security agent have you?" I asked. "I'm getting a bit fed up of looking over my shoulder all the time."

Madeleine sighed. "No, we're still working on that, too. They're not exactly the easiest people to get information out of."

"Well, speaking of getting information out of people, I've had O'Neill hanging round me today, making noises about how he knows me from somewhere."

"Hm, not the most original line in the world," she said.

I almost smiled. Almost, but not quite. "I thought that, but are you sure there's no way he can access any information about me other than what you've planted?"

"We-ell," she said slowly, "reasonably sure."

"What do you mean, 'reasonably'?" I snapped. "I thought you were supposed to be providing me with cover."

"We are," she said, not sounding offended. Not sounding that concerned though, either. "Trouble is, Charlie, you're ex-army, and you're surrounded by other people who are ex-army, too," she went on, her voice patient, as though she was explaining the patently obvious. "I can plant all the info you like, but if someone actually remembers you from that time, there's absolutely nothing I can do about it."

After I'd ended the call I sat for a time, remembering back to my army days. It seemed so long ago it might as well have been another life. Despite my words to Gilby in his study after the first-aid sim, the army *had* suited me. Up until my attack, it had suited me very well.

For possibly the first time in my life I'd found somewhere I fitted, where clearly I had talent. I'd gone looking for a long-term career, and I'd never intended to jeopardise that by having a spur-of-the-moment fling with Sean Meyer.

Things don't always work out quite the way you plan them.

Sean and I had only met when I volunteered for the Special Forces course. I'd been encouraged to apply for it by the commanding officer of my own unit. He'd recognised my skills and had seen a channel for them.

Sean had been one of my new instructors, a sergeant then. He had a tough reputation and eyes that seemed to be able to penetrate your soul. Of all of them, he was the one who scared me the most. He was the one who could see when I was weakening, could sense when I was closest to giving up, giving in.

And he'd exploited that ability to its fullest extent. He was never vicious, never sneering. He was the reasonable one who stood there at the end of an all-night orienteering exercise and asked who would like a hot meal and a shower, and who would like to go the whole route again. Some of them fell for it, opting for the truck back to camp. By the time the rest of us got back, they'd already packed their kit and been Returned To Unit.

So, when Sean started paying particular attention to my every failing move, I thought I was finished. It had hardened my resolve not to let him beat me. I'd trained hard, pushed myself up onto a level of fitness I'd never managed to attain since. Because of Sean, or maybe for him, I'd begun to shine.

Perhaps that was what had marked me out as a worthy adversary, a suitable victim, and had ultimately sealed my fate.

In unarmed combat that afternoon we went through the drills of dealing with crowds. Two of us walked Blakemore down a line-up of the others. He played the visiting dignitary, smiling and shaking hands. Every now and again someone would try and grab him. When they did we had to deal with the problem, quickly and quietly, and keep him moving along to the next.

I was partnered up with Hofmann and together we slowly paraded Blakemore along the line. I was watching eyes and hands, waiting for the first sign of intent. Then a movement to one side caught my attention and I glanced towards the open doorway.

Gilby was standing there, leaning against the frame observing the class, with O'Neill beside him. As I looked, the Irishman seemed to nod in my direction, and Gilby fixed me with his battlefield stare.

It so unnerved me that I missed Romundstad make a lunge for Blakemore's arm. With a small snort of irritation, Hofmann had to lean across and yank him away. Annoyed with myself, I concentrated on the job in hand. By the time we reached the end of the line and I looked back at the doorway, it was empty.

When we finished up there and headed for the outdoor range, the afternoon was already starting its toboggan run into evening. The rain had died, but the cold was thin and biting. My bones ached with the memories of old breaks.

As well as the Sigs, this time out O'Neill and Rebanks had also issued us with belted speed-draw holsters. We spent the first hour practising disengaging one from the other without making fools of ourselves. We were dry-firing to lessen the chances of shooting ourselves in the process. Probably a good job, too.

Rebanks then set up targets at only around six metres on the five-lane range. When we were given the command we had to draw and fire three shots. The first from the hip, and the second and third with the arm extended as we backed away from the source of danger.

Everyone was becoming a lot more relaxed around firearms now. As soon as they strapped on a holster, they suddenly became cowboys. There was plenty of swaggering and references to John Wayne. Even the encroaching darkness didn't diminish the general air of confidence. It was enough to make me nervous.

As if to play on that, the rest of the instructors turned up in time for us to start live firing, so each of the open lanes was supervised. As though they were expecting something to go wrong.

The floodlights were on by this time, creating a pool of light around the firing positions. Our collective breath rose and mingled like smoke into the beams of the lights. Beyond them the trees suddenly seemed very still and very black.

"Keep your wits about you, people," Rebanks shouted as we prepared for the first shoot. "Mr Lloyd, get your thumb out of your gun belt. You are not Wyatt fucking Earp."

Declan dropped his hands to his sides, looking shamefaced.

"OK, when I give the signal you will draw and fire one group of three shots only, as you've been

172

practising, then you will make your weapon safe and return it to the holster." Rebanks favoured us with a hard stare. "Is that clear to everyone? Good, so there'll be no fuck-ups, then."

He waved us into position and pulled his ear defenders into place. I checked the Sig was loose and easy in its holster, and waited for the signal to fire, my mouth suddenly dry. Rebanks was taking his time. *Why are you dragging this out, man?*

Out of the corner of my eye I saw him start to raise his arm, but his eyes weren't on the targets, or on us. He was looking past me, over towards the small wooden shed that formed the range control centre. I started to turn my head, to see what he was looking it. I never got that far.

The floodlights clicked off, and the whole area was plunged into total darkness.

For a moment I was dumb with the shock of it. I kept my feet still, tried to get my bearings, but after the brightness of the lights, I could see nothing. My eyes had completely shut down in the blackout that followed.

I ripped my ear defenders off. Robbed of sight, I needed my hearing as sharp as I could make it.

"All right, all right," Rebanks yelled, "don't anybody panic, let's just —"

The sound of the gunshots was terrifyingly loud. There were two of them, over to my right. I spun my head away, but the muzzle flash lasered across my retinas, burning in and destroying what little night vision I'd just managed to accrue.

"Who the fuck was that?" Rebanks shouted. "Nobody fires! Cease firing, cease firing!"

Then, as my ears began to put away the assault of the shots, other, quieter sounds came into focus. I heard moaning. My heart rate leapt.

Rebanks produced a torch and came rushing past me. "Who's hit?" he demanded. "Who's down?"

Other small lights sprang up across the range as the other instructors clicked on their torches. Next to me, Romundstad had got out his cigarette lighter. The flint sparked twice before it caught, and then I saw his anxious face behind the flickering flame.

The torches converged jerkily on a figure writhing on the ground a few metres away. It was the big Welshman Craddock, his face contorted. Rebanks was on his knees alongside him. So was O'Neill, burrowing under Craddock's jacket, yanking his shirt open. In the unsteady shafts of light that jumped onto him there seemed to be blood everywhere.

Rebanks was cursing steadily under his breath. "Somebody get me a first-aid kit here."

Figgis arrived at a dead run with a canvas pack. He dived into it and ripped open a sterile field dressing.

It was at that point that Rebanks sat back on his heels and looked up at the shocked faces surrounding him.

"OK, Major," he called, his voice calm, "that'll do."

The floodlights snapped back on with a suddenness that made us all blink. For a moment nobody moved, then the realisation slowly began to seep through the layers. We'd been had.

Craddock sat up and grinned at us, mopping the fake blood away from his stomach. "Hellfire, a little of that stuff goes a long way," he remarked cheerfully as he examined his gore-stained clothing. "I hope it washes out. I was fond of this shirt."

Figgis clapped him on the shoulder. "Oscar-winning stuff, lad," he said, "although if you'd really been shot you'd have been screaming like a baby."

Not necessarily, I thought. The last person I'd had to deal with who'd taken a bullet hadn't made a sound, even though they'd had to run with it.

Rebanks climbed to his feet. His hands were streaked with what had looked for all the world like real blood. He glanced down at them and grinned too, more a baring of his teeth. "Let that be a lesson to all of you," he said. "Don't get cocky around weapons. They don't suffer fools gladly, and they always have the last word. Just be thankful this was a simulation, not the real thing. OK, back to your positions and let's go from the top."

Just as I was about to shift back to my firing lane, Blakemore brushed past me and moved in close on Rebanks, Figgis, and O'Neill. He looked the three of them up and down with an expression of distaste on his heavy set face.

When he spoke it was quietly, so that only the few people closest overheard, but I got the impression Blakemore didn't care who was listening.

"So," he said softly. "*That's* how you did it."

CHAPTER
TWELVE

We spent the morning of Day Seven back in the classroom, brushing up on our table manners. I don't know if Major Gilby had been paying particular attention to the way most of this batch of students handled a knife and fork, but they made Napoleonic naval surgeons look refined. If he had it must have made him cringe enough to do something about it.

Gilby had laid out a white cloth onto the desktop in front of him. He identified and demonstrated the correct use of the selection of cutlery he'd placed on top of it with a delicacy that was almost effeminate.

As I watched Hofmann's face crease into a frown of concentration I silently thanked my mother's insistence on nice table manners. He was wrestling with the novelty of having different spoons for soup, dessert, and to stir his coffee.

"So," the Major said now, pointing to the array of wine glasses, "which of these would you use for red, and which for white?"

A few people obligingly indicated different glasses, eager to display their genteel upbringing.

Gilby waited a moment before giving us a chilly smile. "Wrong," he said. "You don't, because the last thing you people should do when you're on the job is drink. You don't drink when you're in a restaurant with the client. You don't drink in a hotel bar even after he's turned in for the night, and you certainly don't ever charge alcohol to the client's tab. Is that clear?"

Chastened, we murmured our understanding and he moved on to restaurant behaviour. It was lightweight, skimming the surface kind of stuff, but there were a few nuggets, even so. How you should always order the fastest thing on the menu so you were finished before the client. How you should tip well so the staff were especially helpful.

"You'd be amazed how fast a waiter will get a meal on your plate," Gilby said dryly, "if you tell him up front that he can add a thirty per cent gratuity onto the bill. You're going to need to eat quickly because when the client stands up to leave, you're finished, whether there's food still on your plate or not."

As a closer, Gilby briefly went over dressing the part. It was at this point that he went completely blind to the three remaining women in the group. "A double-breasted suit is cut best to conceal a weapon," he said, "and make sure the trousers are loose enough to move in if things get nasty."

It was Jan who waved her hand at him. "What about us?" she asked. She managed, for once, to keep the belligerent tone out of her voice.

Gilby had the grace to look uncomfortable, at least. "Just something smart casual," he muttered, which wasn't exactly a great deal of help. "No high heels."

A few of the group were starting to look bored by this time. Clearly this wasn't quite what they'd signed up for. The Major noticed the restless edge and wound it up.

"Right now you probably don't realise the importance of what I'm telling you, but you will," he said meaningfully. "Looking presentable, and not eating your peas off your knife won't, by itself, get you any work in this business, but try behaving like a slob in front of the client and see how fast they dump you."

He allowed his eyes to travel slowly over his students, most of whom suddenly found their interest renewed. "Don't worry," he said, cracking another of those icy smiles, "this afternoon Mr Figgis is going to take you out for some ambush drills in the forest. That should wake you all up a bit."

We went out in a fast convoy made up of all five of the school Audis. Figgis was driving the lead car, which was where I would have preferred to be, given a choice. I wasn't, and ended up in the third, with Todd behind the wheel.

Hofmann had claimed the passenger seat alongside him, with McKenna, Elsa, and me squashed into the back. It was so tight a fit I could barely fasten my seatbelt, despite the comparative skinniness of the three of us. McKenna and I were at the sides, so our forward vision was limited to the small gap between two pairs of beefy shoulders.

Figgis led us at breakneck speed along the rutted driveway and out in the direction of Einsbaden. The

178

weather was dry, but with a hint of a foggy mist hanging in wisps around the dips in the road. Before we reached the village itself the lead car slowed suddenly, turning off the road and onto a side road that was little more than a wide forestry track.

I held onto my door pull and tried not to let my head bounce against the roof of the car as Todd aimed for every pothole. It was like being back in that damned taxi.

Just when I thought I was going to need all my fillings replacing, Figgis brought the convoy to a halt and we all de-bussed.

"OK everyone, as you probably know we're going to practise ambush drills this afternoon," Figgis said. "For this we wanted a space that was a bit more enclosed than the driving arena back at the Manor, to simulate a built-up area."

He waved a hand at the trees that surrounded us. They went off in all directions as far as you could see. The mist had penetrated between the trunks of them now, beginning to thicken.

"Further along this track is a big crossroads, like an intersection," Figgis went on. "Those of you with Mr Todd, Mr O'Neill, and Mr Rebanks will form the principal vehicle and two chase cars and attempt to drive through that intersection. Myself and Mr Blakemore's vehicles will attempt to stop you. We'll run through it once for you, then you'll all get to have a drive." He glanced around at the trees and sniffed. "If this bloody fog doesn't get any worse."

We got back into the cars and waited until Blakemore and Figgis had disappeared. That left Todd with the lead vehicle. He checked his watch, then turned and grinned at me. "Don't look so scared, Fox, you won't need your seatbelt," he jeered. "This isn't a full contact sport and we know what we're doing."

I smiled sweetly at him and pointedly belted up anyway.

Todd set off with lurching gusto, leaving the other two Audis scrambling to keep up. We got up to a ridiculous speed for the conditions, the trees whipping past outside my window. They seemed so close if I'd put my hand out I would have lost my fingers.

Then the trees widened out into the clearing Figgis had mentioned. Suddenly the two ambush Audis were streaking out from the other tracks. One slewed across in front of Todd. I twisted in my seat and saw the other come screaming out from the opposite direction, aiming to cut off our escape route to the rear. It was timed to perfection, I had to give them that.

Todd wrenched at the steering wheel, sending the Audi slithering sideways, and just managed to fishtail round the car that was blocking us. We came within a hair's breadth of slamming into the side of it in the process.

We carried on another fifty metres or so down the track, then Todd stood on the brakes and reversed back to the intersection. Everyone else was already out of the cars by the time we arrived.

"Very good, Mr Todd," Figgis said, and I couldn't help but hear the note of lazy amusement in his voice.

He nodded towards the vehicles which had been following us, and which had been neatly boxed in. "Only trouble is, you're the lead car, not the one containing your principal, which was in the centre. So, although you've managed to evade this ambush, your principal is now in the hands of kidnappers or assassins."

Todd glowered at him. Figgis turned to the rest of us, smiling. "I'm sure you're all aware of the old maxim in this industry — never outlive your principal. It's no good you making good your own escape and leaving your boss behind. It's bad for your professional reputation and besides anything else, if you lose him who's going to pay your wages?"

We grinned back at him. It was difficult not to, and once Todd had finished sulking we climbed back into the cars for another run. This time, Todd was in the passenger seat, with Hofmann behind the wheel. Figgis swapped the order round, too, so that now we were the filling in the three-Audi sandwich, and then sent us back up the track to our starting point.

Hofmann was a big lumbering figure, and his reactions just didn't seem fast enough to evade Figgis and Blakemore's trap, even though we all knew it was coming. Jan, behind us at the wheel of Rebanks's car, did manage to zip past, but received the same criticism that Todd had.

We went back and did it all again. And again.

In fact, we went backwards and forwards a dozen times. I fared no better than the others. I was thankful when my turn was over, and I could relinquish control of the Audi to McKenna. Besides, he drove so badly it even made me look good. Romunstad's rallying experience made him the star of the exercise.

Getting back up the forest track to our starting point had become a race for most of the boys. They were treating it like their own personal closed stage, safe in the knowledge that they weren't going to meet anyone coming the other way. Even the gradually encroaching fog hadn't slowed them down, although visibility was worsening all the time.

Declan was driving the lead car, and Hofmann was behind the wheel of ours, sticking to the Irishman's tail like he was slipstreaming him. I daren't look, but I was pretty sure that Craddock, at the wheel of the car behind us, was just as close to our rear bumper. We were approaching our turnaround point.

"I dread to think what Major Gilby's going to say," I remarked loudly over the frantically revving engine, "if we prang all three cars at the same time."

In the front passenger seat, Todd turned round to grin at me. He opened his mouth, no doubt to make some smart alec reply, but if he actually spoke, I never heard it.

At that moment we seemed to pick up the most enormous stone chip. It landed with a crack in the centre of the front windscreen, which split right the way across in both directions.

Ahead of us, Declan's brake lights blazed. Hofmann hit the brakes and the back end of Declan's car at almost the same instant. The impact was a jarring crunch that threw me forwards against my jammed seatbelt, the diagonal jerking my shoulder. I saw the lead Audi flick out sideways off to the right of the track, bouncing down nose-first into the trees.

If I'd had the time to think about it, I would have put the accident down to sheer bad driving. It was only when Declan's car was out of the way that I saw the familiar black Peugeot sideways across the track less than fifty metres in front, blocking the way.

Behind it stood four men with machine pistols, their muzzles flashing like strobes as they fired at us.

Hofmann suddenly went into overdrive. He spun the wheel over to the left and grabbed for the handbrake without having to be told. The move would have been textbook if it hadn't been for the car behind. Craddock rammed the Audi's rear wing just as we started to swing round.

Our car flipped over, still travelling at speed. My world went haywire and turned upside down. I wrapped my arms round my head as the side window nearest to me crazed and shattered, showering me with chunks of glass. Sticks and leaves and stones were scooped inside as we scraped along the forest track on our roof.

It seemed to take a long time before we came to a stop. The floormat had dropped onto my feet, trapping them in the footwell and for a moment I panicked. I released my seatbelt without thinking about it, dropping painfully into the roof of the car in a tangle of arms and legs. Beside me, Elsa was moving groggily, bleeding from a cut on her forehead. McKenna was hanging slumped alongside her, not moving.

In the front Hofmann was uninjured, but the windscreen pillars had folded down slightly, encroaching on his position, and his size meant he was struggling to get free. He was wrenching at the steering wheel, heaving at it with enough strength to set the car rocking.

The smell of petrol burned the back of my throat. Behind me I could hear the fuel pump still whining, even though the engine had stalled. It was Todd who reached over and switched off the ignition.

"Is everybody OK?" he demanded.

From somewhere above us came the rattle of automatic gunfire. I flinched and thought of the petrol. The desire to get out of that car was overwhelming. I bit down hard on it.

Hofmann had managed to bend the bottom edge of the steering wheel almost double. He pulled his legs free, swivelled in his seat, and kicked the buckled driver's door so hard it exploded open.

Todd grabbed his arm. "Wait," he said. "Where are they?"

I ducked down and peered out through my side window. After he'd punted us up the rear end, Craddock had brought the last Audi to a halt about five metres behind us, slanted across the track. Figgis, who'd been with him, was out of the car holding a Beretta twelve-bore, pump-action shotgun. As I watched, he jacked the first round into the chamber, brought the butt up to his shoulder, and fired. I don't know what kind of slugs he had in that thing, but the noise was incredible.

184

The men from the Peugeot weren't expecting an armed response. They ducked back behind their car.

"Come on," I said. "We've got some covering fire."

My door wouldn't open, but the broken window was plenty big enough to squeeze out of if you were determined you could do it. Elsa followed me out and we dodged round to the other side to help Hofmann drag McKenna clear. By the time Todd was out of the car, one of the school Sigs had appeared in his hand and he looked itching to use it.

We ran back behind Figgis's car, keeping low. I looked across to where the first Audi had taken a nose dive into the trees. The occupants had all managed to scramble out and now they fell back to join us. It was getting crowded back there, but I was amazed to discover that nobody had been seriously injured in the pile-up.

"Keep the bastards pinned down," Todd shouted.

"I'm doing my best," Figgis said with surprising calm. He let off another shot, exploding the rear tyre of the Peugeot and peppering the wing.

"What the hell are Blakemore and O'Neill doing?" Todd snapped. "Can't they hear this lot going down?"

One of the shooters popped up from behind the front end of the Peugeot and let loose another burst. The gun was short, similar to an IMI Mini-Uzi, but with a bulky foregrip just under the business end of the barrel. I didn't recognise the make and didn't feel inclined to spend time finding out.

"We have to get into the forest," Jan said curtly. "With this mist we can find better cover there."

Todd, Rebanks, and Figgis exchanged glances, then nodded. "When I give the signal," Rebanks said, tense, "we all scatter, OK?"

"Who are these people?" Elsa asked, her face dead white. "Why are they shooting at us?" Nobody bothered to answer.

Hofmann picked up McKenna, who was starting to come round, but was still groggy. Rebanks drew a Sig from inside his jacket and cocked it. Did the instructors go armed at all times, I wondered, or had they just been expecting trouble today?

"OK, now!" Rebanks shouted. The three of them jumped up, firing, and the rest of us ran for the trees.

We ran in an outward dispersal pattern. I ended up on the extreme left, a lot closer to the ambush than I would have liked. I resisted the urge to run directly away from the gunmen. Too many of us clumped together presented too tempting a target.

As it was I heard the high-pitched whine of several rounds whistling past me and thunking into the surrounding tree trunks. My imagination placed them closer than reality, but I tried not to think about that.

It wasn't a new experience to be faced with people shooting at me. Still, this time they hadn't been sent with the express purpose of killing me. At least, I hoped not.

A revving engine made me glance back over my shoulder. I'd come maybe a hundred and fifty metres from the ambush site, and already the fog was making the view back dusty and faint. I slowed, jumped over a fallen trunk, and crouched down behind it. As I watched, another of the school Audis slithered to a halt behind Craddock's car and Blakemore and O'Neill jumped out of it. O'Neill was holding another Beretta twelve-bore. He hung the gun round the front of the Audi and pumped three fast rounds into the front end of the Peugeot. The tyres blew out immediately and the car collapsed down onto its rims.

The four gunmen must have realised by this time that the balance of power had begun to swing against them. The arrival of the second shotgun tipped it altogether. One of them jumped back into the car and tried to start the engine. Blakemore, Todd, and Rebanks started pouring shots into the front screen, while Figgis and O'Neill pounded the engine bay with the Berettas.

Within moments there was a small explosive woof as leaking fuel was ignited by the spark from the car's own ignition system. The driver abandoned his efforts and dived out as the flames started to lick around the edges of the bonnet. The four of them fled into the forest.

The other three must have gone in the opposite direction, but I didn't see where. The driver, on the other hand, was heading straight for my location, pausing every half a dozen strides or so to rake the trees behind him with automatic fire.

I ducked down out of sight, adrenaline coursing through my body, shouting at me to get out of there, fast. It was much harder to stay put than to run, but right now I was fairly well hidden and I knew it was my best option. That didn't mean I had to like it. I glanced round, and my eye lighted on a weighty branch close by. I carefully eased it within reach, and waited.

Blakemore came pounding through the forest on the driver's tail, unheeding of the bursts of fire splintering the trees around him. I was reminded strongly again of Sean. That head-down sheer bloody-minded determination.

Blakemore was firing as he ran, keeping the Sig out in front of him. Even so, it was luck more than judgement that he winged the driver in the right arm as he hurdled a pile of logs. I suspect that he was aiming square for the centre of his body.

With a yell of pain the driver let go of the machine pistol and stumbled, going down on his knees less than ten metres from my position. Before he could rise again, Blakemore was on him.

He lifted the man off the ground and slammed him back against the nearest tree.

"What the fuck do you think you're playing at?" he demanded.

When the man didn't answer, Blakemore reached down and gripped him hard round his bicep, digging in cruelly to the leaking wound with his thumb. I saw the driver's body twist with pain, but still he wouldn't speak.

Frustration bloomed across Blakemore's face. He brought the Sig up and shoved the barrel into the other man's mouth. The driver's eyes widened as his head was forced back, smacking into the trunk behind him. The raised foresight dug into his palate, drawing blood.

"You'll speak now or you'll never speak again," Blakemore hissed.

Something in his eyes told me he wasn't kidding. The instructor had the flat cool eyes of someone who could take a life without sweating over it, and look himself in the mirror every morning afterwards.

I knew what it was to take a life, but there wasn't a day went past when I didn't wish the circumstances had been different. That didn't mean I couldn't do it again, but I wouldn't go deliberately looking for the opportunity, either.

I stood up. Blakemore's head snapped round to face me, and didn't relax when he saw who it was.

"Charlie," he said, not shifting the Sig from the driver's mouth. "Get out of here."

I knew what he was telling me to do, but I wouldn't play. Instead I stepped over my protective log and moved forwards to pick up the man's machine pistol from where it had fallen. It was surprisingly lightweight and with the stock retracted it seemed shorter than the nine-mil SMGs I'd fired in the army. I settled the gun in my hands and pointed it in Blakemore's direction. He didn't look surprised about it.

"Either let the police deal with him, or let him go," I said. "I'm not going to stand by and watch you commit murder."

Blakemore snorted. "What do you think this bastard and his mates were trying to do to you?"

I didn't answer, just stood there and kept the gun steady. After a moment Blakemore removed the Sig from the driver's mouth, looking disgusted with himself that he'd been manoeuvred into doing so, and straightened up.

The man didn't need telling twice that this was his chance. He started to scrabble away, but before he'd got far Blakemore leaned down and grabbed his coat collar, pushing his face close and speaking in fast, almost garbled German. Then he shoved the man aside and moved towards me, not even bothering to watch the driver's frantic, lurching escape into the mist-shrouded trees.

Blakemore took the machine pistol out of my hands carefully, as though he still wasn't quite sure if I was going to shoot him with it. I let him take it because my brain couldn't think of a good enough reason to stop him. I jerked my head to indicate the rest of the instructors.

"You knew this was going to happen, didn't you?"

He sighed. "Come on," he said, sidestepping my question. "We need to find the others. Make sure nobody's hurt."

I stood for another few seconds, my feet rooted, then I followed his lead. All the time I was searching through little-used areas of my memory, piecing together a ragged translation of Blakemore's rapid words to the driver of the Peugeot.

My German vocabulary came back to me with painful slowness. When I thought I'd got all the words I didn't believe the sense I'd made of them, so I went back and checked them again.

By the time we were back at the crash site I knew I hadn't made a mistake about what Blakemore had said.

The other students and instructors gradually congregated near the three remaining Audis that were relatively undamaged. I could tell straight away the ones who'd been under fire before. They were taking the whole thing much better than those who'd been civilians all their lives.

O'Neill was one of the last to regroup. He came sauntering in with the Beretta resting on his shoulder like a machete. He nodded at the machine pistol Blakemore was holding. "Did you get one of them?"

Blakemore flicked his eyes momentarily in my direction. "No, he got away," he said. "At least I tried."

O'Neill didn't respond directly to that, just turned and walked away. Blakemore watched him go, not looking any more cheerful than he had done when I'd forced him into releasing the driver.

I barely listened to the exchange. I just stood on the outskirts of the crowd watching the Peugeot burning, but didn't see any of it. My mind was too full of what I'd heard in the woods.

If my translation was correct, I thought, then I now knew what had happened to Kirk, how he'd died, and who had killed him. But that didn't mean the whole thing was solved and over.

If anything, it had just become a whole lot more complicated.

CHAPTER
THIRTEEN

"No," Sean said. I heard his breath escape in a sharp hiss. "No way, Charlie. You're not going to convince me that Gilby's mob are a criminal gang who recruited Salter — a man they'd only known for a couple of weeks — and involved him in the kidnap of Heidi Krauss."

"Is it so far-fetched?" I argued. "Heidi's bodyguards said they fired at the kidnappers as they fled the house. They could have hit somebody and that somebody could have been Kirk. Gilby gets him away, but he dies en route and they dump the body. How else would they explain it? I know what I heard Blakemore say to that guy —"

"You know what you *think* you heard," Sean cut in.

" 'Try this shit again and next time we send you the kid's ears.' He was quite specific," I said mildly. "If you can put another, more innocent meaning on those words, Sean, I'd like to hear it."

I'd already been through the whole story of the afternoon's ambush in the forest and the firefight that had followed. Sean's German was fluent, much better than mine. Even he had to admit that, if I'd heard correctly, my translation was right, too.

He'd asked me twice if I was sure I was OK, and again if I wanted to call the whole thing off and come back to the UK. I'd answered yes to the former question and a firm no to the latter.

Sean had gone quiet, locked down, terse, like he always did when he was in the field himself. He was sending Madeleine out to Einsbaden, he'd told me then, so she'd be close at hand to liaise if things got hairy. She was arriving tomorrow. I'd wished that Sean was coming himself, but would have bitten out my tongue before I'd put that longing into words.

Now, he sighed. "It still doesn't fit," he said at last, sounding tired. More than tired, bone-weary, defeated. "The dates for the Krauss girl's disappearance and Salter's death don't fit. Unless they managed to keep him on ice for a couple of weeks after she was taken."

Disappointment came down over me in a grey wash. "Damn," I said. "It was neat. I thought I'd got it."

"Don't sweat it," Sean said, and there was a smile in his voice now. "We've been going over every permutation at this end and not come up with anything better."

I was alone in the women's dormitory after dinner, sitting on the window ledge with my feet tucked up in front of me. I held the phone cradled in my right hand, next to the glass. It was dark outside, cold enough for snow, but I couldn't suppress the warm delight I felt at speaking to Sean again.

"It doesn't mean that Kirk didn't find out about the kidnap and try and do something about it," I said, screwing my eyes up as I let the memory of Sean's words in that deserted pub scroll back behind my eyes like an autocue. "Didn't you tell me that in his last phone call Kirk said he wished he'd stood up for me, that it had been on his conscience, and that he wasn't going to make the same mistake twice?"

"True," Sean said slowly. "I suppose it could fit with him having discovered that the girl was being held at the school somewhere and not wanting to stand by and do nothing. Did you ever find out where Gilby was going when he was being followed that night?"

"No," I admitted. "There's been rather a lot going on here since we last spoke. I'll give it another try soon."

"OK, but be careful. If we're right about this, the Major could be a very dangerous man to cross. We've checked his finances, by the way, to find out how he can afford his flash new car. He's been receiving large sums of cash from a Swiss account, starting about six months ago."

"Which was when the kidnappings started," I realised. "Coincidence?"

"Could be, but I've never liked them," Sean agreed. "Thing is, they're regular payments and they don't coincide with the ransom amounts."

"Maybe he's just a sub-contractor," I said. "You told me Gregor Venko was thought to be behind these kidnappings, but it was a change of style. Maybe he's farmed the work out and Gilby's on a retainer to get the job done any way he chooses."

Sean was quiet for a moment, but I could hear his brain turning over. "Now that *does* fit," he said eventually. "I don't like it, but it does fit. I'll get Madeleine on to tracing the money, although that's

194

going to be a difficult one, if not impossible. The Swiss are a tight-lipped bunch."

"When I last spoke to Madeleine she said she was working to find out more about the men in the Peugeot. Has she made any headway yet?"

"Not really," Sean admitted. "We know the parent company's Russian, and that's where we've hit a brick wall."

"Russian?" I said. Madeleine had mentioned the Russians and it had rung vague bells at the time that I hadn't been able to clarify. Then it clicked. "The last kid to be taken before Heidi was a Russian. I don't know what circles the kid's father moves in, but there's no chance he's hired in mercenaries to harass Gilby into giving him back?"

"Could be," Sean said and I heard the quickening. "You might have something there. We'll try and trace a link between the two from both ends, see if we have any more success that way. Good work, Charlie."

There was closure in his voice. I realised that he was getting ready to end the call, and almost panicked.

"So, how was your Arab prince?" I said, almost babbling. It was the first thing that came into my head. It sounded crass, even as I said it.

"Spoilt, bored, demanding," he came back with immediately, "but rich enough to pay a double-rate fee without a quibble. For that I'm prepared to put up with most of his bratty ways."

"Oh," I said. My mind had suddenly emptied of all rational thought, except that Sean was going, and that I didn't want him to.

There was a pause. "Charlie," he said gently, "are you OK?" It was that very gentleness that was nearly my undoing.

"Yes," I said, "it's just —" I broke off, bit my lip.

"Just what?"

"Nothing," I said. "It's nothing. Look, Sean, I've got to go. I'll call you tomorrow, OK?" I ended the call fast and leaned my head down so my forehead rested against my knees.

I'd thought I was stronger than that. I'd thought I was over him, but our almost daily contact, even by telephone, had reawakened feelings I'd thought were dead, not sleeping. At that moment I'd come so close to telling Sean just how much I'd missed him. The very fact that I'd been tempted to do so frightened me far more than any dangers presented by Major Gilby and his men.

My mind went back again. It was a long time since I'd thought about that first time Sean and I had got together. Chance and circumstance had played a big part in it, really.

I'd been more than halfway through the Special Forces course by that time and had just gone through a nasty Resistance-to-Interrogation exercise that had been particularly difficult to take. If it hadn't been for Sean's unexpected reassurance part way through, I sometimes wonder if I would have had the stomach to see it to the bitter end.

That evening we'd all been issued with weekend passes, probably by way of reward. Everyone was rushing around getting ready for a night on the piss.

Their first opportunity to let go since the course started. I hadn't felt like celebrating. I'd showered and changed into my civvies, but hadn't planned on leaving camp.

Until, that is, quite by chance I ran into Sean in a deserted corridor. He'd nodded shortly, as he would have done with any of the trainees, and made to move past me. Suddenly I wanted to know why he'd encouraged me alone to keep it together, to keep going. If I'd had longer to think about it, I might not have dared approach him. But I didn't, so I asked him, straight out.

He'd paused for a moment, unsmiling, regarding me with those brooding eyes. "You would have made it without my help, don't worry about it," he said at last, but as he turned to leave I put my hand on his arm.

"Thank you, anyway," I said simply, and meant it.

He'd looked down at my hand and for a moment I thought I'd offended him, crossed the line, been too familiar. I remembered the brilliant smile he'd given me during the exercise, the one no one else had seen, and I couldn't be sure, either way.

Then he'd looked up, straight into my eyes. I'd seen the fire jump there, and the need.

Next thing I knew I was holding onto him, or he was holding onto me. I never knew who made the first move. His mouth was crushed down onto mine with a hunger that left me breathless, and exultant. Those long, clever fingers were framing my face, diving into my hair.

The want was explosive, all-consuming, clawing through my body, the sheer force of it taking me by surprise. I couldn't feed it fast enough, couldn't touch him fast enough, to begin to satisfy the craving. Although I'd known in some corner of my mind that I found Sean physically attractive, something had warned me he was trouble. I'd been both wary, yet minutely aware of him, but I hadn't realised how deep it ran.

By the time he broke away we were both breathing hard. I could feel the heat coming off me in waves.

"I've wanted to do that since the very first moment I set eyes on you, Charlie," he said softly, pinning me with those velvet dark eyes while he stroked my hair away from my face. His fingers stilled. "But I wouldn't have done anything about it if I hadn't seen that you wanted it, too."

"Yes," I said. I would have said anything, so long as he didn't stop.

He smiled at me. No smugness, no triumph. God he looked so different when he smiled. "Question is, what do we do about it now?" he murmured. I couldn't find the voice to answer. He was staring at me like he hated to tear his eyes away. "You have a weekend pass, don't you?" he said.

I nodded.

"So do I," he said. "Meet me outside the main gates in fifteen minutes."

"Yes," I said again. No hesitation.

He let go of me. I ignored the squawk of protest my nerve endings sent up, like having a plaster ripped away from oversensitive skin. As soon as the contact was

198

broken a measure of sanity seemed to return to both of us. I leaned weakly against the nearest wall, unsure if my legs would support me without it.

"Christ. Jesus," Sean muttered, taking a step backwards, almost stumbling when Sean never stumbled. He was the epitome of co-ordinated grace and muscle. "Why am I doing this? I *never* do this."

He shook his head, wiped a hand over his bemused face. "You do believe me, Charlie?" he said, his voice shaken. "That is not a line. I have *never* hit on a trainee before."

"Considering about ninety-nine per cent of them are blokes," I managed, still trembling, "I'm relieved to hear it."

He looked at me again, and something of the cool soldier was back in his face, his eyes. "Seriously, we shouldn't do this. Who knows where it could lead. It just feels so —"

"I know."

I stepped forwards, stepped in to him. I reached up, put my lips against his, and silenced his doubts along with my own.

The next morning, Figgis and Todd ferried us into Einsbaden village to carry out our site surveys, as planned. I was surprised, I must admit, that the Major was still prepared to let us loose off the Manor grounds, but he gave a rousing speech at breakfast.

The gang of criminals who'd attacked us were escaping from an armed robbery and had now been caught by the police, he'd lied, staring us straight in the eye. It was all done and dusted, nothing to worry about.

Looking round the students' faces, I wondered if he saw the scepticism written there as plainly as it was felt.

Nevertheless, none of us voiced our disbelief and we dutifully allowed ourselves to be loaded into the school trucks. The only exception was McKenna, who'd been judged to be suffering from concussion from the crash.

It wasn't like Gilby to show any sympathy for the sick, but maybe he was just worried about being sued. Either way, McKenna had been excused the 5a.m. slog and was reported to be still sleeping when we rumbled down the driveway out of the Manor.

If Einsbaden had been quiet in the evening, it was little better during daylight hours. With the instructors observing, we'd been told to make an inconspicuous survey of the area. The idea was not only to learn the layout of the village from the point of view of ambush and escape, but also so we could generally baby-sit our principal.

"He's going to want to know where to have a coffee, or breakfast, or buy a souvenir," Gilby said to us. "It helps you avoid putting yourself and your client into a vulnerable situation if you know in advance the answers to these questions. Then you have to plan for the possibility of something going wrong. If so, where's the local doctor? Nearest hospital? You will be tested on this knowledge before the end of the course."

Personally, by the time I'd been in the village for an hour, I wondered why any high-powered principal would want to spend more than that amount of time there. It was just a pleasant little place with the usual local amenities, but nothing special enough to make you want to linger.

Besides, despite the sunshine, it was bitterly cold. I finished my tour and headed for the tiny café in one corner of the square, which promised good coffee and was pumping the tantalising smell of fresh pastry out into the street.

Inside, seated at a corner table opposite the door, I found Madeleine.

She looked relaxed, elegant, sitting there reading a guide book to the region and sipping espresso from a cup the size of a thimble. She glanced up as I came in, and her expression was artful. That air of slight resignation of someone who thought they had the place to themselves and is mildly annoyed to find they have not. As soon as she saw I was alone, her face shifted into a big smile instead.

"Well, something agrees with you," she said brightly. "You're looking fit."

I didn't answer that one, just took a seat at the next table, so I could distance myself if anyone else came in. *Yeah sure, Mad*, I thought. *I just love being shot at.*

She must have seen something of that in my face, because she quickly became businesslike. "Do you have it?"

I dug into my pocket and brought out the hollowpoint that I'd retrieved from under Shirley's bed that morning. I handed it to her and she turned it over in her fingers.

"Damn," she said, frowning. "For some reason, when you said you'd found it on the range, I assumed it had been fired. I thought we might be able to get a ballistics match done with the ones recovered from Kirk's body." She gave the round back to me and I tucked it away out of sight. "That doesn't tell us anything beyond the fact that it's from the same manufacturer, and nine-millimetre is the right calibre."

"The men who shot at us yesterday were also firing nine-mil machine pistols," I said. "I got a good look at one. It was a Lucznik PM-98."

"Mm, good choice," Madeleine said casually, as though I'd mentioned a brand of lipstick. "Made in Poland, I seem to remember, but they're becoming very popular with US law enforcement agencies."

I pondered for a moment on the concept of the police in any country using machine pistols. Still, why not? The British armed response units used Heckler & Koch MP5Ks. Why shouldn't an American cop have the capability to fire over six hundred rounds a minute?

"I'm surprised Gilby was prepared to let you all out of his sight this morning," Madeleine commented when I didn't speak.

I glanced through the window just in time to see Blakemore's FireBlade pull up with a flourish near the bar on the other side of the square. He yanked off his helmet as another of the instructors stepped out of an alleyway to speak to him. Todd, I guessed, from the stocky build, though he had his back to me.

"I don't think we're out of his sight exactly," I said. "They're keeping tabs on us."

202

I stood up. "If you can't tell me anything about that round, I'd best get back out there," I said.

I'd made it two strides towards the door when Madeleine called me back. There was something in her voice I couldn't quite categorise. I turned, came back and sat down again with reluctance, keeping one eye on the window. When I looked down, I found she'd leaned across and placed a photograph on the table in front of me.

I picked it up. The image looked to have been taken on the deck of a boat. In the background I could see the rail and wake through the water. To the left of the shot were two people, standing wrapped in each other's arms, smiling into the lens. Madeleine and a tall black man.

He must have been tall. Madeleine was no short-stop, but he towered over her enough to be resting his chin on top of her head. He was eye-catchingly handsome. Regal, with a brilliant smile. Happiness radiated from them.

I handed the picture back. She glanced at it with affection before slipping it into her handbag.

I knew I was supposed to ask, so I said, "Who's the guy?" If I'm honest, I was curious, anyway.

"That's Dominic," Madeleine said.

Of course, he would have to be a Dominic. I just couldn't see Madeleine with a Dave or a Darren.

"We've been together three years now." She smiled, to herself more than to me. A secret kind of a smile. One that wraps you up in a blanket and keeps you warm in the winter. "I think he's a keeper."

"A keeper?"

"For keeps." She looked at me and something of the smile spilled over. I didn't doubt the strength of her feelings for him. "He's wonderful. I'd be mad to let him go."

I dredged my memory and came up with a distant fact that he was a chef, but I'm not entirely sure where it came from. I was at a loss to know where she was going with this sudden outbreak of pallyness.

"He looks . . . very nice," I said, lamely.

Madeleine sighed. "The point is, Charlie, that I love him, but even if I didn't I'd be asking for trouble making a play for Sean when we work together. Besides, I'd be wasting my time. He's not interested."

"In you?" I asked, almost in spite of myself. "Or in having a relationship full stop?"

"Both, I think."

A young, bored-looking waitress appeared from somewhere deep in the bowels of the café. She paused by our tables, scowling. Madeleine asked for more espresso, much to the girl's obvious disgust. I ordered the same, just for badness. She stopped just short of tutting out loud, and sloped away again.

We didn't speak until she'd rattled a cup down onto each table top in front of us and retreated, not bothering to remove Madeleine's empty. Milk and sugar, it seemed, were not an option.

"You seem to know an awful lot about Sean's private life," I said then, taking my first sip of real caffeine for over a week. It plugged straight into my nervous system like a set of jump leads.

204

"I've worked with him since he first set up on his own. I'll admit there was a time when I had hopes in that direction — before I met Dominic, of course," Madeleine said, pausing to smile wryly. "One evening, not long after I'd started working there, I managed to contrive getting Sean round to my flat and cracked open a bottle of wine. I thought once he got some alcohol inside him he might loosen up a bit." She lifted her head and glanced over at me. "Instead, all he did was talk about you."

I said, "Oh."

It was like one minute I'd been walking along a sunny beach without a care and the next a big black cloud had moved across the face of the sun, the tide had turned with a vengeance, and the last step I'd taken had been onto sand that felt suspiciously soft under foot. *Leave now*, my mind shouted at me, *before it's too late* . . .

It's not the first time I've thought I should listen to that voice in my head more often.

But I didn't.

I'd said it as a statement, but Madeleine took my single word as a question. She swirled her coffee round in its cup for a moment, disturbing the sediment at the bottom, then said calmly, without looking at me, "He told me you'd spent an amazing spur-of-the-moment first weekend together in a chalet built into the side of a cliff somewhere on the Welsh coast. Said you'd spent the whole time in bed and that it was sensational."

I felt my face heat at her dryly delivered words, but I didn't deny any of it. There was little point when it was quite true.

The chalet had indeed been built into the side of a cliff, with a long set of winding stone steps leading down to it. They were so steep that if we'd had luggage it would have been a perilous descent, but we hadn't thought much further ahead than the clothes we stood up in. And how fast we could get each other out of them.

I turned away so Madeleine couldn't read the thoughts chasing through my head, and stared out of the window again. Outside I could see a couple of the students standing on the far side of the square with a map in their hands, pointing to various key points of the roof-line opposite. So much for unobtrusive observation. They couldn't have made their purpose any plainer if they'd been wearing sandwich boards proclaiming it.

I turned back to Madeleine and picked up what was left of my own coffee. It had turned cold, and black, and bitter.

"Was that all he told you about me?" I said, with more than a touch of bite. "That I was a good lay?"

Madeleine regarded me with a level gaze, shaming my unworthy comment. "He told me you were fearless, quick, funny, clever, mentally stronger than anyone he'd ever met," she said. "He said you were the best thing and the worst thing that had ever happened to him."

As you were to me, Sean, I thought. *As you were to me.*

206

"He couldn't understand how you came to betray him after what you'd shared together," she went on, into her stride now, relentless. "He couldn't understand how you could tell them about your affair, could claim he'd raped you, to try and save your own skin."

"I didn't," I denied automatically, but without heat.

"He knows that now," Madeleine agreed, "but he didn't then."

When we'd met again last winter, Sean and I had solved the mystery of just how the army had uncovered the details of our clandestine relationship. It had been a relief to find that he hadn't, after all, abandoned me as I'd thought, but by then it had been almost too late for it to matter.

I suppose it might have cleared the air between us.

Human history is littered with might-have-beens.

I'd heard enough. I got to my feet again, throwing down enough change to cover the cost of my coffee.

This time, I almost made it to the doorway before Madeleine's cut-glass voice stopped me in my tracks.

"You've never told him, have you?" she said. "What really happened to you."

I stilled like she'd just jerked a snare around my neck. I swallowed, and my imagination felt the cut of the wire into my throat. Without turning, I asked, "How much do you know?"

"All of it, more or less," Madeleine said. "Don't you think Sean has a right to know it, too?"

Anger lit me. I took another couple of steps towards the door and yanked it open. I gripped the handle tight, making sure I had my escape route before I glanced back towards her.

"He doesn't have to know," I managed through lips that seemed suddenly stiff, unyielding. "It wouldn't do any good for him to know."

"Why not, Charlie? It might make him understand what you went through."

I shook my head. "No. I'd rather he thought of me as a ruthless bitch than a helpless bitch," I bit out. "Don't tell him, Madeleine." In my head I'd summoned up the words as an order, a cool command, but instead they came out shaped as a plea.

She shrugged. "OK, it's your choice," she said, frowning, "but I go home tomorrow and Sean's planning on coming out here himself to take over. You know what he's like. You can't keep something like that from him forever."

"I can try."

CHAPTER
FOURTEEN

The full effect of my dramatic if rather flouncy exit from the café was somewhat spoiled by my immediately colliding with a person who'd been hurrying along the pavement outside. I spun round without caution from slamming the outer door shut behind me and my momentum nearly sent both of us sprawling.

On a reflex, I grabbed at his jacket. It was only when we'd steadied that I realised who it was I'd got hold of.

"McKenna?" I said, my voice sharp and incredulous. "What are you doing here?"

But the youngster just threw me a panicked glance, jerked himself free, and hurried away. I watched, puzzled, until he'd turned the corner. He looked dreadful, his skin grey and clammy. He hadn't come across as the type dedicated enough to the course to drag himself from his sick bed to take part in a group exercise.

I shrugged and let it go. I had other things on my mind as I stalked across the square with my shoulders hunched down into my jacket and my anger bubbling away under the surface.

Blakemore was just the unlucky one. He was the first of the instructors I came across, but even so, he was the one I suppose I had the most faith in. Maybe it was just fate that it happened that way. I caught him just as he was climbing onto the FireBlade, with the engine already fired up and ticking over.

He nodded when he saw me approaching, unconcerned, but when I reached across the tank and hit the kill switch his eyes narrowed under the open visor of his helmet. I stood there and stared long enough and hard enough for him to slowly sit back, undo the chinstrap and pull off his lid. He put it down on the tank, folded his arms and regarded me, stony, one eyebrow raised.

Temper is never the best thing to wear to a confrontation. It has a nasty habit of disintegrating into tatters just when you need its protection most and the colour has never suited me.

Ah well, nothing ventured . . .

I said, "Tell me about Kirk Salter."

Blakemore's eyebrow shifted up another few millimetres. "How do you know Salter?" he hedged. He flashed a quick, almost nervous smile. "What's he to you? Old boyfriend?"

"Old comrade," I said, adding deliberately, "we trained together."

It took a moment for that one to track from starting point to logical conclusion. Blakemore looked up. "He was ex-Special Forces," he said, and it wasn't a question.

"He was," I agreed.

He made a small snorting sound through his nose. His gaze turned calculating and then he nodded. "It figures," he said.

210

"So why did you kill him?" I pushed, ignoring the fact that it was probably unmitigatingly stupid to blow my cover like this, on Gilby's home ground, with only Madeleine for backup. "Did he find out what you were up to and try to stop you?"

"Stop us what?" Blakemore asked. After the initial shock of my opening gambit he'd relaxed slightly. Did that mean he was an accomplished liar, on top of his game now, or that I was so far off the right track he felt secure?

"From grabbing the kid."

He laughed. "Oh no," he said, "he was with us all the way. Salter wasn't the one who threw a spanner in the works."

I could have — should have — pursued that one in any number of directions, but I was blinkered by anger at his amused denial. "So why did you shoot him?" I demanded.

"We didn't," Blakemore said, still grinning at me. "What makes you think that we did?"

"Hollowpoints," I said. "He was killed with them."

"Sorry, Fox," he said quickly, "but we don't use 'em."

He reached for his helmet, but before he could put it back on I brought the round I'd shown to Madeleine out of my pocket and held it up to him.

"So what's this?"

He stopped reaching for the helmet. Instead he took the round out of my fingers, examined it carefully. "Where did you get this?" he asked and any trace of laughter had been sucked right out of his voice, leaving a dustiness behind that was almost arid.

"I found it on the indoor range," I said. "I picked it up the first time we shot there."

"That's against the rules," he said, but he was only going through the motions of rebuke.

"It is," I agreed. "But last time I checked, so was killing people."

Blakemore glanced up then, pinned me with a straight look. "And you would know all about that, would you, Charlie?" he said softly.

I swallowed, pushed it aside and went on doggedly. "Why did you kill him?"

Blakemore sighed. "I didn't," he said. "I thought I knew who was responsible, but now I'm not so sure." He regarded me for a few seconds, that brooding, drawn-down stare he had as though he was mentally walking through his options and not finding any of them to his liking. Eventually he held up the round. "Can I keep this?"

He saw my hesitation. "I want to plant this in front of someone, like you've just done, and see what it shakes loose."

I found a half smile from somewhere. "Didn't work too well on you," I said.

He grinned again, but it didn't reach his eyes. "Yeah," he said, "but that's because *I've* got nothing to hide."

He tucked the hollowpoint into his jacket pocket and fired the Blade up again. I caught his arm.

"What's going on, Blakemore?"

He shook his head. "It's too complicated to go into right now," he said. "You're just going to have to trust me on this."

I hesitated again, then stepped back. He nodded, rammed his helmet on and toed the bike into gear, as though afraid I'd change my mind. It was only as he ripped out of the square that I relayed the conversation through my mind and cursed myself for all the gaps I'd left unplugged with questions.

By the time our allotted research period was up, Blakemore still hadn't returned. I hung around by the back of the truck, hoping that he would still show, until Todd impatiently herded me in with the others.

I scanned the phys instructor's broad face for some sign that I was walking into a trap by allowing myself to be taken from a public place to a private one without a struggle, but there was nothing to alert me there beyond his usual arrogance.

Even so, as we rumbled out of the square I was aware of a tightness in my chest, a prickling in my hands that made me clench them together in my lap hard enough to turn the skin white around the knuckles.

Had Blakemore been telling the truth? Or had he just been stalling for time, putting me off my guard? His denial when I'd first mentioned the hollowpoint had seemed genuine. But faced with the evidence, there'd been something missing. Now, in the back of that lurching truck, it took me a while to work out what it was.

Surprise.

Whatever I'd triggered in Blakemore, whatever I'd said to him that had acted as a spur, it wasn't anything he hadn't suspected already. Suddenly, I remembered the little drama they'd organised for us on the range with Craddock. "*So* that's *how you did it*," Blakemore had said. Did what? And how was it done?

Behind us I could see Todd at the wheel of the second truck, trying to steer with his elbows while he lit his cigarette. When he caught me watching him he threw me a cocky salute that only served to increase my uneasiness.

Then, without warning, our truck braked hard, swerving to the right.

The students were thrown against one another as the heavy vehicle skidded slightly. Declan's shoulder hit mine and I grabbed on to the tailgate to stop myself pitching out over it.

My first thought was that it was another ambush. That the men in the Peugeot had brought in reinforcements and come back for a return match. I strained for the sound of gunfire, realising with a sick dread that the thin canvas tilt sides of the truck would be sliced like butter in a fire fight.

Figgis managed to bring us to a jerky halt, but Todd had been following too close and not paying attention. I saw him rise in his seat as he stamped hard on the brake pedal. Smoke puffed from the offside front tyre as he locked it solid. For a moment I thought a collision was inevitable. When he finally wrestled the truck to a standstill his front bumper was less than half a metre from the tailgate. I could look straight into his startled eyes.

It was only once we'd all stopped that I heard the frantic voices. A man and a woman. It took a few seconds to tune out the panic and latch on to the vocab. I caught it in snatches. Accident. Mobile phone. Ambulance.

I pushed out of my seat and scrambled over the tailgate, just as Todd jumped down from his cab. As we ran forwards I was aware of other people following.

The couple who'd flagged Figgis down were elderly. Both were talking at once, gesturing towards the edge of the road. The woman was crying.

We'd stopped just before a sweeping left-hand bend. As corners went it was a beauty. A long continuously curving entrance and a tightening fast exit. It slanted towards the inside like a banked circuit. A corner designed for speed. And misjudgement.

To the outside, just past the apex, was a lay-by just about wide enough for a single vehicle to pull off the road. Indeed, it was where the old couple had stopped their Westfalia camper van. The road surface broke up there into gravel that had been scraped and scuffed towards the safety barrier in a long ominous twin gouge.

Beyond the barrier was nothing. Open space.

Because Todd stopped to find out from Figgis what was going on, I was the first to reach the barrier and lean out over it. There was a rocky drop on the other side that went down almost sheer for twenty metres before it levelled out into a stream at the bottom, and then away into the trees.

I suppose, if I'm honest, I already knew in my heart what I was going to see down there.

But it still came as one hell of a shock.

Alongside me I heard Declan whisper, "Holy Mary, Mother of God."

I don't know just how fast Blakemore had been going when he hit the barrier, but his trajectory had taken him fifteen metres or so out from the incline. He'd landed a little way from the bike, on his back, with his torso half-submerged in the stream. From this height I could see the current creating whirlpools and eddies around this unexpected obstruction to the flow.

His body was bent and twisted, his limbs contorted inside his leathers. A good set will keep you together, but that doesn't mean it will keep you whole. The darkened visor of his helmet stared up blankly at the sky.

Shards of plastic debris were scattered around his body, splashes of harsh colour against the grey rocks. The faring of the Blade had detached itself in the crash and splintered into fragments, leaving the aluminium box frame exposed.

I was certain he was dead, and then I saw the flutter of one gloved hand.

I've seen dead bodies twitch before, little more than the nervous system shaking out the last few drops of life, but this was different. A controlled movement. A weak signal.

216

I turned. The two instructors were still trying to get sense out of the elderly couple. "It's Blakemore," I shouted, cutting them short. "And he's still alive."

Todd reached my shoulder first and stared down at the drop. "You're fucking joking," he muttered, stepping back, shaking his head. "Forget it, Fox, nobody could have survived that fall."

I glared at him, then inwardly recoiled. Blakemore had suspected somebody of being responsible for Kirk's death. It might be rather convenient for Todd if Blakemore never came out of that ravine alive. Too convenient, perhaps . . .

Figgis came up on Todd's other side in time to hear that last remark. He threw Todd a disgusted glance.

"Let's find out for certain, shall we?" he said and climbed over the barrier.

Todd didn't try and stop him from going. Maybe he was as surprised as the rest of us by the driving instructor's actions. Figgis crabbed across the face to an area where the incline of the rocks was at its most mild. From there he half climbed, half slithered his way down, sending a rash of pebbles skittering in front of him like a bow wave.

His agility surprised me. He made it look easy, but no one else volunteered to follow him down.

At the bottom we watched him pick his way across the rocks and reach Blakemore. I couldn't imagine that the unarmed combat instructor looked any better close up. However strong and fit you are, you're never going to win in a straight fight with inertia, gravity, and impact.

Figgis stepped round the other man's blasted limbs and crouched in the stream alongside him. Carefully, he flipped open the visor of his helmet, but didn't attempt to remove it. He undid the velcro cuff on Blakemore's left glove and pulled it off with a gentleness I wouldn't have given him credit for. Then he pinched the inside of his wrist, looking for a pulse. He seemed to take a long time to find one. Long enough for me to suspect I'd imagined that feeble wave.

Finally, he stood up and looked back up to the road, shielding his eyes. By this time we were all hanging over the safety barrier, staring down. I hoped briefly that the force of the FireBlade slamming into it and catapulting over the top hadn't weakened its foundations or things were going to get crowded down there.

"He's still alive," Figgis's voice floated up. "We need an ambulance — now."

"They're on their way," Todd shouted down, "but we've got some ropes in the trucks. We can use one of the tailgates as a stretcher and haul him up ourselves. It'll be faster."

"I wouldn't move him if I were you," Figgis called. He glanced back at Blakemore for some sign that he had any sense of cognition, but he was patently oblivious. When Figgis spoke again his voice was calm, devoid of emotion. "I think his back is broken."

People's reaction to this piece of news was interesting. Some pressed forwards more fully, stretching their necks for a better look. Declan went and perched on the front bumper of the lead truck and

218

lit a cigarette with hands that weren't quite steady. I was one of those who moved back from the barrier. I'd seen enough, and grisly voyeurism was never in my line.

Elsa turned away, too, and belatedly realised that we'd been shuffling our feet across the gravel where Blakemore's bike had skidded off the road.

"Get back," she said sharply, waving a hand towards the road surface. "The police will need to investigate the scene and all of you are destroying the evidence."

Todd snapped his head round, moved in until he was crowding the German woman. "And just what evidence are you expecting them to find here?" he demanded with a quiet vehemence. "Blakemore's been riding his fucking bikes like a lunatic with half a brain for years. We all of us knew that sooner or later it was going to catch up with him." He registered the startled looks, swallowed down his anger and shrugged. "Today was the day, that's all."

Elsa edged away from him, uncomfortable. Jan moved up to her shoulder, glaring at the phys instructor, but his attention was already elsewhere.

"Dumb bastard," Jan muttered under her breath. "Of course the bloody police are going to want to investigate the scene. What does he think they're going to do?"

"It doesn't matter," Elsa said, but giving her a grateful smile, nonetheless. "He is upset."

I wondered when I'd missed out on the bonding process that had gone on between these two. When had they excluded me, or had I excluded myself?

I eyed the area Elsa had been trying to protect. Casually, I walked a little way back along the road in the direction Blakemore must have been travelling when he'd come to grief, judging from skid marks.

I tried to work out just how he must have ridden that final corner. How I would have ridden it.

I would have approached, braking hard, out to the far right of my lane. It was blind. I wouldn't have cut the apex onto the opposite side of the road and I wouldn't have turned in and laid the bike down into it, wouldn't have creamed in the throttle, until I could see my exit was clear.

The road surface was dry, the day was clear. How on earth had he miscalculated so badly? How had someone of his experience overrun so far that he'd ended up on the marbles and slithered into the safety barrier hard enough to launch him into orbit?

I shook my head, moved back further. OK, so Todd had claimed that Blakemore was a lunatic. How did that change the perspective? I suppose if I'd had that kind of absolute faith in my own invincibility I might have gone in a lot hotter, braked a lot later, and committed to the corner before my arc of visibility opened up.

I paced it out. There was no traffic on the road and I could walk my proposed line without having to dodge other vehicles. As I hit what would have been my perfect clipping point, right on the apex of the bend, something sparkled at my feet. I bent to examine it.

"What is it?"

I tilted my head up, and found both Jan and Elsa standing over me, frowning.

For a moment I mentally juggled the effects of telling them what was on my mind, or keeping it to myself.

"Broken glass," I said at last. When I followed the skids to the barrier they tracked back to the position of the glass like leading lights to a harbour entrance. "It's shaped, patterned — headlight or sidelight, most probably."

It was Elsa, the ex-policewoman, who put it together fastest.

"He was hit by a car," she said. She looked further down the road and her gaze narrowed. She strode away.

"What?" Jan demanded, and we both hurried after her.

"Look at this," Elsa said. "More skid marks, a car this time, not a motorcycle, leading away from the initial point of impact."

"Wait a minute," Jan said. "You both think this was a hit and run, don't you?"

I nodded. It wasn't so hard to put it together, not once you followed the parallel black lines that swept across the road. The car driver, whoever he was, had braked hard enough to lock all his wheels solid and start to broadside, scrubbing off speed along with rubber from his tyres.

"Yes, look at this. He hits Mr Blakemore, loses control and makes a complete one-hundred-and-eighty-degree slide," Elsa said. I don't know how long she was in the police, but she must have been called out to enough road traffic incidents to have learned to read the signs. "He comes to a stop there — see — over on the other side of the road. He was lucky he didn't hit the far barrier."

"Lucky — or skilful," I said, my voice thoughtful. They looked at me sharply, but it wasn't such a wild leap. After all, we'd all spent the previous week watching the likes of Figgis performing just such a move as this. A rapid change of direction after your vehicle came under attack. Viewed from that perspective, suddenly that chaotic slide became a textbook manoeuvre.

"He could just have been lucky," Elsa said. There was a hint of mild censure in her tone, but it was laced with doubt, too.

"So why didn't he stop?" I said. "Why didn't he call the police himself?"

She paced across to the point where the car must have come to a halt, her brow furrowed in focus. "He is horrified that he has clearly hit someone. Maybe he sits there for a moment. He might have stalled his engine. His heart is thundering in his throat at what he has done."

Jan threw me a sideways look at this flight of deductive fantasy. Elsa didn't seem to notice her scepticism.

"Maybe he even gets out of his car, runs over to the barrier, and looks down at the wreckage he has caused. He looks and, like Mr Todd, he too assumes Mr Blakemore is already dead."

Caught up in her snapshot of a life balanced on the edge of instant ruin, the picture began to unfold in my mind. "He thinks briefly of calling an ambulance, and the police, of facing the consequences of his momentary lapse of concentration," I put in. Jan rolled her eyes as if to say, "Don't you start." I ignored her.

"Then it comes to him just how deserted is this stretch of road," Elsa went on, nodding. She was right about that. During the time we'd been stopped not a single other car had passed us. "And he realises —"

"There are no witnesses." It was Jan who finished it, seeming to surprise herself as much as us. We turned to stare at her and she shrugged, embarrassed.

We walked back to where I'd first found the broken glass. There wasn't much of it. Elsa nudged it with the toe of her boot.

"The damage to his car cannot have been severe," she said. "He would still have been able to drive it away."

"It wouldn't have taken much to knock Blakemore off his line," I said. "A glancing blow." That was all it took to deflect something as narrow and jittery as a bike. To send it careering to disaster.

"So," Elsa went on, her voice carrying contempt now for Blakemore's unknown assassin, "he jumps back behind the wheel of his car and he runs like a rabbit." She scanned the area again. "Haste makes him heavy-footed." I followed her gaze and found two thick black lines to suggest that, in his efforts to escape the locality along with the blame, the scared driver had dumped the clutch and lit up his tyres like a drag racer.

We fell silent for a few moments while we replayed the scene, shaping it to fit the scenario we'd just created. It did fit, after a fashion. More off-the-peg than made-to-measure.

"We're all assuming, of course," I said quietly, "that this *was* just an accident."

I felt their disbelief in the way they stiffened beside me. "What are you suggesting, Charlie?" Elsa asked. I tried to read an argument into her voice, but could only find surprise and not a little interest. Should I risk it?

"If you had to pick a good spot for an ambush along this road, where else would you go for?" I said. I paused while they thought about it.

We'd all driven this way several times during our rides out with the school instructors, who'd asked us all just such a question.

I couldn't help the eerie feeling that somewhere along the line the men in the Peugeot had received the same training we had, and probably a good deal else besides.

They'd certainly seemed to know all about ambushes yesterday in the forest, even though that one had blown up in their faces. Perhaps they'd decided that taking the school men out one at a time was a less risky proposition.

But what about Blakemore's threat?

Maybe they hadn't taken his warning seriously. Or maybe they'd taken it very seriously indeed.

CHAPTER
FIFTEEN

Blakemore didn't make it.

He bowed out long before the emergency services reached the scene. He never regained consciousness, never made a sound, never made another movement. It was like his soul was out of there long before we ever reached the crash site. It just took his body a while to get the message.

Figgis stayed down in the ravine with him, laying blankets from the truck over the top of him, talking to him even though he was probably beyond hearing much of anything at all. The rest of us loitered up on the road, waiting for the ambulance. Waiting for Blakemore to die.

When Figgis finally stood up and called, "He's gone," to Todd, it almost came as a relief. I let a shaky breath out slowly, felt the implications sink in like heat on frozen skin, and wondered how this new death changed things.

It was at this point that Major Gilby arrived.

We heard the Skyline approaching for a good couple of minutes before the big silver-grey car snaked into view. The deep throaty growl of its exhaust rebounded through the valley and set up an echoing vibration like the onset of thunder.

Gilby pulled up fast by the side of the road and jumped out. He stalked over to Todd, demanding a situation report. Todd just waved a hand towards the barrier without a word.

When the Major went and leaned over it, he saw Figgis climbing back up the rocks towards the road, leaving Blakemore's still figure lying in the stream at the bottom. After that, he didn't need to be told the man was dead.

Gilby turned away and just for a second he let himself droop. Just for a second he let the mask slip and I saw the tension that was tearing him apart. The Major, I realised with no little surprise, for all his apparent icy cool, was feeling the pressure. And feeling it badly.

Then, as quickly as it opened up, the fissure was sealed. He was barking out orders for us to get back to the Manor. It was just a tragic accident. There was nothing to see here.

Sluggishly, we began to converge on the trucks. As I joined the others I watched the Major walk out the same lines that Elsa, Jan, and I had taken on the road. He saw it all just as quickly — the skid marks, the broken glass — and from the way he was frowning I knew he'd put together a scenario that was very similar to our own.

So what was he planning on doing about it?

As little, it would seem, as he'd done about the ambush in the forest. If my suspicions were correct and he was behind the kidnappings, what could he do?

226

The Major stayed at the roadside waiting for the police and the now redundant ambulance. As we pulled away I watched him move across to talk to the elderly couple who were waiting stoically by their camper van. I had a feeling that by the time the police arrived he would have persuaded them to leave, too.

If you're going to construct your own version of events, it's always better not to have anyone around who might conceivably contradict you.

Figgis and Todd dropped us all off at the Manor's front door. We had been posted to be doing unarmed combat in the afternoon, but even though Figgis was more than qualified to take over the class, they decided to let it drop.

Instead, they told us that after lunch we had the couple of hours to write up our survey reports on the village, while it was still fresh in our minds. By that time I'm sure the only thing that was fresh in any of our minds was the image of Blakemore's broken body lying at the bottom of that drop.

Lunch was a sober and almost silent affair. The only noise that accompanied the meal was the clink of cutlery on china. Even Ronnie had forsaken his usual tuneless whistling as he served up dollops of pasta with meatballs.

McKenna made a reappearance towards the end of the meal, pale and subdued. He sat at a table as far away from me as he could manage, but after I'd dumped my plate onto one of the plastic waste trays I swung by where he was sitting. I quickly realised from his vague answers to the others' questions that he was trying to make out he'd never left the Manor all morning.

"So you've heard about Blakemore?" I challenged.

He looked at me warily. Maybe because I could call him a liar in front of everybody else and know it was the truth. He shook his head even though it could have been the only topic of conversation.

"He's dead. Got knocked off his bike and went off the road," I said bluntly. "It was a long way down."

McKenna turned paler still. Out of the corner of my eye I saw Craddock raise his eyebrows at me.

"Are you trying to make the boy faint, Charlie?" he said in that mild voice of his.

It made me pause, blinking. Then I turned and walked away.

I walked out of the dining hall and slowly upstairs, almost blindly. What *was* I trying to do? Take out my anger at the wilful waste of a life on the nearest person who wasn't going to hit back?

I needed to talk to someone. More than that, I needed to talk to Sean.

I picked up the pace and hurried along the faded corridors to the dormitory. It was empty when I walked in. I went straight to my locker and switched on the mobile phone, but before I could dial a number, it rang.

A generated voice at the other end told me I had one new message and I obligingly pressed the right buttons to retrieve it.

"Hi Charlie, it's Madeleine." On the recording she sounded hesitant and almost breathless. "Look, I've got some information you asked for, some things you ought to know about McKenna and that fight he had with Blakemore. It'll probably explain a few things. I should have told you this morning but, well, other things got in the way. Call me as soon as you can, OK?"

I sighed, suppressing my irritation. She seemed to have plenty of time to interrogate me about my relationship with Sean, so why had something like this taken a back seat?

I dialled in the number she'd left and she picked it up almost right away, as though she'd been waiting for my call.

"Charlie! Thanks for getting back to me so quick. It's about McKenna and Blakemore —"

"He's dead," I interrupted.

"Oh," she said, coming to an abrupt halt. "What do you mean? Which one?"

"Blakemore."

"My God. How?"

"He crashed his bike," I said, "and before you ask, no, it wasn't entirely an accident."

Of course, she wasn't going to let things go at that. I explained, as briefly as possible, what we'd found by the ravine, my suspicions about the men in the Peugeot, and about the conversation I'd had with Blakemore just before he died.

"That doesn't mean he was killed deliberately," she said when I'd finished. I could hear the frown in her voice. "It just means somebody else was involved."

"So why didn't they stop?"

"People often don't," she said, almost gently. "That's why it's called hit and run."

"OK," I allowed, trying not to take offence at her moderate tone. "But it seems a hell of a coincidence that the guy admits to involvement in the kidnapping, tells me he can get me answers about who shot Kirk, goes off and then just happens to get himself accidentally knocked off his bike and killed by a complete stranger. Don't you think?"

"Yes," she agreed slowly. "It does seem a bit unlikely, I'll grant you that."

There was a pause while we both considered the implications.

"Anyway," I said, "what was this news about Blakemore and McKenna's argument the other night?"

"Well, it hardly seems relevant now, but actually young McKenna had a very good reason for taking against Blakemore."

I went very still. "Which was?"

"Well, McKenna had an uncle who was in the Paras. He was only about six years older than McKenna, as it happens. When he came out earlier this year he decided to train to be a bodyguard. So, he signed up for a course at Einsbaden Manor and managed to get himself killed in a car crash during the first week of the course."

Memory arrived like a camera zoom, hitting me flat in the face out of nowhere. Sean's words back in that pub came back to me, hard and fast. "*They had a pupil killed in a driving accident six months ago, and there* were *rumours that it wasn't quite as accidental as it could have been."*

Suddenly, all McKenna's edgy behaviour fell into place. His almost unhinged reaction when we were all buzzed by the men in the Peugeot that first time and his attack on Blakemore in the Einsbaden bar.

"Of course," I murmured. "That's how McKenna knew Blakemore used to be in charge of the driving, not Figgis."

"What?" Madeleine said. "Oh, yes, according to the reports, Blakemore was supposed to be responsible for the class at the time. He claimed that McKenna's uncle was using one of the school cars on his own time, without permission. It all got very messy, but the Major managed to slide out of any suit for negligence. Looking at the financials for the time, it probably would have been enough to finish him."

"So why does McKenna now want to be a bodyguard? And why has he come to the same place that might have been responsible for the death of his uncle?" I wondered aloud, although as I said it, I realised there were two possible answers.

Justice. Or revenge.

"Well, he certainly doesn't seem interested in this as a long-term career," Madeleine said. "He's actually a driving instructor back at home, and before he left for the course he put in an order for a new car, which he's having modified to dual controls for when he gets back. Hardly the action of the man looking to chuck it all in and become a full-time bodyguard, is it?"

"A driving instructor?" I queried. He'd never shown any particular spark during the driving lessons. In fact he'd been awful. But then, I'd tried not to show any in the unarmed combat, either. If he was hiding his abilities, he had to have a reason.

I don't know what Madeleine said next, I wasn't paying enough attention. Instead I was remembering those skid marks at the crash site. There was something precise about them. Something measured. A driving instructor. *I wonder.*

"McKenna was in the village today," I said. "I bumped into him after I left the café, but when we got back, he was here waiting for us."

"I thought you said he had concussion and he'd stayed at the Manor?"

"That's where he was supposed to be, yes," I said.

"So how did he get there — and back, for that matter?"

I didn't answer straight away. None of the students had brought a vehicle of their own to Einsbaden Manor, but that didn't mean there weren't plenty available at the school. The Audis we used every day, for example, always had the keys left hanging in the ignitions. Anyone could take one, if they wanted to.

But if they had . . .

"Listen Madeleine, I've got to go," I said hurriedly. "I need to check on something."

Madeleine did her best not to appear offended at my sudden departure. She just told me to keep in touch and let her know if I needed anything.

I tried not to run back downstairs, but I didn't have to field any awkward questions in any event. I moved quickly across the tiled hallway out of the front door, skirting round the edge of the house to the parking area at the rear.

The school Audis were lined up along the far side, as always, and I took a casual turn along the backs of them. Spotting broken glass wouldn't have been difficult, but only if there'd been any.

I made a return pass along the fronts, but there were no new dents or scratches anywhere. I felt my shoulders slump a little. So I'd been wrong. I started back across the car park for the Manor again, when a flutter of bright blue plastic caught my eye.

Over in the corner, half hidden behind the trucks, were the remains of the three cars we'd wrecked in the forest. They'd been dragged back and covered over with a tarpaulin sheet. I'd assumed they were all written off.

I glanced back over my shoulder at the house, but nobody was visible at the windows or on the terrace. I moved quickly behind the trucks, out of sight, and lifted the nearest corner of the cover.

The car I'd been in — the one Hofmann had been driving — was a mess, completely undrivable. All the glass was gone and the body had deformed sufficiently from the roll that the doors were no longer capable of closing, even if all of them had been still attached.

The lead car, with Declan at the wheel, was also out of the running. When it had bounced off the track it had hit a tree hard enough at the front to fold the metalwork into a sharp vee, splitting the radiator in two.

The rad had sheared right off its mountings and half of the core now dangled out from under the front spoiler on the end of a single piece of rubber hose.

But the last of the three, the one Craddock had run into the back of us, had escaped remarkably unscathed. I worked my way round to the front end. He'd hit us with the right-hand front corner, which was crumpled out of shape and already showing the first tint of rust. All the glass in the headlights and indicators was smashed on that side.

The other corner, though, should have been undamaged. It hadn't even been exposed to the gunfire from the men in the Peugeot. So how had the lights on that side been broken? And what had caused those shiny new gouges in the paintwork along the wing just above the front bumper? I wiped the dirt from my hands and I stood up slowly.

As I did so I heard a sound very like a gasp.

I turned quickly. McKenna was less than half a dozen strides away from me and had obviously been heading for the damaged cars. He stopped dead when he saw me appear, took one look at my glowering face, then turned and ran.

Not towards the house, but out towards the woods that surrounded us. He had no genuine reason to be running unless it was from guilt. There was only one way to find out.

I set off after him. I've never been that fast as a sprinter, but the memory of Blakemore's senseless death was a stark incentive. Still I might not have caught up to McKenna, had he not tripped over a root as he reached the tree line and gone sprawling.

He started to scramble up straight away, but I dug deep for a final spurt of energy and tackled him before he'd made it to his feet. My momentum bowled him over, sending both of us tumbling. He came to rest with his back thumped against a trunk, winded.

I rolled to my feet. Even with the ache in my breastbone that the rough contact had set off, I had my breath back first. When McKenna had recovered enough to focus on me I realised he wasn't just breathless, he was terrified.

Of what? Of what he'd done? Or of being caught?

"Why?" I bit out. "Why did you do it, McKenna?"

He swallowed, twisting his head from side to side as though he could escape the blame that way. I grabbed hold of his chin and held his face straight, but he just allowed his gaze to slide away from mine.

"You talk to me now, or you can explain it to the Major," I threw at him. "It's your choice."

That got his attention. His eyes snapped open fully, then began to fill with tears.

I let go and stepped back from him, disgusted with both of us.

For a while he sat there willing his emotions into submission, then he glanced up at me, sheepish.

"I know you're only here because of your uncle," I said, more gently this time, ignoring his surprise. "Want to tell me about it?"

It took McKenna a little while to find a way into his story. His hands curled into fists of frustration in his lap. Eventually he burst out with, "He would never have just taken that car like they said. He wouldn't!"

"Like you wouldn't just take one of the school cars without asking, you mean?" I said.

He flushed, turned away. "That's different," he said, sulky.

"How is it different?" I said, and without waiting for a reply I added, "Oh yes, I know — he didn't set out intending to kill anyone, did he?"

McKenna's face crumpled again, folding in all the way this time. I remembered, too late, that his uncle had indeed ended up killing someone. Himself.

Damn, I thought, and let him cry.

"OK, McKenna, let me fill in some blanks for you," I said at last. "You played on your concussion from yesterday to avoid going into Einsbaden today, then when we'd all gone you came down here and helped yourself to one of the damaged Audis and set off after us. Don't try and deny it," I warned as his mouth opened. How could he even try, when I'd practically tripped over him in the street?

"OK, so you leave before Blakemore and you wait for him on the road back, at a point where you know one good clout will have him over the barrier. Then you scarper back here, stick the car back, and make like you've never been away. How am I doing so far?"

The boy was shaking his head with vigour. "No," he muttered, "you've got it wrong. I didn't kill Blakemore — even if the bastard deserved it."

I leaned against a tree, folded my arms and indicated with a raised eyebrow that I was still listening.

236

"Yeah, I took one of the Audis, but I didn't know any of the damaged ones were still any good. I just took the first one I came to that had enough fuel in it. I drove down to the village because I needed to talk to Blakemore before I left."

His eyes flicked up to mine, daring me to disbelieve him. I kept mine neutral. "You're leaving?"

He nodded. "Yeah, the taxi's booked. I'd already had enough before any of this happened, but now I just want out of here while I've still got the chance."

"What did you want to talk to Blakemore about?"

"Why they covered up my uncle's death. Why they hinted that he'd stolen the car he was driving. We all know they do driving drills on the road. We've seen them and we all know how bloody dangerous it is. Look at yesterday!"

"That wasn't quite on the open road," I pointed out. "And the circumstances were a little different."

"Yeah," he burst out, "but how do we know something similar didn't happen then?"

I glanced behind me. The afternoon light was turning dull, dropping from pale blue towards a darker shade. Lights were already coming on in the house and the view back across the grass to the car park was hazy with twilight.

"So what did Blakemore say?" I asked.

"Nothing," McKenna muttered. "I never got the chance to speak to him alone. There was always someone else around." He threw me a reproachful look and I realised that I'd been one of those someones.

"So after we bumped into each other you decided you wouldn't talk to him at all," I said, my voice cold, "you thought you'd kill him instead."

"No!" he squawked, pushing himself to his feet and looking poised to flee. "Look, you're not going to pin this on me. No way! I got back into the car and I drove it straight back here. I passed another Audi on the road, parked up. I'm sure it was one of the school cars, but I wasn't paying attention. I didn't get a good look at the driver. He had his head turned away from me. Why don't you go looking for him instead, if you're so desperate to know who killed Blakemore? Me, I don't give a shit. I'm out of here."

"So why did you run just now?"

"After everyone got back and they told me about what had happened, I wondered about the car I'd seen, that's all, so I came to check," he swallowed, embarrassed. "Look, I don't know who was in that car. I didn't see them clearly, but that doesn't mean they didn't see me. They could think I'm a witness, you know? I don't want to get caught up in that, and if it was someone from the school who's responsible, well, I don't want to become the next victim, either."

"What about your proof?" I asked. "Wasn't that what you came here for?"

"What good's proof if I'm dead, too?" he threw back. "This place is a death trap. I don't know what game the Major's playing, but he's gambling with lives. I'm not going to hang around long enough to find out if he's on a winning streak."

238

He pushed past me, started out across the grass. After only a few strides he paused and turned back to me. "If you had any sense, Charlie, you'd be doing the same."

CHAPTER
SIXTEEN

It took me a few minutes after McKenna's departure to put my thoughts in order.

To begin with, out there at the scene, I'd been so certain that the Russians were responsible. I remembered the fear and the loathing on the Peugeot driver's face after Blakemore had threatened him. His need for retribution had been fierce and blazing, to wipe away that paralysing moment of weakness. Was it enough to override the danger to the child?

But after I'd spoken to Madeleine, McKenna seemed to fit as a suspect on all fronts. Yet when he'd told me about seeing the other school car my instinct had been to believe him. I wasn't entirely sure why.

I looked up. Evening was dropping rapidly over the Manor now. The interior lights were harsh in their brightness, beginning to cast outwards. It was cold, too. I shivered inside my sweatshirt and wished I'd stopped long enough to put on a jacket.

With a sigh, I trudged back towards the house. I walked across the parking area and up the steps to the smokers' terrace. I was halfway up before I realised someone was standing out by the French windows, in the shadows, waiting.

I climbed the rest of the way cautiously. It was only as I reached the top that the figure moved out into the light and I recognised him.

"Charlie," Hofmann greeted, his voice expressing neither happiness nor displeasure at finding me. "Was that McKenna I saw you talking to?"

For a few seconds all I could do was stare back at the big German, my mind furiously working up a reasonable excuse for my actions.

Eventually, I said, "Yes, he told me he was leaving. He just wanted to say goodbye," I added, hoping Hofmann hadn't been around for long enough to see me grappling McKenna to the ground. I might have a little trouble convincing him that kind of behaviour was an English tradition for those departing.

"We were just realising how close a shave we had the other day," I went on quickly, hoping to distract him. "Something like Blakemore's accident really brings it home to you." I waved a hand in the general direction of the blue tarpaulin that covered the wrecked Audis over in the corner. "We survived a roll and being shot at, and walked away without a scratch, yet Blakemore makes one mistake and poof, he's gone. Doesn't it make you think how lucky we all were? How fragile life is?"

Hofmann considered for a moment, his heavy face reflecting the slow turn of the machinery inside his head. "Motorcycles are dangerous things," he said at last.

I felt my shoulders drop a fraction at his response, made to move past him, but as I did so I noticed the narrowed shrewdness of his gaze as his eyes rested on me.

The next moment he'd turned away and that dull, almost vacant air had settled over him again. Like his mind was totally occupied with the processes of walking upright and operating his lungs.

So, I wasn't the only one who'd come to Einsbaden Manor pretending to be less than I was. Why was he?

Before I could form that thought into a question that stood any chance of an answer, Hofmann said abruptly, "I was sent to fetch you. Major Gilby wants to speak with you in his study."

He stayed by my shoulder as we went in through the French windows, like he'd been told to stop me making a break for it. If that was the case, why send a student, rather than one of the instructors? Maybe the Major thought such a move would put me more off my guard.

Hofmann almost marched me down the set of corridors to the Major's study without pausing to consider the way. I wondered briefly if he was just efficient, or if there was more to it than that, and I remembered Sean's warning that the German security services had infiltrated this course. The more I thought about Hofmann as a possible for that, the more he seemed perfect.

"Ah, Miss Fox, do come in." Gilby said in his deceptively polite voice and I realised we'd reached the open study doorway. "Thank you, Herr Hofmann," he added in dismissal. Hofmann hesitated for a moment, then nodded and walked away.

I stepped over the threshold into the study, aware of a sense of low background panic. I wished I'd had time to prepare for the Major's questions. More than that, I wished I knew what they were.

The door closed behind me. I forced myself to be casual as I glanced over my shoulder. Todd was standing behind me. When I looked across the room to where Blakemore had sat the last time I'd been here, Rebanks was in the same chair.

The Major was watching me carefully for signs of nervousness. I tried not to show him any.

My chin came up. "You wanted to see me, sir?" I said blandly.

"Yes," he said. He didn't invite me to sit. Instead, he rose, started to walk round the study so I had to keep turning my head to follow him. "I understand you were the last person seen speaking to Mr Blakemore." He paused, both in speech and movement. "I don't suppose you'd care to tell me what you and he talked about?"

Now it was my turn to hesitate. No way was I going to replay the conversation word for word. In view of Blakemore's throwaway admission that the school men had indeed been behind the kidnapping, it would have been suicide.

Damn, why hadn't I called Sean as soon as we got back to the Manor? If only Madeleine's message hadn't distracted me. If only my earlier conversation with her hadn't made me so wary about getting in touch with him. Together we could have formulated something that would have been believable.

I should have known that Gilby would get to find out Blakemore and I had spoken. We'd been standing in the middle of the square, for heaven's sake. Not exactly keeping it secret.

Now, I looked the Major in the eye and said, "I don't see what relevance it has, but if you must know we were talking about bikes. I have one at home. I've ridden them for a few years."

I don't know quite why I added that last bit. Maybe I just wanted to warn him that if he was intending to pass this off as sheer bad riding on Blakemore's part it wasn't going to wash. "I was asking about the FireBlade," I went on, another nail. "We were discussing cornering technique. He was telling me how well it handled."

Todd gave a derisive snort at that last statement, but I refused to back down from it. Gilby glared at him.

"Might I remind you, Mr Todd," he gritted out, "that I have just lost a good man today. This is not the time for levity."

Todd's face snapped to attention. "No sir!" he said smartly.

For several seconds the silence hummed between them. Now seemed a good time to leave, but I've always been bad at choosing such moments. Besides, when would I get an opportunity like this again to probe?

"So, do the police think they'll catch him?" I asked instead, keeping my tone absolutely neutral.

All three heads turned slowly in my direction. I read degrees of shock and guilt there in all of them.

Eventually, it was Gilby who challenged stiffly, "Catch who?"

"Whoever it was who knocked Blakemore off his bike," I said patiently, shrugging as though it was an obvious question. As though there was never any doubt that the accident wasn't purely accidental. I looked at them with an expression of puzzlement on my face.

"Surely you saw it all — the skid marks, the broken glass?" I said, diffident. "You must have seen how narrow the tyre tracks were when he hit the barrier. He was travelling almost in a straight line, braking hard. If he'd simply gone in too hot and lost it, he would have been almost broadside, or he would have been on the ground already and sliding."

"And you worked all this out how, exactly?" Todd demanded. "How come I was there and I didn't see it?"

I shrugged again. It was getting to be a nervous habit. "You spent most of the time concentrating on what was happening down in the ravine," I pointed out. "A few of us had the chance to have a look at the road surface."

Todd had been with us in Einsbaden for the morning. He hadn't been in plain sight, but it would have been a logistical nightmare for him to have got from the village, to the Manor, and back again, pausing only to commit murder on the way.

Rebanks and Gilby, on the other hand, had apparently never left the Manor. And they weren't the only ones.

"It's fortunate the police caught that gang of criminals who attacked us yesterday, isn't it, Major?" I

245

said, keeping my face level as I fed his own invention back to him. "Otherwise you might almost suspect they were to blame."

"Mm, quite," Gilby muttered, looking as rattled as I'd ever seen him. *Where were you, Major, when Blakemore was being murdered?*

Up to that point Rebanks himself hadn't spoken. Now he took advantage of the death of the conversation to lever himself out of his chair. He moved casually in front of the desk with his back towards me.

"I don't suppose you can shed any light on this, can you?" he asked. And when he moved aside there was a single hollowpoint standing on the polished wooden surface.

I knew, don't ask me how, that the round was the very one I'd found on the range and given to Blakemore. If they'd had me wired up to a heart monitor it would all have been over at that point, because my pulse rate went storming off into cardiac arrest territory.

Outwardly, I tried to stay calm. Inwardly, my mind went totally blank, which I suppose is another kind of calm. I tried to figure the innocent response, but couldn't find one.

Then, with a mental lurch, my brain reconnected and started running again. *Deny everything. Nobody was close enough to know for sure that you gave the round to Blakemore. Unless they were watching you through binoculars . . .*

I shook off that last unwelcome thought and looked Rebanks straight in the eye. "Why should I be able to?"

I asked pleasantly. "Munitions are your field, aren't they?"

A quick flash of something chased across his narrow face too fast for me to identify.

"All right, Miss Fox," Gilby said then. He sat on the edge of his desk, suddenly looking as tired as he had done earlier that day, when he'd realised that Blakemore was dead. "That will be all."

I nodded, grateful of the chance to escape. He let me get the study door halfway open before he called me back, the frozen relief at almost making it out of there in one piece grabbing me by the throat.

"Just one last thing," the Major said with that deceptive quiet. When I turned back I found him watching me with the dispassionate stare of a stone-cold killer. "The police will be investigating the crash and they will present their findings in due course. In the meantime I will not have anyone shooting their mouth off about what happened today that will unsettle the staff or the students here. Is that quite clear, Miss Fox?"

People have made that kind of mild threat to me before and it's never ended well. I didn't think this was the time to say so, so I nodded meekly. "Yes sir," I said, not nearly as smartly as Todd had done, and made my exit.

I was out of the study and had almost reached the end of the corridor when a voice behind me made me stop.

"Charlie, can I speak with you?"

I turned to find Rebanks had followed me out and was hurrying after me. Without waiting for an answer, he took my elbow as he came past and hustled me towards the hallway, as though afraid Gilby would appear and call back both of us.

I let him walk me well out of earshot before I twisted my arm out of his grasp.

"What's this all about, Rebanks?" I demanded. "What's going on?"

"Why did you ask about hollowpoints the other day?" he said, ignoring my question to pose one of his own. "You asked if you'd be firing them. Why?"

"Just something somebody mentioned," I said, wary enough to be deliberately vague.

"Who?"

"I don't recall."

He let his breath out, exasperated. For a moment he regarded me with his head slightly cocked, as though he couldn't quite make up his mind if I really was innocent, or whether I was just stalling him.

"Look, Charlie, there's stuff going on here that you can't begin to understand," he said suddenly then, speaking low and urgent. "Blakemore was into it and look what happened to him. You and I both know that crash wasn't an accident, but the Major's stonewalling." He glanced over his shoulder, just to make sure the corridor leading to Gilby's study was still empty.

Surprised by this unexpected confidence, I said, "Surely the local police will turn up evidence of the other vehicle."

248

He gave me a withering look. "The local plod will toe the line," he said. "What they turn up is immaterial. Gilby's got influence. If he wants it kept quiet, that's the way it will stay. Trust me on this."

And how would he know that? Of course, Gilby had done it before. Kirk had died in the most suspicious of circumstances, but the school had not been put under the microscope, hadn't been closed down. The whole matter had been dusted under the carpet.

I feigned puzzlement, tried to push aside everything Blakemore had told me right before he died. "But why the hell would the Major want to cover up the man's death?"

"Ah," Rebanks said, giving me a bleakly knowing look. "Isn't *that* the question? Maybe what you should be asking is why he wanted him dead in the first place."

"What do you mean?"

"Oh come on, Charlie," he said. "You said yourself it wasn't an accident!"

"No," I said carefully, dismissing the doubts I'd shared with Elsa and Jan. "That's not what I said. It could very well have been an accident. I meant it wasn't simply down to rider error. The other driver could just have panicked and run, that's all. And now you're telling me that Major Gilby wanted Blakemore dead. What possible reason could he have had for that?"

Rebanks stepped back away from me abruptly, staring, and a combination of thoughts flitted across the screen of his face too fast for me to unravel any of them.

"I thought —" he began, then stopped, shook his head. "Never mind, Charlie, forget it." He turned and started away from me, but I grabbed his arm, pulled him back.

"Hang on a minute, Rebanks," I said. "You can't just drop that one on me and then walk away. What the hell are you talking about?"

Rebanks shook his head again, more forcefully this time, his mouth compressed as though I wasn't going to force another wrong word out of it. "Forget it, Charlie," he repeated, urgently. "I mean it. If you value your safety, you won't pursue this any further."

That evening we handed in our reports on the fleshpots of Einsbaden village, which Gilby warned us he would mark and return the following morning, like junior school homework. I wondered who'd be getting a gold star and who'd be getting a "See me".

I was aware, also, when I'd finished mine that it was a shoddy piece of work and unlikely to earn me particular praise, but that was just too bad. I had other things on my mind.

Why would Gilby have killed one of his own men? And why choose such a hit and miss fashion to do it? There was always the chance that Blakemore might have avoided the ambush. Kirk's death had been much more certain, much more precise.

Maybe Gilby had realised that he wouldn't get away with two such obvious executions. It made it all the more important to find out what he was up to.

Just after supper McKenna had walked out of Einsbaden Manor, as he'd said he would, to meet a taxi down at the main gate. I watched him go from the dormitory window, but didn't feel inclined to go down and indulge in any kind of fond farewells. Not many of the other students did, although I was surprised to see Jan talking to him outside the front door. Maybe she had a softer heart than she'd like us all to think behind that sharp exterior.

McKenna hadn't tried too hard to make friends during his short spell in Germany. I doubt he was going home with answered questions. Still, at least he was going home in a seat in Economy, rather than in the hold.

Elsa came into the dormitory then and disappeared into the bathroom announcing her intention to soak in the bath before turning in. I didn't want to risk being overheard, so I grabbed my jacket and the mobile, and headed back out to the woods where I'd collared McKenna that afternoon.

It took me a while to wind myself up to call Sean, but even so I had no clear idea what I was going to say when he picked up the phone. In the end I needn't have worried.

"I know about Blakemore," he said as soon as he came on the line. "Madeleine called me."

I didn't know whether to be relieved or disappointed. "Did she tell you about McKenna's uncle as well?" I asked.

"Yeah. Do you think he could be our boy, or do you think the Russians took Blakemore out?"

251

"Neither," I said, and I told him what had happened since I'd got back to the Manor.

"So McKenna's claiming he saw another of the Audis near the scene, and Rebanks is hinting that Gilby's responsible?" Sean said and there was no mistaking the incredulous note in his tone. "And you believe either of them?"

"I don't disbelieve them," I said. "It's a moot point as far as McKenna's concerned anyway. He's packed up and left."

"Hm, either lost his nerve or accomplished his mission," Sean murmured. "Take your pick."

"I keep coming back to the fact that Blakemore admitted they had some involvement with the kidnapping and that Kirk was in on it, too."

"We've been through this before, Charlie," Sean said, rather tiredly, "he couldn't have been."

"Yes, he could," I said. "He just couldn't have been shot by Heidi's bodyguards, that's all."

"*He was with us all the way,*" Blakemore had said of Kirk. "*Salter wasn't the one who threw a spanner in the works.*"

Threw what kind of a spanner? "Supposing Gilby's not the one who planned the kidnapping?" I demanded then. "Supposing it was his staff who did it, and when Gilby found out he went ape shit, and *that's* when Kirk was killed?"

For a while there was silence at the other end of the line. I could almost hear the gears whirring. "It's close," he conceded, and just when I'd begun to feel pleased

252

with myself he added, "But how do you explain the money Gilby's been banking over the last six months?"

I swore under my breath.

"Quite," Sean said. "Sorry, Charlie, but Blakemore must have been spinning you a line."

"I didn't get that feeling from him," I insisted, stubborn.

"And you can tell when somebody's lying to you?" Sean said, and there was just a hint of taunting there. "Just like that?"

"Sometimes, yes," I threw back at him, stung. "You remember you once told me you'd never hit on one of your trainees before? Well, I believed you. I didn't ask for evidence, I just *knew*."

Oh God, where did that come from? It was the last thing that had been in my mind, but as I said it I realised it had never really been away.

A full five seconds went past before Sean spoke again.

"Well, I have to hand it to you, Charlie," he said drily, "you certainly know how to stop a guy in his tracks."

"I'm sorry," I said quickly. "I don't know why I said that, I just —"

"Don't," he cut in, fierce enough to surprise me. "Don't ever apologise for having faith in me. Christ knows I didn't think you'd ever want anything to do with me again when I've meant nothing but pain for you. Why do you think I sent Madeleine to fetch you from your parents' place?"

It was my turn to be speechless, to feel my mouth working but no words waiting behind it to emerge. My tongue was dry and empty.

I leaned back against a tree and listened to the quiet rustling of the forest around me. It was almost soothing.

So, where do we go from here? I had no idea. A picture had unfolded suddenly in front of me that was too big to see the end of it. I needed time to digest, for Sean's words to sink in.

"But you were over in Germany," I said, forgetting completely for a moment which countries we were both in.

"I didn't have to be," he admitted. "I'm hoping you won't need to be for much longer. How's Gilby taking Blakemore's untimely demise?"

"Badly," I said. "He's feeling the pressure and he's starting to suffer for it."

"And you think that's more likely to be guilty conscience because he's bumping off his own men," Sean said, back on track, "rather than the more natural anger and frustration because somebody else is doing it and he's powerless to stop them?"

"But why is he powerless?" I shot back. "If he's nothing to hide then why doesn't he bring in the authorities and let them clear it up? Why is he letting people ambush his students with machine pistols and run one of his instructors off the road? Gilby's up to his neck in this kidnapping somehow. I'm waiting for him to show now, to see if he might lead me to anything interesting on his nightly walkabout."

Gilby hadn't turned out for the last couple of nights. Either that or I'd missed him. It was difficult to maintain an effective watching brief single-handed. It was when you had to be up and running your guts out at five o'clock the next morning, at any rate.

"You just be damned careful, Charlie," Sean warned.

"I will," I promised.

"At least wait until I get out there tomorrow before you go confronting anybody else."

"Don't worry," I said. "I'll take it easy."

He paused, as if trying to find a nice way to call me a liar then changed the subject with a teasing note in his voice. "So how are you getting on with the course, or has that all gone to hell in a handcart?"

"Sort of," I said. "I've just handed in a very scrappy location survey that might just pull in a C-plus — if I'm lucky."

"You're not there to pass the course, Charlie," he pointed out.

That took me aback slightly. *Wasn't I?* I'd never liked failing, that was the trouble. Perhaps I hadn't realised how much I'd hated that aspect of getting kicked out of the army. My relationship with Sean had been a failure, too.

"You remember that chalet we stayed in, that first weekend in Wales?" I asked suddenly. I really was going to have to learn to keep my mouth shut. It was running away with me tonight.

"Yes," he said, with a quiet intensity. "I remember."

I wished, more than ever, that I could see his face as he spoke, could gauge him. Mind you, if we'd been face to face then probably this conversation would never have happened.

"It was quite a place," I ventured at last, mentally cursing my own cowardice.

"Yes, it was," he agreed. "All that wildness, that untamed element." He paused. "I thought it would suit you."

I listened for, but couldn't find, the ironic note in his voice. Instead I asked, "How did you know it was there?"

"Is that a tactful way of asking me how many other girls I'd taken there?" It was the way he said "taken" that made my bones melt.

"Not necessarily."

"Well if it was, the answer's none — before or since."

I leaned my head back, stared up at darkened branches and past them, to the stars. My heart had started to thump painfully behind my breastbone, like I was preparing to run. I had to swallow before I could speak again.

"So how did you know it was there?"

"My mum knew about it," he said. "I think my dear departed dad took her there in the happy days before he started to drink. She used to tell me about it and I remembered the name. What made you think about that?"

How could I not think about that weekend in Wales? We'd run purely on instinct and feeling. No thought. No doubt. No regret. I'd remember it until I died.

"Something Madeleine said, that's all."

"Oh yes," he said. What was that in his voice — surely not embarrassment? "I seem to remember her prising that information out of me one night. There were times when it was good to have someone to talk to." *About you*. He didn't say the words out loud, but I knew they were there because I'd felt the same way.

It's amazing what people will admit to over the phone. Encouraged, I said, "She showed me a photo of her boyfriend."

"Dom?" Sean said and he sounded surprised. "Why would she do that?"

"I think," I said carefully, "that she was trying to tell me that she wasn't a threat."

Sean said, "Ah," as though a lot of things had fallen into place. There was a long pause, and when he next spoke there was something serious in his voice. "She never has been, Charlie."

I closed my eyes, felt the pull of a smile across my lips. "Good," I said. "That's all right, then."

CHAPTER
SEVENTEEN

Major Gilby walked out of the Manor house about twenty minutes after I'd finished talking to Sean, and strode briskly along the path towards the ranges. He wore a heavy greatcoat that flapped around his legs as he walked.

It was bitter out, just on the point of freezing. The ground was crystalline with a heavy frost that reflected the moon like a cut diamond.

As for me, for once I didn't feel the cold.

I waited until he'd moved past my position, then slipped out into the darkness and followed. I clung to the edge of the trees, not only watching his progress, but also keeping an eye out behind me, just in case the Major's mystery shadow had chosen tonight to make a reappearance. If he had, he was better at hiding than I was at spotting him.

It didn't take me long to realise that I'd picked a bad night to trail Gilby. His footsteps along the path showed as flattened prints on the concrete, plainly visible through the frost. Where I'd walked along the edge of the grass I left telltales that were clearer still. Crossing the open ground that lay between us was going to be impossible without leaving tracks a blind man wouldn't need a Labrador to be able to follow. Was it worth that risk?

I'd promised Sean I wouldn't take risks, but I'd also promised him results, just by being here. It was a wrench to know which to keep, but for the moment I settled for a watching brief, got as close as I dared and stayed in cover. It was a good job I didn't break out of it.

Gilby checked behind him twice, coming to a standstill and revolving slowly, listening as well as watching for any sign of movement, of something out of place. I kept motionless and tried to think like a tree.

Eventually, seeming satisfied, he strode the last few metres to the indoor range, took a key out of his pocket, and let himself in. I watched the door swing shut and in the stillness of the night I heard the lock click behind him.

I felt my shoulders drop a little. I had my Swiss Army knife in my pocket, as always, but I couldn't pick a lock to save my life. Even if I had ventured after him, I would have needed to be right on his heels to stand any chance of getting in. Not a move that was likely to pass unnoticed.

I realised too, that if I made my way back to the Manor now, Gilby was likely to spot my footprints across the grass when he came back. I checked my watch. It was edging towards ten. I thought regretfully of my lost beauty sleep and decided to wait him out.

The Major was only inside the range for a quarter of an hour, which was more than enough time for me to have lost most of the sensation in my toes. I watched the lights in the Manor start to blink out as people called it a night.

When he reappeared, locking the door behind him, Gilby walked quickly straight back along the path, not bothering to check who might be following. He reached one of the sets of French windows on the ground floor and let himself in.

I wondered briefly if they went round locking all the exterior doors at night. In which case I was going to have fun getting back in myself. Perhaps it would be a good idea not to find out. I started forwards, but a movement over to my left stopped me in my tracks.

I wasn't the only watcher in the woods, it seemed.

Another figure emerged into the moonlight about thirty metres away and made for the range doorway that the Major had just come out of. I was suddenly thankful that I hadn't been whistling to myself to pass the time.

Apart from the fact that the figure was clearly a man, I was too far away to recognise who it might be. He was bulked up in heavy clothing, a wool hat pulled down low around his face. Now why didn't I think of that? My own ears were pulsing with the cold.

Whoever he was, the man also had a key to the range. Did that mean he was one of the instructors, or a light-fingered pupil?

This time, though, as the man entered, the range door didn't fully close behind him. I hesitated for a moment, briefly remembered my other promise to Sean, that I wouldn't confront anyone else, then hurried across the frigid grass before my nerve failed me. It was a stupid manoeuvre, I knew, but too good an opportunity to miss.

I couldn't remember for the life of me if the door squeaked. I pushed it open very carefully with my fingertips, like that was going to make a difference. It swung silently aside and I slipped through the gap, making sure it didn't latch behind me.

There were no windows in the indoor range. There wasn't any need for them and the lack of glass enabled the interior to be almost completely soundproofed.

I discovered when I got inside that the lights in the cramped vestibule had been switched on, too. After the clean silver blue of the moon outside, the ceiling tubes threw out a dull harsh glare the colour of stagnant pond water onto the blockwork walls.

The range area itself, off to my right, was still in darkness. I bypassed that and crept through to the room next to the armoury, where we'd been shown how to strip and clean the Sigs. It was very dark in there. I had to pause long enough just inside the doorway for my eyes to adapt.

I moved cautiously across the floor, trying to recall the exact layout of the room. There was a large table in the centre, its dirty plywood top ingrained with burnt powder and gun oil. Even though it was so dark I crouched below the level and crabbed my way across the room. Where was he?

Beyond me was the armoury section. Normally this area was blocked off by a steel door, held shut with a selection of locks and padlocks that would have had

Harry Houdini muttering nervously about not realising that was the time.

But not any more.

The locks were disengaged and the padlocks hung open to one side. I slunk through the open doorway, trying to blend into the paintwork on the jamb. Across in the corner was the weapons' store, a secure caged area. The lights in the cage were on, bleeding out across the floor, but because the sides were stacked high with gun cases, it was difficult to tell if my mystery man was inside.

With a dry mouth and damp palms I edged forwards until I was right up against the bars. I peered in through a tiny slot between two cases. Something moved across the other side of the gap, close enough to make me jump and recoil. With a silent curse I glued my eye back to the gap.

I could just make out part of a workbench against the far wall. It had a vice bolted down to the corner with wall-mounted plastic boxes for nuts and screws above it. On the bench itself was a small wooden crate.

As I watched, the man moved in front of the bench and began levering the lid off the crate. It was cold enough in there for him to still be wearing his hat, his breath clouding against the light. Because of the position of the bench, his back was towards me. I still couldn't make out the details of his face.

When the lid of the crate was off he dumped it to one side and disappeared from view. I tensed, in case he was about to walk out of the cage. The walls of the armoury were bare. There was nothing big enough to hide a rat under. *Damn, why did I have to go and think about rats?*

Even if I did find a place of concealment, what the hell did I do if he walked out of the range and locked the door behind him? It wasn't the kind of place where there was likely to be a convenient fire exit.

Fortunately, the next moment I heard him dragging something across the floor inside the cage. I couldn't see what it was, but if his grunt of effort was anything to go by, it was heavy.

When the man reappeared in my field of vision he was carrying three packages, wrapped in oiled cloth. He carefully placed two straight into the crate, hesitated for a moment, then started to unwrap the other. I had a frustrating few seconds unable to see much more than his back and arms as he worked, then he shifted his position slightly, and it all became chillingly clear.

The contents of the package was a compact submachine gun. The man slid out the wire stock and tried the weapon for size into his shoulder, ducking his head to squint through the open sights.

Beyond firing a few during my time in the army, I was no particular expert on submachine guns, but I had no difficulty in recognising the Lucznik PM-98 the man was holding. I'd had one in my own hands only two days ago, when I'd picked up the Peugeot driver's fallen weapon.

I'd no difficulty recognising the man who held it now either. As he turned I caught my first proper full view of his face.

Rebanks.

Question was, what the hell was Gilby's weapons' handler doing with a case-load of machine pistols?

I didn't have the chance to expand much on this train of thought. Behind me there was a clatter from the other room, followed by a deafening clamour as somebody punched the fire alarm.

I flinched back. The alarm bell seemed to be ringing right next to my head, incredibly loud, but it didn't quite mask the faint slam of the outer door. I didn't think I'd been followed in, but whoever had done so obviously wanted to make sure I wasn't going to get out again unobserved or unhindered.

Shit! I jerked to my feet and began to make a dash for the doorway into the darkened room next door. I didn't stop there, but went full pelt for the exit, hoping shock had gained me enough of a head start.

I almost made it.

I was only half a dozen strides from the outer doorway when I felt Rebanks make a grab for the back of my jacket. His fingers closed down hard, and I was caught. In the darkness my capture took on nightmare proportions. I fought down the spike of panic and tried to rely on cool, logical thought.

He hadn't seen my face near the cage, didn't know it was me. It was dark enough in the outer room so if I could escape now, I could get away with this. I hadn't zipped my jacket up and, all too briefly, I considered jettisoning it. Pointless to leave it behind. It would lead them straight to me.

Instead, I braked suddenly and dodged sideways. Rebanks had been at full stretch reaching for me. The additional movement unbalanced him. He stumbled, went down onto his knees, but he didn't let go.

Using his hold on my jacket to steady me, I locked down hard on his wrist, pivoted on my right leg and kicked him, twice, with my left foot where I guessed his body would be. The first blow landed square in his diaphragm, in the fleshy vee just beneath his ribcage. I heard the explosive whoosh as his lungs were blasted empty. He floundered for air, his grip slackening.

Even though I couldn't see any more than a dim outline, I instinctively understood the size and the shape of him. I could map the vulnerable areas of his body. Before he'd recovered enough to shout, my second kick connected to his throat, straight across his windpipe.

His hands fell away. He dropped backwards and rolled slowly onto his side, making quiet little gasping and gulping sounds that were hideous in their softness.

I didn't stop to check how badly I'd hurt him. It was enough to know that I had. At that moment, I really didn't care.

I ran.

I ran out of the building, heedless of who might be waiting in ambush outside, and hared along the concrete path back towards the house. It was the most exposed route, but it was the quickest, too. I'd hoped that the alarm in the range might have been linked to the Manor's entire system, to add confusion, but there my luck failed me. The only sounds came from behind me.

I reached the house and flattened against the wall, burying myself into the ivy that clung to the stonework. The alarm was clearly audible across the grounds from there. It must have been wired in to some sort of central control system in any case, because lights had suddenly come on in the centre section of the house. The instructors' quarters.

I had to suppress a gasp of shock when a door was thrown open less than four metres from me. Two dark figures rushed out. They pounded back along the path in the direction of the building. The kind of power that sprinters have, born of muscle.

I waited, silent except for the thunder of my heart, until they'd almost disappeared from view. Then I slipped out of my hiding place and back into the house.

I resisted the urge to run back to my room. On that floor it would have sounded like a stampede. Mind you, with the amount of noise going on in there anyway, nobody might have noticed.

I darted up the main staircase, hearing shouting and running feet above and below me. Then I tiptoed along the edges of the corridor until I reached the women's dormitory. I opened the door as little as I could get away with, and slid through the gap into the room. I closed it quickly and stilled in the darkness that met me. Nothing.

I crossed to the bathroom, closed the door and stripped down to my T-shirt and knickers. Then I flushed the loo, just in case, washed my hands, and padded back across to my bed, bundling my clothes into my locker as I did so.

As I lay awake, listening to the far-off noises of panic and disorder, a terrible coldness swept over me. I began to shiver violently, like I was in the grip of a fever. The bedclothes suddenly felt chilled and damp against my skin.

I told myself, over and over, that I'd only done what I had to. That I'd acted in self defence. I hadn't hit Rebanks hard enough to do him any real harm. Hadn't hit him hard enough to kill him . . .

But I knew I had.

I went over it again and again in slow-motion replay. The first blow to his solar plexus, I recognised with a sickly taste in the back of my mouth, had winded him, effectively silenced him. It could have been enough to allow me to escape. I should have made it enough. Should have taken that chance.

The second blow was the killer in every sense of the word. Running down either side of the trachea are the vagus nerves. They control just about everything of importance in the body, from the heart and lungs to the abdominal organs. Hit the vagus nerves hard enough and your victim ceases to breathe, his heartbeat stutters, his nervous system crashes.

And then he dies.

I remembered again the dreadful noises Rebanks had made as he'd fallen. I shut my eyes, but it only made the images in my head more vivid.

I hadn't hesitated. Not for a second. I was in danger and I'd reacted with potentially deadly force. Perhaps if the army had known what was inside me, what I would eventually turn into, they might not have been so keen to let me go.

It seemed like I lay there for hours, wrestling with my conscience. According to the red digital figures of my alarm clock, it was actually seven minutes before the door was rammed open and the lights flashed on.

Elsa sat up almost as a reflex action, with a startled cry. I raised myself up on my elbow and engineered a groggy, just-woken-from-sleep expression onto my face. Jan barely stirred under the blankets.

Gilby stood in the doorway glaring at the three of us, with O'Neill by his shoulder. They both had faces that should have come with a severe weather warning.

"All right, let's have everyone out of their beds and downstairs immediately!" Gilby rapped out.

With reluctance I didn't have to feign, I pushed back the covers and swung my legs out of bed, trying to ignore the way O'Neill's eyes flicked over them.

"Major, what is the meaning of this, please?" Elsa demanded, her German accent becoming more pronounced as it tended to do, I'd noticed, when she was angry or upset. She groped for her glasses from the bedside table and peered at the clock.

"We've had an incident, Frau Schmitt," he said shortly. "One of my staff has been seriously assaulted."

Elsa gaped at him. "And you think one of us was responsible?" The incredulity was clear in her voice. "When did this 'incident' take place?"

The Major checked his watch automatically. "About fifteen minutes ago," he said, but his anger was beginning to dissipate into discomfort. Elsa, I considered, must have been a formidable police officer. Jan had come round by this time and was eyeing the intruders with some malevolence.

"Then you are wasting your time looking here," Elsa dismissed contemptuously. "We have all been asleep in our beds, as you can plainly see."

"All of you?" the Major said sharply. "None of you has been outside?"

Elsa glanced briefly in my direction, sending my pulse rate skittering. "Both Jan and Charlie have been to the bathroom," she said solemnly, "but I hardly feel that counts against them."

"Nevertheless," Gilby said, his face hardening as he recognised her ironic tone, "I must insist that all of you are searched downstairs."

That suggestion brought a brief, but to-the-point expletive from Jan. Elsa regarded the Major coldly. "I do not think so, Major," she said. "And if you insist in this matter I will have no alternative but to press charges for sexual harassment against you and your men. I am sure Charlie and Jan will agree with this."

We both nodded. It's difficult to retain any degree of authority when you're facing someone who's fully clothed and standing, and you're lying down in a flannelette nightie, but Elsa managed it with style. And besides, she knew her law. It would have taken a better man than Gilby to have defied her.

In the end he gave a frustrated short nod, his neck rigid, and retreated. His control was such that he didn't even slam the door behind him. For a few moments after they'd gone there was silence.

"What the fuck was that all about?" Jan demanded.

Elsa shrugged. "I'm not entirely sure."

There was something in her voice that made me glance towards her. I found her watching me thoughtfully. "If you are going to expect us to cover for you in future, Charlie," she said calmly, "it would be a courtesy if you would explain to us what it is that you are up to."

CHAPTER
EIGHTEEN

I fobbed Elsa and Jan off. Of course I did. Jan in particular scowled as I made excuses about having been outside talking to Sean on the mobile and come rushing back in when I heard the alarm go off. I told them I hadn't wanted to get into trouble, to get involved.

If only they knew the kind of trouble I might be in.

As it was, my lame piece of invention was rewarded by looks of disbelief and even of reproach from both women. Jan *would* keep asking insistent questions about where exactly I'd been, and what exactly I'd been doing, as if she was deliberately trying to increase Elsa's suspicion of me. I did my best to ignore them. After all, I had other more pressing things on my mind.

Eventually we turned out the lights again. I lay awake in the darkness and listened to their breathing soften and slow, but my own sleep didn't come easy.

The panic was a trapped beast inside me, thrashing to get out. Keeping it caged took all my concentration as I forced myself to face up to the possibility that I might have killed a man.

And it wasn't the first time.

The first time I'd been under intense pressure, intense threat. It wasn't so difficult to convince anyone that I'd acted in self-defence on the most primitive level. Kill or be killed. I wasn't quite so optimistic of getting away with the same plea twice. Not in these circumstances.

The guilt and the sheer weight of what I'd done settled slowly onto me. I could feel it crushing down, layer upon layer. Weight without measure, like rock. I buckled under the force of it.

The thoughts swam round and round as the digital figures on my alarm clock marched inexorably on, out of one day and into the next. It was only then that I finally surrendered into fitful slumber.

Hardly surprising then, that I was wasted during the morning run. Mind you, so was everybody else. The ones that hadn't decided to quit, at any rate. Another two people had taken the night's events as the last straw. I gathered from a disgruntled Romundstad that Gilby had given them all the third degree in the wee small hours, despite protests somewhat more vehement than Elsa had put forward.

It went to show, I thought grimly, that he hadn't really believed a woman capable of inflicting Rebanks's injuries. The bile climbed up the back of my throat, burning brightly when I swallowed it down again.

Todd was in charge of phys, as usual, but for once he didn't push us to our limits, which was unusually lenient of him. I suppose what had happened to Rebanks, coming on top of watching Blakemore die

272

down in the ravine the day before, was an experience that would have a subduing effect on anyone.

Or maybe he was taking it steady because he had O'Neill out with him. The scarred instructor ran with a grimace of stony determination twisting his face further out of kilter. Every now and then I caught him with a hand to his ribs, like he'd got a stitch. But when Todd jogged back and threw him a single enquiring glance, it was met with an angry glare.

"So, what do you reckon's gone on then?" said a panting voice by my shoulder, and I turned to find Declan running alongside me.

I shrugged. It required less breath than speech.

"Old Gilby was going spare last night," he went on. "I don't know what's happened to Rebanks, but it can't be good if he can't even describe who clouted him, can it?"

"No," I managed, "I suppose not."

Declan paused. "You know, of course, that Hofmann was outside last night."

That broke my stride. "Hofmann? What on earth was he doing?"

"Said he'd gone out for a last cigarette," Declan gasped. "But he came bolting in when those alarms went off, I can tell you."

We ran another dozen strides or so in silence while I let that sink in. Then I ventured, "How did Gilby react to that?"

Declan grinned at me. "Ah now, girl, d'you think we'd rat on the man?" he demanded, adding, "Even if he is a big numb German."

This morning Todd didn't put us through any extra tortures on the dew-misted grass in front of the house. Instead, when we got back we were allowed to fall back to a walk and trudge wearily straight across the gravel to the main doorway.

My eyes searched for Hofmann's broad figure and found him almost immediately. As if aware of my scrutiny, he glanced round, his gaze sweeping across me as he did so. Surely, if it was Hofmann who'd been watching outside and who'd followed me into the armoury, he must have seen enough to know my identity, mustn't he? But there was no hint of recognition on his face.

Then I remembered that flash of cunning I'd seen in him after I'd confronted McKenna, and I couldn't be sure.

Major Gilby was waiting for us inside the hallway. Waiting and watching. He didn't move at our approach, so we were forced to part and flow round him, keeping our heads down, trying not to be noticed. He was like a stockman eyeing up the herd for the weak and the slow.

There was that stillness to him again, that single-minded ruthlessness unveiled now. I could well believe that here was a man who'd marched his prisoners across a minefield without a second thought and had satisfied himself that it was the logical thing to do.

As for me, I daren't make eye contact. I had a nasty feeling that I wouldn't be able to hide what he might see written there. The urge to break down under that

274

scrutiny and confess what I'd done was almost overwhelming.

Breakfast was a solemn affair. The students were still shell-shocked from the events of the last couple of days. Rebanks's abrupt and apparently unexplained departure was just the latest in a catalogue of events designed to make even the most dedicated trainee bodyguard begin to doubt his or her calling.

None of the depleted group of instructors were any more chatty. I noticed that the dining hall staff had used a smaller top table, so the two empty places were not so glaringly obvious.

When the Major came in with amendments to the day's schedule, he couldn't help but take in the lack of focus within the group. The apathy was coming off everyone in waves.

"This morning we'll be doing a little team-building exercise on the assault course," he announced. "You'll need to present yourselves at the front entrance at oh-eight-hundred." For a moment he looked about to say more, but he closed his mouth with a snap and stiffly left the room.

I knew that I should really have used the intervening time to call Sean and update him on the latest events before we went out on the assault course, but when the Major's deadline rolled round I hadn't plucked up the courage to do so. How could I tell him what I'd done now without also having to reveal what had gone before?

Besides, I don't know if Jan and Elsa had made a pact between them to stop me getting into any more trouble, but one or other of them seemed to be there whenever I turned around.

Todd, O'Neill, and Figgis were all waiting for us on the gravel when we went back outside, but for once they didn't give us a hard time for being late. It wasn't hard to understand why.

Pulled up just about where the Major's new car had been delivered was another transporter, but this held a very different load.

The remains of Blakemore's FireBlade had been retrieved from the site of the accident and had been brought to Einsbaden Manor. For what purpose I can only guess. I don't know how the police work in Germany, but I would have expected them to want to hang on to the wreckage of the bike to examine it for evidence of another vehicle's involvement in the crash. Looks like the Major had managed to successfully fudge the verdict to suit his own purposes.

We watched in silence as the driver dragged out the ramps and removed the webbing straps that had held the bike's carcass onto the load bed. Not that it was going anywhere. The buckled front wheel was bent right back into the radiator, the forks twisted well out of true.

Gilby appeared at this point, rapping out sharp commands in German that the driver should drop his load off in the car park at the rear of the building. With a sigh the driver lifted the ramps again, muttering that the bike would not even push, he'd had to winch it on to the truck, and he would need a hand to unload it.

The Major hesitated, as though he realised that using any of the students for such a task wasn't in the best possible taste, but he had little choice. He commandeered Hofmann and Craddock, being the biggest of the lads, to help the instructors assist the driver.

We didn't need to, but the rest of us followed round to the rear parking area to watch the process. The driver had been right about the immobility of the bike. The clutch and gear levers were gone, snapped away, so there was no way to free up the transmission which was locking the rear wheel tight.

The men had to practically carry the dead Blade off the truck and over into the corner with the damaged Audis. Todd even tucked a corner of the tarpaulin over it, like a shroud. He turned away, wiping his hands, and caught sight of me.

"So, d'you still think those bastard machines are better than a car then, Charlie?" he demanded with surprising bitterness.

I shrugged, aware I had the attention of the others, but pride was at stake. I'd ridden bikes for enough years to know the risks. Blakemore would have known them, too, but that wasn't what had killed him.

"Well, everybody's birth certificate expires sometime," I said. *Yeah, but sometimes it's earlier than they expected . . .*

Todd shook his head in disgust and came stalking past me. "You're one hard-faced bitch," he said under his breath. "That attitude's going to win you no friends here."

The instructors had been expecting us to be spending the morning in a nice warm classroom and they hadn't looked too happy about the change of plans. Maybe that partly accounted for Todd's sour mood. What the hell, he'd never liked me anyway.

By way of retribution they fast jogged us the half-kilometre or so through the forest to the assault course location. It turned out to be not far from the CQB range, out of sight of the Manor house itself.

We were split into four teams of four, which accounted for all the survivors of the course so far. I remembered the number who'd started out, and wondered how many more we were destined to lose before the full fortnight was up. Only a few days to go now. I'd found out plenty of answers in the time I'd been here, but I realised I just wasn't sure I knew what the questions were.

Todd split the three women up between the teams. I ended up with Craddock, Romundstad, and Declan. Hofmann was in the one team without a female constituent and looked smug at the prospect of not being lumbered with such a weak link. That self-satisfied air didn't last long, though, when Todd explained the purpose of the exercise.

"You will designate one team member as your injured principal," he announced. "They are unconscious and must be carried to safety over the assault course." He grinned nastily at our consternation. "Preferably without causing them any further injury. If we spot any of them lending a helping hand, or generally not behaving like dead weights, you go back to the beginning and start again."

Three pairs of eyes swivelled in my direction.

"Now hang on a moment, lads," I protested, backing away. "Declan's skinny. Why can't we carry him?"

Craddock smiled and swept me up easily off the ground. He didn't even grunt with the effort, which was kind of flattering, I suppose. "He is," he agreed, "but he's not nearly so much fun."

"OK," I muttered as he set me down again, "but I warn you now, boys, if I feel anybody's hands where they shouldn't be, you'll get them back minus a few fingers, all right?"

Todd was setting the teams off at two-minute intervals. We watched Jan's lot go first, getting themselves well knotted up in the climbing net. They bundled her over the six-foot wall like she was a sack of potatoes. For an unconscious VIP her language was loud and colourful. Then Elsa's team was away.

By dint of the fact that Elsa was what might politely be termed statuesque, a smaller bloke had been designated as the principal. Even so, they were struggling by the time they reached the rope swing.

Hofmann's mob made a better job of the net. He was clearly the powerhouse of the team and even though his principal was much bigger than the others, he seemed to be managing to carry him without immediate danger of herniating himself. Or maybe he was and it was just taking a long time for the message to fight its way through the muscle to his brain.

An image of Kirk sprang to mind. He'd had been blessed with that same casual strength. It had made him inclined towards bravado. He'd had a tendency to show off, carrying more and more weight in his bergen for cross-country runs, completing high numbers of one-handed or even one-fingered press-ups. Stupid stuff that had made us all laugh.

"If you're *quite* ready, Miss Fox?" Todd's voice snapped me back to the present. We stepped up to the start line. Craddock hoisted me over his shoulder and held me steady with a meaty hand perilously high up the back of my thigh.

I reached down his back and grabbed hold of a fistful of the elasticated waistband of his jogging trousers, then pulled up, twisting hard.

"Let's not hurt each other here," I hissed.

The Welshman's hand immediately dropped six inches further down my leg and I let go cautiously.

"OK, go!" Todd shouted, clicking his stopwatch, and we were off.

Being carried over someone's shoulder in a fireman's lift is not only extremely undignified, I discovered quickly, but it's also bloody uncomfortable, particularly when they're running. Fortunately, Craddock had big shoulders, coated with slabs of muscle, but even so it wasn't long before the pressure set up a dull ache in my sternum, making it difficult for me to catch my breath.

I didn't have to feign helplessness as Craddock bundled me over the net and rolled me down the far side where Romundstad and Declan were waiting to slow my descent.

As we progressed further round the course, over the six-foot wall and across the rope swing, the pain in my chest increased. I bit down on it, forced myself not to make any sound of complaint. We were catching up the people ahead of us. The rest of my team would not have appreciated any request to slow down or take things easier. Besides, the end was in sight.

I nearly made it, too.

It was the final obstacle that was my undoing. A single-piece rope bridge stretched between two sections of scaffold, nearly four metres off the ground. How to get a supposedly unconscious principal across this gap had caused discussion and disagreement in the other teams. Nobody had come up with the definitive answer.

If you left it to the strongest member to simply carry them across, he couldn't hold on to both the principal and the guide ropes at either side. It was a precarious operation, and it seemed much further down from up there than it had from the safety of the ground.

Jan's team only managed to hold onto her by the skin of their teeth. By the time they reached the other side she was dangling precariously by her wrists and cursing her team's cack-handed technique.

Hofmann went for the brute force approach, hoisting his principal and muscling his way across, leaving his two team-mates to struggle after him. He made it about halfway before his grip and his balance both failed him. I was right about it being a long way down. They were both lucky to escape injury.

Elsa, who seemed to have taken charge of her team, solved the problem by having one person carry their burden draped over their shoulder, holding on to the guide ropes with both hands. The other two, one in front and one behind, held on with one hand only, steadying the principal with the other. It was probably safer, but it was numbingly slow.

By the time they'd inched their way to the other side we were the only team left and everyone, instructors included, was waiting under the bridge to watch our crossing.

"What d'you reckon?" Craddock asked. "Mad dash or slow but sure?"

I was in enough pain by this time to favour a mad dash, just to get it over with faster, but the other two voted for the other alternative and I had no choice but to go along with it.

With Declan in the lead and Romundstad bringing up the rear we edged out across the void. Dangling over Craddock's shoulder all I could see was the back of his legs and Romunstad's feet that came nervously after. Below them, it was a hell of a long way down.

Every now and again their collective movements would set up a swaying motion on the rope and they'd have to freeze until the lurching subsided. It was painful progress in every sense of the word and a good job, I contemplated tightly, that I wasn't seasick.

Then, when we were just over one-third's distance, I felt Craddock slip slightly to one side. It was enough for me to start slithering off his shoulder. I waited a heartbeat for Romundstad to grab hold of me, but he must have had his own balance to worry about. I didn't want to be the one who incurred a forfeit from the ever-watchful Todd, but I didn't see I had much option.

In the end, I left it too late to save myself anyway.

Craddock's boot slipped off the rope entirely. With a bellow that could have been anger, or could have been pain, he managed to get a fistful of guide rope with his left hand, but I tumbled off his shoulder and started heading for *terra firma* at a nastily accelerated rate.

For a split second my vision was a cartwheel of ground and sky, then I thumped down hard, mainly head first, and landed on my face in the dirt.

The impact left me stunned and sick. For a few moments I lay there, disconnected from myself, watching with vague interest as numerous pairs of booted feet congregated around my head. Eventually, I was rolled over onto my back. The rope bridge seemed miles above me in the sky. Had I really fallen all the way from there?

Figgis's long mournful face appeared. "Charlie," he said, slowly and carefully, "can you move your hands and feet for me?"

I obligingly wiggled my limbs to show my spinal cord was still attached, but when I sat up it was like I'd been punched in the chest. I wrapped my arms round my ribs, gasping.

"Steady, girl," Figgis said. "Take a minute. You might have cracked a couple of ribs."

Light-headed, I gave a wheezy laugh and muttered, "Been there, done that."

Somebody snorted and when I looked up I found Todd staring down at me. "This is why female bodyguards are a waste of space," he stated, his voice acid with contempt. "You just haven't got the physical strength to get the job done."

"I'm plenty strong enough when I'm fully fit," I threw back at him, and regretted the words almost as soon as they were out of my mouth. There was a long pause.

"What the fuck does that mean?" he demanded.

I tried to think of an excuse, but none came. The throbbing in my chest was making it difficult to think much. In the end the truth just came dribbling out.

"I fractured my sternum two months ago," I said, part shamefaced, part defiant.

"And you still came on the course?" O'Neill asked, and I couldn't tell from his tone whether he thought I was a hero or a fool.

I shrugged. "It's supposed to be mended."

Figgis held his hand out. For a moment I stared at it stupidly, as though he was offering it to shake. Then it dawned on me that he was helping me up.

I got to my feet. The other students moved back silently to give me room. The whole of my ribcage felt tight, like I'd been crushed by a snake. I tried a couple of deep breaths, with varying degrees of success.

Todd stood and looked at me with his hands on his hips. "I think you'd better get back to the Manor," he said, dismissive. "Talk to the Major. He'll arrange you a flight home."

"Hang on," I protested. "You can't just chuck me out."

"I think you'll find we can do anything we like, Miss Fox," he said with a grim smile. "Injury is one of the commonest reasons for people failing this course. It's against school policy to let you continue. Like it or not, you're out."

CHAPTER
NINETEEN

It was a long way back to the Manor and nobody offered to walk with me. Before I was even out of earshot I could hear Todd resuming the lesson, sending the students off round the assault course individually. O'Neill and Figgis were shouting insults and encouragement.

As I walked back into the teeth of an uncouth wind I felt instantly forgotten. The sands had closed over me and now there was nothing to show I'd ever been there.

I was out. Finished.

But there was always the chance, I realised, to argue my corner with the Major. Somehow I didn't think he was going to bend the rules in my case, but it was worth a try. I would call Sean as soon as I got back, I reasoned, and seek advice before I braved Gilby.

I tried not to worry about Sean's reaction to my expulsion from the course. I didn't think for a moment that he'd blame me for it, but that didn't make it any easier to believe I hadn't failed him. I closed my mind to telling him about Rebanks. Sean should be in Germany by now. I would wait until I could tell him face-to-face.

I thought about a lot of things on the way back. It helped keep my mind off the pain in my chest. The bitter weather was sidling in through my jacket with negligent disregard for its apparent insulation properties. The sweat had cooled on my body and shivering made things hurt all the more.

It was better to have something else to concentrate on, not least of which was the fact that Romundstad should have saved me, and either couldn't or wouldn't do so. It was an interesting point to ponder. I shifted from that to wondering what he might have had to gain by letting me fall.

Kirk had let me fall, too. A calculated act of cruelty from a man with a big heart. Not surprising in some ways that it had been on his conscience as Sean had claimed. Didn't stop him standing against me at the time, though. Peer pressure is a powerful method of inducement.

Eventually, the back of the Manor came into view and I trudged across the rear parking area. I'm not entirely sure why, but as I drew level with what was left of Blakemore's bike, I slowed. It was a mess, even more so than I remembered. How could I just give in and leave here with my tail between my legs when there were still so many unanswered questions?

When I looked back towards the house, there were two men with machine pistols walking across the terrace.

I ducked quickly behind the wrecked Audis, trying not to wince as I did so, but they hadn't seen me. If I hadn't made that brief pause I would have been out into the open. On killing ground. The thought made me start to sweat again. I didn't need to be told that these weren't Gilby's regular men. So who were they?

If these were a couple of the mercenaries that the Major was using for the kidnappings, then I needed to know. Particularly if he wouldn't budge on kicking me out. The more information I could take away with me for Sean, the less this whole painful business would have been a disaster.

I peeped round the corner of the tarpaulin and watched as the men scanned the whole of the area carefully and methodically. Then they started round the side of the house, keeping sharp, moving like professionals. They were carrying IMI Mini-Uzis on shoulder straps. How many more of them were there?

I thought all too briefly of hightailing it back to the assault course and fetching the instructors, but then I thought of the distance, and the time it would take, and realised that I was on my own. Besides, what if they were all part of it? All I'd be doing would be exposing the rest of the students to danger.

The only weapon I had on me was the small folding knife in my jacket pocket. I don't think even the Swiss Army are expected to actually engage the enemy with one of those. Ah well.

As soon as the men had disappeared round the corner of the house I sprinted for the cover of the terrace wall. I blanked out the pain in my chest, pushed it down to another level. There'd be plenty of time to worry about how much it hurt later. I crept up the steps, keeping low, but there was nobody on the terrace itself and nobody else waiting behind the French windows.

The windows themselves were unlocked. I opened them as little as I could get away with and slipped in through the gap. I had a sudden flashback to my covert entry to the indoor range, and hoped this wasn't going to end the same way. Besides anything else, I didn't think I was up to much of a fight.

I moved through to the open front hallway, staying on my toes across the echoing tiled floor. It was empty. For a moment I stood there, listening, assessing my options. Then I heard muffled guttural voices coming from the dining hall.

Something told me that opening the dining-hall doors would not be in my best interests. Instead I took the small corridor off to the side, the one that led direct to the kitchens. On the run-up towards lunch the place should have been a hive of activity, but even the overhead lights were off. Cautiously, I moved deeper. There was enough daylight coming through from the adjoining room for me not to trip over anything noisy on the way.

I stayed down below the level of the industrial stainless steel kitchen units, comforting myself with the thought that at least if anyone started shooting at me there'd be plenty of furniture that was solid enough to hide behind.

Big serving hatches had been knocked through between the two rooms, so it wasn't difficult to get a view of what was going on in there. What I saw didn't exactly reassure me.

Two more men with Uzis were holding the Manor's cooks and domestic staff spread out along one side of the room. They'd been forced to their knees facing the wall, far enough apart not to be able to communicate in whispers, their hands on their heads. Judging from the way they were drooping, they'd been in that position for some time.

One of their guards stood up on the dais, while the other patrolled along the backs of them, walking with measured footsteps, occasionally pausing behind one or another. It was a move designed to play on their nerves, keep them frightened and on edge. These men were not just professionals, I realised, they were experts at intimidation too.

Carefully, I backed away and returned to the main hallway, with my brain turning over furiously. If they were holding the staff hostage, surely the men couldn't be working for the Major. In that case, alerting Todd, O'Neill, and Figgis was probably a damned good idea, particularly if any of them happened to be carrying the keys for the armoury.

Footsteps coming from the corridor opposite the dining hall snapped me into action. I leapt for the nearest doorway, only to find the door itself was locked. The footsteps were growing louder every moment. Cursing under my breath, I flattened myself against the door, gripping the knife in my pocket.

I didn't even have time to extend any of its array of useful blades before the man appeared. He passed within inches of my doorway, but fortunately his back was towards me and I remained unseen. He was wearing a good quality dark brown leather jacket and his hair was long, tied back into a ponytail with an elastic band.

He paused and for a second I thought the game was up. My heart bounced, I stopped breathing, but all he did was tuck something under his armpit so he had both hands free to light a cigarette.

My first thought, whimsically enough, was that the Major would strenuously object. My second, with some amazement, was that the object under his arm was the barrel of a handgun. He'd momentarily let go of it to work his lighter.

I knew I wasn't going to get another chance like this.

I stepped forwards and silently jammed the cold hard end of the folded knife against the back of the man's neck, just under the base of his skull where his hair was pulled back. I was close enough to see the dusting of dandruff on his collar.

He tensed instinctively, then froze, too much of a pro to even attempt to outmanoeuvre the gun he clearly believed I was holding on him. I suppose I was just lucky I wasn't dealing with an amateur.

Still without speaking I reached for his gun. He thought about clamping his arm down tight onto it, but when I jerked the handle of the knife a little harder into his neck he capitulated. It dropped heavily into my hand.

The sight of it made me swallow. The damned thing was enormous, a .50 calibre chromed Desert Eagle Magnum with the optional ten-inch barrel. It was a gangster's trophy piece — and a rich gangster, at that.

291

Not quite what I was expecting from the urban commandos who'd apparently taken over the rest of the Manor.

I slipped the knife back into my pocket and stepped back away from the man, covering him with the captured Desert Eagle. I could feel the pull as my biceps flexed with the effort of keeping the muzzle up. He risked turning his head to look at me then, revealing razored sideburns cut to emphasise the line of his cheekbones.

The surprise and anger flared briefly in his eyes, then died, replaced by a cold blankness that almost made me shiver. This man was a killer without doubt, and would be only too willing to prove it when I gave him the opportunity. There was no "if" about it.

He wasn't a bulky man. In fact, he was surprisingly slender under that big coat, which gave me the impression he was higher up the food chain than just hired muscle.

Not taking my eyes off him for a second, I indicated with the Desert Eagle that he should retreat a little way back down the corridor he'd just come out of. I was acutely aware that I'd been standing with my back to the dining hall doorway and was terribly exposed. If either of the men in there chose this moment to answer a call of nature and search for the bathroom, I was going to become the filling in a bad guy sandwich.

I gripped the huge gun in both hands with my arms out straight, keeping it high enough to bring into position fast if Sideburns made a move I didn't like the look of. As he backed away from the hall he never took his eyes off me once. The intensity of his gaze was unnerving. He was totally focused on me, waiting for that moment of weakness that he knew would come.

"OK sunshine," I said when we were out of earshot of the dining hall. "Just what the hell are you up to?"

His contempt was palpable. If I was important, it said, I would obviously know exactly what the game was. He shrugged, and spat out what could have been total gibberish in something that sounded a little like Russian. He might have been pretending that he didn't understand English, but the gleam in his eye told me a different story.

I raised my eyebrow and let the barrel of the gun drop a little.

"OK, if you insist on doing this the hard way," I said, conversationally so there was no way he could pick up the meaning just from my tone. "If I have to ask you again I'm going to put a bullet into your right thigh. With this cannon I'm almost certain to hit your femoral artery, in which case you will bleed out within minutes. Does that make things any clearer for you?"

Just for a fraction of a second, he hesitated. Whether it was because he genuinely believed I might carry out my threat, I wasn't sure. With a gun this big he must have known that if I did he'd most likely either die from the shock of losing his leg in the blast, or at best he'd face amputation. It seemed that his comprehension of both my words and their meaning was excellent. The reason he hesitated was because neither option appealed to him much.

"We're here to find the boy," he said reluctantly, his English heavily accented, but perfectly idiomatic.

Of course, the Russian kid.

"Where's the Major?"

He flicked his eyes back further along the corridor, in the direction of Gilby's study.

"OK," I said. "After you."

He balked at that, getting his second wind. After all, his courage had faltered for a moment and because of it he'd let himself be captured by a mere woman. Now his pride was goading him towards some reckless action to compensate. By my reckoning it made him roughly twice as dangerous.

I smiled at him, a thin smile, full of ice. "I know you will kill me if you can," I said, my voice low and strangely detached, so that it didn't sound like it belonged to me at all. "If stopping you from doing that means I have to kill you first, I won't hesitate, I promise you."

For a moment we eyed each other, then his gaze dropped away. I don't know whether it was the words or the smile that convinced him, but one or the other must have done the trick. He led me right up to the study door without trying any form of evasion.

We both paused there for a moment. Behind the door I could hear a mixture of voices I didn't recognise until Gilby's clipped tones filtered through.

"Who's armed in there?" I whispered to Sideburns. The contemptuous look he threw at me told me I should know better than to ask.

"OK," I murmured, "in a moment you're going to open the door and walk in." I returned that cool gaze

294

with one of my own, raked him with it. "Let's just hope you're not expendable — for both our sakes."

Again he thought about resisting, but I kept the gun hard in the small of his back. He turned the handle and gave the study door a nudge to swing it open.

We stepped into the room with me staying as close up behind Sideburns as I dared. My eyes instantly tracked the first person who reacted. He was off by the fireplace to my right. Bigger than Sideburns, and slower for the extra weight. I brought the gun out into plain sight as he reached for his own weapon. He was carrying an Uzi dangling by its shoulder strap and it took him a second to go for it. The sheer size of the Desert Eagle's distinctive, slightly triangular barrel made him falter.

Sideburns took advantage of my distraction to try and make a grab for the gun himself. I could have punched him, but the jacket he was wearing was heavy enough to cushion the blow. Besides, I was badly positioned to deliver anything that would have been effective, particularly considering the delicate state of my ribcage.

Instead I chose a move that required little more than balance and accuracy. I twisted out of his reach and stamped down sideways onto the outside of his right knee. Something structural inside the joint gave way with an audible crack.

The knee joint is a straightforward two-directional hinge mechanism. It has almost no lateral stability and that makes it especially vulnerable.

I knew I'd pulled a dirty move, one that owed more to street fighting than to martial arts, but I needed to do something that was guaranteed to drop him in a hurry. Even if it didn't, I could always outrun him afterwards. In the event, he went down faster than a South American football player, but letting out a genuine grunt of pain.

After the action came silence and immobility.

I stood there, breathing hard, with the gun up and steady, centred on the second bodyguard. He flicked his eyes to one of the other men in the room, but I didn't see what signal he received. It must have been in my favour, though, because he reluctantly surrendered the Uzi.

"That's probably a wise decision," Gilby said calmly. "I have no doubts that Miss Fox is more than capable of pulling the trigger. And she's certainly an excellent shot."

I flicked a glance in his direction, briefly taking in the whole scene. He and the two other men in the study were sitting around the desk and hadn't stirred during my arrival. The Major was showing little emotion on his lean face beyond the slightest hint of a smile.

To his left was a grey-haired man in thin wire-rimmed glasses and a good suit that he appeared to have slept in. He was staring at me with horrified disbelief. I knew his face, but momentarily couldn't place him.

I wasn't too surprised to find that the Major wasn't the one in the position of authority in the leather swivel chair behind the desk. That honour had been taken by a new player.

He was a big broad man with the look of a wrestler about him. His pinned-down shirt collar strained around a neck thick with muscle. His face, with its full lips and heavily hooded eyes, was unreadable.

"OK boys," I said to the two thugs, "let's have you two kneeling down facing the wall over there, feet crossed at the ankles, hands on your heads."

They did as they were told without enthusiasm. Sideburns showed a distinct reluctance for the idea until I persuaded him it was in his best interests. He ended up hunched sideways on the floor, trying to keep the weight off the knee I'd kicked.

When they were down I checked the Uzi, finding it fully stocked and ready to go. My hands worked automatically without a fumble, even though I barely glanced at them. I made sure I had everyone covered with the machine pistol while I took the magazine out of the Desert Eagle and checked that, too. It was filled with hollowpoints. As if something that calibre wasn't enough. Nice people I was dealing with.

The man behind the desk watched me do all this without speaking, keeping his hands still and in view. He didn't fidget and at no time did he show surprise or anger at my intrusion. When I was done he turned to Gilby.

"Very impressive, Major," he said, ignoring me completely. "I was not aware that you had any women on your staff." His deep voice rumbled up from somewhere in his chest, and he had a thick accent straight out of a Cold War thriller. He had a particular way of saying "women", like he usually regarded them as a commodity, something to be bought and sold.

Gilby smiled thinly, and now there was a touch of smugness about him. "Oh Miss Fox isn't staff." he said. "She's a pupil here, but her hidden talents are proving a constant source of surprise, as I'm sure you'll agree."

He put his hands on the arms of his chair to start to rise, but froze when I brought the Uzi up sharply.

"Sit down, Major," I said. "Nobody is going anywhere until I get some answers about what's going on here."

He stilled, affronted. "And what makes you think we're going to give you any?" he snapped back in that clipped voice he reserved for dressing downs and lectures.

I hefted my expanded arsenal. "I can think of a couple of reasons," I said. "But before we start I think you should at least introduce me to everyone. Herr Krauss I already recognise, of course," I added, motioning to the man in the rumpled suit.

It had finally clicked who he was and where I'd seen his picture before. Elsa had brought in photographs of Heidi Krauss and her father, Dieter for her presentation about the girl's kidnapping. So what was he doing here?

I flicked my attention to the third man. I remembered Sideburns's admission that they were here to find the boy, and Sean's briefing about the young Russian who'd been grabbed. The boy's bodyguard, I recalled, had to be identified from his dental records.

That probably accounted for the artillery. Was this man his father?

"Let me guess," I went on when nobody spoke. "You are another grieving parent here to reclaim your child — by force if necessary."

The man behind the desk inclined his head, allowing his heavy eyelids to close briefly as he did so. "You are very astute," he said. "I can see that you are someone who might be able to help me in this matter. Miss Fox, wasn't it?"

"That's right," I agreed. "And you are?"

The man smiled, a white bright smile. "My name is Gregor Venko," he said. "And the good Major here has kidnapped my son."

CHAPTER
TWENTY

I let out a low whistle and raised my eyebrow in Gilby's direction. "You are either a very brave or a very stupid man, Major," I said, "but right now I'm not sure which."

Having subsided back into his chair, the Major had gone still again. The kind of stillness only rage produces. I had a feeling my only possible ally in the room was changing his mind about who he would choose to shoot first if it came to it.

I glanced at Dieter Krauss, who was visibly unravelling in front of me.

"So what's your story, Herr Krauss?"

"*Please*," he said. He twisted his hands together in his lap, sounding close to tears. His high forehead was shiny with sweat. "You don't know what you're doing. He will kill my daughter!"

"I see," I said. I waited half a beat before asking, "Who will?"

He floundered for a moment, then folded into himself and closed his mouth with a snap, as though he realised that he'd already said far too much, but just hadn't been able to help himself. Fear jumped in his eyes. Flames behind glass. Gilby and Venko, meanwhile, were trying to outdo each other with the Sphinx impersonations.

"I don't suppose you'd care to enlighten me?" I said to Venko.

He considered my request, weighed it up carefully. The fact that I had a gun on him was of no consequence. "I am a businessman, Miss Fox," he rumbled at last. His voice had the projection of a Shakespearean actor, designed to be clearly audible even in the cheapest seats. "Let us just say that we each of us have a product which the other desires. I am here to propose a simple exchange."

Out of the corner of my eye I caught Sideburns's companion shifting stealthily. Without taking my eyes away from Venko's I stepped sideways far enough to prod the bodyguard in the back of his head with the barrel of the Desert Eagle. I made sure I did it just hard enough to bump his nose against the wall.

"Ah, ah," I said. "No cheating."

I moved back to my original position again. "I hear what you're saying," I told Venko, "but I'm afraid I'm inclined to believe that you were intending to leave without paying up your half of the bargain." I tilted my head towards the two men kneeling. "For a businessman you travel with *unusual* associates."

Venko shrugged, momentarily causing his neck to disappear entirely. "My line of business often takes me to dangerous places," he said. He still had his hands flat on the desk in front of him. Not a coward, but too experienced to want to make me nervous, either. There were gold heavyweight rings on three fingers. "These men are simply my insurance. To enable me to arrive and depart without hindrance."

I stared at him without blinking for several seconds then said, "Not very good, are they?"

He laughed. A deep belly laugh, a burst of genuine amusement despite the tension, or maybe because of it. "No, you are quite right," he said. "But this is something that will be remedied very shortly, I assure you."

I had the feeling that when a man like Gregor Venko terminated your employment, your cards came pinned to a wreath.

Venko had tired of sparring with me. His deceptively sleepy eyes flicked across to Gilby and any trace of humour faded from his features.

"So Major, can we come to some mutually agreeable arrangement in this matter? You, more than anyone, must appreciate my distress as a father at having my son taken from me in such violent circumstances."

The deliberate tone set the hairs up on the back of my neck.

Gilby stared at him coldly for a moment, forcing himself to relax even though it clearly cost him to do so. He crossed his legs, taking his time to make sure the crease in his twill trousers was perfectly aligned.

When he didn't immediately throw Venko's offer back in his face Dieter Krauss half-lifted from his chair in protest. "What are you talking about?" he cried. "Valentine, for God's sake. You're not seriously thinking of trusting this — this murderer?"

"Shut up, Dieter," Gilby said softly, and the other man fell silent as though he'd shouted. "Just what do you know of my son?"

Venko met, matched, and maybe even outplayed the Major's stare. "That he followed you into the army and was blown up by an Iraqi mine," he said calmly. "I understand you were present at the time. Very unfortunate."

My God, I thought.

"My family is my business," Gilby said, still quietly, but there was a brittle quality to his voice now. "I'd thank you not to mention the subject again. That is not the issue here."

"Of course." Venko nodded, allowing his eyelids to droop briefly. To cover what? Triumph as the barb went home? He opened them again and returned his gaze to me. I braced under the force of it. "So, Miss Fox, you are the one with the guns here. How do you propose that we solve this unpleasantness?"

"*Solve it*? We don't have to solve it!" Krauss squeaked, flapping his hand towards me. "You've just said yourself that she's the one with the gun. She will shoot you if you do not give me my daughter!"

I raised my eyebrows a fraction at that. "I hate to break this to you," I said, "but things may not be quite so black and white. I saw at least two men patrolling the outside of the Manor, plus another two who have the domestic staff held at gunpoint in the dining hall. I shouldn't imagine they're the only ones. The moment I start shooting anyone I expect they'll come running."

"Quite so," Venko agreed, taking the possibility of his own demise with graceful equanimity. "So, it would appear that we have something of a stand-off situation, no? But, this can be easily resolved," he went on. "Give me my son now, and don't try to prevent us leaving, and your daughter will be released within twenty-four hours."

It would have been an impressive speech, cold and commanding, but there was just the faintest suggestion of a tremor underlying Venko's sonorous tones.

"Please," Krauss begged, pouncing on the words regardless. "I just want my little girl. I'll pay your ransom, anything! I just want her back. I didn't know what they —"

"No deal," Gilby sliced across him curtly. He sat back, calmer now, smoother, more confident, and I knew he'd seen that tiny waver too. "Release the girl now or no deal."

"You are hardly in a position to bargain, Major."

Gilby cocked his head in my direction. "Neither are you," he said.

Venko leaned forwards, resting his thick forearms on the desk. The cuffs of his wool cashmere overcoat rode up to reveal a gold Rolex plastered with diamonds. He stared straight at the Major as he spoke, trying to hypnotise him into capitulation by a sheer act of will.

"Give me my son. You have my word that Heidi will be released unharmed."

Gilby gave a short, harsh bark of laughter. "Not good enough," he snapped. "He isn't here. It will take a little time to retrieve him. And even if he was, Europe is

304

littered with corpses as testament to the value of *your word*."

"Then, indeed, we have a problem." Venko sat back and just for a second he allowed his frustration and his anger to show through in a swirling heaving mass. Under that unruffled surface, it would seem, the currents were as diverse as they were deadly.

Ah well, in for a penny . . .

"You're approaching this from the wrong position, all of you," I said. Three heads turned slowly in my direction. I think I preferred it when their concentrated spite was focused on each other. I took a deep breath and kept going. "What do you all want to happen here?"

"I just want my daughter," Krauss said, sounding close to tears.

"And I want my son," Venko said, expressionless.

"I want the safe return of Heidi, and a guarantee of the future safety of my school and its remaining personnel," Gilby said, with a narrowed glance at Venko which I ignored.

"OK," I said carefully. "Well, as far as I can see none of these demands preclude any of the others. We know where we want to go. The question is, how do we get there with the least amount of blood being spilled?"

Venko suddenly switched on a big smile. "Bravo," he said, all jolly as though his flash of steel was just an imagining. "You see, Major. All it needed was the logic of a woman."

"Wonderful," Gilby drawled acidly. "So, Miss Fox, how do you propose that we achieve these aims?"

I turned to Venko. "You leave now, and you pull your men out with you. You return here in twenty-four hours, with Heidi. By which time the Major will have retrieved the boy from wherever it is he's got him stashed. You make the exchange and you leave. No tricks, no ambushes, no double-crosses. And no retribution."

Silence followed the outlining of my plan. If I'm honest I hadn't expected anything else. At least they didn't laugh it straight out of court.

Venko smiled again, rather sadly this time, and shook his head a little. "Impossible," he said. "You have good heart, Miss Fox, but what guarantee do I have that the Major will deliver my son?"

"He'll deliver." My chin came up. "On that you have *my* word."

He regarded me, brooding, unconvinced.

"What's your son called, Mr Venko?" I asked.

"Ivan," he said, a father's pride putting roll and drama into it. "His name is Ivan."

I nodded. "And how old is Ivan?"

Venko hesitated before he answered, as though the question was some kind of a trick. "He is just twenty," he said at last.

"I see," I said, choosing my own words with care. "And how would you feel if Ivan never lived to be twenty-one because *you* couldn't bring yourself to trust me?"

Venko stared at me again, as though his gaze alone could bore through the outer layers of skin and skull and lay my brains out on a slab looking for the dark cancerous stain of lies.

I forced myself not to flinch under the onslaught, just stood quiet with the Desert Eagle resting in my hands, and the Uzi hanging from my shoulder. Difficult to take the word of someone who forces you to listen to it at gunpoint, but Venko didn't seem to mind.

Eventually, long after I'd given up hope, he favoured me with an austere smile. "Very well, Miss Fox, we will leave now and we will bring the girl here at ten o'clock tomorrow." He stood, the cashmere coat closing around him with the silent floating grace of old-fashioned velvet theatre curtains after the last encore.

He moved out from behind the desk, not much taller than my own height, but twice as wide and barrel-chested. I backed up as he came past me, kept my finger on the trigger as he waved his disgraced bodyguards to their feet with a brusque, "Come, we go."

Sideburns would have liked to have made a bigger production out of getting to his feet, but a glance at his boss told him sympathy would not be forthcoming. In fact, staying as invisible as possible was his best chance for survival. He didn't even have the courage to demand the return of his personalised gun.

Just as they reached the study doorway Venko halted and turned back, encompassing all of us in a visual sweep that singed where it touched. It finished up on me and I could feel it burning.

"Just remember, Miss Fox," he said, sombre, "what I risk by trusting you. Yes, I will return the girl to her father, just as I wish to have my son returned to me. I will keep my side of this arrangement." His voice roughened then, grew harsh with the emotion that vibrated through him.

"But let me promise you one thing," he went on. "If anything happens to Ivan I will raze this building to the ground and make it my life's work to destroy you — all of you — and hunt down what is left of your families. I hope I do not regret making this bargain with you, Miss Fox."

And with that cheery farewell he and his entourage stalked out of the study.

"So do I," I murmured, watching them go. "So do I."

CHAPTER
TWENTY-ONE

"Here," the Major said, splashing a decent couple of fingers of brandy into a lead crystal tumbler and placing it into my trembling hands. "I think you need it."

"Thanks," I only managed to keep my voice steady with an effort. "I'd rather have a single malt, though, if you have it."

"No," he said. That familiar arrogant tone was back, but he almost smiled. "Drink what you're given, madam."

Venko had gone. His men had gone. Dieter had gone, too. He'd allowed the Major to lead him out of the study. I'd heard him protesting in staccato German all the way along the corridor.

I was left sitting in the chair Gilby had so recently vacated while he went to calm the staff and organise them into a makeshift security patrol. The ease with which Venko and his men had walked into the Manor and taken control of it had obviously galled. The instructors and pupils were all still down at the assault course. Run ragged, but oblivious. No doubt there would be time later to explain what had happened here to those of them who needed to know. I had a feeling

Gilby wasn't going to make this invasion common knowledge.

So I sat by myself in a room made more empty by the sudden absence of violent men, and tried to stop the cracks joining up and becoming tears. By the time he came back I'd more or less got them papered over enough to fool him. Maybe for a couple of seconds.

He closed the study door and looked at me for a while before moving over to the drinks' cabinet. A long thorough inspection like I was a racehorse none of the pundits had fancied much, but who'd somehow put on an unexpected spurt at the finish.

Me, I *felt* like a racehorse who'd run out of their distance and damned near burst my lungs to do it. I was exhausted.

Holding the sheer weight of the Desert Eagle out and ready for that length of time had overstressed my biceps where they blended with the deltoid muscle at the front of my shoulders. With every movement I was aware of the stretched and torn fibres. Even lifting the glass was painful.

My sternum, which had been keeping a low profile, was throbbing like crazy. Breathing hurt. Sitting hurt. Now the adrenaline was slowly bleeding from my system I felt thoroughly second-hand.

The Major poured himself a brandy and took it to the other side of his desk. I'd put the Uzi and the hand cannon down onto the surface and he moved them aside with a frown of disapproval, like he was worried about scratches. Then he sat and looked at me some more.

310

A sudden thought rocked me. I sat up so fast I nearly slopped the contents of my glass into my lap.

"Major, please tell me that you *do* have Ivan to trade, don't you?"

"Of course," he said, not seeming in the least surprised by the question.

The relief had me nearly sagging back into my chair. "Where is he?"

"Somewhere close. Somewhere safe," Gilby said, short, sharp. "Even my own men don't know his location." To his credit he didn't point out that I was considerably further down the chain of command and I didn't press him. There would have been little point.

"That wasn't the first time you've been in this kind of situation was it, Miss Fox?" Gilby said then.

I took a slug of brandy, trying not to wince as it ripped down the inside of my throat like bleach. Whatever the Major siphoned into his decanters, it certainly wasn't a five-star Cognac.

"Not exactly," I agreed. "No."

He nodded slowly. "I thought not," he said. "Venko isn't a man who would allow himself to be held captive by a woman unless he believed absolutely that she would kill him." He paused. "You have that air about you."

If only you knew . . .

"Yeah, well," I muttered into my glass. "It's a knack."

"Yes," the Major said. "Yes, I suppose you could say it is."

I looked round a little then, tried to pull it together, and said, "Where's Herr Krauss?"

"I've persuaded Dieter to let me handle things. It's going to be difficult enough tomorrow without having to cope with an emotionally unstable civilian."

"You can hardly blame him. The poor bloke's obviously frantic."

"Yes," Gilby agreed, his voice giving away neither sympathy nor irritation. "But that makes him unpredictable. A liability."

I took another gulp of brandy. It seemed to be improving as I got into it. Maybe it had just burned away all the more vulnerable taste buds.

"So what's the connection between you and Krauss?" I asked.

For a moment I thought the Major was just going to tell me to mind my own damned business, then I saw his gaze skim over the weaponry on the desk top. If I *had* minded my own business. If I hadn't interfered . . .

"He owns fifty per cent of this place," he said at last, circling a hand to indicate the Manor as a whole. "He bought in about six months ago." And having decided to be frank, he really pushed the boat out. "Got me out of a bit of a hole cash-wise, if you must know," he added stiffly, burying his nose in his glass. "It's only since then that I've been able to pay the staff decent wages."

Talking about money was a subject the Major clearly found rather vulgar. It was probably how he'd managed to get himself into a financial mess in the first place.

Six months. The words suddenly clicked. Six months ago was about the time that the money Madeleine uncovered had started arriving in the school's accounts.

Gilby had re-equipped, put in a new heating system, hired some decent cooks. And once he'd done that he'd bought himself a flash car.

It fitted, I couldn't deny. Better still, it had the ring of truth about it.

"So when Gregor Venko kidnapped Krauss's daughter, you naturally offered to kidnap Venko's son to get her back?"

"I didn't offer, but Dieter was convinced that unless we had some kind of sword of Damocles hanging over Venko's head, he would kill Heidi. He was probably right." Gilby glanced at me. "But good God, woman, it was a ludicrous idea. Venko's organisation across eastern Europe makes the Mafia look like the Women's Institute."

"My mother's in the Women's Institute," I said drily. "They're a pretty tough bunch."

I was rewarded by another near-miss of a smile. "I didn't know they had a swat team."

"You be amazed," I said, "what she can do with knitting needles."

The smile broke out fully. He paused for a moment, then shook his head. "What the hell are you really doing here, Charlie?" he asked, and there was no anger, just a kind of tired amusement.

I hesitated for a moment, drained the last of the brandy, made my decision.

"I came," I said bluntly, "to find out if you'd murdered Kirk Salter."

That shook him. He sat up straight, the fatigue momentarily dropping away. "Good God," he murmured.

"We knew there was something about you." His eyes slid away unfocused into thought, then flicked back to my face, turning shrewd. "And if I had?"

I shrugged and found that shrugging hurt, too. "Find some evidence and take it home," I said. "I'm not here on a vengeance kick. Hell, I didn't even like the bloke."

"So why did you come?"

"I made a promise," I said, thinking of Sean. And because the Major seemed to be waiting for more than that, I added, a little reluctantly, "Kirk saved my life once."

"I see," Gilby said. I noticed his eyes had shifted to my throat, where the scar lay hidden under a high-neck sweatshirt.

Sean had once made the mistaken assumption that the injury dated from the same time as Kirk's opportune intervention. I hadn't corrected him, either. Maybe it was just easier that way.

"So," I said carefully, "are you going to tell me what happened to him?"

There was silence while the Major rose, walked over to the drinks cabinet and refilled his brandy glass. He turned and waved the decanter at me, but I shook my head. There was only so much of that stuff I could take and still hang on to the lining of my oesophagus.

When he was seated again he said, "I'd been following the kidnappings since they started, so when Heidi was snatched I already had a pretty good idea that Gregor Venko was the man behind the operation. I also knew that Heidi's chances of survival were very poor." He allowed his distaste to show through. "The man's a monster."

I watched him sample his drink. He saw me watching and set the glass aside, as though he'd had enough already. "Anyway, I had Dieter going ballistic for me to do something, so I pulled in a few favours with contacts in the security services. Getting anywhere near Venko himself was going to be impossible without months of preparation, but I did manage to find out the location of his son, Ivan."

He scanned me for any sign that I considered the targeting of Gregor's only child made him a monster, too. I kept my face neutral.

"Taking him seemed the logical thing to do at the time." He gave a wry smile. "Perhaps if I'd had the chance to think things through more I would have hesitated, but I didn't. We had less than a week to put a team together. Salter was here when Dieter arrived, overheard enough to know what was going on and volunteered immediately."

There was a hint of something close to admiration in the Major's voice as he reached for his drink again. "I was glad to have him," he muttered fiercely. "Damned good soldier."

"So what happened?"

"I'm not entirely sure," Gilby admitted. "We had a plan of attack. Not a foolproof one, by any means, but a good plan nonetheless. Somewhere along the line somebody blew it. We were compromised. It was a miracle we made it out with so few casualties and still managed to achieve our objective."

"And Kirk was one of those casualties?"

The Major lifted his head and looked straight through me, his eyes blank to everything but the recall. "He was last man out," he agreed. "Told us he'd cover our withdrawal, but the field of fire they put down was incredible. They were using machine pistols and just emptying magazine after magazine at us. Made the Gulf look like a picnic." He shook his head, grim-faced at the memory. "We got him into the truck, did everything we could, but our medic was injured too. Salter didn't make it."

Our medic? Ah, so that was the problem with O'Neill.

"So you dumped Kirk's body in the forest," I said. I didn't think I had any feelings about that, one way or the other. I was mildly surprised therefore, to hear the contempt in my voice. "Nice way to treat a *damned good soldier*."

Gilby ducked his head in acknowledgement of the jibe, but he didn't flinch. "I agree," he said. "Officially, we couldn't explain to the authorities what we'd been up to, so we left him. It was a tactical decision, but not an easy one, I can assure you. Making choices like that is one of the burdens of command." It should have sounded pompous, but somehow it didn't.

I sat in silence for a while. So there it was. The gospel of Kirk's death, according to Gilby. If I believed him then my work here was done. And if I had any sense I would report back to Sean and get the hell out of there before the shooting started.

I didn't even have to explain my departure to the other students. They'd all heard Todd telling me I was finished. They were all fully expecting me just to pack up and leave . . .

But then there was just the small matter of my promise to Gregor Venko. A promise bound by blood, in all its forms.

"Who were the men in the Peugeot?" I said suddenly. "The ones who ambushed us in the forest. Were they Venko's men?"

"Father, or son?"

"Either," I returned, just as succinctly, "or both."

"Son. His bodyguards, I believe. I rather think Venko sent them to try and intimidate or force us to give him back without having to use him to trade for Heidi. It's only after their attempts failed that he's come prepared to make a deal. It would explain why we haven't come under significant fire until now."

I remembered again Blakemore's words to the Peugeot driver. "*Try this shit again and next time we send you the kid's ears.*" It all made such perfect sense now. How would they have talked *that* one away to a man like Gregor Venko?

"And now Gregor's decided to handle things personally," I murmured.

Gilby inclined his head. "As you've seen."

"So if that's the case," I said slowly, "who was behind Blakemore's death?"

"That was an accident," Gilby said quickly. Much too quickly.

I met the Major's gaze level, held it there. He had the grace to break away first. "You looked at the scene as much as I did — probably more. The fact he was hit before he went over isn't in doubt," I said. And because the need to know was deep and biting, I added with an edge dipped in acid, "And now you've lost another man. Your forces are being depleted, Major, at a faster rate than you can sustain."

The hit was a direct one, but the response wasn't quite what I expected. "Oh, Mr Rebanks isn't lost," he said tightly, a flush forming along his pale cheekbones. "Although in my opinion he more than deserves to be dead." Shock kept me silent, and my silence pulled more out of the Major than questions would have done.

"Dealing weapons from *my* school," Gilby gritted out with quiet vehemence, more to himself than to me. "Dealing them to the very men who would use them against us!" He sucked in a breath, fought for control. After a few moments his colour began to subside, calming as his temper ebbed.

Rebanks was still alive. Thank God for that!

"Oh yes," he went on bitterly, "he deserves to be dead." He looked up sharply then and I can't have hidden the emotions that were rioting through my mind.

Astonishment and disbelief came and went across the Major's own features. "Good God," he said softly. "It was you." As he said it another realisation came riding in on the back of the first. "You thought you'd killed him," he said, and I saw him take another mental step back.

318

"Yes," I said. There wasn't much else I could say. I could only hope to distract him. "What's happened to Rebanks?"

Gilby gave a grunt. "This place was built to house an extensive wine cellar," he said, briefly showing his teeth. "Mr Rebanks is languishing in new underground quarters until I've cooled down enough to decide exactly what to do with him. You probably did me a favour there." His voice was mild. Only the expression on his face told me he might be lying.

"I wasn't the only one at the armoury last night," I said quickly. "Somebody else set that damned fire alarm off. You do know you've got the German security services on your tail, don't you?"

"I couldn't ignore the possibility," he acknowledged, but his face darkened at this new infringement on his territory. "They indicated that they would allow me to act with autonomy in this matter until Heidi was released. I should have known they wouldn't play by the rules."

Startled, I asked, "They *know* you've kidnapped Ivan?"

The Major inclined his head reluctantly. "Not officially, of course, but yes, they know we've got him, all right. In the manner of governments the world over," he added, his voice sour, "they're more than happy to overlook it — providing I hand him over when the girl is safe."

I sat up straight, feeling my scalp prickle with apprehension, ignoring the aching protest of all corners of my body. "Does that mean you've no intention of going through with this exchange?" I said carefully.

Something like a spasm twisted across the Major's face. He passed a hand across it, then let it drop into his lap, his shoulders rounding in defeat.

"God knows," he said. He tried a smile but couldn't really raise it. "The words rock and hard place spring to mind. I'm down on manpower and running out of options." He eyed me again. "You seem to be the one with all the answers today," he said with heavy irony. "Any suggestions?"

It was thrown down carelessly, so he could snatch it back without dishonour, but underneath I knew the Major wasn't joking. He was deadly serious.

For a few moments I sat without speaking, then said, "Have you heard of a man called Sean Meyer?"

"Of course," Gilby said promptly. The name had resonance for him, I saw. It changed things. "After that business in Colombia last spring, how could I not? The whole industry was buzzing with it."

I'd no idea what had gone on in Colombia, or what Sean's involvement might have been, but now didn't seem the time to ask.

Instead I said, "Well Sean's the reason I'm here. He asked me to come and find out what happened to Kirk."

He looked surprised at that, and not a little sceptical. "But why, of all the highly-trained personnel undoubtedly at his disposal, did someone as good as Meyer choose *you* for such a mission?"

320

I shrugged, and learned that I hadn't loosened up much since the last time I'd tried it. "Sean was one of my instructors in the army," I said. "He felt that someone from outside the industry, as you put it, would stand a better chance of passing unnoticed."

The Major said, "Ah," and the way he said it spoke volumes. I remembered, too late perhaps, our conversation after the abortive first-aid sim, and the excuse I'd given then for leaving the services. I knew I couldn't deny the link he'd just made without it seeming that I did protest too much. Better to keep quiet and hope I could gloss over the significance.

"Sean's here," I said now. At Gilby's raised eyebrow, I added, "In Germany. I can give you his number. Call him."

Still he hesitated. I leaned forwards in my seat, picked up a pen and scrawled the digits across the corner of his virgin blotter.

"Look, you've just said yourself that he's good. Let's face it — against Gregor Venko's private army you're going to need all the help you can get."

"Including you?" the Major asked, and his voice was wry again.

"Including me," I concurred.

I got to my feet, trying not to stagger, trying not to groan out loud. Movement outside the window caught my eye. When I looked, in the distance I saw the first of the pupils beginning to straggle back from the assault course.

The Major caught my distracted gaze and turned his head, following their progress across the grounds.

"You might have a bit of a problem with Todd about keeping me on," I admitted, somewhat belatedly. "That's the reason I'm back early. He thinks you're going to send me packing because I'm injured."

The Major turned back to me, raked dubious eyes up and down. "Injured?"

I explained briefly about my fall from the rope bridge and the cracked breastbone such a move had exacerbated.

"Well, I wouldn't have guessed, but perhaps it might be best if you weren't in this fight," he said, but there was no enthusiasm in his tone. "You've done enough."

"Oh no," I shot back, fast and fierce. "I'm the one who gave Gregor my word on this. It's my neck on the line just as much as yours. I hardly think he's the kind of man who'd accept a sick note from my mother if I don't show. I'm in this now, whether you like it or not, and I'll see it through."

For an agonising few seconds Gilby hesitated, then he nodded slowly. "All right, Miss Fox," he said and, more purposeful, "leave Mr Todd to me."

I started for the door. If I could manage to break into a jog up the stairs I might even be able to snatch the bathroom before Elsa and Jan got back. I wasn't banking on it, though.

"Oh, Miss Fox." The Major's voice caught me when I'd nearly made my exit. "If what I've just seen is anything to go by, I'd rather have you when you're injured than half the men I've worked with when they're fully fit."

He was back on top, his voice clipped, shoulders straight. Any hint of weariness was gone. He was already reaching for the phone to dial the number I'd given him for Sean.

In his eyes I read a new determination. For the first time since Gregor Venko had left that study, I could see that Gilby really believed he might win this.

I hoped to God he was right.

CHAPTER
TWENTY-TWO

Even with a head start, I didn't make it to the shower first. Elsa beat me to it easily without having to resort to any undignified elbowing techniques. While she was in there Jan collared me with all the concentrated determination of an average domestic cat faced with a wounded sparrow.

"Come on then, Charlie, what happened when you got back here?" she demanded. "Give me all the gory details!"

For a moment I stared stupidly at her, thinking she somehow knew about Gregor Venko's armed invasion. It took a couple of seconds for my brain to click round into the right gear.

Actually, I thought she was being thoroughly nosy considering how closed-mouthed she was about her own motives for being on the course, but I refrained from saying so. In truth, I suppose I was glad of the opportunity to try out the rhythm of my concocted story on her before I faced the third degree from Elsa. The German woman, I'd discovered, was not easy to lie to. Maybe I just found the fact that she'd been in the police instinctively intimidating.

So, I told Jan how Major Gilby had decided to exercise his executive power and let me stay on, as he had done when McKenna had concussed himself during the ambush in the forest. It was a recall of a conversation Gilby and I had never spoken, but I was pretty sure it was what he would have said, if he'd thought of it at the time.

I told her how it was up to me to prove I was fit enough to complete the course, how there'd be no quarter asked nor given. There was a certain ring of truth to that last bit, bearing in mind the kind of stick I just knew I was going to have to take from Todd, but still she frowned at the rest of it. I shrugged and didn't try too hard to persuade her. I was too tired to put up much of a fight, in any case.

My near-indifference must have worked, though, because when Elsa appeared, her wet hair combed back flat from her face, it was Jan who told her I was staying, with hardly a hint of cynicism in her voice. Elsa raised an enquiring eyebrow in my direction and I repeated the bones of my story for her benefit.

When I was through Elsa regarded me gravely for a few moments, then nodded. "Good," was all she said, almost cryptic. "It is right that you should be here."

In light of the morning's events, that could have been read in any number of ways.

The three of us went down to lunch together. When I walked in to the dining room I swear the conversation dried up in direct response. As I walked across to the hot buffet I was self-consciously aware of the eyes following my progress. I was glad of the show of

325

solidarity from the two women flanking me, whatever their private doubts might have been.

I received a few cheery nods of encouragement, though. Declan gave me a, "Good on you, girl." Craddock's reaction was one of relief rather than pleasure, and I realised that he'd been feeling guilty that he'd let me fall in the first place.

I was more wary about the behaviour of the domestic staff than of anyone else, but fortunately they seemed unaware that I'd played any particular role in the proceedings. I don't know exactly what it was that the Major said to them after Venko's thugs had gone, but if you knew where to look and did so very closely you could just about spot that they'd all had the fright of their lives.

Now, I held my plate out and Ronnie slapped a couple of slices of roast beef onto it, his movements jerky, his normally good-natured whistling silenced. When I glanced round I saw that all of them were much the same, but very few of the pupils seemed to have noticed anything was amiss. It's amazing how often people dismiss waiters and porters and cooks without really looking at them.

Elsa, Jan, and I sat together at the end of a half-occupied table. There seemed to be more empty spaces than filled seats down here now and I tried to work out how many had left the course so far. I wondered if the Major calculated his costs on the basis that half the students would drop out before the end of the two weeks.

The doors opened and the instructors came stalking in. I could see straight away that Gilby had filled them in and they hadn't liked what he'd had to say. Some of them less than others. O'Neill was glowering at everybody in general and — when his eye lighted on the three of us women — at us in particular.

"Looks like you've ruffled a few feathers, Charlie," Romundstad commented from along the table. I gave him a wan smile. *Oh yes, Tor, but not quite in the way you're expecting.*

In fact, I wasn't sure that Gilby's pride would let him tell his men about my intervention, but it wasn't until Todd swung by the end of our table that I found out for sure.

The bulky phys instructor paused so close to my chair I had to lean back slightly and crane my neck to look up at him. His whole body seemed to be vibrating with anger.

"So what did you have to do to get him to let you stay, Fox?" he muttered, his voice tight and nasty. "Give the old man a blow job?"

I should have kept my mouth shut and my head down, I know, but in twenty-four hours Gregor Venko was going to come in here all guns blazing, and if he didn't get his son back there was going to be a bloodbath. In the light of that I couldn't find it in me to be diplomatic to the likes of Todd.

"Why?" I shot back. "Is that how you got him to take *you* on?"

The silence arrived along the table on a gasp of surprise that quickly turned to a splutter of astonished amusement.

"Ah now, Mr Todd," Declan said almost gently, shaking his head, "but you surely asked for that one."

The flush started just above Todd's shirt collar and rose up past his ears like coloured smoke. He opened his mouth to drench me in vitriol, but the dining hall doors swung open again, and suddenly nobody was paying him any attention.

Major Gilby walked in, smart and upright. By his shoulder was Sean Meyer.

I told myself that I'd known Sean was coming. That I was the one who'd told the Major to call him, but the shock of his arrival still hit me like a mental and physical double blow. My brain reeled even as my body reacted, prickling my scalp, tightening my stomach, making my shins itch.

I could hardly believe it was less than three weeks since we'd sat together in that little country pub in Yorkshire and he'd asked me to go to Germany. It was like none of the events of last year had ever happened and we were back in the army again, with all the baggage that implied.

It didn't help that Sean was wearing the old familiar garb, or something so close to it as to be almost indistinguishable. He had on a khaki T-shirt because he never had felt the cold, and neatly pressed camouflage trousers that sat snug around his narrow hips, secured by the same webbing belt.

He'd even abandoned the expensive Breitling somewhere along the way. Instead he'd retrieved his plain battered old watch with the leather cover that snapped over the face. It was the sight of that watch, more than anything else, which sent a shiver through me.

I recalled Madeleine telling me that Sean was coming to Germany, but I'd never actually got around to asking her about it. Why would he bring an old watch with him other than because he knew he was likely to be going into combat?

Now he strolled into the room managing to convey the impression the Major was merely preceding him, rather than that he was following. He allowed his eyes to skate over the occupants with that same old flat scrutiny, the one that had so terrified me back then.

His gaze passed over me just once. It was cold, indifferent, giving away no hint that he knew me at all, but I couldn't prevent the stab of remembered fear.

Even after we'd spent that first breathtaking weekend together, and I'd returned to camp dazed and not a little staggered by the depth of the experience, Sean had not allowed his control to slip, had not changed in his outward behaviour towards me. Most of the time, at any rate.

Just occasionally, when we were alone together, or out of sight and earshot of anyone else, he'd launched one of those slow-burning smiles at me, or touched my face. I'd found those tiny unexpected gestures, coming after such a rigid adhesion to protocol, quite devastating in their erotic effect.

And the next time we'd had the opportunity to be together, without fear of interruption or discovery, the release of that long over-wound tension had been both explosive and profound.

I'd fallen for him utterly, without restraint, so that when he seemingly abandoned me I found I'd kept nothing in reserve to sustain me. Looking back, it was a wonder I survived the ordeal.

Now the Major took Sean straight through the middle of us and up onto the dais where the instructors were giving him the same suspicious appraisal as the students. He weathered their inspection with easy contempt. No defiance, just indifference. I know what I am, his attitude said, and I don't really give a damn what you choose to make of me.

Gilby turned to face us. By this time he didn't really need to call for silence, but the impresario in him meant he paused a moment anyway.

"If I might have your attention for a moment," he said, needlessly, "I'd like to introduce a new instructor."

Sean stood alongside him, hands low on his hips, eyes raking over us as though in search of weakness. The students shifted in their seats and kept their gaze fastened safely on the Major.

"This is Mr Meyer," Gilby went on. "Those of you who've taken an interest in the close protection world will undoubtedly be aware of his reputation. We've been lucky enough to secure his services at short notice to come and join our team for the remainder of this course. I hope you'll do your best to impress him with the skills you've already learned."

Gilby was nervous of Sean, I realised with surprise. If not actually afraid of him.

Sean stepped forwards and nodded briefly to the Major, who relinquished control without a murmur, like we were watching the arrival of a new alpha wolf in the pack.

"Good afternoon," Sean said. It was as much of an introduction as he was going to give. "We'll be picking up your unarmed combat training right away after lunch. You can forget everything you've achieved so far because now you're going to have to prove how good you are all over again." He paused, looked around the still faces, then added grimly, "The bad news is you're going to have to prove it to me."

I'd heard him speak those words before. Exactly those words.

I told myself that I'd been through this before, that I knew what to expect, but I found myself unconvinced. The time and distance since the last time did nothing to make me fear the prospect any less.

I suspect that most of the students — the ones who hadn't heard of Sean, at any rate — thought he was much too full of himself. Until we started the lesson, that is.

For openers Sean set up a free-for-all scenario where he picked Declan as his principal and told the rest of us to try and get to him, any way we liked. It was a walkabout situation, a packed crowd, common enough. The only difference was that instead of just one of us being an assassin or a simple nutcase, all of us were.

It was a brave gambit, but one I'd seen Sean play before. It was designed to expose the chancers, the ones who thought they'd show what a big man they were by going in hard, aiming for damage. Those with that kind of macho temperament could rarely resist the temptation.

Sean dealt with all our efforts with the kind of casual grace that was an innate part of him. Nobody came close to grabbing hold of Declan, and after a few minutes the Irishman was grinning at the increasing wildness of our attempts and the apparently careless ease with which they were foiled.

Where people went in quietly, Sean repulsed them the same way, but where others tried to hurt him he responded with instant violence, a mirror of their own aggression.

Sex didn't matter, he made no distinction. When Jan went for a nasty armlock, he flipped the positions and jerked her up short and tight with a painful lock of his own. He held her just long enough for her to recognise that he knew what she'd been trying to do, then released her.

After fifteen minutes of failure, Sean called a halt.

"OK, that wasn't bad," he said calmly. "But now it's my turn."

A ripple of disquiet ran through the group. It was well justified, as we were soon to discover. For the remainder of the lesson he took on the role of attacker, calling forwards and defeating one after another of the students in their role as bodyguard. He made the small seem weak, the big seem merely clumsy. And he made everybody seem painfully slow.

By the time the clock above the doorway was within a few minutes of time up he'd gone through just about all of us, except me. I stayed slightly back, grateful for the respite, assuming that Gilby must have warned him about my excursion on the assault course.

And so, I was totally unprepared for what was to come.

Sean finished evading Hofmann's overreached defence, turned slowly, and his gaze landed squarely on me.

"You," he said. "Charlie, isn't it? Step forward and let's see how you get on."

No, Sean, I prayed silently, *don't do this to me*. But, with limbs that felt leaden, I complied, moving onto the crashmat. He was staring at me with that unfathomable gaze, face set.

"So, Charlie, I'm a threat to your principal, you're between the two of us." He smiled, but I felt no more reassured. He spread his arms, so arrogant that he needed to ready no defence against me. "Come on then," he taunted. "Come and do your thing. Stop me."

For a moment I met Sean's eyes. Why was he doing this? So I'd spilled the beans to Gilby, but surely if he hadn't wanted to be here, on the inside, he would have refused to come? What did he have to gain by picking me out like this?

Sean was so difficult to read accurately at the best of times, but now he was impossible. The other trainees stood and shuffled their feet. A few of the blokes were grinning like they were watching a pit bull terrier who'd been unexpectedly matched against a toy poodle.

Before I could form a plan, Sean lunged forwards. I saw the blow coming, but did nothing to avoid it. I guess a part of me wanted to know how far he was prepared to go with this charade.

I soon found out.

A moment later I was levering myself off the mat and wiping a trickle of blood away from the corner of my mouth. If looks could kill, they would have been zipping Sean into a body bag right about that point.

"Come on, Charlie. Your principal's dead now. I've just disposed of you and I've stuck a knife in his guts. I let you out on the job and you'll be dead inside a week. Get up. Do it again."

I made it to my feet slowly and took up a stance. Going down the first time had sparked my ribs into grumbling complaint. I'd no desire for a repeat performance, but I'd no idea of the game plan Sean had agreed with Gilby. Until he'd brought me up to speed I knew I was going to have to play by the rules I'd agreed. The injustice of it burned.

Sean came at me again. This time I blocked him and slid out of harm's way. Was it me, or did his movements seem more obvious than they once had?

The last time I'd done any serious hand-to-hand with Sean, he'd walked all over me, but that was years ago. I'd learned some hard lessons since then. And a whole host of dirty tricks. It dawned on me that if I was prepared to really let rip, if I stayed on the ball, and I was lucky, I could probably take him.

But what about the job I'd set out to do here?

The prospect of imminent humiliation battled against the danger of exposure. One or the other. There had to be a loser.

In the end, I let him take my pride.

When I hit the mat a second time, he graciously gave me a hand up. Glanced at his watch as he did so. "OK everyone, that's it for this time."

Nobody met my eyes as they filed out. As I went to walk past him, Sean touched my arm, but when he spoke, his voice was dispassionate, detached. "You should get that lip seen to," was all he said.

I nodded, swallowed the hurt and angry words that were bubbling to the surface, and moved away without speaking.

CHAPTER
TWENTY-THREE

There was a short gap before we had to be down at the ranges for the next lesson. It gave me time to go up and mop at the cut on my lower lip with paper towel from the bathroom, and grab my jacket.

My lip seemed to have stopped bleeding anyway, but it was swollen in the centre like a collagen-enhanced starlet. I looked in the mirror and my pale reflection stared back at me, much bruised around the eyes. The sight of my own defeat annoyed me, put some steel back into my spine.

Sod this! You can't get away with treating me like this, Sean.

What did breaking cover matter any more? Tomorrow Venko was coming and if we didn't work as a team we were going to be dead. Whatever game Sean was playing, when it came to the crunch I needed to know if I could trust him.

After their earlier attention Elsa and Jan seemed to be avoiding me, but I would have ignored them anyway. I made my way back downstairs with brisk determination.

Sean was in the hallway, deep in conversation with Hofmann. If the hand movements and gestures were anything to go by, they were discussing some finer point of combat technique. It surprised me to note in passing from the big German's body language that he was listening with an almost deferential intent. Neither man looked pleased when I stalked up between them.

"Mr Meyer," I said, forcing out a smile through gritted teeth, "I wonder if I could have a moment of your time?"

Sean regarded me darkly for a second, then nodded with a show of reluctance that was a little too convincing. "If you'll excuse me?" he said to Hofmann and followed as I marched out through the main doorway.

I carried on walking round to the side of the house where we were out of immediate sight, then wheeled to face him.

"Do you want to tell me what the fuck is going on here?" The anger forced a crack in my voice. I swallowed it back. Dammit, I would not cry in front of him!

Sean dropped a shoulder against the stonework and folded his arms across his chest. For a moment he didn't speak, and that infuriated me all the more.

"Come on, Sean!" I snapped. "You sent me in here. You wanted answers about how Kirk died. Well, I've done my part. I've found out what you wanted to know. What the hell have I done to warrant that kind of —"

"You lied to me, Charlie." His voice was so soft, so quiet, but it cut me down better than any shout.

Oh. Shit.

My anger backed and died, dragging my shoulders down with it. I didn't need to ask him to explain any further than that. I knew exactly the lie I'd told him, if not in so many words, then certainly by omission.

"How did you find out?" I asked in a small voice. I couldn't entirely keep out the bite as I added, "Madeleine?"

Sean threw me a warning glance. "No, as it happens," he said and his grim tone told me that Madeleine's silence on the subject had not met with his approval either. Then he let his breath out hard through his nose. "Does it matter how I found out? What matters is that I know and *you* should have been the one to tell me."

It was the note of accusation in his voice that did it. The pain in my body now extended right the way to my soul. Before I knew it I'd pushed Sean roughly against the stone at his back, with my arm across his throat and my face close in to his. He could have stopped me, but he didn't do it.

"What did you want me to tell you, Sean?" I hissed. I wanted to hurt him, like he was hurting me. I bunched my fists into his T-shirt at the shoulder, gripped until my hands ached.

"Did you want me to just come right out with it? That the four of them beat me up, and then they held me down and they raped me, one by one?" I said, deliberate, my eyes fixed on his face. "When would have been a good time to break that kind of news, hm? You tell me. Over a quiet drink perhaps? Dinner?"

He made an impatient gesture, a shrug like a horse trying to twitch off flies, then he stilled and I felt his muscles give.

"I don't know how you should have done it, Charlie, OK?" he said, sounding unbearably tired, as though he'd been holding out some last slim hope that it had all been a mistake. "All I know is that you kept it from me. Why didn't you tell me?"

I let go of him, stepped back not meeting his eyes. It suddenly struck me how cold it was. My jacket wasn't enough to keep it out and when I wrapped my arms around my body I discovered I was shivering.

"How could I bloody tell you?" I said. "At the time I thought you'd abandoned me, and then later you thought *I'd* accused *you* of rape because they'd thrown me out of the unit." My voice cracked again. "You actually believed that of me, Sean. The army fed it to you, and you swallowed it whole."

"I didn't abandon you, Charlie, you know that," he said in a perfectly reasonable tone. "But how could I not believe them when all the evidence at the time was pointing that way?"

The anger clawed back up my throat like bile.

"Oh well, if you were working on evidence alone, I would have been twice damned, wouldn't I?" I threw at him. "After all, the *evidence* was shown to prove that I decided to indulge in a gang-bang with the four of them, then panicked when things got a bit rougher than I was expecting. How's that for fucking evidence? In more ways than one."

I swear I saw him flinch, but I could have been mistaken. He hid it fast and rounded on me.

"So how did they explain you getting your throat half cut?" he bit back. "Did that not count against them, or was it just dismissed as part of some bizarre sexual game?"

Scorched and wounded, we were just aiming to score points. It was the way I'd feared it might go when I'd walked through the possibilities of coming clean with Sean, of telling him everything. It was precisely why I'd never had the courage to do so.

My temper subsided, leaving me hollow and shaky in its wake. "They didn't cut me," I said, weary myself now. "That happened last winter. Somebody tried for a repeat performance."

"What happened?" Sean said. There was an odd note in his voice, as though he'd realised what we'd been doing, too. I glanced at him, but could read nothing in his face.

"They didn't succeed," I said, my voice flat.

"So this is the final version of this story is it, Charlie?" he said softly. "No more nasty little surprises in store?"

"No. No more surprises," I said, bitter. "What is it, Sean? You think I *let* them do that to me. You think I —"

"You were good enough to have stopped them, Charlie," he said, close to vehement. He was staring out across the Manor grounds to the far tree line, avoiding my gaze. "I know you were. *You* know you were. You were the best."

It sounded like a recommendation, but underneath it his ultimate lack of trust burned like a needle in my arm. I shook my head. "Not when it mattered I wasn't. I froze up. I panicked, OK? And you forget — they knew exactly the same moves I did. Exactly the same counters. They were one step ahead of me all the way."

"I've seen you in action. You didn't freeze up then."

"No, I didn't," I agreed, "but there's been a lot of water under the bridge since then." I paused, then offered quietly, "Maybe knowing exactly what the penalties are for failing makes it easier to be brave."

He turned so abruptly it almost made me start, moved in close. He put his hands on my shoulders tentatively, as though afraid I'd break. "I'm just so sorry that I wasn't there for you, Charlie," he said, and I realised that all his anger and revulsion had been directed inwards.

The unexpected relief caught me off guard, crumbled me. Tears sprang into my eyes, rolled down my face. Sean took one look at them, gave a sound that might have been a sigh, and gathered me into his arms.

Just briefly, I struggled against him, but he tightened his grip, almost crushing me. In the end I gave in and simply clung to him, my cheek pressing wetly against his shoulder.

He held me so tight I could hardly breathe, but I didn't care. We stood like that for what seemed like a long time, not speaking. The whole school and Gregor Venko's private army could have descended on us, and still I doubt we would have broken apart.

Eventually I felt Sean's head lift, felt his chin graze against my hair.

"I am — so — damned — sorry," he said, and I heard the anguish ripping through his voice as I registered that he'd been masking his own overspill of emotion as much as my own.

He let me go then, stepped back from me, letting his hands drop away as though he couldn't bear to touch me any more. "And it's not enough, is it? Not nearly enough to even begin to heal what you went through because of me."

A cold dismay clutched at me. Sean's anger I could deal with, anything else terrified me. I reached forwards and grabbed his arm, spinning him to face me.

"Either you take me as I am today Sean, or you get out of my life and you leave me alone," I said, my voice low with feeling, close to breaking altogether. "Make a choice, because I won't have half measures from you."

And with that I turned my back and stalked away from him, not knowing if I'd just opened up the future for us, or cut it off at the knees before it could even begin.

I found I was heading for the back of the Manor and having started in that direction, I kept going. There was the customary gaggle of smokers on the terrace, stamping their feet as they cupped their cold hands around their cigarettes. A grabbed opportunity to feed their addiction before the next lesson.

As usual, Elsa was among them, even though I'd never actually noticed her light up. I saw her head lift as soon as I rounded the corner of the house, and she watched my progress from there intently, hurrying to intercept me as I climbed the terrace steps. Her eyes darted over my face.

"So, Charlie, what is this between you and Mr Meyer?" she asked right away. Loudly.

I cursed inwardly even as I forced a smile between stiff lips.

"What do you mean?" I asked, playing for time so I could move closer, force her to lower her voice a little. Even so, it was clear we had the full attention of everyone present. Romundstad and Craddock had edged nearer with barely disguised curiosity.

"Oh come on, Charlie," Elsa said, recognising my stall for what it was and giving me an old-fashioned look from behind the tinted lenses of her glasses. One that said, clearly, you're going to have to do better than that.

"There's nothing to tell," I said, shrugging. "I did a course he was instructing on once, in the army. From what I can remember he was a right bastard back then, too."

"But apart from that, you don't know him?" she insisted.

I could feel the jaws of the trap opening on either side of me, but she was leaving me nowhere to go but straight in between them. "Not especially, no. Why?"

Elsa smiled, almost gently. "Hofmann has just seen the two of you having what would seem to be a very personal argument," she said.

Ah. OK, Fox, now get out of that. It wasn't going to be an easy escape, either. Even the non-smokers had come out onto the terrace now, on their way to the range. They were instantly aware that they'd walked into an atmosphere you needed a chainsaw to cut through. Although they hadn't been in at the start of this encounter, they certainly seemed set to stay around for its climax.

I glanced around at the avid faces long enough to discomfort them, for their eyes to shift away, before I looked back at Elsa. "Maybe," I said, calm, level, "I just take a very personal exception to letting *anybody* kick me around."

Elsa stayed a studious distance during the walk down to the armoury, where Figgis had taken charge of distributing the Sigs and speed-draw holsters to the lot of us. Most probably, she would have liked to have kept away from me after that, too, but fate in the form of O'Neill had other ideas.

He led us to the outdoor range where we'd first practised our speed-draw drills, and announced that we would be working on threat-reaction exercises, and we'd be doing it in pairs. As he read off names down his list my heart dropped at the same rate.

"Charlie," O'Neill said, inevitably, flicking his eyes briefly in my direction, "you'll be with Elsa."

We walked to our designated lane without making eye contact. I plonked my carry tray down onto the bench at the back and concentrated on loading the Sig's magazine from the box of nine-mil shells, keeping my head down. Out of the corner of my eye I could see Elsa doing the same. If the layout of the bench had allowed us to work with our backs to each other, we would have done it.

By the time we were all loaded up and ready, Major Gilby hadn't put in an appearance. Neither had Sean. No doubt they were taking advantage of having the remaining three instructors nursemaiding us to formulate their strategy over Gregor Venko. I couldn't suppress a pang of churlish disappointment that I hadn't been included in that briefing. After all, it was as much my neck on the block as theirs.

I forced myself to concentrate on O'Neill's words as he went through the drill. In turn each of us would play bodyguard to the other, he said. At a shouted signal we would assume an armed threat had been made to our principal. We would shield them with our body while retreating towards cover and firing at the target. He made it sound so simple. First lightly grease camel before passing it through eye of needle.

We had half a dozen practice runs first, safeties on, stumbling over our own — and our partner's — feet. Hoisting another person's weight onto your back, one-handed, takes as much technique as brute strength. Romundstad, in the next lane along to our left, seemed to have mastered it. Beyond them Jan was swinging Declan over her shoulder with an ease that he couldn't match when it was his turn, much to his clear discomfort. The likes of Hofmann and Craddock simply relied on their muscles.

On the first of the real deal Elsa grabbed me and managed to drag me away from the designated source of danger, jolting my tender ribcage with a roughness than might, or might not, have been deliberate on her part.

The second time it was my turn. Todd's bellowed warning sounded muted under the ear defenders we were all wearing. I grabbed a big handful of the German woman's collar, twisted my body in front of hers as I started to turn, getting my hips under hers to lift her feet off the ground like I was going for a judo throw.

I'd already drawn the Sig, acquired my target, and I squeezed the trigger with my arm still bent, feeling the gun kick in my hand. As I backed away I snapped off two more fast shots, my arm fully extended now. I knew before I'd fired them that they were good. That they would hit the target right in the centre, would be closely grouped.

And then, behind me, Elsa jerked herself half out of my grasp and went dead weight. I'd taken such a firm grip on her collar that I couldn't immediately disentangle myself. My only option was to go with her as she went down.

We fell in a mess of arms and legs with me mainly on top, which saved me from further damage, but can't have done Elsa much good. She gave a single low cry, little more than a loud gasp, as I landed on top of her. In trying desperately to stay light I inevitably made myself heavier. Sod's law. I rolled away untidily onto my knees, wondering what the hell was wrong with her.

Elsa was lying on her back, pupils dilated with shock, staring up at the sky. Her hands flapped weakly against the ground a couple of times, like the last beats of a drowning fish.

I unsnapped the catch on her holster, yanked down the zip on her jacket. Underneath it she was wearing a black fleece and I opened the collar, trying to help her breathe. She didn't speak, didn't move her head, but her eyes flicked to mine, wide with panic and with pain. I ran both hands up her sides from waistband to armpit. My left one came away wet and sticky.

A shadow loomed over me. Todd.

"Made a mess of that one, didn't you, Fox?" he sneered, and then he saw the blood on my hands.

"If you can stop being a smart-arse for one fucking minute, get a medic," I snapped. "She's been shot."

O'Neill arrived at a run, carrying a medical pack. He moved me aside with the confident but slightly puzzled air of an actor who thought he'd already played this scene and isn't sure if he should be improvising or sticking to the same script.

Once he knelt by Elsa's side, though, and saw the blood now staining the ground beneath her, he faltered, hands fluttering. In the end, it was Romundstad who took the half-opened field dressing from his nerveless fingers. Me who slit Elsa's shirt and fleece open so we could see what we were dealing with.

She'd been lucky. The bullet had struck her side, but at a shallow angle, ploughing a livid gouge along the groove between her lower ribs before exiting skin and clothing at her back. It was a flesh wound, little more.

Bloody and dramatic rather than life-threatening, but it could clearly have been so much worse.

Elbowing O'Neill aside completely, Romundstad packed the dressings along the course of the wound, wrapped them tightly to staunch the flow. He seemed to be coping so well that Todd and Figgis didn't try to take over from him.

One of them must have been in touch with the Manor as soon as the incident occurred, because Gilby appeared at this point, along with Sean, who went straight to Elsa's side. The Major asked O'Neill for a prognosis, but grew quickly impatient with his vague replies.

Romundstad handed over responsibility for Elsa's immediate care to Sean with obvious relief. He got as far as one of the loading benches, which he slumped onto like a man who's just unexpectedly run the hundred-metre sprint in a world-record time. As he wiped the sweat from his bushy moustache, his bloodstained fingers were shaking.

As for Elsa, Sean's increase in pressure on the site of the wound provoked a moan of protest, but he didn't let up. All the while he spoke to her quietly, letting his tone soothe as much as his words.

"I think we need a rapid medevac, Major," he said quietly over his shoulder, as polite and calm as though he was suggesting a choice of wine with dinner.

Gilby nodded and pulled out his mobile phone, moving off to one side to bark orders into it in quick-fire German.

It hit me right about then, in the lull after the action, that Elsa had actually been shot. It might have been an accident, but it could just as easily have been a calculated attempt at murder.

The question was, was she the intended target, or was I?

The rest of the students milled about, abruptly lost and directionless. Eventually it was Figgis who went round collecting up the Sigs for return to the armoury. It was only at this point that he realised we were one missing. Student plus firearm, that is.

"Has anyone seen Miss King?" Figgis asked, anxious.

No one answered. I cast back. Jan had been there on the terrace, listening unashamedly to my exchange with Elsa and she'd been behind me in the queue when the Sigs were handed out.

Then I'd seen her expertly manhandling Declan in the next but one lane to mine. The next lane but one to the *left*, I recalled. Mind you, Romundstad had been positioned on that side of me, too, as had Hofmann.

I allowed my gaze to skim over both men. Romundstad was still looking dazed, but Hofmann's expression was harder to read. Grim, masked. If I'd had to put an emotion on him at that moment, I would have gone for a deep and abiding anger.

The Major finished his phone call and started organising us into search parties, claiming that Jan might have wandered off suffering from shock. It was clear he didn't believe this supposition any more than we did, but none of us felt inclined to stand around and argue the point with him.

I started off with the others, but Gilby called me back.

"You were closest to Frau Schmitt," he said. "Perhaps you have some idea what might have happened?"

But before I could answer Figgis came running from the direction of the armoury. He wasn't a natural athlete, his anatomy more suited to being behind the wheel of a car than on his feet. The sight of his ungainly frame at full pelt was all the more alarming because of that.

"Sir," he said breathlessly to Gilby as he reached us, his face ashen, "I think you'd better come quickly. There's something you need to see."

The Major shot Figgis a daggered glance and let out his breath in an annoyed spurt. "What is it man?" he snapped.

Figgis's long face screwed into discomfort. His eyes flipped from Gilby, to Sean, to me, and back again. He all but shuffled his feet.

"Well sir —" He stopped, but decided there was no other way of saying it, regardless of who might be listening in. "It's the boy, sir," he blurted then. "He's gone."

CHAPTER
TWENTY-FOUR

This time the Major didn't exclude me from his war cabinet. He would have had a fight on his hands if he'd tried.

So, I found myself back in the same chair in his study that I'd taken after Venko's departure. Was it really only a few hours ago? At least, I realised, my body seemed to be aching less than it had done then. I was either working through the stiffness or I was going numb.

"Well I still don't like it, *sir*," Todd said on a growl. "It seems a mite too convenient that he arrives and the next moment the kid's snatched from under our noses." He glared, taking in both Sean and me in the same sweep. "How do we know we can trust either of them?"

"We don't have a choice — not now," Gilby said. He was slumped in his chair behind the desk. Defeat gave him a sulky air.

Figgis and O'Neill were sitting on the far side of the room, as though trying to put distance between us. Sean was standing, leaning against the wall by the window. He'd never liked to sit when there was something going on. It was the only giveaway to his inner restlessness, but anyone who didn't know him wouldn't have doubted his calm at this moment.

I studied the thoughtful set of his face, trying to read what was revolving behind those liquid dark eyes. It wasn't easy.

Despite everything that had happened since, I couldn't help myself going back to our last conversation. I sweated at the realisation that I'd thrown down an ultimatum, a take-it-or-leave-it flat choice, to a man who wouldn't be bullied or cajoled into making any decision. Had I blown it?

I looked away, flushed with a sudden guilt that I could be wondering about my relationship with Sean amid all this chaos and bloodshed. The truth was, I couldn't help it. I craved some small sign of his acceptance of my past, my failings, like an addict craves the reassuring twist of foil. Logic just didn't come into it.

Sean had his arms folded again, those long fingers resting lightly against his own skin. He and I had washed Elsa's blood off our hands, literally if not metaphorically. She'd been whisked off to the nearest hospital with brisk efficiency. Although the paramedics who'd attended the scene hadn't seemed unduly worried by the severity of the wound, it could just have been part of their act. As yet there was no word of her condition.

We'd searched the immediate area both for Jan and for Ivan Venko long after the light had gone and darkness had come down cold and hard. Just before eight o'clock Gilby had called a halt and we'd stumbled back to the Manor for hot showers and hot food. We'd found nothing out there in any case. In reality we hadn't expected to.

352

It transpired that the Major had been keeping Ivan in a small room, almost a cell, behind the back wall of the indoor range. He seemed to have had no qualms about the effect our barrage of gunshots must have had on the boy's psychological well-being, every time we'd fired in there. Gilby appeared to think that obeying the basic Geneva Convention rules of food, water, and no actual physical cruelty had been luxury enough for the son of Gregor Venko.

And now he was gone. I still couldn't believe that Jan had done it. Not just that she seemed to have stolen Ivan away, but that she'd cold-bloodedly shot Elsa to provide enough of a distraction while she did it. I was convinced, as we all were, that it hadn't been an accident.

The worst of it was that I'd never suspected her for a moment. After all, she'd been with Elsa in the dormitory the night I'd had my run-in with Rebanks at the armoury. Or had she? Why wouldn't Elsa have told me if she'd been out of the room as well? And then I remembered her exact words. "*Both Charlie and Jan have been to the bathroom,*" she'd said. Surely she couldn't have failed to notice?

Now, Gilby's men were discussing the possibility, which we couldn't ignore, that Jan had been working for Gregor from the start. But if so, why wait until now to snatch the boy?

"Maybe she couldn't find him before," Figgis suggested, adding pointedly, "After all, sir, you only told *us* at lunchtime where you'd put him."

"Yes," Gilby said sharply, "and soon after I do, he disappears. What am I supposed to make of that?"

Figgis's long face hardened, his limbs contracting as he made to rise from his chair. Sean moved across and put a placatory hand on his shoulder.

"There is always the chance that she'd known for a while where Ivan was," he said. "Ever since Charlie discovered Rebanks's little sideline and was ambushed doing so. That could be why Jan set the alarm off," he added to me, "to stop you finding him, which is what she must have assumed you were after."

"Wait a minute," Todd snapped. He looked disgustedly from Sean, to Gilby, to me, and back again, as though someone was playing a joke on him, one that was not in the best taste. "You're never telling me that *she* was the one who clouted Rebanks, but —"

"I'm afraid so," Gilby said. He paused and gave me his own assessing stare, as though he couldn't quite believe it, either. "She's a tough little bitch," he said then. His tone was dispassionate, as though I was a dog he was thinking of breeding from. Only the slightest smile spilled over. "You have to give her that."

"I rather feel that a discussion of Charlie's undoubted abilities is beside the point," Sean said, managing to pass me half a smile of his own as he did so. "Finding out who Jan was working for is a bit more important right now."

"Why?" Gilby demanded bitterly. "It's obvious Miss King was working for Gregor Venko. He agrees the exchange, then breaks his word." He reached for the generous glass of brandy he'd poured as soon as we'd

354

all adjourned to the study. I eyed the rate he was knocking it back with no small measure of alarm. "I should have known I couldn't trust the man," he muttered. "Scum of the earth."

"You're overlooking another possibility, of course," Sean said quietly. "That Jan could be working for the German security services."

Gilby's head came up, surprise dusting across his face. "But we had an agreement," he said. "They gave me their word." He fell silent, seeming to realise the similarities of what he'd just said with his comments on Gregor.

Sean saw his hesitation and went for it, moving in to the desk. "Major, I deal with security services around the world all the time and most of them would sell their own grandmothers if they thought it was to their advantage to do so. What makes you think this mob are going to stick to anything after the event? And anyway, what are you going to do about it if they don't? You're not even a German national."

"No, but Dieter is," Gilby said immediately. "One with influence. If this cock-up *does* turn out to be down to the security services and anything happens to Heidi, Dieter will make waves from here to Bonn. Of that you can be quite certain."

Sean let his breath out hard and slammed his hands onto the desk top, making us all jump. It was a calculated display of temper rather than the real thing, just to get the Major's attention. Sean leaned in to the other man's face. "You're talking about repercussions, Major," he said tightly. "What we need now is a plan of action. You're going to have to evacuate this place for a start. Get all the civilians out of here."

Gilby almost snorted. "What does that leave me with?"

"Fewer hostages for a start," Sean shot back.

"But what do I tell the students?" Gilby's voice was almost plaintive. His authority seemed to have dulled to grey, like an old shirt one time too many through a mixed wash.

Sean stood up straight, stepped back as though he'd lose his temper for real if he didn't put some distance between the two of them. "Tell them there's going to be an investigation over the shooting," he said. "Tell them what you like. What does it matter?"

"You could always tell them the truth," I said.

Gilby threw me an acid glance. "And what does that gain me, precisely?"

I shrugged. "You've got a good bunch of people out there," I said, undeterred. "They may not be quite up to the standard you're used to," I couldn't resist a sideways look to the three instructors as I said it, "but they still have a lot of valuable experience between them. Tell them the truth and you never know, some of them might decide to stay."

I stood, unable to sit and do nothing any longer, and looked down at the Major. "Let's face it," I said, "at this stage you need all the help you can get."

Todd rose also, muscled his way into the Major's line of sight. "What about Rebanks? He's a useful man and he's probably the best shot we've got."

I caught the flicker of the Major's eyes in my direction, and knew he was remembering that day on the CQB range, but he didn't point that out to the stocky phys instructor.

"How can I rely on him when he was cheating me so flagrantly?" he said instead. He wouldn't meet anyone's gaze as he admitted, "Besides, he might also have been involved with Teddy Blakemore's death."

"There's one way to find out," Sean said, impatient now. "Ask him."

From the other side of the room I heard O'Neill swear under his breath. "You're serious aren't you?" he said. "What makes you think for a moment that he'll tell you the truth?"

The look Sean passed over the Irishman was cold and flat. "I don't know," he said. "Does he enjoy pain?"

Gilby led the way down to the cellars. There was a doorway under the curving staircase that I'd always assumed was a store cupboard. It turned out that it dropped straight down a set of stone steps that were rough almost to the point of being crude in their construction. The architects of the Manor had not wasted their talents on finesse for an area they only ever expected the servants to see.

Once we were down a level the Major moved off confidently along a narrow corridor, snapping on unshielded light bulbs as he went. Most of the men had to duck to avoid sending them swinging, but I didn't have that problem.

Several generations of wiring additions were clipped to the bare walls and our feet crunched on years of dust and grit on the stone floor. It was a grim place, full of foreboding. I couldn't resist the urge to keep checking behind me, making sure I could recognise the way out when the time came.

Eventually the Major paused by a small heavy wooden door, secured by an iron bolt that was so decorated it was almost ornamental. He shot it back, pushed the door open, and stepped through.

Inside the cellar Rebanks was sitting on an unmade camp bed wedged up against the back wall. He half came to his feet when Gilby walked in, but when he saw the other three instructors, then Sean and me, he dropped back again. His eyes had panic in them, but he put on a good show of being unconcerned.

He looked small and scruffy, unshaven so that he'd sprouted the beginnings of a ginger beard that didn't suit his narrow face. There was a big livid bruise across his throat and when he spoke his voice was rusty with it.

"Well well, Major, to what do I owe the pleasure?" he said, aiming for a light casual note and just failing to carry it off.

Gilby stood and stared at him for a while, not trying to mask his distaste. "Venko's coming," he said, "but I'm sure you knew that already, seeing as you've been supplying him with the armaments to attack us."

Rebanks waved a tired hand in the Major's direction, as though he'd heard all this before and was bored with it. "Yeah well," he drawled, "at least his credit was good."

Gilby's features locked down tight. He took a quick step forwards and backhanded Rebanks across the face, hard enough to send his former weapons' handling instructor reeling.

And all of a sudden the atmosphere in that cramped cell had changed. I found myself parachuted in on the side of the interrogators and I didn't like the view from there.

I moved in, put my hand on Gilby's arm. "Valentine," I murmured, deliberately using his first name, trying to humanise him. "This isn't helping."

For a second Gilby looked at me with that film of madness covering his eyes, then it lifted. He blinked a couple of times, came back to himself, rolled the tension out of his neck.

Rebanks checked out the inside of his mouth with his tongue and dabbed a couple of finger ends at his cheekbone. It had started to swell, but the blow hadn't broken the skin. He was shaken, clearly, but still defiant.

"Since when did you start taking orders from a girl?" he jeered.

"Considering Charlie was the one who caught you in the act," Sean told him, eyes narrowed, "I'd watch your tone if I were you."

Rebanks swung his gaze back to me and I read part hatred, part fear there. The desire to be in a room alone with me for a short period of time was both an urgent desire and a phobia, all rolled into one.

359

"Why did you do it, mate?" Figgis broke in then, sounding saddened rather than angry.

Rebanks leaned back, aware he had his chance of an audience, and looked round the gathered faces. It was only me he avoided eye contact with. "The money, of course," he said. When nobody responded to that he laughed. "Come on, we were all of us sick to the back teeth of the pay cheques bouncing back every month." He threw a disparaging look in Gilby's direction. "Whatever else the army trained you for, Major, it certainly wasn't accountancy."

The Major's face darkened again, but this time he didn't make any moves towards him.

Rebanks eyed him for a moment, as if waiting to be sure before he continued. "I have contacts who can supply just about whatever you could wish for in the armaments line. That's my job," he said, almost boastful now. "And when you have those kinds of contacts, people get to know about it. I was approached by a buyer who wanted PM-98s. He offered good money and I took it, that's all. I'd have been a fool not to. I didn't ask any questions."

"What about when Venko's lot jumped us in the forest?" Figgis demanded.

"They might not have been the same guns," Rebanks protested. "I mean, why the hell would a guy with Gregor Venko's connections need to come to a comparatively small-time player like me for weapons. It didn't make sense."

"Blakemore knew they were Venko's men, as soon as they jumped us," I pointed out, recalling his vicious words to the driver of the Peugeot. "Is that why you ran him off the road? Because he was getting too close to finding out about your little deals?"

Rebanks looked at me blankly for a second, then laughed. Really laughed, letting his head go back carelessly against the stonework behind him. He rubbed at it, rueful. "Wow," he said at last. "I would have put you down as closer to being a redhead than a blonde, Charlie. But coming out with crap like that, are you sure you don't dye your hair?"

He sat forwards then, let his eyes drift slyly across Gilby's men. "Oh I can tell you who killed old Blakemore and I can tell you why," he said. "But what's it worth to you to know?"

Gilby let out an annoyed breath, little more than a hissing puff down his nostrils. "Don't you know the penalties for gunrunning, Mr Rebanks?" he rapped.

"No," Rebanks said, shaking his head, insolent. "But tell me, Major, are they worse than the ones for armed kidnapping?"

He let that one drift for a moment. In the confines of that dirty cell I could hear each man breathing.

"All right, Mr Rebanks," Gilby said through his teeth. "What do you want?"

Rebanks never got to state his terms. I barely caught the flash of movement out of the corner of my eye as someone made a dash for the doorway. There was a scuffle behind me. By the time I'd turned, O'Neill was on the floor, thrashing about with Sean's knee firmly planted in the middle of his back.

Sean looked up and nodded briefly to Figgis. "Nice moves," he said.

Figgis gave him a faint smile as he uncoiled that long body back into its normal inoffensive mode. Todd was fast enough himself, but he was left just gaping at the pair of them.

Gilby watched O'Neill's struggles impassively, then turned back to Rebanks. "Well," he said, "I suppose we won't be needing your help in this matter after all, Mr Rebanks." He tried to keep the smugness out of his tone, but couldn't quite manage it. To Sean he said, "Get him up."

Sean stood, yanking the Irishman to his feet, seeming totally unconcerned by the other man's weight and exertions. At one point O'Neill managed to get an arm loose and took a savage swing at Sean's head.

Sean ducked out of the way almost negligently, hooked both O'Neill's arms up behind him and locked him tight. He applied just enough pressure on the joints so that O'Neill had to rise up on his toes to try and lessen it. Sean kept him there, teetering.

Gilby frowned at his man. "Why?" he said. "What the hell had Blakemore done to you?"

O'Neill just glared at him, the scar twisting his face into a sneer.

I stepped forwards. "I think I can help you here," I said. I took the Swiss Army knife out of my pocket and folded out its largest blade. For a second as I approached, O'Neill's eyes bulged and he renewed his struggles, nearly popping a shoulder out in the process.

"Don't be an arsehole, O'Neill," I said mildly, and cut his military-style green jumper in two straight up the centre. I put the knife away and unbuttoned his shirt, pulling it wide open. He was one of those men with a distinct hollow at his breastbone. The skin covering it was pale and he was visibly sweating.

Below his ribs on the left-hand side — the same side where Elsa had been shot, I noticed — was a large square of white dressing, held in place with strips of surgical tape. I looked straight into O'Neill's eyes as I reached for it, saw the dismay there as it came away from his ribcage with a faint rip.

Underneath was nothing. No wound, no blood. Just unmarred, smooth, clear skin.

I glanced down at the dressing. It was clean.

"Looks like I'm not the only one who's not a team player," I murmured, then turned and dumped the wad of dressing into Gilby's hand. He was staring backwards and forwards from me to O'Neill.

"But he was wounded," he said, confusion making his voice blank. "I saw him —"

"He faked it," I said. "It wasn't hard. He has to fake something very similar on every course during the night shoot. Blakemore knew that he'd panicked under fire and bottled out, and he was threatening to tell. That's how you were compromised, Major. That's how Kirk was shot." As I said this last part I met Sean's gaze. *That's it*, I thought. *Now the job really is over. But where do we go from here?*

Gilby looked at O'Neill, and saw the truth of what I'd just said written in the other man's face. He

363

gestured to Sean, unable to speak over the top of his disgust.

Sean released O'Neill, throwing him contemptuously onto the camp bed next to Rebanks. The Irishman bounced against the wall and huddled into the corner.

I looked at Todd and Figgis. Their faces held much the same expression, not of shock, but of recognition. They were going back over the same events, viewing them in the same new light, as the depth and scale of O'Neill's betrayal hit them.

"Congratulations, Major," Rebanks said then, his voice dripping with sarcasm. "If you lock all of us away down here, who's going to fight your battles for you?"

"I'd rather have a handful of good men than a battalion of rotten cowards," Gilby shot back. He turned for the door, then paused and added grimly, "Besides, Mr Rebanks, if Gregor Venko does carry out his threat to slaughter every one of us, I'll make it my last mission in this life to personally make sure both you and Mr O'Neill are included."

CHAPTER
TWENTY-FIVE

Gilby gathered the students and the rest of the Manor staff together in the dining hall to deliver the bad news. He took to the dais, with Figgis and Todd flanking him, seemingly unaware of how lonely a figure he presented up there.

Sean preferred to stay down on the main floor, hitching a hip onto one of the window ledges, watching the reactions from the ground. I leaned against the wall off to one side of him. Close enough, but still keeping my distance.

I felt rather than saw him turn his head to study me, but I refused to meet his eyes. I'd said what I had to, for better or worse. It wasn't up to me to push him for a response. Besides, we had other more pressing things to worry about right now.

I checked the time on the clock on the wall high above the Major's head. It read nine thirty-two. Just over twelve hours to go before Venko's invasion.

Perhaps Gilby was aware of the shortening of time, also. He spelled it all out for them in brief, clipped sentences. Somehow the situation sounded so much more desperate laid out that way, with no attempt to soften the blows he was delivering.

365

At first there was a kind of uncertain astonishment, teetering almost on the edge of amusement. As though this was all part of the course and their reactions were being monitored towards a final graduation mark. It was only as the Major ploughed on, relentless, that the gradual realisation spread.

The cooks and domestic staff didn't need much convincing. They'd already experienced a taster of the kind of treatment they could expect from Gregor Venko's army at first hand. I caught their nervous glances and knew there wouldn't be many who'd have the stomach for a second run.

When the Major wound up his short speech by extending an offer to leave immediately to anyone who wanted it, for a moment there was a silence brimmed with shock. People shuffled uncomfortably in their seats, began making surreptitious eye contact with their neighbours. Desperate to leave, nevertheless nobody wanted to be the one whose nerve was first to break.

Eventually, one of the cooks stood up, truculent as he unknotted his apron and dumped it firmly on his chair. His actions broke the surface tension. More people rose, students and staff alike, gathering momentum with mass. By the time the movement slowed, only a pathetically small group remained resolutely in their chairs.

The big Welshman Craddock had stayed put, but he probably would have done the same if you'd told him nuclear war had just been declared. He just had that kind of placid nature. Michael Hofmann was another, his face blank as he rolled slowly through some inner thought process. Maybe the realisation of the danger he was in was just taking a long time to reach his brain. Romundstad was hunched forwards, looking poised for flight as though he might change his mind at any moment, but he stayed in his seat.

There were two surprises. Declan Lloyd was one of them. He was lounging back in his chair putting on a good show of airy lack of concern, with only the jerky swinging of his casually crossed foot to call him a liar.

The other unexpected volunteer was Ronnie. He was the sole member of the domestic staff who'd stood his ground. The Major's gaze tracked slowly across everyone, showing neither approval nor disappointment at their decisions. He nodded once, briefly, to those who'd elected to stay.

"Thank you," he said with quiet dignity. Then he shifted his attention to the others, told them to pack their stuff and take one of the trucks into Einsbaden village. "Although you may like to consider a fallback position," he warned, almost taking delight in trying to make them squirm. "One somewhat further away from the front line, as it were."

We who'd elected to stay sat and watched as they filed out. Mostly they didn't look at us, or if they did it was with a pitying disbelief. We were mad, their thoughts clearly said. We didn't stand a hope in hell.

Maybe they were right.

The door closed behind the last of them, echoing slightly as if on an empty room.

Gilby and the two instructors stepped down from the dais, coming to sit among us. The sudden breakdown in formality showed a nice common touch on his part. It gathered us to the cause.

The Major needed all his communication skills once he started to outline the situation in more detail. He didn't make it sound any better than it had done in broad strokes.

"So let me get this straight," Declan said when he'd finished. "This Gregor Venko feller, who's as nasty a piece of work as ever walked the earth, is coming here in —" his eyes swivelled to the clock on the wall high above the Major's head "— a little over eleven hours from now, expecting to exchange the young lady he's kidnapped, for his son, who *you've* kidnapped?"

"Yes," said Gilby.

"But now you don't have the lad *to* exchange because young Jan, who's turned out to be a darker horse than any of us would have given her credit for, has — for reasons all of her own — stolen him away?"

"Yes," Gilby said again.

Declan threw his hands up and sat back in his chair. "Holy Mary, Mother of God," he muttered. "We're all fecked."

"Thank you for providing that succinct summary Mr Lloyd," Gilby said tartly. "But what we need now is a plan of action." He had the grace not to look Sean straight in the eye while he stole his words.

"It would help if we knew who Jan was working for, no?" Romundstad put in, tugging at his moustache.

"That we don't know," Gilby said. "If she *is* working for Venko then he probably already knows Ivan is loose and he has no reason to turn up tomorrow except for a revenge attack."

"Or he might not show at all." It was Ronnie who spoke, looking absurdly hopeful. I wondered if he was already regretting his show of bravado.

"That's correct." Sean nodded at him, encouraging. "But I would suggest we need to formulate a plan that *isn't* based on the premise that Venko isn't going to show. If he turns up tomorrow, with Heidi, we need to know how to try and retrieve the situation. Preferably without getting anyone killed."

Todd stood up. "We need to get Venko's men into a controlled location and go for a first-strike ambush," he said. "Hit 'em hard and fast, before they've got a chance to react. We don't stand a cat in hell's chance in a straight fight, so we're going to have to fight dirty." He glanced sideways at the Major. "At least we've now got access to a crate load of submachine guns."

Gilby was clearly unhappy with this suggestion, but the frown on his face showed he couldn't think of anything better to counter it.

"And what about Heidi?" Sean said, sounding as though he was tiring under the effort of being calm and reasonable. "We're back to the problem of whether Gregor knows about his son or not."

He was still leaning against the window ledge. He had that caged restless air about him. The one that said the time for talking should have long been over and the time for action was here. I was watching him to the point where I didn't immediately see Hofmann get to his feet.

"Major Gilby," he rumbled. "I must speak to you. In private."

"If you've anything to say, Herr Hofmann, then say it here," Gilby said sharply. "This is no time for further secrecy."

Hofmann sighed. "In that case," he said, his voice burdened, "I can assure you that Gregor Venko does not know about this latest development. There is no reason why he will not show for your rendezvous."

"And how, exactly, can you be so certain of that?"

Hofmann seemed to grow more depressed at the question. "Because I know for sure that Jan is not working for Venko."

Gilby didn't say anything to that, but his face said it for him. Hofmann glanced round at all of us and knew that he wasn't going to get away with leaving it there.

He sighed again, frowning into the space just in front of him, as though hoping that life's autocue would provide him with the correct next lines. The autocue had stuck. He was on his own.

He made his decision, came straighter in front of us. Something seemed to change under the surface of his face, a subtle shift of bones and skin, so the vacant muscle-bound look vanished and was replaced by a hard, keen-eyed stare. I'd caught a glimpse of it once before, but I hadn't realised how complete an act Hofmann had been putting on. He'd relied on the assumption that men big in body are slow in mind. It had been a very effective disguise.

"Because, Major," he said and even his speech seemed faster now, "she is my commanding officer. Her correct name is Jan König, and she is a major with the German security services."

König. German for King. If I'd had to point to anyone as being the German infiltrator I would most likely have suspected myself before I'd thought of Jan. She was just such a Londoner.

"So," Gilby said now, face pinched, "what does that make you?"

"At this precise moment," Hofmann said crisply, "probably guilty of treason, but I've spent the last two years as part of Major König's team, tracking Gregor Venko. I understand a little of the way his mind works. Those who are loyal to him are well rewarded, but those who betray him, well —"

He shrugged, letting his palms spread. "We have yet to find all of the bodies. If he turns up here tomorrow and you do not have Ivan to trade, he will not rest until you are all dead, and he will bring enough men with him to ensure this. Trying to lay a trap for him with the resources at your disposal is a pointless act of suicide."

Declan gave a hollow laugh. "Michael, me boy," he said. "You're not helping."

"Well, Herr Hofmann — assuming that is *your* real name?" Gilby said tightly. "If what you say is correct, we are in a rather difficult situation. Unless you have any idea where Major König might have taken the boy?"

He threw out this last as a sarcastic challenge, but Hofmann nodded with all seriousness.

"Yes," he said. "I think I do."

We all stared at him, but it was Sean who asked the question first, quite calm and matter of fact. "How do we know we can trust you?"

Hofmann smiled at him. A quick smile, out of character. "Because I am the only chance you have of getting out of this alive," he said simply. "Major, ask yourself this: What reason do I have to come forwards now, if not to try and help you? In theory, my job here is done. Why would I not just keep quiet, leave with the others, say nothing? You would never have known until it was too late."

"So why are you still here? Why didn't Jan take you with her when she left?"

"That I can't answer," he said and his expression hardened. "I was not privy to the Major's plans or I would have done my best to stop her carrying them out in the way she did. Perhaps that was why. Of late, there have been many aspects of Major König's strategy with which I have not agreed." He paused, then added, with reluctance, "I begin to doubt her judgement in this matter."

"Where has she taken him?" Sean demanded.

"A safe house," Hofmann said. "She will want to debrief him herself before she officially delivers him to her superiors."

Sean rose and glanced at Gilby. "Let me call one of my colleagues at home," he said. "She can get us a list of safe houses in the area. We can narrow them down."

Hofmann looked shocked. "You have access to that kind of information?"

Sean flashed him a grim smile. "Give her a computer and a high-speed internet link and there isn't much Madeleine can't find out," he said.

"I know where Major König will have taken Ivan, and it won't be on any official safe house list," Hofmann said then. "Venko has slipped through our fingers so many times in the past that she has become convinced that the service has been compromised by someone from his organisation. She would have taken the boy somewhere she has arranged personally. She has become so paranoid about security, that's why I am so sure that Venko does not know about his son's capture."

"Where is this safe house?" Gilby asked, his interest keen.

Hofmann looked at him rather sadly. "It is on the outskirts of Berlin," he said. "Major König would have flown him out of Stuttgart by helicopter thirty minutes after she'd taken him from you. I'm sorry."

He looked round at our shocked and disappointed faces. The hope we'd begun to build was gone, sucked away like the air from a dead balloon.

"Where *exactly* is the safe house?" Sean wanted to know, even though it could only have been an academic question.

Hofmann sighed. "It's more than six hundred kilometres from here, Herr Meyer," he said heavily. He checked his watch. "You now have less than eleven hours to make it there and back. It is a hopeless task unless you have access to a private jet."

Sean smiled at him, but it wasn't a pleasant smile. "No, but I think we can come pretty close to a flying machine." He turned to Gilby, and there was a quiver about him now, a scent he'd picked up and was ready to run with. "Major," he said. "Can I borrow your car?"

Although he didn't want to admit it, Gilby seemed to agree with Hofmann that trying to cover that kind of ground in the time we had just couldn't be done. Sean met their dissension with a silent, determined disregard, refusing to be deflected.

There was something about Sean that inspired a kind of confidence. He could have told you he was going to jump over the moon on the back of a cow and you'd have found yourself merely asking, "Jersey, or Friesian?"

Maybe that was why Gilby handed over the keys to the Nissan Skyline without the kind of argument I'd been expecting. The only thing that did cause controversy was Sean's assertion that he wanted me to ride shotgun with him.

Todd was keen to go himself and even Major Gilby would clearly have preferred to have had one of his own men in on the trip. Sean shook his head.

"We must have Hofmann, and this car's a two-squash-two at best, not a four seater," he declared. "With any luck there *will* be four of us on the way back."

"So why let her fill up one of the seats?" Todd challenged. "Me or Figgis would be twice as much use."

"I don't think so." Sean eyed him coldly. "Charlie and I have been in action together before," he said.

374

"She won't let me down. I know just how far she's prepared to go."

He met my eyes, just briefly, and I saw a calm and steady trust there. A tangible sense of relief breezed over me.

Todd was looking disgusted. "Yeah, all the way, by the sounds of it," he complained.

Sean turned and pinned the phys instructor with a savage glare. It would have taken a better man than Todd not to flinch under it. "You have no idea," Sean said softly, and walked away from him.

Outside someone had switched on the floodlights. They blazed out over the gravel to where the Skyline sat waiting, giving a faintly oily cast to the car's paint.

It was a brutal machine, resting rather than merely parked. Somehow you knew that the folds in its bodywork had been sculpted like skin over muscle, rather than the components living within the limitations of exterior line. No compromise.

Without knowing why, the car scared me. It was the kind of vehicle that tempted you to kill yourself all too easily, like a big bike, or an offshore powerboat. It was bred for speed, for risk. I had no illusions that Sean was going to take it steady just because it was dark with a hint of ice in the wind. I glanced across at his set face. This was going to be a battle of wits and wills. All or nothing.

Figgis met us then with a fistful of Sigs in speed-draw holsters and three of the PM-98s hanging over his shoulder. "Take your pick," he said.

"We'll take the lot," Sean said. "Don't bother to wrap them."

"What about him?" Figgis asked quietly, nodding towards Hofmann.

"Not yet," Sean said. He glanced at Hofmann's impassive face. "No offence."

Hofmann shrugged. "In your position," he said, "I would do the same."

The back of the Nissan looked tiny, but the big German managed to fold his large frame up small enough to squeeze in behind my seat. It was only as Sean climbed into the driver's side that I registered for the first time that the car was right-hand drive.

"How the hell are you going to manage overtaking anything in this when you're sitting on the wrong side of the car?" I asked.

Sean flashed his teeth as he twisted the key in the ignition and the twin-turbo engine growled into life like the ringmaster had just prodded it with a chair and a whip.

"You'll have to call gaps in traffic for me," he said. "Just give me the same amount of room you'd go for on a bike and I'll get us through."

I rolled my eyes and suppressed a groan.

Gilby leaned past me into the car and pressed something in the centre console. There were three faint beeps and then part of the stereo slid out and unfolded upright into a TV screen about seven inches across.

"Don't tell me you've got Alpine navigation as well?" Sean said, surprise in his voice.

"Naturally," Gilby said, unable to suppress the note of pride. "It covers the whole of Europe. Just punch in your destination and it'll give you the fastest route."

Hofmann leaned forwards and gave him the street name on the outskirts of Berlin, spelling it out for him.

"When you bought this puppy, Major," Sean murmured as he quickly programmed the Alpine, "you certainly went for all the toys."

"Just keep your eye on the exhaust gas temperature and try not to melt the turbos," Gilby advised, trying to make light of it even though his voice showed the strain he was under. "And don't trash it. Nissan don't make them any more. It's practically irreplaceable."

I looked up from stowing the PM-98s in the bottom of my footwell. "Valentine," I said gently, "if we don't make it either way then I think finding you another car is going to be the least of our worries."

He nodded at that, face serious. "Good luck then," he said and ducked back out, closing the door on us.

"OK, is everybody buckled up?" Sean asked. That quick grin again, like a schoolboy who's found his father's hidden car keys. That restless edge. "I would ask you not to move about the cabin while the fasten seatbelts sign is on. We may be experiencing some turbulence."

From the back I heard Hofmann groan. "Now, for sure," he said, "we are all going to die."

CHAPTER
TWENTY-SIX

Getting from the narrow twisting back roads around Einsbaden to the main autobahn heading for Stuttgart took a perilous nineteen minutes. It made my wild taxi ride on the way in seem like a Sunday cruise.

I tried not to clutch faithlessly at the base of my seat during that first part of the journey, but I feared that Gilby was never going to get rid of the indentations my fingers made in the leather upholstery. Suddenly I understood why Hofmann had opted for the rear.

The headlights on the Skyline were far better than my Suzuki's glow-worm in a milk bottle effort, but at that kind of speed they took on a delayed reaction, as though we were constantly arriving at the edge of darkness before the xenon bulbs had the chance to fully illuminate it.

Sean drove to the very limit of visibility, which by my reckoning was some distance beyond the limit of sanity. The lights cut jagged swathes through the scenery as signposts, rocks, trees, and junctions leapt towards us with a terrifying lack of clarity, blurring into a subliminal image before they'd ever had the chance to solidify. The broken white lines in the centre of the road became a single continuous streak.

378

As for the corners, I'd thought Figgis had taken the bends more than fast enough on his demonstration drives in the school Audis. But that was in daytime. Midnight's veil lent an extra hallucinatory dimension to the trip that I'd been unprepared for and I surreptitiously hauled my lap belt as tight as it would go across my hips.

I needed to. When we came up on the occasional sleepy piece of lumbering traffic Sean had to stand on the brakes so hard I ended up hanging forwards against my seatbelt. Even little old ladies seem to drive like demons in Germany. By comparison, when we were balked by them I felt I could have got out and walked faster.

To begin with my fear kept me from calling the gaps that Sean had demanded. I rapidly discovered that if I didn't do it he pulled out anyway, putting my side of the car into the firing line first. Gradually, as I realised just how quick the Nissan was, just how catapult-like its acceleration, I relaxed my death grip enough to begin to participate more fully.

And almost — but not quite — to enjoy the ride.

The Alpine navigation system not only showed a small-scale map of the immediate area on the screen, but also gave out verbal instructions in female tones so calm they were almost tranquillised. The only trouble was that whoever designed it obviously hadn't been expecting its end user to be driving like a lunatic. Once or twice it directed us to take turnings which seemed to flash up too fast for us to make them. When that happened the system instantly re-routed, without so much as a sigh to rebuke the driver. Sean was very taken with its uncritical approach and I mentally christened it Madeleine II.

Although I trusted his abilities, it was still a relief when we hit the main A81 to the west of Stuttgart and I no longer had the responsibility for our safety. Sean flexed his fingers on the steering wheel as we pulled on to the twin-lane road, and then he really put his foot down. It hadn't occurred to me until that point just how much he'd been holding back.

Over the next half-dozen kilometres or so I watched in amazement as the speedo needle climbed. Where before it had never dropped below sixty, now it rocketed past a hundred, then one-fifty. Was that in kilometres an hour? The peril sensitivity section of my brain shut down, totally refusing to compute the numbers.

"Sean," I said carefully as a truck in the next lane was sucked backwards past us like it was falling, "just how fast are we going — in real money?"

His eyes dipped fractionally. "In miles an hour?" he said. "About one-seventy."

His face was cast pale in the instrumentation lighting, his jaw clenched in pure concentration, eyes narrowed. But I could tell that some small part at the back of his mind was smiling. This must have been every car-mad schoolboy's fantasy come true, and Sean lived for danger. It was his life, his work.

If I let it, it could be mine, too.

The LCD display at the top of the centre console gave out vital engine temperature readings as the car thundered relentlessly on into the night. It was hot enough to grill steaks on just about any part of the motor you could name.

At Heilbronn the Alpine's voice politely directed us to turn east onto the A6 for Nürnberg. For a long time none of us spoke further, trying not to distract him.

Sean had settled into a rhythm that kept the Skyline barrelling along at around a hundred and fifty miles an hour. After a while the speed became almost hypnotic. At Nürnberg we took the A9 for Bayreuth and Leipzig. We were eating up the miles, tearing them up and scattering the pieces behind us, but Berlin still seemed an impossible distance away.

"At this rate," Hofmann said from the back seat, his voice betraying his surprise, "there is a chance we will get there in time."

I twisted round just far enough to be able to see Hofmann's face. "By the way," I said, loud enough to be heard above the roar of engine, wind and tyre noise. "What did you and Elsa argue about that first day, on the terrace?"

Hofmann leaned forwards slightly to catch the words and frowned, remembering. "Ah yes," he said. "She thought she recognised me, from her time in the police no doubt. I thought my cover was blown. I had to tell her she was mistaken more forcefully than I would have liked."

I shifted my feet, my boots disturbing the weapons piled in the footwell. The action jogged my memory. "And it was you, wasn't it, who set off that damned alarm in the armoury?"

"Yes," he admitted. "It wasn't my idea to do that to you, Charlie, but Major König was in the bathroom in your quarters relaying orders over her radio. She thought you were also trying to locate Ivan and she wanted you stopped."

I recalled Jan's particular irritation the night I'd attacked Rebanks. Unlike Elsa, she hadn't been interested so much in what I'd been up to, I realised now, as in how I'd managed to get away with it.

"I didn't know anything about Ivan at that point," I said. "I was just trying to find out what happened to Kirk."

"Ah yes, Kirk Salter," Hofmann rumbled, "we knew all about him, of course."

"And you did nothing about it?" I asked, incredulous.

"What could we do?" he asked with a shrug. "By the time we found out what Major Gilby was up to, the boy had already been taken and Salter was already dead. We would not have sanctioned such an operation had we been told about it in advance, but afterwards, well, we would have been foolish to ignore the possibilities." He sighed heavily, his contrition apparently sincere. "It might have helped prevent more deaths. There have already been so many."

Ahead of us, a car pulled out to overtake a convoy of trucks. The driver must have been doing over a hundred, but to us he was little better than a moving roadblock. Sean swore softly and I just had time to snap round straight in my seat as he stood on the brakes and dropped down two gears. As soon as the obstruction had cleared he was back hard on the gas again, romping the big bruiser of a car back up to its cruising velocity in sixth.

It was only then that I turned to Hofmann again. "If you wanted to prevent further bloodshed, why did Jan take Ivan now," I demanded, "when all our lives are at stake?"

"We knew that Herr Meyer had been asking questions about Venko," he said, nodding to Sean, "and naturally we knew of his reputation in hostage situations. When he turned up at the school Major König assumed that an exchange was imminent and she must have decided to act."

"Without consulting you," Sean put in, his voice clipped either with anger or just by the fact that the majority of his brain was taken up with keeping us rubber side down on the black stuff.

"I know you find it difficult to believe that I am being honest with you," Hofmann said, "but I had my own theory about these kidnappings. One Major König did not want to entertain."

"And that was?"

Hofmann paused, as though reluctant to put his ideas forwards just in case we, too, dismissed them out of hand. He hutched forward a little further, so his head was nearly between the seats and he could speak to both of us more easily. I hoped he realised he was in perfect launch position for the front screen if we crashed.

"These kidnappings are not Gregor Venko's style. They're too violent, too unpredictable. He's an old-style gangster who still believes in honour among thieves," he said, and I still had difficulty hearing him speak so fast and fluently. "To leave children slaughtered for no reason, to go back on his word — it's just not Gregor."

"You almost sound as though you like him," Sean said tightly.

"Gregor's a ruthless criminal. You need have no qualms that I'm going to go soft on you, Herr Meyer," he said grimly. "Two weeks before Christmas I went to the funeral service of a man from his organisation who had agreed to pass us information. Gregor sent the man's tongue and his ears to his widow gift-wrapped in a Tiffany box. We never found the rest of his body."

He shook his head and finished with great sadness that seemed for all the world to be genuine, "A pair of ears and a tongue do not go far towards filling a coffin."

"And still you think these kidnappings are not his style?" I said with just a hint of sarcasm.

"No," Hofmann said seriously, then added, "but they are Ivan's."

"Ivan?" Both Sean and I said the name simultaneously. He flashed me a quick grin. *In tune*, it said, *together*.

"Yes," Hofmann went on, not noticing our brief, silent exchange. "He's shown all the classic psychopathic tendencies since childhood. He started torturing animals, then worked his way up to other children. His mother sits in a sanatorium just outside Odessa and drinks like there will be no tomorrow. Who or what do you think drove her to do that?"

384

I listened to Hofmann's speech and yet I remembered Gregor's pride when he spoke his son's name. Parents could be blind to the faults of their offspring. Or were supposed to be, at any rate. Sometimes I wondered if mine had my shortcomings under a magnifier instead.

"And what does Gregor do about his son's nastier side?"

"He's aware of it, of course. He's taken him to every disreputable shrink in Europe, but they can do nothing." Hofmann shrugged. "So, all Gregor can do is surround him with bodyguards and try to keep him out of trouble."

"So you think Ivan's been doing the kidnaps off his own bat, that Gregor really didn't know about them?"

"That's what I believe, yes," Hofmann confirmed. "It's why Ivan had to buy guns from a two-bit player like Rebanks — because the last thing he wanted was for his father to find out."

"So *that's* the real reason why Ivan's minders were so desperate to get him back," I realised out loud. "Not on behalf of daddy, but before he found out what had been going on and came down on them like a ton of hot bricks."

"I think that Gregor only discovered his son was missing shortly before he paid Major Gilby a visit. That is why he is willing to do a trade — to put right what Ivan's done. He's been clearing up after him since the boy was seven."

"Ivan is Gregor's weakness," Sean said. "He'll be his downfall."

"I agree, and I have told Major König in the past that we should concentrate our efforts in that direction," Hofmann said. He sat back in his seat, so that his voice became disembodied in the gloom. "It's just unfortunate that she's chosen this moment in time to decide to listen to me."

We romped on northwards through Germany, only stopping briefly to satisfy the Skyline's voracious thirst for high-octane petrol. The normally generous seventy-litre fuel tank was diminished by the severely reduced fuel economy of running at these speeds. We were forced to stop every hundred and thirty miles or so.

The kilometre countdown signs for Bayreuth came and went, and then we were heading for Leipzig and I, too, began to allow the faint hope to form that we might just make it.

I asked Hofmann another question over my shoulder, but there was no answer. When I squirmed round in my seat I found the big German had lolled his head back against the side glass, his jaw hanging slackly. Unbelievably, he'd gone to sleep.

"It's nice to see someone's relaxed," I said quietly to Sean. I jerked my head. "Hofmann's spark out."

"You can tell he's been a soldier," he said. He smiled. "You might want to grab some kip now yourself. You never know when you'll get the opportunity again."

"I'm OK," I said, "and I'd rather stay awake."

As I said the words it struck me how frightened I should have been feeling. I did a quick mental search, just in case a huge example of classic denial of the situation was sitting lurking in the back of my mind, but found nothing. I was keyed up, yes. My stomach

386

was clenched tight like I'd done a rake of Todd's sit-ups, but there was no panic there.

I'd been in action with Sean before, stared death in the face and been terrified. But not for myself, I realised.

For him.

"I'm sorry, Charlie," Sean said suddenly and for a moment I frowned at him, backtracking to try and work out an immediate reason for him to be apologising to me. It took a moment to register that there wasn't one. So we were back to that confrontation we'd had outside the Manor. It seemed so long ago I could barely remember what had been said. Maybe that was my denial.

As the Skyline motored on Sean kept his eyes on the road, almost fixed to the vanishing point ahead of him. "I don't know what I can say or do to change things," he went on, his voice low and tense. "I wish to God I could!"

"I don't want you to do or say anything, Sean," I said, surprised at how calm I sounded, how perfectly reasonable. "I know you weren't the cause of any of it, but that doesn't change what happened."

I paused, tried to put some kind of order to my jumbled thoughts. "When you look at me," I came out with, "all I want is for you to still see *me* underneath it all. Not some faceless victim. Does that make sense?"

For a few seconds he didn't answer and the heavy frown was back. "You're asking me to pretend it never happened," he said, neutral and cautious. "Is that it?"

I sighed. "No," I said. I stared out of the darkened glass of the side window, aware only of the flash of the passing road markers like a continuous stream of stars in hyperdrive and the morbid pulse of my thoughts. I turned back to Sean. His face was set.

"I'm just asking you to accept that it did, but underneath, inside, I'm still me," I said. "A bit ragged at the edges, maybe, but still me."

There was a long stretch of silent deliberation then he said, at last, "I'll try and remember that." He smiled, but it was a sad, tired smile. "There is no instant rewind button in life, is there?"

"No, I guess not," I said, trying to smile myself although there was a sudden taste in the back of my mouth that was hot and bitter, like smoke.

If there was I'd go back and edit out a whole heap of things. But the time I'd spent with Sean, I realised, would not be one of them.

We stopped for fuel again just outside Dessau at a little after 2.15a.m.

As we slowed for the exit I reached awkwardly behind me to tap Hofmann's leg to warn him. By chance my hand landed on his solid calf just above the top of his combat boot. My fingers grazed across something, but at that moment he jerked awake, shifted his position.

"What is it?"

"We're stopping to fill up," I said over my shoulder. "If you need a break of any description, speak now."

He nodded. "I will stretch my legs," he said.

388

I watched him pace away across the filling station forecourt, rolling his neck and swinging his arms to ease the constrictions out of his considerable muscles. I moved round to stand with Sean, leaning carefully against the dirt-streaked rear wing of the Nissan. Sean had left the engine running, to try and save the turbos from self-destructing. It hummed now under my hip.

"You do realise that Hofmann's carrying a knife, don't you?" I murmured, low enough for the German not to overhear.

Sean's eyes flicked sharply to Hofmann, but he didn't look surprised. "Where?"

"Top of his right boot."

Sean nodded. "OK," he said. "Leave it for the moment, but just be ready for him if he tries anything."

I shivered, and not just at the wind that whipped between the pumps. "That's easy for you to say," I muttered. "You're not the one who's got him sitting right behind you."

I'd faced knives before and had the scars to prove it, but the prospect of taking on someone with the kind of military training Hofmann had been through took it up to another level altogether. He'd been an elite soldier. If he was planning to double-cross us, the chances were I wouldn't see the knife until it was hilt-deep in my throat.

After Dessau we crossed the river Elbe and then Berlin was suddenly within our grasp. I was used to distances unfolding in miles, rather than kilometres. That, combined with the sheer speed we were travelling,

389

made the city seem to be actively rushing forward to meet us.

Once we reached the outskirts Sean slowed to a less obtrusive pace. It was raining steadily here and the road surface sparkled in the dance of the lights.

The Alpine directed us to the street we'd asked for, then Sean switched off the unit, folding the screen back into the dashboard, and relied on Hofmann's instructions from the back seat. It was almost 4a.m. and the run-down residential district he took us into was so quiet it was like it was under curfew.

Hofmann guided us without any hesitation. I wanted to trust him, but when we finally pulled up in the gloomy shadow of a dilapidated apartment block, I couldn't help the feeling that this could all be one hell of an elaborate trap.

Sean left the engine ticking over to cool down while he twisted in his seat. "OK, what are we likely to be facing here?"

I glanced at him. He'd driven nearly four hundred miles at the kind of speeds that would have challenged a Le Mans racer, but somehow he was still alert, on his toes.

"If we are lucky, and Jan is *not* there," Hofmann said, "I may be able to talk the boy away from them. If she is —" He broke off and shrugged, plainly unhappy. "Then it may come to a fight. Maybe three men. Maybe four. MP5Ks and sidearms. We tend to favour the Heckler & Koch P7 pistol."

The "we" in that last remark really brought it home to me what we were expecting of Hofmann. That we were asking him to stand against his own comrades. Hardly surprising that he might show some reluctance to engage them in a fire fight.

I picked one of the PM-98s out of my footwell and handed it to Sean. He caught my eye and nodded almost imperceptibly. I picked up another, handing it back over my shoulder.

Hofmann took the Lucznik with a slight bow, recognising the act of faith for what it was. He checked the magazine and cocked the first round into the chamber with the practised ease of a man who's done this many times before. Sean and I did the same, easing the safety back on. I dumped one of the Sigs into my right-hand jacket pocket, just as a backup.

As we got out of the Skyline I felt the fresh bite of the rain on my face. We left the big car crouching by the kerbside and crossed the empty street with the submachine guns held close. Hofmann led us round to the front of the block and up the front steps, with me behind him and Sean bringing up the rear.

We climbed to the fifth floor under the dim, vacant gaze of the naked lightbulbs on each landing. The matting on the stairs was worn to the woven backing in the centre of each tread. Our boots sounded harsh against the night, but the faded doors we passed stayed resolutely shut. The residents had clearly heard too many intruders in the early hours and had long since chosen total deafness as the way to deal with them.

Finally, we stopped in front of a doorway no different from any of the others. Hofmann silently motioned to us to stay a little behind him, and to keep the guns out of sight of the Judas glass. My heart was trying to jump out of my chest as he knocked on the woodwork, firmly, with no apparent pattern. I heard the shuffle of movement from inside the apartment.

Whoever was inside must have recognised Hofmann, even if we were strangers. There was only a short pause before the door was opened by a man remarkably similar in build and manner. Hofmann brushed past him impatiently and, before he had the chance to object, we followed.

"Where is the boy?" Hofmann demanded in German. "We have a security breach. Major König wants him moved immediately!"

I managed to contain my surprise at this tack. There was, I noted, no other easy way to do it. If Jan was here to contradict him we were neck-deep in trouble anyway, and if she wasn't? Hell, it might just work.

Hofmann strode further into the shabby apartment, glancing round him. All the time he was barking commands, berating his colleagues for their lax procedure. Someone had been sloppy he told them. Gregor Venko's men could be breaking the door down at any moment.

As he stalked from room to room Hofmann was carefully pinpointing the four men in the apartment, calling them together, improving our field of fire. Sean moved casually sideways, giving him a better angle. I held the PM-98 negligently down by my thigh, but the safety was off now and my finger was inside the trigger guard.

The men were indeed using HK nine-mil handguns, as Hofmann had predicted, most with a silencer fitted to the end of the barrel. Someone had been in the middle of cleaning an MP5K submachine gun, too. It was stripped to its constituent parts and laid out neatly on the chipped yellow formica table in the living room. Well, that was one less to worry about.

"So where is Ivan?" Hofmann snapped. "We need to withdraw him to a more secure location and we are wasting vital time!"

"But Major König will return in less than an hour," protested the man who'd answered the door, his eyes drifting to the wall clock. "She will want to supervise his removal personally."

"The Major has sent us to get the boy now," Hofmann said, which was the truth — if you didn't ask which Major. He pushed his face in close to the other man's. "If we wait an hour," he ground out, also no lie, "it will be too late. We must go now."

"Is there any word of the girl Venko's holding?" another man asked.

I turned at the question, flicked a glance to Sean and found him frowning. So, the security services were far better briefed on the situation than we'd thought. *And still Jan took Ivan.*

Hofmann straightened up. "No," he said, expressionless. My translation might not have kept up, but I could have sworn he added, "Unless some miracle happens it will be too late for Heidi."

For a moment there was silence. Nobody spoke. Then the man nodded slowly, got to his feet and led the three of us to the entrance to one of the cramped bedrooms.

They'd handcuffed Ivan Venko to the iron head of the narrow bed, which had been pulled into the centre of the room away from the walls. He was wearing a purple silk shirt, one sleeve of which had been ripped at the shoulder. He'd been stripped of his shoes and the belt was gone from his designer jeans. His ears were completely covered and he'd been blindfolded, too.

I'd been through something similar myself during my army training. No sight, no sound. It had been hard to take, even when I'd known it was just an exercise and I could almost feel sympathy for the kid.

Hofmann held out his hand for the keys, which the man gave up without demure. Ivan cringed when he was touched, blinking away tears as the blindfold came off and the light stung his eyes. Hofmann used the boy's discomfort to refasten the cuffs behind his back without a struggle, pocketing the keys. Then he hauled Ivan to his feet and shoved him in my direction.

I grabbed hold of him with reluctance, not least of which was because, close to, the boy stank of stale sweat and abject fear. It rolled off his body in waves. Even so, the look Ivan cast me was one of haughty disdain, but I expect he must have been used to having girls hanging on to his arm.

A lucky combination of a sinuously slender build and an arrangement of features that included high slanted Slavic cheekbones had provided him with good looks that would have turned heads anywhere. Allied to his father's power and money, I'm sure it had given him a social position that was practically unassailable.

Only the eyes scared me. There was nothing behind them, as if the price for all that exquisite external structure was a black and rotting soul. I was reminded of a pedigree dog. Beautiful to look at, but with hidden inbred defects.

Ivan didn't want to walk with me and he was just crazy enough not to respond to being prodded with the barrel of the Lucznik, either, digging his heels in. Hofmann leaned down and pulled the knife out of his boot. It came free with a metallic slither that snapped the boy's eyes round.

"Here," Hofmann said, handing me the knife. "If he gives you trouble just make that pretty-boy face of his a little more — interesting."

After that I only had to offer the tip of the blade up towards Ivan's cheek for him to comply with docility. Even when Hofmann tipped a rough cloth hood over his head, he did little more than squirm briefly.

With me on one side, and Sean on the other, we hustled the boy blindly back through the flat. All the time I was waiting, heart painfully contracted, for Jan to burst in at any moment, for the game to be up, but our luck held.

The four men who'd been guarding Ivan were gathered in the tiny hallway. One of them was holding an MP5K and for a moment I feared we'd been rumbled.

One of them put a hand on Hofmann's arm. "You do know what Major König will do," he said with a heavy foreboding, "if you should — lose him."

"Yes," Hofmann said firmly, "I do."

The man shrugged, then he stepped back and allowed us to go.

It was still raining when we hit the street and Ivan faltered as his sock-clad feet tripped into soggy puddles. We ignored his protests and half-dragged, half-carried him to where the Skyline was waiting for us.

Getting him into the car proved a struggle until Hofmann hissed, "What's the matter, Venko? Don't you want to see your father again?" Then Ivan folded with a stunned compliance.

We shoved him in behind Sean's seat. Hofmann recuffed the boy's hands to the grab handle above the rear window and squeezed in alongside him, swapping the Lucznik for one of the Sigs to keep him covered. I gave the big German back his knife. He took it without comment, tucking it away inside its usual hiding place in his boot.

Sean and I snapped the front seats back into position and jumped in. The Skyline's engine cracked up on the first turn, despite the prolonged abuse it had just suffered. Before he put the car into gear Sean glanced over his shoulder.

"They knew, didn't they?" he said quietly. "What you were really up to, and yet they let us do it."

"Yes," Hofmann said, his impassive face giving away nothing. "Now, Major König may return at any time and when she does, she will not be happy with any of us. I would suggest we go."

It was 4.28a.m. We had almost exactly five and a half hours.

CHAPTER
TWENTY-SEVEN

If the return journey to Einsbaden had been a mirror image of the way out, we would have made it back to the Manor with nearly a couple of hours to spare before Gregor Venko's deadline.

But it wasn't, and we didn't.

To begin with, it all went according to plan. I used Sean's mobile to call Gilby and let him know, briefly and cryptically, that we'd retrieved his present and were on our way back with it, hopefully in time for the party. He took the news with a tense abruptness, so that I couldn't tell if he was pleased or if he felt we'd dragged our feet over the task.

We reactivated the Alpine and let Madeleine II's dulcet tones guide us out of the residential district and back onto the road past Potsdam heading for Dessau. There were no other cars taking the same route behind us, no sign of sudden pursuit or interception. As we regained the A9 I couldn't help a feeling of relief that we'd made it this far unmolested.

It was raining steadily now, coming down slash-cut through the beams of the lights. Even with the Nissan's intelligent four-wheel drive, Sean had instinctively backed off. Having said that, we were still thundering south at a little over a hundred and forty miles an hour. In hardly any time at all Dessau was in the rear-view mirror and Leipzig was looming.

I was aware of a sense of blasé relaxation about our speed. I had to remind myself that although my Suzuki would do just short of one-forty, I'd only maxed it out once on a deserted stretch of bone-dry motorway. Even so, it was a grit-your-teeth, hang-on-for-grim-death kind of experience, and I'd been secretly quite glad when I decided I'd had enough. In the big Nissan it was just all so easy.

After staying quiet for the first section of the journey, Ivan became vocal just south of Leipzig. He demanded to know, in German first, then in what could have been Russian, and finally in English, who we were and why, if we were working for his father, we were keeping him shackled like this. There would, he warned in a voice that trembled with outrage, be trouble of a kind we could scarcely imagine when Gregor found out how we'd treated him.

I twisted in my seat. Hofmann rolled his eyes at the rhetoric, but didn't make any answer. I grinned at him and turned back forward. We continued to ignore the boy's childish bluster until finally, in a small voice, he admitted to feeling car sick. Only then did Hofmann reach across with a heavy sigh and remove the hood from Ivan's head.

If anything, that move seemed to frighten him more than being kept in the dark had done. I remembered back to a time when I'd been attacked by two masked men who'd ransacked my Lancaster flat, a year before the fire that had eventually driven me out of the place. At the time I'd been comforted by the fact that they'd hidden their faces from me. Taken it as an indication that, whatever else their intentions, at least they didn't want me dead. If so, why bother to conceal their identities? The same possibility had obviously occurred to Ivan now, but he was too stubborn or too proud to voice it.

His eyes flicked from the Sig Hofmann was loosely but expertly pointing in his direction, to the Lucznik I had slung across my knees. As much as he could do with his wrists manacled above his head, he allowed himself to slump back into the corner of the seat and fell into a petulant silence.

When I next turned to glance at him, he was apparently sleeping, with his head tilted sideways, resting on his upraised arms, and his lips slightly parted. In that guise he looked too young, too innocent, to have masterminded the kind of vicious killing spree that was suspected.

Nevertheless, I made a silent vow not to turn my back on him if I could help it.

Ahead of us and off to the left the sky was just beginning to lighten as the sun rose out over the Czech Republic and stretched long shadowed fingers towards the eastern border of Germany. I watched Sean putting every ounce of effort into piloting the car safely south and tried not to think about the last time any of us had seen our beds.

As it was, someone had weighted my eyelids when I wasn't looking. I blinked and realised several kilometres had passed in the meantime. God, I was so tired everything had begun to ache again. Sean had the car's air con system turned down cool enough to keep him sharp, but it was just making me more sleepy.

Well, maybe I could allow myself just five minutes . . .

I jerked awake almost instantly, it seemed, to find that we were barely moving and an hour had passed.

"Where are we?" I demanded, my pulse suddenly stepping up with guilt at my lapse in concentration.

"Just outside Nürnberg," Sean tossed across and the exasperation showed clearly in his voice. "Bloody traffic."

I sat up from the slithered position I'd drooped into and looked around me. Ahead all I could see was the tailgate of a massive truck on Swiss plates. Alongside was a pair of middle-aged suits in a BMW. They were either too world-weary, or too polite, to look perturbed at having a car filled with armed desperadoes and a hostage right next to them.

For the next forty-five minutes we barely made a couple of kilometres. The loudest noise inside the car was the slap of the wipers on intermittent across the screen, like an irregular heartbeat. The traffic grew steadily thicker as the morning filled out into rush hour. It was agonisingly slow.

"We're going to have to stop and fill up again," Sean said at last, glancing down at the instrument panel. "It may as well be now." He caught Hofmann's eye in the rear-view mirror and nodded towards Ivan. "Do you want to hood him up again?"

Hofmann put the Sig in his pocket and slid the knife out of his boot again.

"No," he said ominously. "If he makes trouble I can deal with him quietly enough."

Sean left the engine running again, despite the obvious disapproval of the filling station attendant, while he poured in litre upon litre of *Super bleifrei*. The Skyline seemed to have an appetite for fuel that was of alcoholic proportions. It had consumed an exorbitant amount since our last stop, but economy was not supposed to be one of its assets under these conditions.

I ran in to pay to lessen the time we were off the road and also so that Sean could move the car further away from prying eyes. Even without his hood, Ivan was still handcuffed to the grab rail and looked suspiciously like he was being taken somewhere against his will rather than being rescued. It wasn't a scenario we wanted to have to explain in detail to anyone, least of all to the police.

It all took up precious time, minute after minute of it. When we rejoined the A6, now heading west towards Heilbronn, I was aware that Gregor was probably already en route to Einsbaden. The wheels were in motion and couldn't be called back, nor cancelled out.

I tried to ring Major Gilby again to let him know our progress, but this time the Manor's phone line rang out without reply. There's rarely something good will come about from an unanswered phone. My mind started constructing its own spurious reasons, each more fantastical than the last, but I couldn't ignore the likelihood that Gregor Venko was already there, and that the Manor had already fallen to his forces.

I caught Sean's anxious gaze as I ended the dead call. His eyes were red-rimmed from staring into the artificial airflow, fatigue pinching his cheeks into hollows.

I wondered if he could force himself to this kind of stamina naturally or if he'd taken anything in order to sustain it. I couldn't think of a way to ask that wouldn't insult him.

"It'll be OK," I said, more to reassure myself than him. "We'll get there."

"That's not the worry," he said, raising a half smile even though his voice was flat. "It's what we'll find there when we do."

At Heilbronn we turned south again, back onto the B10 for Stuttgart and the penultimate leg. The traffic stayed obstinately thick and cumbersome. Since Nürnberg we'd been able to average barely eighty miles an hour. I was almost glad when Madeleine II began to give us the countdown warnings to our final junction. That feeling didn't last for long.

By the time we were onto the tortuous back roads heading for our destination, Sean's temper was racked to breaking point by sheer overwhelming exhaustion.

He drove with a kind of controlled violence now, taking blatant risks to get past other vehicles. Yet still he seemed to maintain a light deft touch on the Skyline's controls as it screamed and scrabbled and snorted along the narrow roads. Like a master rider on a horse that was totally insane.

Ten o'clock.

The deadline came and went, and still we were half a lifetime from Einsbaden. The village had always seemed so close to the Manor, but now some giant joke of fate kept moving it further away.

But, when we finally skittered between the griffin-topped gateposts and I checked my watch, I discovered that despite the increased congestion we had shaved a further two minutes off the outward trip from the Manor to the autobahn. Nevertheless, it was now ten-ten.

Ten minutes too late, perhaps?

The barrier on the driveway was down. Sean cursed, shifting his foot off the accelerator and beginning to brake. We'd barely shaken off speed when two figures stepped out from behind the guard hut and pointed submachine guns meaningfully in our direction.

For a second I thought that Major Gilby had posted a couple of his men to watch for our return, but as soon as the thought had formed I dismissed it. He didn't have two to spare.

I registered the fact that they were strangers at the same instant that the Uzis they were carrying began to sing. The flashes from each muzzle became a continuous blaze as they opened fire. I ducked down behind the level of the dash top as my side of the windscreen crazed.

Sean got back on the power without any thought to a progressive throttle. The Skyline leapt forwards, snarling, and ran towards the men with the guns. I heard the whiz and twang of the rounds hitting the bodywork, but the big car shook them off and kept coming.

Too late perhaps, our attackers realised Sean wasn't trying to evade them. The front edge of the bonnet hit the barrier, snapping it off and hurling it aside like a broken lance. One of the men jumped for cover, rolling into the trees.

We clipped the other man's thigh with the front wing as he moved just too slowly to avoid us. He flew backwards with a grunt, dropping the Uzi and disappearing from view. Sean never even looked in the mirror.

"Well, that gives you your answer about Gregor," he said tightly. "He's here."

I sat up again and shook the fragments of broken glass off my clothing. I'd picked up a couple of scratches from the splinters on the backs of my hands. Other than that I'd been lucky.

The holes in the windscreen would have been at head height if I'd been taller. Sean's height, for instance. I realised they'd been aiming for the driver, but they'd been thrown by the fact that — to them — he was sitting on the wrong side of the car.

I took the safety off the PM-98, although keeping my finger outside the trigger guard for the moment. Hofmann released Ivan's hands from the grab rail, recuffing them in front of him so we could get him out

404

quickly. Gregor's sighting of his son could be vital if we were going to avoid being shot to pieces.

The front of the Manor forecourt was deserted, but Sean must have spotted something because he snatched the wheel over at the last moment and headed for the parking area at the rear of the house.

Gregor Venko had parked his bullet-proof black Mercedes stretch limousine at a slant under the terrace. His men held the high ground above it. Gilby and his ragged crew had been forced into retreat as far as the rear of the car park, and were dotted among the school Audis and the wreckage. By the looks of the damage to the stonework and the cars, they'd been exchanging cordial amounts of ammunition.

Two separate sets of guns swung in our direction as Sean made his dramatic entrance. We had a few seconds' respite while shock kept fingers away from triggers. Gilby, of course, must have recognised his own car, but to Gregor's troops this was an invader, to be repelled. They began to do so then, with enthusiasm.

Sean slewed the Skyline into as sheltered a space as he could find in the split-second he had to make the decision. We ended up between the trucks, nose facing outwards, so when we flung the doors open they afforded us a little protection at least. The bullets splattered around us, zinging off metalwork like hailstones. Gilby's men started to lay down covering fire.

The Major had strung his people out into sniping positions along the back line of the parking area. Considering the length of time he'd had to plan his campaign, and the fact that he was severely outnumbered, he was well dug in and holding his own.

Sean dragged Ivan out of the back of the car without regard to hurting him, yanking his head back so Gregor could get a look at his face. Hofmann and I dived behind the back end of the car with Hofmann yelling, "Hold your fire!" over and over in half a dozen different European languages.

I glanced at Sean, standing half exposed with Ivan gripped wriggling in front of him. He refused to drop into cover with the boy and his defiant stance made me shiver. To come this far and then lose either of them to a stray bullet would be unthinkable.

Gregor recognised his son in an instant, bellowing to his men to stop shooting. He had to give the order three times before the firing finally ceased, and the look he threw at the last man to take his finger off the trigger was pure poison.

After the noise, the silence deafened me. The only sound that emerged over it was the quiet tickover of the Mercedes's engine and the breathless whirr of the Nissan's cooling fans as they battled to stop the overheated turbos from going into terminal meltdown.

And then, into the stillness, came the click and rattle of a dozen magazines being changed and hastily rammed home, and first rounds being racked into chambers.

Gregor Venko, no personal coward, stepped out from behind the limousine. He was wearing another beautiful long cashmere coat, this one the colour of a field of summer corn, over a double-breasted suit that was well cut enough to almost conceal his expansive gut. He advanced as far as the front wing of the Merc, then stopped and gestured impatiently to someone still behind the car.

Sideburns, the bodyguard whose knee I'd kicked out from under him, appeared then, propelling a young girl in front. I recognised Heidi Krauss from the photographs Elsa had displayed.

She seemed to be in a better physical condition than Ivan perhaps, but I wouldn't like to vouch for her mental state. Her eyes showed a mind well past being terrified and into a shock so deep it was almost catatonic. She was shuffling like a convict who's been too long in leg irons, stumbling over her own feet. If it came to making a run for it, I calculated, we were probably going to have to carry her.

"So," Gregor called across the distance between us. "We make the exchange without further — unpleasantness, yes?"

"Yes," Sean agreed. "Two men only. We meet in the middle."

Gregor nodded slowly, but was unwilling to surrender complete control by accepting the suggestion without his own stipulations.

As Hofmann went to walk out with Sean, Gregor stopped them. "Wait!" He pointed at Sean, eyes narrowed. "I don't know you. I don't trust you," he said. He waved in my direction, the light flashing from the diamonds on the Rolex at his wrist. "Miss Fox can bring Ivan. Just her and the German. She gave me her word."

I cursed under my breath and edged out from behind the car. Aware of the eyes watching me, I took over Sean's grip on Ivan's collar. The boy curled his lip at me. I smiled sweetly back at him and jammed the Lucznik into his ribs.

"You don't have to do this, Charlie," Sean muttered in my ear, scowling. "There's no way he'll refuse to make the swap because of it."

"No, I'll do it," I said, sounding more confident than I felt. "And he's right. I did give him my word."

With Hofmann alongside me, we moved forwards. Every step seemed to make us more exposed, more vulnerable. The parking area had grown in size until it was a very long way to the middle. Opposite us Sideburns and the other bodyguard I remembered from Gilby's study shifted carefully to meet us, shoving Heidi before them.

I was watching Sideburns's face carefully. The look on it was sly and I knew he was itching for a chance of revenge for the humiliation he'd suffered at my hands. I kept my eyes locked on his, waiting for the first indication that he was planning to double-cross us, despite his boss's wishes.

It just so happened, therefore, that I was watching at the precise moment that the right-hand side of his face exploded in a welter of bone shards and brain, and the high-pressure spray of viscous, scarlet blood.

CHAPTER
TWENTY-EIGHT

I didn't know who'd fired the shot that killed Sideburns, but I didn't really need to. It was enough to know that somebody was shooting at us.

I grabbed the back of Ivan's neck, ramming my fingers and thumb into the sensitive points there to force his head down. I was already twisting him back towards the cover of the Skyline before Sideburns's body had completed its final dive.

Heidi had been so close to Gregor's bodyguard when he died that she was immediately splattered. The noise was like she'd been hit with a wet tea towel. A great swathe of gore was flung across her face and upper body. The pig's blood scene from *Carrie* was just a pale rehearsal for this.

The horror of what the girl had just witnessed jerked her mind out of its zombie-like state and sent her reeling into the far reaches of hysteria. She darted away from the other bodyguard's clutches, screaming fit to strip her vocal cords raw. Her popping eyes were fixed on the blood on her hands in front of her, her fingers stiffly outspread.

Hofmann took two calm strides forward and snatched her off her feet as though she weighed

nothing. The relentless chatter of automatic weapons'
fire battered our senses from all sides. My bearings
were shot. Then I saw Declan beckoning frantically
from behind the wreckage of the Audis and
Blakemore's FireBlade off to my right. I ran hell for
leather in that direction, dragging Ivan along with me.

Sean had tried to come out to us as soon as the
shooting started, but was forced back almost instantly.
Out of the corner of my eye I saw the dirt at his feet
puff up from the hits. He fired a short burst from his
PM-98 in the direction of the house, then threw
himself back behind the Nissan and wisely stayed
down.

Whoever had joined the fight had done so with a
complement of full clips and the will to spend them.
For almost a minute hundreds of rounds came down
like hard rain into the parking area. I crouched behind
the Audi, instinctively keeping Ivan down, while
Hofmann wrapped himself round Heidi's still-shrieking
figure and held on tight. Ivan, for once, didn't try and
get away from me. I guess he was just waiting to see if
I was going to get myself conveniently killed then he
could shrug me aside.

Then, as suddenly as it had all started, it stopped. I
lifted my head cautiously and risked a peep round the
bottom corner of the crumpled FireBlade. Sideburns's
body lay where it had fallen in the middle of the open
ground. One leg was still twitching.

Gregor's men were lying low and the man himself
was crouching behind his bullet-proof car with two of

410

his largest bodyguards sticking to his back. So who the hell was attacking us?

And then, high up on the roof of the Manor, I saw movement. Black-garbed figures, armed to their cammed-up teeth. Professionals.

Declan had crabbed himself round into a position where he could look over my shoulder.

"It's the feckin' Germans," he said. He glanced back at Hofmann. "No offence, but it looks like your mates have arrived."

Hofmann nodded, not looking too surprised about this turn of events. He met my eyes. "Major König," he said.

If it was indeed the German security services, they'd picked the best spot for an ambush. The flat roof of the Manor offered a superb vantage point over the whole of the rear of the house. We must have all been laid out below them like a map.

I wondered why Gregor hadn't planted a couple of his own men up there just to hold the ground. Then my eye found Sideburns's corpse again and realised that probably he had.

From down here I could see along the edge of the parking area. Thinly stretched out to my right were Figgis, Gilby, and Todd. They were in good defensive positions, tucked in behind the cars. Providing Jan didn't have anything larger than the submachine guns they'd used so far, they were safe.

But pinned down.

For Gilby to get either over to Gregor, or to fall back to the woods in the opposite direction involved crossing open ground that was just crying out for the work of a decent sniper. I'd be willing to bet Jan had brought a couple of those with her. There was just too large a gap between the last parked Audi and our position for Gilby to reach us, either.

As for Sean, he wasn't going anywhere. Up hard against the back end of the Skyline he had minimal cover, but he was completely stuck or he'd make an easy target.

"Major Gilby!" Jan's voice rang out above us, strangely unfamiliar and harsh with command now. "We want Ivan Venko. Bring him out and save yourself a lot of trouble. Otherwise, my men will open fire."

That got Gregor's attention. He twisted round to stare across at our position. "I want my son!" he roared. "Miss Fox, you gave me your word!"

"Yeah, and I want a brand new FireBlade," I threw back at Gregor, reckless, flippant. "We can't always have what we want."

Ivan tried to wriggle free at his father's voice. I cursed under my breath and dug my fingers in harder.

Sean twisted round, careful not to expose himself to the snipers. "Charlie," he called across, "for God's sake let the Germans have him. You try anything else and they'll cut you to pieces."

"I made a promise, Sean," I said and looked away so I wouldn't see the pain in his face.

I shuffled backwards, hauling Ivan with me. Ronnie, Craddock, and Romundstad were sheltered by the remaining school truck. They managed to duck across to join me behind the wreckage of the Audis and the

412

bike. "Well, Charlie, it looks like you're the boss," Craddock said. "What's the plan?"

I took a deep breath. "We're going to have to walk Ivan over there," I said.

"Oh you have to be feckin' kidding me," Declan muttered.

"Why not?" Romundstad said, more robust. "This is what we have been training for, is it not?"

Ronnie didn't answer that one. I couldn't see this kind of thing being on the syllabus at catering college, but to his credit he didn't raise an objection.

I glanced at Craddock. After a moment's hesitation, he nodded. "OK," he said, "let's do it. Why not?"

"Michael," I said. "How many of the men Jan's got with her will speak English?"

He shrugged. He was still holding onto Heidi, hands automatically smoothing her matted hair. "Most will probably understand a little," he said, frowning. "Why?"

"In that case, you're going to have to tell them in German," I said. "Tell them we're civilians, we're unarmed, we're just pupils here. And keep telling them."

He nodded, not liking it, but not about to talk me out of it, either. "You do realise," he said slowly, "that I could just take charge of the boy and save you from making this decision."

Declan brought his gun up and grinned. "You could try, me old lad," he said. "In fact, we'll be sure to tell your boss up there that you did."

"I should be with you," he said, but I shook my head.

"You've already taken enough risks and I think, once Jan sees whose side you're on, that might only encourage her to aim for you, don't you think? Besides, Heidi needs you." He couldn't refute that. Indeed, the girl looked permanently attached to the big German. Disengaging her was going to take some time and probably a strong solvent.

We crowded round Ivan.

"Just remember," I told the boy in a savage whisper. "You try and run for it and there's a dozen men up there who'll win a prize for being the first one to shoot you. We're your only chance, OK?"

"OK," he said, the single word torn out of him. He would almost rather get himself shot than submit to this indignity, I realised. I tightened my grip and nodded to Hofmann.

He started shouting up to Jan, his voice loud enough to carry to all the men up along the roof line. He told them we were coming out, and who we were, and that she would be murdering unarmed civilians if she ordered her men to open fire.

I looked across to where Major Gilby had crawled to the edge of the last Audi. He met my eyes but didn't speak. Maybe he just couldn't bring himself to plead with me. He knew, as well as I did, what had been threatened if we didn't match Gregor's half of the bargain. We were risking our lives by this, yes, but even more so if we backed out now.

"Charlie," Sean said urgently, "for God's sake don't do this."

I swallowed, ignoring him, bearing down on the fear that was threatening to overwhelm me. We dumped our guns and positioned ourselves around Ivan, with Craddock and Romundstad in the front, Ronnie to his left, me to his right, and Declan bringing up the rear. We were so tight in that we could hardly move without standing on each other's feet.

Then, before any of us could have second thoughts, we stepped out into the open ground.

Above us, Jan was going practically apoplectic, screaming at her men to shoot us, not to let Ivan reach the safety of his father's limousine. But Hofmann's words were hitting home. They hesitated.

Jan drew her own gun and started firing down at us, but there's a limit to what you can hit with a handgun at that sort of distance. Besides, we were keeping too tucked around Ivan for her to have a clear shot at the boy.

Still, it was only a matter of time.

And then Ronnie gave a shrill cry, spun away to the side and dropped. He'd taken a round through his left thigh, just above the knee, but that wasn't the real problem. The blood was pumping out between his clamped fingers, a thin jet of it, pulsing to the beat of his heart.

Artery.

Ronnie sat up and almost tried to hutch away from the sight of his own blood, as though it was a separate entity that was attacking him and he could somehow escape it.

He was screaming now, in terror as much as pain. He knew as well as the rest of us how little time he'd got. You can't work with big sharp chef's knives for a living and not have it hammered into you about the dangers of accidentally slicing your femoral artery. Untreated, he had minutes.

We faltered, our advance stumbling to a halt.

"Close up, for God's sake," I hissed.

Declan stared at me with eyes that were wide with shock. "For feck's sake we can't just leave him!"

"We don't have a choice," I snapped back. I grabbed his arm and yanked him back close round Ivan. "We stop now and they kill the boy and all this is a total waste of time. You wanted to be a bodyguard, Declan, well this is what it's all about, not those Hollywood babes you're so keen on. Now live with it *and let's move!*"

Just for a second he looked at me as though his dearest wish was that I was the one writhing on the ground in a growing pool of my own blood. Then he nodded darkly and we moved forwards again. The whole thing had taken only a moment, hardly a break in stride, but it felt like hours.

We were almost in the lee of the terrace now, and close enough to Gregor's Merc to make a dash for it.

Gregor grabbed hold of his son in a quick fierce bear hug, then his bodyguards were bundling the boy into the limo. Gregor climbed in behind him, but just before he slammed the door he looked directly into my eyes, his own bright and hard like pebbles.

416

"I will not forget this," he said, his voice a deep bitter rumble. "And I will not forget *you*."

It was hard to tell if it was said as a threat, or a promise.

Then the heavy door slammed and we had to jump back as the Merc was gunned forwards, fishtailing wildly as it swerved out of the parking area. What was left of Gregor's invasion force retreated behind him, covering his escape with well-drilled precision.

If Jan had had the time to assemble a larger force, they might have stood a chance of preventing Gregor's escape, but as it was they were woefully outnumbered. Their elevated position had only given them the advantage while we were all pinned down in one place. As soon as the Merc left the parking area, that superiority was lost. I heard her barking commands into a radio, but by the growing ire in her voice, she knew she was beaten.

As soon as Gregor had taken Ivan off our hands, we'd turned and run back to Ronnie. Jan's men were still firing after the limo. Shots seemed to be landing just about everywhere. Craddock and I piled ourselves over the top of the cook, shielding his body. Romundstad had grabbed a spare magazine out of his jacket and turned it, with a strip of Ronnie's shirt, into a tourniquet. Ronnie was chewing through his bottom lip in an effort to stay quiet.

Gradually, the firing petered out, leaving a ringing in my ears. The drift of gun smoke left a dirty smell in the air. I sat up, risked raising my head. Craddock did the same and gave me a quick grin. I looked down.

Romundstad had managed to stem the bleeding and Declan was holding Ronnie's hand, telling him he was going to be fine, and this didn't mean he was let off making our lunch.

My God, I thought. *We're actually a team.*

Declan looked up and caught my eye. He gave me a brief nod of apology. I shrugged my acceptance. Nothing further needed to be said.

Gilby's men moved out of cover then. Todd went to carefully prise Heidi away from Hofmann, sweeping her up into his arms and carrying her across to Gilby, uncaring of the blood. Figgis produced a medical kit, elbowed us aside and began patching up Ronnie's leg more scientifically than we'd been able to.

The tension drained away from us, sapping the adrenaline that had kept us going with it. I got to my feet and staggered back, wiping Ronnie's blood onto the legs of my jeans.

I saw Sean start in my direction, but Gilby waylaid him on his way across to me, shaking his hand, thanking him. I was glad of the respite. He had that head-ducked look about him, the one that said he was spoiling for a fight. I didn't think I was quite up to a confrontation with him just yet.

At that moment, above us on the terrace, the French doors clattered wide open and Jan came stalking out, with four of her men behind her carrying MP5Ks. Jan herself was holding a nine-mil calibre pistol, like the ones we'd seen in the little apartment in Berlin. I wondered vaguely what she'd done with the Sig she'd taken with her from the outdoor range.

The gun she'd used to callously shoot Elsa.

Jan had always had an air of underlying resentment about her, but now she was halfway to ballistic and she made a beeline for me.

"You!" she yelled at me, her thin sallow face made ugly by her anger. "How dare you interfere!"

"I made a promise," I said. It was becoming a catchphrase.

Jan's temper spilled over. She darted forwards and kicked my legs out from under me. If I hadn't been so damned weary I probably could have done something about it, but as it was I went down as far as my knees. She jammed the barrel of the P7 under my jawbone and lifted my head back with it.

"You have no idea who you're dealing with here," she bit out. "I can disappear you, Fox, for what you've done today."

I stared up into her eyes with my heart racing, but I wouldn't flinch. "I know," I said.

"That's enough," Sean said in that deadly quiet tone I knew so well. "Leave her alone."

Without moving my body I flicked my eyes sideways to find that one of the Sigs was out in Sean's hand and was aimed at Jan's head. I hadn't seen where he'd been carrying it. From the shimmer that ran through them, no one else had, either.

Sean was dog-tired, grey with exhaustion from the tension and the twelve-hundred-kilometre drive, but the security service agent must have seen the cool intent in his eyes. It cut through the layers, penetrated. She carefully took her gun away from under my chin.

At the same moment one of Jan's men came forwards and planted the muzzle of his MP5K, almost leisurely, into the side of Sean's neck. He may have hesitated over shooting us when we were unarmed and protecting Ivan, but I had no doubts at all that he was capable of pulling the trigger now.

Stand-off time.

There was a moment's hesitation, then Sean sighed and surrendered the Sig. The man took it and stepped back away from him. I could almost feel the others' relief that Sean had gone down without a fight. Even surrounded by armed opponents and utterly fatigued he'd still represented a serious threat. He just had that air about him.

Jan tucked the HK back into its speed-draw holster and moved in close, putting her face into Sean's. "I'll have the pleasure of dealing with you later," she sneered.

She brusquely ordered Sean searched and cuffed, and Gilby's men, too, just for good measure. Major Gilby handed over Heidi into Romundstad's care and submitted to the restraint with quiet resignation.

Jan eyeballed him as the cuffs went on. "Not quite so superior now are we, *Major*?" she said, spitting out the last word. She stabbed a finger to her own chest. "At least I earned my rank, I didn't cheat my way into it!"

Gilby eyed her calmly, but didn't speak. His silence only seemed to inflame her further.

"I could have you shot here and now for your treachery, Gilby," she said. That didn't raise a response, either, even though Jan looked as though she was seriously considering such an act.

I climbed slowly to my feet. Two of Jan's men were standing over me, but they didn't make any attempts to keep me down. They were too busy eyeing their commanding officer with something approaching concern.

"I am taking command of this operation," Hofmann said then, loudly, in German. "Major König, you are relieved."

Jan didn't have much colour to start with, but now what little she had was driven out of her face by a clenched fury. The last thing she looked was relieved.

"You can't fucking do this to me, Hofmann," she flared. "I outrank you. I'm not the one who's removed a suspect from custody and helped him to escape. You're a fucking traitor!"

Hofmann regarded her rather sadly and as her eyes slipped past him to the faces of her own men, the realisation of who they were prepared to follow must have hit her like a smack in the mouth.

"Oh I might have expected that," she said bitterly. "You're nothing but a brain-dead bunch of chauvinistic morons." She nodded to Hofmann, her disgust plain. "He's the man, so he's got to be right. Is that it?"

"Major König, you have overstepped your authority and you *will* stand down," Hofmann said, ignoring her. "Your weapon please."

He stepped forwards, peremptorily holding out his hand. Jan yanked the P7 out of its speed-draw holster again, tight-lipped and livid, and started to surrender it.

And that's when Hofmann made his big mistake.

He allowed the faintest hint of a patronising smile to creep across his mouth.

Jan saw it, and snapped.

I saw the change come over her. Her eyes went wild, opaque, her grip shifted slightly, her stance hardened. The means of retribution was in her hand and all logical thought had fled in the face of fury.

I don't know how Jan was planning on getting away with shooting Hofmann in cold blood in front of so many witnesses, but maybe she just didn't give a shit any more.

I had a sudden almost subliminal flashback to the day when my four attackers had been acquitted and had smiled at me with gloating conceit as they'd left the courtroom. If someone had handed me a gun then, I would have pulled the trigger without hesitation and kept pulling it, rage-blind, until there was no one left standing.

Something bumped against my hip and I suddenly remembered the Sig I'd dropped into my jacket pocket outside the apartment in Berlin. I'd left the Lucznik behind the FireBlade, but no one had thought to check me for any other weapons.

The nearest of Jan's men was standing less than a metre away from me. He caught the sudden flurry as I wrenched the pistol out of my pocket, thumbed the safety off and started to bring it up level, all in one move.

For all his apparently careless lapse in not searching me, he was a trained man and his reactions were damn near instantaneous. He was already turning before I'd got the barrel clear of the fabric. Already launching himself towards me in a ferocious tackle as my target fell between the sights.

Now or never.

I fired.

I got off one clean shot before the German's momentum took me straight off my feet. He was big and heavy and we landed solid enough to crack the air right out of my lungs, leaving me gasping.

He recovered first, viciously twisting the gun out of my unresisting grip and jamming the business end of it hard under my right ear, jarring down to the bone. He dragged me up as far as my knees.

Everybody seemed to be shouting at once. I closed my eyes, waiting for it all to end. Either way.

Nothing happened.

The gun eased away from my skull, the hand on my jacket relaxed its hold. When I cautiously opened my eyes again I found Hofmann was crouching in front of me.

He put a meaty hand on my shoulder. "Thank you," he said solemnly, and stood again. Uninjured, I noticed. Unharmed.

When he moved aside I found myself staring into Jan's shock-glazed eyes. The rage that had transported her to the edge of madness was dissipated, spent. She was sitting hunched on the ground half a dozen metres away, breathing quick and shallow, with her right hand curled lifelessly in her lap. I don't know what happened to the P7 she'd been holding.

Even so, two of the men so recently under her command were standing close by, their MP5Ks trained on her. Another had a medical kit open on the ground and was dealing efficiently with the wound. I'd managed to plant the shot high through the fleshy part of her right arm across the swell of her bicep and despite his best efforts she was losing blood in a steady stream down the sleeve of her jacket.

Hofmann ordered the release of Gilby's men and Sean. The squaddie who uncuffed Sean moved back from him quickly when he'd done it, as though afraid of reprisal. Sean merely dropped the handcuffs contemptuously at his feet and came straight over to me. He skimmed his gaze over Jan as he passed, coldly expressionless, but she was unaware of his presence.

"Can you get up?" he asked me. When I stared at him stupidly he grasped my upper arms and hoisted me gently to my feet. I doubt I would have got there without his help. Once I was upright I found I could stand of my own volition providing I didn't try doing anything absurdly athletic. Like breathing deep, or walking.

Sean continued to hold me steady even when there was no longer any need to do so, head bent close in to mine so I could see the individual tiny flecks of colour in the irises of his eyes. His thumbs were unconsciously brushing circles against my arms.

He was watching me with that darkly brooding frown on his face, the muscles bunching under his jaw. It took him a while before he was in control enough to speak.

"Don't do that to me, Charlie," he managed at last on a growl. "We've only just got things out in the open

424

between us and now you've got some kind of a death wish!" His fingers gripped harder, making my shoulders hunch.

"Sean, go easy," I said, but my voice wasn't as steady as I would have liked it to be.

He almost shook me. "Christ, there you were on your knees with your eyes shut like you were waiting calmly for your own execution, and you tell me to go easy!" He stopped, lips compressed, eyes skating over my face. "Jesus, Charlie," he said, softly now, "sometimes you terrify me."

"What did you want me to do? She would have killed him," I protested, shakily. "I'd have stood a better chance of reasoning with a shark than of talking her out of it. You saw how she was! Besides, you were the one who walked up and stuck a gun in her face. And that wasn't supposed to frighten me?"

"I know," he said, and being forced to admit it made him glower even more, "but I didn't actually try and kill her. Governments take a very dim view of foreigners who shoot their security services personnel — however crazy they're acting at the time. For God's sake — they would have thrown away the key."

I looked at him blankly for a moment, then shrugged out of his grasp and backed away from him. Suddenly cold, I rubbed at my arms where he'd been touching them, whispered, "Just what exactly did you think I was trying to do, Sean?"

He stilled, but before he could speak Gilby came over. "Venko got away," he said quietly. His eyes flicked to me. "I hope you realise what you've done, Charlie."

425

"I gave him my word," I said, unrepentant. "If I'd gone back on it he would have murdered all of us, then gone after our families. You were there, Major. You heard him say it."

I glanced across to where Romundstad and Declan were standing with Heidi Krauss, looking faintly embarrassed. She was still clinging to Romundstad, crying inconsolably into the front of his jacket, hands meshed into the fabric like she was never going to let him go. I remembered Dieter's hysteria, that day in Gilby's study. They'd both suffered more than they could bear. More, probably, than they would ever completely recover from.

"He may still try," Gilby pointed out now, "but if the Germans had got him Venko wouldn't have had the chance to carry out any threats."

I thought of the size and scope of an organisation like Gregor Venko's. It didn't die away because you cut off its head. It just grew another. More ugly.

"I don't think so," I said, shaking my head. "I did what I thought was right."

I thought of Gregor's parting words. *I will not forget this. I will not forget you . . .*

I'd risked my life, and those of the others, to save his son. I blanked out the possibility that he might blame me for the ambush. Any other way of handling it was too scary to contemplate.

"I'll deal with it when I have to," I said, weary to the point of tears. "Right now I just want to go home."

The Major nodded, exchanged a look with Sean that I didn't fully catch, and moved away.

I started to move, too, but Sean put his hands on my shoulders and turned me back to face him. "Don't do it, Charlie," he said.

His sudden intensity confused me. "Don't do what?"

"Don't go back to Cheshire," he said. "Not permanently, anyway. They'll smother you. Come back to King's Langley with me."

For a moment I was frozen by both hope and fear.

"What are you offering here, Sean?"

He saw my wariness, responded with caution of his own. "Whatever you're prepared to take," he said carefully. "A job, for a start. A home."

If I'd taken half a step towards him he would have matched it. I know he would. I couldn't quite bring myself to let go of that final reservation. Maybe Sean felt the same way.

It would come, though. If we let it.

"OK Sean, I'll do it," I said, and knew by his face that he remembered the last time I'd said those words, back on the day of Kirk's funeral when he'd first asked me to go to Germany. I saw too that he realised, possibly for the first time, that what I agreed to now I'd also agreed to then.

He didn't try and hide the relief, just smiled at me. After a moment or so I smiled back.

After all, we'd both accepted that there was no going back to what we'd had before.

But that didn't mean we couldn't go forwards.

Epilogue

I flew home three days later. Alone.

Sean had stayed on to help sort out the mess Ivan's capture, retrieval and release had caused, and to finally close the case on Kirk's death. Major Gilby had decided to come completely clean about what had really happened there. About O'Neill's part in Blakemore's death, too, and Rebanks's nasty little sideline. Even the truth about the accident which had claimed the life of McKenna's uncle might finally emerge.

Gilby was going to be lucky to stay out of prison, never mind keep Einsbaden Manor intact. I just hoped he was right about the spread of Dieter Krauss's influence. He was going to need it.

It was, Sean told me with a weary smile, all going to take some time. He would call me as soon as he got back to the UK. We would take things from there.

"No backing out now, Charlie," he'd murmured, touching the side of my face as he said it.

"No," I'd agreed. "No backing out."

Before any of the rest of us were allowed to go we went through a debriefing by the Germans that reminded me almost of the Resistance-to-Interrogation exercises I'd endured in the army. In the end, though, they decided the line they were going to take was that none of this had ever happened. We would all do as well to remember what it was we had to forget.

I asked Hofmann what they were going to do with Jan, but the look on his face told me I didn't want to know. He warned me that Gregor Venko seemed to have gone underground and had taken his family with him. It had been read as a sign he was about to get dangerous, to start a campaign, and I should watch my back.

The only good news he brought was that Elsa was set to make a full recovery from her flesh wound, even if she was going to have to wear a one-piece bathing suit in future.

Madeleine managed to reschedule my ticket so I flew direct to Manchester without the hassle of the stops and changes I'd gone through on the way out. I carefully scrutinised my fellow passengers as they boarded, but none of them looked like an eastern European assassin except the head stewardess. I didn't eat the airline food, just in case, but I probably wouldn't have done so anyway.

I rang home before I left and my father agreed without hesitation to meet me at the airport. He was waiting at the barrier when I cleared through Customs.

He studied my face gravely for a few moments without speaking. I don't know what he saw there, but the smile he gave me was hesitant. As though he recognised the events I'd gone through and he was just a little afraid of what they'd done to me.

It wasn't until I was in the passenger seat of his Jaguar, heading along the M56, that he spoke, his voice neutral.

"Was it —" he paused, as if searching for the correct phrase and came up with, "— very bad?"

I stopped peering into the mirror on my sun visor, trying to watch the cars following us, and turned to face him. His fingers rested apparently lightly on the rim of the steering wheel, but his eyes were a little too fixed on the road ahead.

What could I tell him? That I'd gambled with his safety. That I'd recklessly endangered his secure, comfortable existence and that of my mother. And for what? To help the psychopathic child of an equally psychotic father escape justice. What had I achieved by that?

Heidi's future, I told myself. *My own survival.* Suddenly it didn't seem like a convincing argument.

Finally, I said, "Yes."

He nodded. "So what are you going to do now?"

"Sean's offered me a job again," I said. "This time I think I'm going to take it."

"What kind of a job?"

"Close protection," I said. "A bodyguard."

He glanced across quickly. "Quite apart from my feelings on the subject of Sean Meyer," he said grimly, "are you sure that's a wise decision, Charlotte?"

No, I wasn't. Especially not when I couldn't shake the feeling that Sean didn't entirely believe my intent when I'd winged Jan. He knew first-hand just how good a marksman I'd been in the army, but even so he'd still been certain that the shot I'd so carefully calculated to wound and disable had been aimed to kill. What kind of long-term prospects did that leave open to us?

Now I shrugged rather helplessly. "The army didn't want me," I said, aware of the tiredness in my voice. "What else am I good for?"

He made no answer and we didn't speak again until he pulled up onto the gravel outside my parents' house forty-five minutes later. I looked up at the ivy-strung walls and measured architecture. I knew that it looked just the same as it had done when I'd left. It must just be me who was different.

I climbed out and moved towards the front door mentally gearing myself up for a reunion with my mother. I was wondering how I was going to break the news that they were going to have to get a panic alarm installed, when he stopped me.

"There was a delivery for you yesterday," he said. "Don't you want to see it?"

Just for a second I tensed with a thousand nasty possibilities before common sense took over. I shrugged again. He eyed my apathy with a moment's concern, then pressed the button on the Jaguar's alarm remote which also operated the garage door. It lifted gradually.

Inside, right at the back, was my old RGV Suzuki. Next to it, looking so much bigger by comparison, gleaming like an oiled-up bodybuilder, was a Honda FireBlade on a brand new plate. I walked towards it slowly, feeling the prickle of the hairs rising at the back of my neck.

My father followed me in and was watching my reaction. He reached past me for a manila envelope that was tucked behind the front screen and handed it over.

"It came with this," he said. "I thought perhaps you ought to be the one who opened it."

I slit the top flap with my thumb and pulled out a sheaf of papers. The top one was a bill of sale from a London dealer, made out in my name and stamped Paid in Full. Stapled to the top left-hand corner was a piece of plain white card. On it, a flamboyant hand had written just a mobile phone number and the words, "Sometimes you CAN have what you want. Thank you." It was signed, "Gregor."

"Who's Gregor?" my father asked.

I put the papers back into the envelope and looked at the bike. It was gorgeous. I ran my hand over paintwork on the tank that was so smooth and so unblemished it was silky to the touch. There was zero mileage on the clock, and the release agent still shone like skin on the virgin tyres.

"Oh, he's just someone I did a favour for," I said softly.

Definitely a promise then, not a threat.

My father looked at me, waiting for me to go on. At last he said, "It must have been some favour."

"Yes," I said, and realised that I was smiling. "Yes, it was."